THE SUMMER KITCHEN

Karen Weinreb

ST. MARTIN'S PRESS

NEW YORK

THE SUMMER KITCHEN. Copyright © 2009 by Karen Weinreb. All rights reserved. Printed in the United States of America. For information, address St. Martin's Press, 175 Fifth Avenue, New York, N.Y. 10010.

www.stmartins.com

Library of Congress Cataloging-in-Publication Data

Weinreb, Karen.
    The summer kitchen / Karen Weinreb. — 1st ed.
      p. cm.
    ISBN-13: 978-0-312-37925-4
    ISBN-10: 0-312-37925-0
  1. Housewives—Fiction. 2. Nannies—Fiction. 3. Rich people—New York (State)—Westchester—Fiction. 4. Life change events—Fiction. 5. Baking—Fiction. 6. Bakeries—Fiction. 7. Female friendship—Fiction. 8. Westchester (N.Y.)—Fiction. 9. Domestic fiction. I. Title.
    PS3623.E432446S86 2009
    813'.6—dc22

2008046326

First Edition: July 2009

10 9 8 7 6 5 4 3 2 1

FOR HUNTER,

HAYDEN,

AND HUDSON

Acknowledgments

Many thanks to my amazing editor, Elizabeth Beier, and to Dori Weintraub, Michelle Richter, Rachel Ekstrom, Mimi Bark, Tara Cibelli, Meg Drislane, and all the hardworking staff at St. Martin's. I am also grateful to Dan Menaker, who first suggested I write a novel. I owe my gratitude to many others. These include the boys' dad, for the journey; Carolyn Ford, for our never-ending conversation; Jill Gibbons, for her insights; Cristine Gelwicks, for never wavering; Hiroko Suzuki, for the same; Eileen Lambert, for the teas; Lee Forni, for the hospitality; Paige Levine, for lake days; and the two women who inspired in me the love of good food that emerges in this book: the Jam Lady of my childhood, Dee Fielding, and my adored cookbook-author mom. It's my greatest sadness that she died before meeting her grandchildren. Speaking of them—thank you to Hunter, Hayden, and Hudson for putting up with their mom writing on the sidelines of their soccer games while other moms watched every play and never forgot water bottles.

Prologue

It was raspberry season in Bedford, New York. The local private-school mothers whose families were not that week vacationing in the Hamptons or on Martha's Vineyard had left their children splashing in their home pools with their nannies and were pulling up along Nora Banks's drive in their Suburbans and Range Rovers and BMW X5s. Though there was no valet at this casual gathering, the cars glided into line along the Belgian-brick curb. These women were practiced at parking in groups on one another's estates. They all knew to park against the left curb, too, leaving room to the right for any other car leaving earlier to pass and use the lushly landscaped island bed up ahead.

Though the cobblestone-paved drive stretched perhaps 180 yards from the dirt road out front—the best addresses in Bedford were on dirt roads, which required more tax money in upkeep, but were preferable for the horses—the last cars to arrive still needed to utilize Nora's empty paddock to the right. It did not do to park on the dirt roads. The dust was not the problem. If these women had been concerned about their cars needing always to appear clean, they would have requested silver enamel rather than the black most preferred. Silver hid the dirt; black displayed it. Which was partly *why* black cars were preferred. Dusty cars were something of a status symbol. They told the community you lived on a dirt road and not a paved one. It was also just what everyone did. Drove black cars. Not just black cars, but black four-wheel drives. Beyond that it didn't matter whether your four-wheel drive was a Suburban, a Range Rover, or a BMW X5, though Suburbans had a slight edge, since they had three rows of seating, suggesting one had a large family, and a nanny, and perhaps a dog. Large families were also something of a status symbol, though only if your children attended the private school, and had not needed, as had one family, to move to the public one. Well upward of $100,000 a year after taxes to keep four at the community's only private nonsectarian lower school had become more in that case than could be managed. That family was never mentioned again. But if you had lots of children, *and* they attended the private school, *and* you vacationed every holiday, *and* your kids rode horses or skied, well then, you were along the road to being embraced. And pulling up at the school drop-off each morning in a dusty black Suburban told all the other drivers of dusty black Suburbans at school drop-off that you had all this and so were just like them. If you had ski racks on the roof, all the better. It was not an uncommon sight in the school parking lot to come across a mother clicking her remote central-locking device behind each black Suburban, one after the other, until hearing the telltale sound of car locks unlocking. There was sometimes no other way to find your car, unless you remembered where you had parked it—not likely at eight A.M. before you had picked up your five-dollar coffee from the upscale bakery Phillip's en route to the Sawmill Club for aerobics with Claude.

No, it was not because of the dust. These women avoided parking along dirt roads because season after season of inconsiderate winter weather had washed roadside ditches perilously deep. They knew their heavy vehicles would not ruin Nora's paddock, either, since the

sun had baked the ground hard—though they would park on one another's paddocks even in the winter when those paddocks were
muddy and snow-encrusted and their sometimes-skidding tires
plowed the ground as well as tractors. All knew that the mass of
Central American immigrants who resided in their shared apartments and row houses out back of the local train stations in Mount
Kisco and Bedford Hills would emerge from behind the snowplows
in the spring to refertilize and reseed all the grounds. These quiet,
hardworking men would then materialize weekly to mow and blow
the lawns. They understood that nary a leaf must discompose the effect of rustic storybook fields. Imperfect grounds were enough for an
inquiry or two by a neighbor into the welfare of the family. Was
everyone well? Did they need a meal brought over? Someone to pick
up the children from tennis? Less subtly put, a referral to a new landscape gardener?

These women never hesitated to park on one another's paddocks,
either, because many of them lived throughout the seasons in their
riding boots, having often come from or being about to go to their riding lessons or preparations for equestrian events upstate or down in
Palm Beach, Florida. (It was never considered that some women might
wear real riding boots—and not just the Ralph Lauren–style Riding
Boot, which anyone could wear—to *imply* they had an impending
equestrian event. Conversations about horses were so prevalent that
imposters would be caught out in a flash.) Though it was accepted
practice for these women to appear at school drop-off in the mornings in their workout or tennis gear, by afternoon pickup they were
"D"ressed. The entrenched women almost all appeared in variations
of low-cut, straight-leg Barbour or Ralph Lauren corduroys (school
was in session mostly only in the cooler months), or riding pants, turtle-
neck sweaters, reversible channel-quilted puffer vests with mock-neck
collars and shaped back yokes, waterproof microfiber jackets, some
hoods trimmed with coyote fur, and often their Ralph Lauren calfskin

boots. So it was rarely a matter of a Manolo Blahnik heel sticking in the mud. That was a potential problem only when they attended one another's houses on winter evenings, but then they had their husbands to assist them by elbows from car to house.

These husbands were yet another status symbol among the women of Bedford. First off, you had to have one. To arrive alone to any evening function would be to upset a symmetrical table-seating arrangement, but that would never happen because a single woman would never be extended an invitation. Single women were relegated exclusively and without discussion to the daytime activities, coffees, tennis, play dates, volunteer organization meetings. It was not like Manhattan—although Manhattan was just forty-eight miles and a one-hour drive south, and all the husbands worked there during the week, almost all of them on Wall Street—where you could, if you were single, attend functions with a Beard. Doing something like that in Bedford would raise too many Presbyterian eyebrows. This affluent family community was about black and whites: You either had money—serious money (if it was serious, it didn't matter whether it was new or old, and Bedford was increasingly filling with new money, in any case)—or you did not; you were either married or not. Not even boyfriends existed, or at least they were not recognized until they became husbands. But none of this was much of a problem, in any case, because there were very few single women in Bedford. The second point about husbands was that they must be rich. Very rich. The size of their end-of-year bonus mattered. It was all the talk when one woman's husband made $55 million on one deal; she became among the women in this community something of a celebrity herself. Age, looks, intelligence, creativity, sense of humor, physical presence in the family during the school weeks—none of that was necessarily required of husbands. What mattered was that you had one, and that he made a truckload of money. It was also helpful, though not required, if he was good at golf. He could that way earn the respect of the other husbands at the private local golf clubs, though it *was* expected that he could afford without hesitation the membership fees that ranged from $50,000 to $250,000 and then cover the stream of bills for entertaining at the club. Sending him off to coach the Saturday-morning Bedford Youth Soccer League matches could always make up in respect among the men for any lacking golfing ability.

Having a rich husband was up there in importance with having a nanny (and one had to have children first to need a nanny; it went without saying that the key to entry into this private-school world was children). Most had a full-time nanny and a part-time housekeeper—this though none of the women of the houses held jobs. Well, perhaps one or two worked as doctors or pediatric dentists, but since they were never around during the day to coffee or volunteer or chatter at play dates, they did not as a rule register in this world. At least they were rarely mentioned. Not for any nasty reason like suspicion that they might *need* to work. No one would ever say that. Only a few private-school mothers successfully straddled the two worlds, one of them a horse veterinarian. The equestrian women of the community valued her more even than their eyebrow artists: this despite some of their exclusively male Manhattan eyebrow artists being married also to rich men. When she donated as an auction item for the Boys and Girls Club Humanitarian Award dinner a day at work with her for a child, the bids amid the chinking of glasses at the $25,000 tables went as high as for the use of another couple's private jet, and another's second—or was it their third?—vacation home (well, not quite as high, but still).

Under no circumstances could these women do without their nannies. How else could they manage with young children at home to play morning tennis, attend the gym and riding lessons, meet with their architects overseeing new houses being built or old ones being renovated, coffee with other mothers, manage the crews of landscapers, florists, housepainters, exterminators, and appliance repairmen, plan dinner parties and luncheons and vacations, consult with a professional over the perfect design for stationery for their children, scream at the Mercedes dealership for not including the extras with your husband's new S-class sedan that the dealership had promised, divine the most imaginative donations for the biannual school auction, and then others still for the yearly Boys and Girls Club Humanitarian Award auction (imagination became valued at these times of the year), host or attend baby showers each time one of your own became pregnant again, volunteer at the school book fair, attend school Parent Council meetings, bake cupcakes for your children to share with their classmates on their birthdays at school while arranging parties for them as lavish as coronations, RSVP to the streams of invitations to children's birthday parties, purchase the perfect presents and wrapping paper to take to those parties, arrange for limousines to collect your five-year-old daughter and her classmates from school on Valentine's Day to whisk them into the city for a private afternoon tea, make other arrangements to visit your private jeweler to select a black diamond to wear to that black-and-white business affair to which your husband had been invited in Europe, shop for gourmet food items at Balduccis across the border in Greenwich, Connecticut, and then prepare dinner to share with your husband when his driver returned him from Manhattan around nine P.M.

Though the nanny was charged with preparing the children's meals—usually macaroni and cheese, chicken nuggets, white pasta with or without sauce, or hot dogs (nutrition was as big a deal here as recycling, both being the mainstay really of people closer to the ground than these lofty perches)—wives almost always insisted on cooking for their husbands themselves, or rather taking credit for those meals by performing the last step in recipes otherwise fulfilled

by the morning or afternoon housekeeper. It was the special something they brought to their marriages, besides their children, of course,
to keep their all-important husbands from running off with mis-
tresses in Manhattan. One local husband had twice left his family
for different younger assistants, but children and good food had both
times brought him home. There had to be a good reason indeed to
give up the family in Bedford when the fact of your family being in
Bedford allowed you to lead both lives. Why else did so many of the
men of Wall Street set up their families here but to keep their family
life out of New York and their New York life away from their families? All it took to keep their wives quiet and their guilt assuaged was
an invitation to an affair in Europe now and then, and a black diamond to wear to it. It was also no small factor for these men to consider that there were few eligible men in Bedford. Not even the
buffed Caucasian pool boy existed to tempt their wives. Cental
American laborers cleaned the pools. Take a walk through any of the
Westchester County towns during working hours and you were unlikely to see any men but a few real estate brokers and construction
workers between the ages of eighteen and sixty-five. One Bedford
mother had lately fallen to succumbing to one of those (married, as it
happened) construction workers every Wednesday during school
hours, though the other mothers frowned upon this unlikely affair:
They understood what was expected of them in the deals that were
their marriages.

SUMMER
THROUGH
FALL

One

Expecting their mother's friends to arrive later in the morning to make jam for their school's bake sale in the fall, Nora Banks's children, Thomas, Nicholas, and Charlie, aged seven, five, and three, had set out to collect as many raspberries as they could after first filling and staining their mouths crimson with them. Their nanny, Beatriz, had tried stringing prunes over their little torsos—a technique she had learned as a girl to leave both hands free, one to lift the thorny branches, the other to pick the plump fruit— but, no, the boys had wanted to use their Halloween buckets, the child-sized orange plastic ones with the black handles to match the jack-o'-lantern print. Past the barn, across the stream, and along the twenty-six-acre property's old stone walls the boys in their protective jeans and long-sleeved shirts had stumbled and giggled and jostled for prime place, Beatriz leading the way ably to the thickest clusters.

Now they were all headed back with their loot just as their mother's perfumey friends were stepping down from their cars as high as crane-elevated director's chairs. The women greeted the boys effusively, priding them on their spilling buckets, though none acknowledged Beatriz. Each probably would have done so and felt good about it at a play date, when it was just another mother or two and the children and their nannies. Those were perfect opportunities to show off your Spanish, never mind that almost all the nannies understood English. But in such a crowd as this it was better to seem preoccupied with balancing your hundred-dollar platter of sandwiches and pastries ordered by telephone in the morning and picked up en route from Bedford Gourmet. Though they all knew a sumptuous lunch would be provided, it was not the done thing to arrive empty-handed. The outcome of the platters was given little thought really, except in a roundabout way on garbage-collection days, when these women wondered how their households produced so much trash.

Appearing on the porch to greet her guests, Nora made the perfect picture of a young Bedford wife and mother. Behind her for a start was the 1890 crown-pedimented homestead she had restored. When her husband presented the house as her wedding gift, he had joked that the real gift was the "tender loving care" it required. It would save her facing empty days into the horizon while he worked long days back in Manhattan. She had given up her fledgling career in banking. Working just no longer seemed worth it. She would bring home just pennies relative to how her husband's newly founded hedge fund was performing. She threw herself into renovating happily and understood only later that this was what Bedford women did: renovated. Renovated and volunteered. But she had not been part of the community long enough back then to expect invitations to join boards of prestigious local preservation organizations such as the John Jay Homestead or the trust to preserve the Bedford Oak—Bedford's five-hundred-odd-year-old white oak tree—and so she had renovated. Well, baked and renovated, baking having been a passion since childhood Friday nights braiding challah with her Jewish father, Humbert Rosenfeld, or Hum, as everyone called him on account of his being a trombonist in the Rhode Island Philharmonic Orchestra—Rhode Island being where she grew up. Her father had taken as much pride in his challah as in his music and his only child.

It was by accident, too, that Nora *looked* just the part in this community. If she inherited her father's love of baking, she looked every bit her Scandinavian mother; glowing skin and high cheekbones, her long blond hair pulled now artfully out of the way in a French twist atop her regal five-foot-seven frame. The only aspect to her appearance that might have betrayed her humbler origins was the apron tied around her neck and hourglass waist. She had spent the morning stacking crates of cherries, blueberries, blackberries, raspberries, figs, and early apples. Her famed supplier trucked them in yesterday just after daybreak from the Hudson Valley, the region's bread basket a little west of Bedford running north along the Hudson River. Heavy lifting, getting messy—it was all simply a part to Nora of the deep love she had for working with her hands in the kitchen—an oddity in a community that expected that everyone had enough domestic help, though her affluent circumstances were otherwise incontrovertible.

Her summer kitchen played no small part in the women considering her affinity for baking an adorable hobby. There were not many still standing of these kitchens once designed for the privileged to keep the heat of preserving in the summer away from the main house. Hers was just why her estate was registered as a historical property. She had started the property's renovations inside the barnlike outbuilding, to make a place for her growing collection of pastry-making antiquities. But once the antique shelving had been restored, the latest baking equipment installed, and antique rugs were spread, the space soon enough become a salon of sorts for charities needing a fresh luncheon venue.

The sun was now at its zenith and bright in her eyes. Nora cupped her hand over her brow, her almond-sized diamond engagement ring glinting so that her forehead appeared bejeweled.

"Good morning, ladies! Welcome! I hope there was enough room for you all to park. I've been meaning to talk to Evan about having our landscape architect pave a parking area for parties, but you know how it is: One just never has the time."

"But you do have little escorts for us," quipped Pamela Hanson.

Nora smiled down at the tiered blond heads of Thomas, Nicholas, and Charlie, the sudden creases around her eyes the only sign of her thirty-six years. She looked behind the boys to Beatriz. It was no surprise that Beatriz was still neat in her usual skirt, blouse, stockings, and heels, not a single hair straying from the intriguing braided bun she created daily with her long, black hair. The women laughed on occasion that Beatriz was a fashion victim of the fifties, acknowledging in the same breath that she was the Mexican Mary Poppins of nannies and wishing she worked for *them*. They would never have hired her, though, in the circumstances she had, Nora knew. She had never mentioned this aspect of Beatriz's past for Beatriz's sake, which if truth be told, amounted to her own: for it reflected well to be envied for your nanny.

Nora found herself reminding the women again now of her luck.

"And a fabulous escort for the little escorts in our dear Beatriz," she added.

Clearly preferring not to be the center of attention, Beatriz began herding the boys around the house to wash their berries.

The boys hardly needed the encouragement and skittered ahead.

"But where are my manners?" Nora stepped inside to hold the door. "Please, come through, come through. We're heading out back, of course, to the summer kitchen."

As the women filed through with their platters, chattering of their summers so far and their plans for the summer still ahead, Bonnie

Taggart complimented Nora's apron. "I absolutely love it," she gushed in the powdery voice that tried to belie the power of her tall, broad frame and flaming red hair.

"I'm glad you like it. I thought the design with all the strawberries was so thematic I had the store make forty, one for everyone to use today and take home."

"How novel! I can't remember the last time I wore one."

As they crossed the garden out back, the women thrilled to its lemony beauty, and to the delicious fun ahead. Each felt there was no place in the world she would rather be. These gatherings were addictive that way, and once addicted, there was no way a woman of Bedford would contemplate going back to work and missing all this midweek fun. Many had been in their twenties, and some even in their early thirties, employees on Wall Street, television reporters, marketing directors, models, but like Nora they found few reasons to keep working once they married their multimillionaire husbands or their husbands clearly on their way to a great fortune. Then came the babies and entry into the life of nonworking Bedford mothers and they were out of reasons altogether. Besides, their type A industrious natures were not wasted here, only put to different endeavors, like making jam to raise money for a multimedia room at the school.

To that end they eagerly took up, once lunch was cleared, the tasks Nora assigned, cutting circles of gingham fabric, washing berries, squeezing lemons, measuring sugar. All chatted in their aprons as might Southern women gathered to quilt a bedcover.

"You know, Nora, you're a Martha Stewart clone," ribbed Lacy Cabot. "You're a self-taught and exceptional pastry chef, you think of things like gingham hats for jam jars, and just look what you've done with your summer kitchen and house and garden!"

"You're much more Martha than Martha," Pamela corrected. "You not only also have a gorgeous husband—but you're not under house arrest!"

The homemaker magnate lived one Bedford hamlet over from Nora's, Martha being in Katonah and Nora in Bedford Hills, around the corner from actress Glenn Close's estate. The third hamlet was Bedford Village. Well, Martha had yet to properly begin a life in Bedford, but she had still become another billionaire neighbor to Ralph Lauren and George Soros. She had purchased her 150-plus-acre parcel back in 2000. Contractors had since been renovating the dozen or more existing buildings on the estate. They were also building a greenhouse, a henhouse, and a house for her collection of horse-drawn carriages. Hammers kept banging even through her surprise incarceration from last fall to this past spring of 2005 on charges to do with obstructing justice on an insider-trading investigation, though the pace had picked up through her almost completed subsequent home confinement in the main house.

"I was over at Martha's the other day," Gina Cushing interjected through the laughter. "Everyone has to go to her, of course, since she can't leave the house because of that ankle thingy. She's putting together her new TV shows. There were teams of people passing through, and her private chef was cooking for everyone, and it was really funny, because she made everyone, everyone, take off their shoes. Everyone was barefooted!"

The laughter heightened.

"What's more weird," said Caitlin Maynard, "is that nobody cares."

"About being barefooted?" queried Gina.

"Noooooo . . . that she's on house arrest!"

"Why would we?" quipped Pamela. "She's still rich. Richer than any of us."

"Imagine having that much money," pondered Bonnie, who had just returned from a month with her family and nanny in the South of France.

"She's lucky she didn't lose it," said Pamela. "Charlotte's brother-in-law in the city lost almost everything when the State Attorney General started an investigation into his insurance company earlier this year and he was ousted as CEO."

"Ned says it all the time," Lacy chimed in about her husband, "says he wonders whether he should have accepted partnership last year after all. He says the buck stops with him now and if he does just one thing wrong—"

"Bonnie, would you please pass the lemon juice?" interrupted Nora. Her tone hid her budding boredom. The women often repeated their husbands' raw talk of money. Lately the men of Bedford were forever talking about the changed climate on Wall Street. She was tired of hearing of the new, intense legal scrutiny of the white-collar world.

The fruit was now peeled, sorted, and washed, and Nora stirred through the acidic juice to prevent browning. After mashing the fruits in their ready-to-boil pots, she tipped in packets of dry pectin, the trick to turning out set jam every time. She needed to move fast now. The steps came in rapid succession. It was easier to do the rest alone.

The women loved watching Nora move about her kitchen, handling everything with such expert ease. It was like being on set at a cooking show.

"Okay, girls, now the fun part," Nora said. "If some of you could set out the jars from the dishwashers—be careful, they're hot—we can all start filling them."

There was suddenly much bustling in the room. Glass clanking against marble sounded like percussion. Fruity steam rose like a dry-ice fog. Filled and lidded jars were passed along. Some women stuck on hand-decorated name labels. Others secured gingham hats with ribbon tied above skirted brims. Nora stood back to sip water from her tumbler. Conversations about the room layered over one another. Jenna Newhouse was sharing ideas for where to hold the next annual Boys and Girls Club Humanitarian Award Dinner, Caitlin Maynard told of how cute she found the tennis coach who filled in for her regular one that morning, Lacy of the vacation home she and her husband had just purchased. Nora was happy just to listen, to take in this scene in her kitchen. How happy she felt . . . yes, she was. She was happy. Of course she was. How did she even hesitate? It was not possible for life to be better. She had it all, the Bedford estate, the Manhattan pied-à-terre, the private school, the home numbers of the most heavily booked contractors on speed dial. She could not think of another thing she wanted, well, save a paved parking area. How ridiculous then to feel once more that none of it was right.

And everything did feel right again when Thomas, Nicholas, and Charlie ran into the kitchen ahead of Beatriz.

"Look what we've made, boys," exclaimed Nora, gesturing to the jam jars.

"But where are our berries, Mom?" asked Nicholas.

"In the jars, darling. We turned them into mixed-berry jam." Nora crouched down to their level and took them all into a communal hug. Drawing back to look at Nicholas, she asked, "Can you find the labels that say 'mixed-berry jam,' Nicholas?"

Nicholas and Thomas both pulled away and started running around the bench, trying between seated and standing women to spy the sought labels. Charlie joined the dodging, thinking it a new game, not realizing it had a purpose, squealing with glee, stopping occasionally to wonder if he should hide, if this game was hide-and-seek.

In their rush, one of them shouldered out of alignment a reproduction on the wall of one of Nora's most beloved paintings, *Freedom from Want*. The original hung in the artist's eponymous museum in Massachusetts. Nora set down her glass. As she straightened the image of a kind-faced family happily gathered around a table to enjoy a turkey, Bonnie asked over the racket, "Who painted that again?"

"Norman Rockwell."

"Oh, yes, of course. It's a very, well, simple Thanksgiving they're having in the picture, isn't it? When I think of our table at Thanksgiving—" Bonnie's face took on a rapturous expression. She went on, "Our herringbone-weave tablecloths and napkins, the oversized fine china, the silverware with the braided-design handles, the lead-crystal champagne flutes, the artwork and antiques around the walls—"

"That's entirely the point," Nora interrupted, her back turned still while she tilted her head one way and then the other to ensure that the painting was hanging square again. "Rockwell once said, 'The commonplaces of America are to me the richest subjects in art.' His paintings depict the dignity of everyday people, like the books of Charles Dickens, who in many ways was like Rockwell, appreciated by the masses in his lifetime, but not until after death by critics, and they were both the most fabulous storytellers. . . ." After a few minor alterations the painting was square, and Nora turned back to the women. Wide-eyed silence met her, a silence that heightened the boys' whooping and the squelching of muddy boots and sneakers.

She had become carried away and had forgotten that discussions of art and literature were as welcomed in this private-school-mother world as books. It had shocked her to learn that there was no bookstore in Bedford. She had always read voraciously and trips to bookstores brought her as much joy as a bowl of fresh-picked strawberries and vanilla-bean-touched cream. Even the tiniest out-of-the-way New York towns had bookstores! The one in Millerton was a favorite, in fact. But the Bedford-mother life of volunteering, renovating, entertaining, and gossiping about high-end local real estate transactions left no time for reading—and the men could not even think of books between long hours on Wall Street and time on the golf course—an understanding of the community potential owners of bookstores had evidently arrived at before her.

She could have kicked herself now for exposing the women so in-delicately to terrain no longer familiar if it had been once, though a restless side felt unsatisfied and longed to engage in a discussion about how far from the sentiment of *Freedom from Want* the country had come. *That* was a conversation she would have enjoyed! It didn't always come freely, being good in the eyes of her world, but she knew it was better to keep in line. She differed enough already in her pas-sion for the art of baking. This was her world now, and a privileged one at that, and one played along, if one wanted to be in it. It was like a high-end card game. There were rules. To sit at the table you had to have a hell of a lot of money. To stay at the table you had to throw a lot of it into the pot. And you never questioned house rules.

Nora concealed her rebellious urge behind a decorous smile.

"I see them, Mom!" Thomas screamed proudly, not prepared to let Nicholas take such a prize as their mother's pride. "These ones here, at the end."

"These ones here, at the end," repeated Charlie, pointing in the same direction as Thomas, not yet able to read, but wanting to ap-pear as clever as his oldest brother.

"That's not fair," complained Nicholas, falling cross-legged to the floor, elbows on knees, uplifted fists impressed into grumpy cheeks. "Mom asked *me* to find them."

The women were as delighted by the change of subject as Nora was glad to be saved from her embarrassment, though her relief was not so intoxicating as to render her oblivious to the need now of some distraction to draw Nicholas out of his fury.

"Beatriz, perhaps the boys are tired," she said.

Beatriz stood quietly by the door.

"You've been so good to keep them occupied all day," continued

Nora, "but they need to wind down now. Would you take them inside to watch a movie?"

"*Sí, señora,*" replied Beatriz, and then looking at the boys, "Come, *mis niños.* I will put on *Charlie and the Chocolate Factory.*"

Nicholas bounded up like a spring to rush out with his brothers.

But then Nora moved quickly to the door and called out to Beatriz. "*Sí, señora?*"

"Beatriz, don't use the media room. Use the DVD player in the family room."

"*Sí, señora.*"

Turning back to her guests, Nora put her hand over her heart and gave an exaggerated sigh. "That was close," she said. "I remembered I hadn't yet removed the labels from the new armchairs in the media room. I would hate for Beatriz to see how much I spent on them. It was more altogether than her whole year's wages!"

Bonnie gushed, "I do the same thing! I always run boutique bags up to our bedroom before Carmelita can see how many I brought home. But you know, I feel angry later, that I have to hide in my own house, that Carmelita might dare to feel ungrateful. I'm forever giving her clothes, and putting up with her arriving late, and moping about her boyfriend always cheating on her. I'm even sponsoring her green card!"

"It's still better to hide your bags," Sara Woodward added while tying a pink-checked hat over a jar with white ribbon. "I once left out an invoice from Badrutt's Palace in St. Moritz and suffered this passive-aggressive thing from Adonica for a week."

None of this was quite what Nora meant. She had meant simply to be considerate of Beatriz. But that instinctive good intention shifted now to the greater pull to keep her seat at this lovely, privileged, irresistible table and she forced a laugh of complicity.

Though the laugh, the day, it exhausted her. Settling later that evening into the cushions of the family-room sofa, she relished the moment alone in the comfort of her home. Amid the textures of rib-knit, velvet, leather, and fur, the hues of paisley, tea-stained cotton, and gold embroidery, thick blue bullion rugs beneath, the interior of her house felt as luxurious as Bergdorf's during the holiday season.

She closed her eyes to restore her balance after her busy day. The heady aroma of the glass of Cabernet Sauvignon in her hand soothed as if heated lavender oil. Beatriz had hours ago put the boys to bed before leaving, and Evan was finishing the shower he now always took immediately when he arrived home. Showers hadn't always been his first thought walking in the door. She remembered the early years of their marriage, when he had longed to come home, to unbutton her blouse, bury his face in her breast. Things were somehow different now in the middle of their marriage. It had occurred to her recently that she could no longer even remember the last time she and Evan had even enjoyed one of their intense cultural discussions. It seemed strange to her now that she had once taken it for granted that they both loved literature and art. In the early years of their marriage they had read the same books just to talk together about them afterward. They had spent hours sipping wine and discussing exhibits, theater, films, architecture, food. It had all felt so natural that it had never occurred to her that people lived otherwise and for other things, or that there might come a time when their life also would become about other things. No one had warned her, either, that it was possible for two people so alike still to become one day so uncomfortably separate.

She wondered now whether another romantic vacation might breathe some life back into their relationship. It had been five months since they had returned from their annual clothes-shopping trip to Milan. She and Evan always went in February, while Beatriz stayed home with the children. The sales were on then—though they still managed to spend twenty-odd thousand each trip even before the bill from Milan's Four Seasons, the hotel they adored for its concierge, who got them into the best restaurants, and could always produce otherwise-unavailable Teatro alla Scala opera tickets. There were no plans to go away again until the holiday season, when the whole family together with Beatriz would go down to the Caribbean or over to Aspen to ski, she had yet to decide. They always went away in the holiday season, partly because neither she nor Evan had family still alive with whom they wanted to spend the holidays. Evan's mother had died in his teenage years as her father had died in her teen years, and Evan's father was as impossible in his character as her stepfather was jealous of her rise above him in lifestyle. Neither of them had siblings, or grandparents still living. She had not made plans to rent a house in Martha's Vineyard next month, as they had done last August. Evan had told her he needed to stay close to the city. She and the boys and Beatriz could have rented a house without him. Many of her friends did that, and liked vacationing this way so much that when their husbands who funded these $100,000-a-season beachfront homes visited, it felt to their wives like an intrusion. But Nora sensed that a separation like this would not be good for her marriage right now.

She opened her eyes when she heard Evan enter the room. She watched as he poured himself a glass of wine from the opened bottle she had left for him on the bar. His damp dark hair was combed back—the gray at the temples to be expected in men edging toward forty—his well-groomed feet bare, his tall, broad frame enveloped in the favorite white toweling robe that Beatriz managed to keep as soft in its eternal washes as a baby's blanket. He was an extraordinarily handsome man, her husband; no one could deny it. Long dark lashes and thick dark brows framed apple-green eyes as striking as his strong cheekbones and perfect aquiline nose. His face caused reactions, lesser men to feel intimidated, people to give him things for no other reason, women to become flustered or flirtatious. His looks so overpowered some women that they would completely ignore the existence of a fiancée—the salesgirl from whom Evan bought her engagement ring at Tiffany's had passed over her home number with the ring—or a wife. Nora would never forget one lunch she and Evan had shared at the restaurant '21' in Manhattan when she had been pregnant with Thomas. The woman lunching at the adjacent table had spent the entire lunch ignoring her own luncheon partner and talking to Evan. Nora had suspected from then on that Evan enjoyed the attention.

"Evan, I've been thinking." She waited for him to pad across the room and sit opposite her in his favorite armchair. "Why don't just you and me get away? Beatriz would stay with the kids, and we could spend a few days on a beach. Let's fly down to Barbados again. We loved that resort Sandy Lane with the kids last year. It was nicer even, I think, than the Four Seasons in Nevis. We could just lie in the sun, and get facials and massages, and linger over long lunches and dinners. What do you think?"

He stared silently at the wine stem he twirled slowly between his thumb and four fingers, and then looked up at her through eyes awash with a pallid anger.

What was he so angry about? Or was she mistaken?

He said flatly, "I've got too much going on right now." He took her in then, her worn straight-legged jeans, blue shirt, bare feet, hair still tucked in its French twist.

"How was your jam-making thing?"

She knew her husband well enough to know when he wanted to change the subject.

"Good. Fine. Lacy and Ned finally decided how to spend Ned's bonus last year. They've just bought an eight-bedroom beachfront vacation home on the Cape."

"Good for them." He was looking down into his glass again.

"You know," Nora went on, "it reminded me with all the cars here today that we really should do something about a guest parking bay."

Evan sighed heavily, his eyes seeming to will a long life for that sigh as if it were a curling puff of cigar smoke blessedly hiding his emotions. When the cover had evidently dissipated he took a long swallow of wine.

It was finally clear to Nora that her husband had no intention of engaging in any meaningful conversation. She stood with her glass and headed into the kitchen, resignedly throwing over her shoulder the mention of dinner. The caterers had left a tomato and onion salad for two, and a roasted chicken smeared with a cumin-accented olive oil and stuffed with apricots, slivered almonds, raisins, and cumin. She turned on the plasma television. It was mounted on the wall beyond the end of the island bench. Last night she had recorded their favorite show, *Curb Your Enthusiasm*. Watching it over dinner would fill the lack of conversation, and might get a laugh out of Evan. As she was finishing clicking all the right buttons, Evan walked in with his glass, sat on one of the island stools, and focused on the flickering picture. She felt sad for him suddenly and wanted to hug him. Perhaps that look of anger she thought she saw earlier was the deadness of fatigue. He had needed to stay in the city at their pied-à-terre so often recently. His impossible workload left no time even to commute. And it wasn't as if there weren't *any* great days anymore. But another part of her still rankled that he had barely validated her presence that night, and so she took up the carving knife and sliced breast meat for her, and for Evan, who preferred red meat, carved drumsticks. It occurred to her after she had plated the meat and was spooning Mediterranean stuffing beside it that she had forgotten to tell Evan what had happened the other day.

"I know this is not the right time, darling, that you're tired, but you'll probably leave in the morning before I get to mention it, and I need you to call and scream at our banker tomorrow. I forgot to tell you, but when I was buying aprons for the women in this little kitchen store in New Canaan, the damn bank wouldn't approve the charge. It was only sixteen hundred dollars! You put your Porsche on that card! Probably it's a security thing. Maybe you've been using our credit cards more than usual lately, or something. The store owner said I could pay later, but it was embarrassing."

Evan looked at her blankly, closed his eyes, and nodded that he would take care of it.

Two

After her dinner of beans and rice and her dessert of fresh warmed berries ladled over *la señora's* shortbread, Beatriz had tidied her apartment and gone to bed after a shower with a book. She had taken to reading biographies of women in business. It gave her an hour or two of delight at night to scrutinize the stories for ideas for what to do next with her life, and for clues to how to go about it. She was sensible enough to feel grateful for her current circumstances, but she was also sensible enough to know circumstances changed. Though the days with her *niños* still felt wonderfully long, the years with them were flying past. All too soon they would be independent. That would be her time to become independent, too. She had achieved it already, of course, rented her own apartment now, paid her own bills, but she wanted to be her own boss. She knew what had sparked the idea. Sometimes a word was all it took to light ambition. That was how it had been: just hearing in passing of fellow domestic workers who had started their own cleaning business and now sold franchises. So far she had outlined strategies for a dozen different businesses or careers as an independent contractor. Thumbnailed, then discarded them. It was not that she was a dreamer. Had she been only that she would not have enrolled in the night course in business administration that she loved. Rather, she was awaiting the next epiphany. She had learned it paid to wait for answers to reveal themselves.

In truth she had taken to reading also as a distraction from inopportune bodily urgings—really none were opportune. In the last year or two since forty had become closer than thirty-five, the ticking of her clock had begun to feel physical. She knew exactly now when yet another of her eggs set off from the starting block. It was as if she felt every one of its trusting strokes. She would think of lambs bleating innocently en route to the slaughters that would void their potential. She would think of lambs when she was not thinking of sex. For along with the scratching in her womb came this urging. It felt like all she could do sometimes to keep from asking almost any man in the street right out whether he would mind taking a few minutes to make love to her. As easy as asking him to sign a petition: Either he would consent or not. That was how desperate she became sometimes, trying to summon the courage through reasoning to go through with it. Though it was always unreasonable reasoning, since it was not within her even to ask for a signature. She hated asking for anything. Not only could she never ask a man on a date, she had come to believe she put out the wrong signals. Now that she had been sober and self-sufficient for so long, she suspected men looked at her as someone who did not need a man. And mostly that was true. Really she did not even want a man. Sex, yes, but not a man afterward: at least not the sort of man with whom she had last shared a night, more than ten years ago. He had been her last for good reason. Though in the way that all bad things had silver linings, he had done her a great favor without knowing it.

Her first impression of him had been that he smelled of liquor. She had found the smell reassuring. It reassured her he drank the way everyone she knew then did. She had sat next to him on a sofa at a party in a house shared by three times as many people as rooms. He was flirting with another woman, but she could tell after a while he liked her better. When he asked her would she like to go somewhere, she had just stood up, ready to follow. They had shared a bottle of something in the car on the way to wherever it was. They had taken her car, the falling-apart thing that it was, though he had said it was better he drove. That was all she remembered. She woke up the next morning naked under a canopy of trees. She could hear a man— no two, three—barking laughs somewhere in the trees behind her. For a moment she thought she was dreaming, but when the barks came again and louder she scrambled to her feet, grabbed her blouse and skirt and heels, and dressed without stockings while running to her car. She only realized later how lucky she had been that the keys were in the ignition. She drove looking for a highway. The police found her instead. She thought she had been raped, she told them. A hospital examination could not support her story. All she would ever know about what had happened that night was that it could not have been good but might have been worse. She was charged with driving while intoxicated and referred for treatment to an outpatient rehabilitation program.

It was beneath the fluorescent lights of that state facility that she finally realized she was an alcoholic. The first day she did not think she was. She still did not think she was the third week. She sat in group sessions resentfully, silently underscoring the ways others' stories differed from her own. Then in the fourth week a girl had walked into one of the sessions. She had been working the streets down by the Port Authority in the city since she was fourteen. Drinking was the only thing that numbed the fear and pain so that she could keep working, and she had needed to work because if she did not keep up payments on her drunken father's gambling debts, they would burn his trailer. Only her father had satisfied his own debts by dying of

cirrhosis of the liver, and she had contracted so many diseases by being too drunk to insist on condoms that they had told her she would
never have children.

Beatriz had taken a good long look at herself in the mirror that night
and had asked the emaciated image where she thought she was headed.
She and that girl in the session were fundamentally the same. Both of
them had allowed alcohol to keep them from rising out of damaged
lives, as though deep down they did not believe themselves worthy of
anything better. She had earned her green card by slaving for a family
her first three years, had studied English so untiringly to improve upon
the amount she learned in the convent she attended until she was fifteen that people asked was she born here, and all for what? She drank
so much and so often that when she felt hungry she thought of filling
her stomach with a drink. When she did eat something—usually
spoonfuls of peanut butter or rank-smelling leftover Chinese food—
she felt so sick she needed a drink to feel better. She had made herself
as invisible as she often felt.

All she had to show for her life after selling her car and the little
else she owned to pay her fine and supplement her living costs while in
treatment were a few clothes and bathroom accessories. And she
had her hair, she thought, managing to make a little joke about the
mess that had become her life; it made her feel there was hope when
she could laugh about it. What made the idea of her hair so funny
was that more than once she had considered selling it. She had beautiful hair, she had always been told, long, thick, silky black hair that
almost enveloped her petite frame. It was the picture of that hair
that did it. It was as if she were noticing its beauty for the first time.
It was the spiritual moment someone might have beholding a miracle
or discovering God. Selling it seemed suddenly preposterous. It was
not vanity, but an awakening. After so many years of being clueless
and lost she was finding self-respect. She did not want to lose any

more of herself; she wanted to value what she had and to make her place in the world finally sturdy.

Three months later, she found herself almost miraculously at *Señor* and *Señora* Banks's. The instantaneous attachment she felt to their house surprised her. After *Señora* Banks's call the previous afternoon she had felt only vague hope, and gratitude to the neighbor of her first employer. The week before, this neighbor had seen her leaving an office-cleaning business. It had not taken much to persuade the owner to divulge Beatriz's telephone number. Her unexpected benefactor of sorts had taken it upon herself to find Beatriz better work, and it happened that her son was an acquaintance of *Señor* Banks.

It was odd that she felt such a powerful sense of promise at the house. It was falling apart. Shutters hung as awkwardly from their hinges as the roof slanted in the wrong direction. The paint was so badly peeled it took a guess to know the house had once been white. Boards covered two front windows. A tree branch had grown into a side porch. There were no other gardens to speak of, unless sideburns of high grass and weeds counted. Someone else might have been incredulous that a family had moved in. But she saw only a home-in-progress. Though this property was still a place apart from her world, there was something about it, something that felt overwhelmingly right. She wanted to get inside, remove the dust and grime, bring the floors and windows to a reflective shine, sort every drawer and cupboard, water drooping plants, revive life. She found herself wanting desperately to make this house better, as if its rebirth offered a tangible image of her own.

"Beatriz, is it?" *La señora* answered the door. If Beatriz had formed a picture of the voice on the phone the previous day, she would have imagined a thin middle-aged woman in a skirt and matching sweater set. The voice had been that pearly. After Beatriz had disclosed in that conversation that she was a recovering alcoholic, *la señora* had responded, "We don't need to dwell on that. You've been given a glowing reference." So it was a surprise to see this tall *señora* standing in bare feet, jeans, and an oversized white T-shirt.

"Do come in." *La señora* wiped flour dust from her face. "I'm making tea."

Beatriz became aware then of men's voices and laughter. As *la señora* shut the door behind them, she also noticed the silver-framed photographs of her and presumably *el señor* on the console. They looked incredibly happy. It was hard to feign that kind of happiness. There were no pictures of children.

La señora ushered her into a kitchen. It was flooded with sunlight and messy in an endearing way. At least a dozen men huddled around a bench, sipping from large mugs, filling their mouths in between with muffins lifted from a rack. The men looked comfortable, like they ate here every day. They all wore jeans and T-shirts and work boots, in various states of grubbiness. It was clear that the call of muffins accounted for the deserted construction materials out front.

Beatriz noticed the gaze of a few fall unself-consciously to her legs; men often looked at her legs. She supposed the shimmer of her stockings caught the light. She understood when their glances did not rise: The rest of her revealed little, her attire buttoned up, the plumpness of her bun the only suggestion that her hair was long. She liked that her appearance closed her in, safe from prying eyes she feared would find her terrible secret. Not her alcoholism. That secret was no longer her own. Her secret she could never reveal. Never, though it still seared inside like acid every morning when she woke. The noises on the street below would come to her first, always the same wherever she stayed lately—the clanking, booming sounds of Dumpsters, the din of cars, horns blowing, tires screeching—and then the weight of needing to find a job, start over, would seep into her consciousness. Just as her optimism and determination would begin to counterbalance that weight, the acid would hit her stomach with the power of tequila shots before she became used to them.

After *la señora* had introduced her, the oldest-looking of the men put down his mug, wiped his mouth with the back of his forearm, then slapped the fronts of his thighs.

The cracking sound roused his workers.

After the men had returned outside, *la señora* invited her to sit up at the bench. She handed her a mug of tea. "I hope you like the tea that way," she said, stacking a few more baking trays into the sink. She wiped her palms on the front of her jeans. The informality of her manner made Beatriz feel at ease. She imagined *la señora* had that effect on everyone. "I find it complements these muffins better when it's creamy and sweet. Have a muffin, too. They're delicious."

The phone had started to ring then, though just as *la señora* said she would leave it, a clinking drew their attention toward the glass door to the back porch. A large dog had a paw raised, scratching at the glass as if waving at them.

Behind the dog stood a man.

La señora moved quickly to open the door. The dog bounded into the house, his paws up on her stomach in no time, as if reaching for a kiss of greeting. She took his head into her hands and ruffled his jowls. "Hey, boy, I've missed you."

"It seems he's missed you, too." The stocky man dressed in jeans and a cotton shirt followed his dog into the house. His clean attire contradicted his smell of dirt and fish emulsion, or it might have been kelp. One of his hands rested in his pocket. In the other he jangled a set of keys. His handsomeish face was freshly shaven and he wore his oil-black hair almost as cleanly buzzed as a marine. "He's not so friendly with most people. But you know that, of course. God, he nearly tore that contractor to pieces last time, didn't he? Guess the old boy figured he was protecting you. . . . Come on, Digger, give your lady friend a little space, boy."

"It was sweet, Digger protecting me. And the carpenter was good about it."

The man looked over at Beatriz. She noticed then that his eyes were misaligned, so that his left eye seemed to look at a different object to the right.

"Beatriz, this is Reuben," *la señora* said. "He supplies me with my fruit."

"Do you work in a shop?" Beatriz asked.

"Shop?"

"Do you run a store?"

"Ah. No, I have an orchard."

"Not just any orchard," *la señora* said enthusiastically. "*The* orchard. He grows the best organic fruit in the state, supplies some of the leading restaurants in Manhattan. He's something of a celebrity in the food world."

"It sounds big, your orchard." Beatriz smoothed the front of her skirt.

"Actually I like to keep it small enough that I can still work the soil myself."

"Reuben grew up the son of a fruit-picker," *la señora* said.

He laughed. "The soil got into my blood, the smell of it, the warmth of it. Most men dream about fancy cars, I guess. My dreams are of fancy shovels and trowels."

Nora smiled. "I'm talking to Beatriz about working here."

He nodded. "Well, you couldn't work for a nicer lady, Beatriz. When I first came to this house the garage door was open and I found Mrs. Banks—"

"Reuben, please, *please* call me Nora!"

"I found Nora bottle-feeding a heavily bandaged doe. She had found the deer injured on her property and was nursing it back to health." He chuckled. "Of course, some would say that Nora is just a romantic and doesn't want to acknowledge the ravager behind the shiny eyes. Anyone else would have had the thing put to sleep. People around here hate deer. They eat all the landscaping."

The phone started to ring again.

Reuben turned to *la señora*. "Want me to take your crates down to the cellar?"

Nora nodded. He looked at Beatriz again. "It was a pleasure to meet you."

"And you."

La señora crouched down. "See you later, Digger."

Then she stood to pick up the phone.

It was not until more than an hour after she arrived that Beatriz and *la señora* began to talk. Life in the house was that busy. She could tell that her answers pleased *la señora*, and not far into the conversation *la senora* offered the position. Beatriz offered in return her Social Security number. She assumed *la señora* would want to do a background check. But she shrugged off the offer. Beatriz could see she was partly too busy managing her house and its renovations and its flow of people to be bothered with background checks. But there was something else. *La señora's* shrug had seemed more a physical recoiling from unpleasant realities. Something told Beatriz that Reuben had been right when telling the story of the doe that *la señora* had a tendency to romanticize. She suspected *la señora* wanted her to fit the idea *la señora* had of a housekeeper in her world.

La señora had given her the option of living in when she had told her how she was living. They had spent that afternoon furnishing her room with pieces from other rooms and stocking her bookshelves with books borrowed from the house library. *La señora* thought of things like that. She even filled a vase on the bedside table with flowers from the bouquet in the foyer. They ate dinner together that first night, and the following morning *la señora* took her shopping for clothes. She still wore those skirts and blouses and sweaters and heels, she cared for them that meticulously. Though *la señora* would become increasingly busy over the years, and the times they were alone together would become less frequent, she would feel eternally indebted for the generosity *la señora* extended to her at this lowest point in her life. She believed she would go to the grave wishing for some meaningful way to repay the kindness.

✳ ✳ ✳

Beatriz put down the book she had been staring at and rearranged the pillows. The air felt clammy and she slid off the bed in her full-length white cotton nightgown, her hair unbunned and braided down her back, and turned on the air conditioner protruding out her bedroom window. She glanced through the blinds at her view of darkened shopfronts. The air lolled between buildings like a corpulent presence that had moved in and refused to budge. A man smoking a cigarette hurried down the street. There were no other pedestrians. Her apartment took up the second floor of an old, narrow, three-story building in the Stamford, Connecticut, commercial district, and though in business hours the rhythmic street noises shook her lights, after dark virtually nothing moved. The night street reminded her of an abandoned movie set. Not even a dog barked. Her eyes landed on the malfunctioning neon letters of the grocery sign down the street. Really it was a newsstand that sold fried-egg sandwiches and coffee in the mornings. The flickering wash of lights appeared to her as an image of the jittery torment she had been battling since what had happened that very morning.

La señora had urged her the night before not to arrive early. But she knew *la señora* was just being considerate. She knew that once the children awoke and Reuben delivered the crates of fruit there would be no stopping before the guests arrived for the jam-making day. When she had turned up the drive that morning, the first light of dawn was softening the blackness of night in the country. She cut the lights on the car. She did not want to wake anyone. Deer were trying to nose their way through the landscape fencing. At first she thought the figure that rose slowly above their outlines was one rearing on its hind legs in frustration. Then the figure began moving toward her car and she realized it was that of a man. In the moment it took her to decide whether to get out and scream or to keep driving around the circular driveway at the risk of hitting him, a face came into focus. It was *el señor*. His face was pulled tight. She got out of the car. He was so close then she could smell his wet hair and warm breath. He was dressed for work, his tie knotted, his shirt crisp. His cuff links glimmered. He had something to say to her, she could tell. She stood quietly and waited. But rather than say anything, he sat on the bluestone curb by her feet, rested his elbows on his knees, and hung his hands and head between them. She could not walk away, nor could she stand there, superior to his pain. She sat quietly beside him, pulling her skirt securely over her bent, pressed knees.

They sat that way without a word as a fragile light overtook the darkness. She had seen her father in this position once, on the ground with his head between his knees. She had seen her father like this many times. But only once when he was not vomiting. She knew seeing her father that day that life had become too much for him. She had only been eight then, but she knew, the way she knew almost everything he felt. He had taught her without knowing it how to read him well. His moods would change so often that she had needed to learn to gauge them so she could manage him. Studying people carefully was the sort of self-preserving skill a child in an unsteady home learned quickly—not that she needed to protect herself exactly, at least not in any physical way. She had needed to understand how best to help this person she loved. She had taken the skill with her into adult life. Most times it helped her to get along. She could read what was needed of her. It was how she now guessed that it was best she stay still and quiet.

It was odd to see *el senor* this way. She had always loved most about him his expansive powerful energy. It felt uplifting being around him, and he was always so kind to her. He often wanted to know if she was happy and if she had enough money. Every other month he pressed a bonus check into her hands. But something was wrong in the house. She had known it for six months, could pinpoint the day things started to change. It was the day she found a hole in the wall of *el señor*'s home office. She had lost count of how many times she had called the carpenter to repair yet another of those fist holes in that room. Of course she always gave different explanations for the crumbled plaster. She had no idea if the carpenter believed her or not. She guessed he did. If you tipped people enough they went along with anything. *La señora* always kept plenty of tipping money for contractors and delivery people. She had never told *la señora* why she called the carpenter so often. *La señora* had long ago given her reign over managing the house. *La señora* never questioned the bills, either. She rarely read any bills she paid. It had worried her that *el señor* was capable of such aggression. But then she knew *el señor*. He would never hurt his family. That was why he punched the wall in no other room but his office. Even while angry he knew to hide its effects.

Other days when there were no holes in his office, *el señor*'s energy seemed more euphoric than positive. She always expected the announcement of extraordinary news those days. But all was usual, except that the volume was higher and the talk nonstop. And he could rarely be persuaded to sit down. The children loved those days, of course. Their playmate was tireless, and always brought gifts. Loads of them often. She always came around to liking those days, too. When the children and their father were screaming with delight, she always felt that nothing terrible could ever happen. But after days like that *el señor* would seem to disappear for a while. She always knew when he had not come home. His side of the bed was still made in the morning. When he reappeared he would look exhausted and seem distracted and clumsy. He had dropped his briefcase one of those times. It sprang open and spilled an assortment of papers. He had looked stricken as he scrambled to gather them. When she had tried to help, he snapped at her to go away, though he apologized later.

"I need your help, Beatriz." *El señor* lifted his head now and turned to look at her. A tear rolled down his cheek. The tear seemed incongruous. His voice sounded still so steady and strong. There was a mellifluous quality to his voice, like he might have been one of those soloist singers with a deep crooning voice women swooned over, only he was too much a manly man for an artistic profession to suit. Wall Street fitted him like a glove, with his powerful aura and almost military posture, the poker face that could belie the warmth and consideration she knew in him. "I know that I can trust you."

"*Sí, señor.*"

"I have installed a safe in my office. I got the idea there was space behind the wall when I put my fist through it the first time. . . ."

He looked at her intently. If he had not known for certain that it was she who had the holes repaired, he knew now. She showed no surprise at his remark.

"The safe is behind the wall in that same place." He made an attempt at a smile. "It took me a while to do as good a job at the plastering as your carpenter."

She lowered her head.

"If something happens to me, Beatriz, I want you to tell Nora it's there."

She looked up again. *"Señor?"*

"I don't want her knowing about the safe unless something happens to me."

He hung his head again between his knees. She did not understand what he was talking about. Then it came to her: *El señor* was speaking of suicide. Everything all of a sudden made sense. His strange behavior lately; he was severely depressed.

Though she knew it was inappropriate for her to touch her boss, she reached out and took his hand in her own. "You cannot do this thing, *señor*. Your family loves you."

"It's too late, Beatriz."

"It is never too late, *señor*."

He took back his hand and gave a chuckle at once frightening and frightened.

"It's over, all right. It's most definitely over."

She sat quietly a moment.

"Señor, I think that maybe we should tell *la señora."*

The sudden resolve in *el señor's* eyes told her that this was not going to happen.

"Beatriz, listen, it's over for *me.* I'm asking you to help me to help Nora. You need to trust me as I'm trusting you. It'll be better this way for everyone."

They were quiet again for a while.

"I don't know when this might happen, Beatriz. But I need to know that Nora will have what's in the safe. Will you do this for me?"

She looked up and away from him at the morning. She looked back at him. "I will do this if you assure me that you will get some help."

"Believe me, Beatriz, I'm getting all the help I can afford."

She nodded.

"Is there a code I need to give to *la señora?"*

"Tell her to remember the place I proposed to her."

That had been it. He stood up and said thank you, in a way that added sadness to her acute worry. His soft tread over the grass sounded so lonely. Thoughts crowded her head as she stood to watch him drive out and away. She was remembering how *el señor* had asked her a few months back where the landscape gardeners stored the rope. She had not thought anything of it at the time. Though she should have. *El señor* was putting his fist through the wall by then. As soon as she had the opportunity she would search for and hide any rope on the property. But surely there was more she could do. She could not just stand by and let this happen. Perhaps she could investigate anti-depressants. Maybe that was all he needed. And that would save *la señora* having to question her husband's state of mind. She understood why *el señor* had looked at her with such resolve when insisting she not tell *la señora*. *La señora* would never be able to face such a thing as her husband not fitting his designated role. That had been, after all, why she, Beatriz, had hidden *el senor's* fist holes.

She kept glancing at *la señora* that morning in the house. She seemed in such a truly happy mood again. She laughed when Digger reached up to nuzzle her as always when he arrived with Reuben. She hummed as she stacked the crates Reuben left. Her eyes lit up when one of the *niños* ran to show her their latest origami creation.

Surely *el señor* would never leave this, she had told herself.

Surely, surely, she told herself again now in bed.

Three

Evan and Beatriz escorted the boys up the garden path of another perfectly restored 1950s suburban home to the front porch where a man dressed as a vampire was handing out to dozens of children miniature chocolate bars. The path was crowded with adorable little giggling ghosts and witches and skeletons comparing levels of candy in their buckets. Spiderwebs covered the bushes to either side of the path, and up ahead a fog machine worked its eerie magic around a foam tombstone. Charlie clung to Beatriz's leg. Watching from the pavement, Nora imagined his eyes under his costume wide and darting. She was happy to hang back for a bit and watch. It was one of her favorite nights of the year. Every Halloween, the residents of downtown Katonah—the most folksy of the three hamlets in the town of Bedford—decorated their classic homes with scarecrows and orange-and-purple string lights and inflatable scary things and then camped out in costumes on their front porches. The local children would run from one porch to another, forgetting to feel scared for the excitement. Sometimes they would also forget to say "Trick or treat," but just hold out their bags, expecting them to be filled. Others were just too shy or young to say anything except "Thank you." In other cases the children were older and more savvy:

Who would go to the trouble of decorating their house this way only to invite a trick? Those were the children whose buckets at the end of the night overflowed, and they no longer carried child-sized buckets, either. The younger children always stepped aside for these bigger children, frightened of them and wishing they were them at the same time.

Her boys looked darling dressed as the Three Musketeers. Costumes in their sizes for the Three Musketeers had been impossible to find. She had ordered pirate costumes in the end, with high black boots and thick matching belts. She made the musketeer hats and long cardboard swords herself. It seemed they had barely taken their costumes off these past weeks. At the John Jay Homestead annual Halloween event they had decorated giant cookies and had followed a haunted trail around the property and outbuildings. The trail ended in high grass rushes where a dead man hung from a tree. On a sugar high the dead man seemed real. Then there was Thomas's class social at the local apple orchard famed for its cider donuts. The children had rattled down from the hills in a hayride to select a pumpkin to take home to carve. The boys had all attended private Halloween parties, and that morning they had paraded with their classes through the school playground for the parents, a smaller version of the annual Halloween parade through the quaint village of Bedford itself. Childhoods hardly came better than the life of a child here. She became particularly appreciative of the fact at this time of year. She was all the more appreciative this year because Evan also seemed back to his old wonderful self. For the past month he had been coming home in time for dinner with the children, and he was mentally and emotionally there for his family again. Not that the boys could possibly know it, but their parents' love life had also lit up. It was again as tender and exciting almost as their first years together. She had been conscious lately of mothers looking at her at school pickup in a way that seemed subtly envious, and she had wondered whether they sensed her renewed sexual activity and contentment.

Or perhaps she just looked younger suddenly, her face no longer tight with worry. Things between her and Evan had become truly awful for a while. At first it was just that Evan's sleeping patterns became highly irregular. If he went to bed at a normal hour, he rose in the middle of the night. During a family weekend in the Hamptons in August she awoke to a call from the husband with whom she had the previous night gone to bed. He had inexplicably risen in darkness and driven back to Bedford. In the early fall, his behavior took a darker turn. She and Evan were driving one afternoon up to the Berkshires for a weekend without children. Evan was driving her car because a recent accident destroyed his beloved Porsche. The ranges to either side of the Taconic were afire with golds and reds, but the song of their beauty was brief, for she noticed a police car in the trees ahead. Its driver directed a hand-held radar device at cars traveling back toward the city. She looked over at the speedometer. Evan was speeding. She asked him to slow down. He did for a minute. And then suddenly he planted his foot on the accelerator. She turned to him. His face was blank, as if there were no one inside any longer. "What are you doing?" The chill of fear stabbed like a blade. "Evan!" And suddenly she was thinking that his story of the other driver being in the wrong in his accident was perhaps not the truth.

She had never thought she would be grateful to see police lights flashing in the side mirror. After the ticket was issued, she insisted on the wheel. She considered driving home, but there was nowhere to turn, and after a while she had driven too far to think about going back. It felt easier to keep going straight, in any case, to be still with what had happened. It was just a moment, a moment in a long marriage, but it had shifted something. She could not imagine there was anything more terrifying than your life being driven out of control by someone else's behavior, much less your own husband's.

In their room at the inn later, she screamed at him for twenty minutes. The next day her fatigue after a restless night made all that was becoming wrong in her marriage seem overwhelming. Each time when she had the opportunity she let her anger fly. Not once did Evan answer her back. Their second night there, he told her he needed to go out to make a phone call. She barely had the stomach even to mutter, "Whatever." Two hours later he came back drenched in skunk stink. He had gone walking in the woods and frightened one. It might once have been an incident to have them rolling on the floor in fits of laughter. Instead, she lifted the bedside phone, dialed the concierge downstairs, ordered her husband a separate room, and went back to her book. She had not even asked was he all right. And that was why a week later she felt contrite. Contrite, and selfish, and ashamed. The way she had reacted to the skunk stink was symptomatic of her general appalling lack of concern for her husband. What was wrong with her that she was incapable of empathy?

As soon as the children settled back in school, she made a reservation at a resort in Bermuda. It was a place suffused with a feeling of such calm that she was sure she and Evan would be able to talk finally there. Only he had not made their flight. He had told her to go ahead. He would meet her at the hotel. But each day the concierge gave her the message that her husband would be coming the day after that. She could not remember ever feeling so lonely as she did dining each night alone amid other couples in the romantic setting of the resort's clifftop restaurant. She wondered whether the maître d'—who asked every night would her husband be joining her that night—believed after a while that she even had a husband. Many of the women guests had certainly started looking at her with eyes suspicious that she was shopping for one of theirs—when they were not looking at their husbands narrowly for also glancing her way. She flew home alone after four days. At home Beatriz said she had thought *el señor* was with her in Bermuda. She did not return any of Evan's calls from his office and their pied-à-terre that week. Then that Saturday he also failed to show to coach soccer. That morning *he* didn't answer *her* calls. She had to apologize herself to the parents hugging thermoses and struggling to restrain dogs excited to play with the dozens of five-year-olds in muddied cleats. When he came home later that day, it was evident he hadn't slept.

In their room alone, she said it, the thought she had kept stomping down, but that still kept pushing up again and again.

You're having an affair, goddamn you!

He just stared at her with agony in his eyes, then shook his head ever so slightly, as if in disbelief that she would say such a thing. What happened next was so quick that she only realized at the sound of shattering glass that Evan had thrown a book that was on the bed at the mirror. There were no more words after that. She cleared the glass shards and then walked downstairs in a daze to put jackets on the children. She drove with them to a city hotel. Evan had needed to pry them back. He took over the hotel suite with bouquets of flowers sent by the hour. On the second night he stood crying outside the door. She let him in only because the children would not have understood otherwise. In whispers while the boys giddily took on the adventures that were their room service dinners, he swore he was not seeing anyone and that he would never throw anything and frighten her or the children like that again. He begged her forgiveness and implored her and the children to come home. She consented to both things subject to his behaving again like a husband and father should. The next day after she had taken the children to school, she answered a call from their insurance agent. He wanted to know did Mr. Banks want the papers sent to the home or office? He and Evan had worked all through Friday night on them apparently. Evan had wanted to update the family policies, among other things. At least he had not spent Friday night with another woman.

But leaving him for a spell had seemed to prod him back to life.

Now nothing was too good for his family. He forewent the showers he had grown dependent on as soon as he walked in the door. He joined the children straight off instead for another game of Monopoly or Parcheesi. After dinner he sat patiently through Thomas's and Nicholas's reading howework. If one of the boys screamed out at night, he rose to adjust their covers and stroke their brows until they fell back to sleep. One night he brought home a squeezable, lightweight, bright yellow vinyl ball the size of a softball. It had a big black smiley face on it. Whenever it hit a surface, like the palm of a hand when being caught, it would send out a cascade of laughter. It was impossible not to laugh with it. Whenever one of the boys would get into a bad mood, he would throw that ball at them and have them laughing in no time. The boys adored this father and had already come to expect his early arrival home. Often they would be waiting at the door to the garage, ready to jump forward and frighten him when he walked in. Those nights reminded her of how she once ran down the street to greet her own father as he got off the bus after orchestra rehearsal. She remembered an abandoned lot on that street. Someone kept a white horse in it. She would sometimes take a carrot with her, to feed the horse while she waited for the bus. Only one day the horse bit her jawbone and she had been afraid of horses ever since. It was why she did not keep horses on her estate, though it was suited to an equestrian lifestyle.

Other nights Evan seemed happy just watching her. She would move about at her baking, and he would sit and take her in, like a sailor committing his new bride to memory before being shipped off to sea. The intensity of those evenings aroused her. Once they tipped over a saucepan of melted chocolate in their hurry to take one another. She loved the way he made love: at once powerful and selfless. He went about bringing her pleasure with such confidence that she abandoned herself to him every time.

Last Sunday they had all gone hiking along one of the trails in the

4,700-acre Ward Pound Ridge Reservation. At one point the trail seemed to grow narrow and thicker with vegetation. Evan had told them to wait while he explored ahead. He disappeared into the shrubbery and soon they could not hear him, either. It seemed like he was gone for a long time. Thomas said eventually, "When's Daddy coming back?" and it felt like her heart skipped a beat, though she smiled and said, "Oh, he won't be long, darling." After a while she had told them he was probably waiting for them, after all, and they had all filed one after another along the narrow path after Evan. But he was nowhere to be seen. The boys had started to think that he was playing hide-and-seek and she encouraged the notion, though she had started to think herself about the Australian novel *Picnic at Hanging Rock*. In the story three private-school girls and their teacher mysteriously vanish after climbing the eponymous rock on a school country outing. She felt a quiet panic take hold of her and it was all she could do to keep up the conversation about anthills and how it would have been smarter if we were built like camels and did not have to carry water bottles. "Are leaves powerful, Mom?" Thomas had asked at one point. "Well, they're not thought of as powerful exactly," she had responded distractedly. "So how do they make wind?" Then just as she took a break from feeling panicked to marvel at how a child might so easily imagine that leaves pumped out the wind rather than blew in it, Evan appeared above them breathing heavily and looking desperately relieved. He had explored a side trail and when he turned back there were several trails and they all looked the same. He felt like he had been lost forever. But he had found his way back to his family, and she knew then somehow he always would.

※　※　※

She could hear Evan and the boys talking as they headed back down the garden path with miniature chocolate bars added to their buckets.

"Dad, why does everyone have jack-o'-lanterns at Halloween?" Thomas asked.

"Ah, here's a scary story for you . . ."

They all stopped and the boys looked up. Nicholas's hat fell off when he tilted his head. He left it lying on the ground, he was that enthralled.

"It all goes back to a greedy old farmer named Jack . . ."

Evan smiled down warmly at their eager faces.

Beatriz hung back and clasped her hands loosely at hip level.

"Well, this Jack, he once tricked the devil—"

"What's the devil, Dad?" Charlie interrupted.

"An evil thing," responded Thomas.

Charlie and Nicholas looked at Thomas, then back up at their father.

"People have different ideas about the devil. I think the devil is a way of understanding temptation. Old Jack was tempted by money; that was his devil."

"My devil is chocolate," announced Thomas.

"Mine, too," said Nicholas.

"Me, too," Charlie chimed in without understanding.

Evan laughed.

"So what about Jack?" Thomas asked.

"Well, one Halloween, Jack was in a tavern and the devil walked in. Old Jack decided to play a trick on him. He screamed loudly for all to hear that he would sell his soul for a purse of money. Quick as a wink the devil turned into a purse of money. Old Jack grabbed the purse and put it into his pocket, where he knew the purse that was really the devil would be trapped. For in his pocket was a cross. And the one thing that could destroy the devil's powers was a cross. Now, old Jack made a deal with the devil. He would let him go if he promised never to lead old Jack's soul to hell. The devil kept his promise

and when old Jack died and was not let into heaven the devil closed
the gates to hell, too. So the devil got the better of him in the end.
Old Jack's soul was left to roam with no place to rest. To see his way
through the darkness, he hollowed a vegetable he was munching
when he died and filled it with embers. Now at Halloween when evil
spirits come closest to tempting us, we carve jack-o'-lanterns to remind us never to be so tempted as old Jack."

"Wow," said Nicholas.

"Wow," echoed Charlie.

Thomas paused a moment. "Does that mean I'm supposed to re-
sist chocolate?"

The boys assumed a posture of sudden concern.

Evan laughed again.

"No, I have it on good authority that chocolate is good for you on
Halloween."

"In moderation." Nora had joined them on the now emptier path.

"You're such a buzzkill, Mom," Nicholas said.

"Nicholas, don't talk to your mother like that," Evan reprimanded.

"Just joking."

"Even in jest. You should always, always speak to your mother respectfully."

They all headed along the pavement to the next house, Beatriz
and the boys ahead, Nora and Evan side by side a good way behind
them already, the boys were that fast. The crunching of leaves underfoot in semidarkness sharpened the drama of the night. Flash-
lights darted every which way. Almost all the children carried them,
though really they were not needed. Porch lights and string lights lit
the pathways well enough. Up ahead on the pavement a resident was
roasting rows and rows of marshmallows on a spit. She held out one
of the long skewers and children slid off the gooey blobs, tossing
them from palm to palm like hot potatoes to cool them. Farther along
on the pavement other children were putting their hands and buck-

ets behind their backs and bobbing for apples. The air was crisp—
soon it would get too cold for the boys without jackets; maybe they
would do just another couple of houses, then head home for a bath.
She also found herself consumed with a desire suddenly to be intimate with Evan.

She slipped her hand into his. He squeezed it and bent to kiss her.

"You two lovebirds!" It was Bonnie and George, waving from
across the street. They were a witch and a wizard, their daughter
Chloe in a miniature version of her mother's costume. She and Evan
had not dressed up, though Beatriz had dressed as a female musketeer. Together, she and Beatriz and the boys had made her costume.

"Your costumes are spectacular!" Evan shouted over the street.

George hollered back, "I said to Bonnie, 'I'm not going to wear this
thing, I tell you!' But you know how women are. She said, 'Fine'—well,
we all know *fine* really means anything but fine—and then I get the
silent treatment."

"Come on, look at you two: You're made for each other," Evan reassured.

George rolled his eyes. He titled his head at the same time, to make
the gesture more dramatic. "Made for each other, huh!" he shouted.

"You're lucky to have me!" Bonnie said sourly. "Who do you think
is going to make you such superb dinners, for a start? Nobody cooks
better than me!"

"Huh, who do you think got the better deal in this marriage?"

People were looking, but George thought it was hysterical.

Bonnie stooped to readjust Chloe's costume. She was not smiling.

"So when are we going to hit the links, Evan ol' boy?"

"Soon, soon," Evan said.

Nora hollered, "We've got to catch up with the boys! I can't even
see where they've gone." She waved good-bye. "See you at drop-off
tomorrow, Bonnie."

But Bonnie was busy fluffing Chloe's purple hair.

"What was *that* all about?" Evan asked after they had moved on.

"Well, let's see . . . George hasn't slept with Bonnie since Chloe was born. . . . He's embarrassed about her collection of vibrators; not least because his penis is apparently a lot, lot smaller than them all. . . . He's had two affairs she knows about. . . . She has cleverly assumed over the years control of their money so that it would cost him a lot now to leave her. . . . She fantasizes about bondage. . . . He had always been predictable in bed. . . . She has tried on occasion to write pornographic novels. . . . When he shows disgust she threatens to use a vibrator in front of him, which makes him more disgusted. . . . He's a bottom man, she has no bottom anymore, and he has no appreciation for her enormous breasts. Which explanation do you want?"

"You're kidding, right?"

"Nope."

"How do you know all this?"

"You know how Bonnie asks me over for an afternoon cocktail whenever George travels? Well, one of those nights a few months back she had quite a few drinks. . . ."

"And she told you all this?"

"Uh-huh."

"Why didn't you tell me?"

She gave him a look.

"Oh . . . it was during that time with us. . . ." He looked at her with a furrowed brow. "I had no idea you girls talked about such things."

"Wait, are you surprised at what I told you, or that it was me who told you?"

"Well, the latter, really. Imagine if one of our boys started explaining what a prostitute was. You'd be shocked that he understood."

"Evan. I'm not a child."

"You're as virtuous as one, though."

She laughed.

But as she nestled her head into his shoulder, her smile died, for her eyes landed on that husband whose manner toward her was always so unsettling. He was standing alone on the side of the pavement up ahead, talking on his cell phone, staring at her under his brow with those eyes that always radiated searing intelligence, mingled with cunning, narcissism, and a rippling energy that seemed to want to burst open his shirt buttons. Fox Silverworth was a little older than she and Evan, his full head of slightly curled hair all gray, though he combed it back neatly in a way that made it appear still slick from the shower—presumably the effect of some type of hair product. He evidently took pride in his appearance. He was not much taller than her, but his powerful build told of a regular gym routine. His skin was always clear and freshly shaven, his nails were always neatly clipped, and his fingers remained remarkably unstained for a chain-smoker.

This was the first time Nora had seen him dressed casually. Those mornings he delivered his daughter to school he was dressed in expensive dark Italian suits. Presumably his sense of style worked only office hours. He was dressed now in unstylish loose blue jeans and a black bomber jacket. How had his wife let him go out dressed like that! Anyone might have thought there was no wife.

Now that she was staring back at him, he flashed her a smile full of . . . what was that in his smile that made her uncomfortable? She could not put her finger on it, only understood some vague intention. And then the word came to her: *ambition*. It was one thing to make no bones about raw ambition, but to direct it at her turned it to sexual impertinence. And then he just as suddenly turned to the conversation on his cell phone, took a long, deep draw on his cigarette, and crossed the street without giving her a second look. She was left feeling that perhaps he had not been appraising her after all and that *she'd* been narcissistic to think it. She looked after him as he disappeared into giggling shadows and felt annoyed with herself for letting this virtual stranger's manner affect her so that she was always left bemused after crossing paths with him.

As she continued along with Evan still kissing her forehead on his shoulder, she recalled what Evan once said of this man he had evidently not noticed this evening.

"He came from nothing and graduated top of his class at Temple University School of Law and partnered with a fellow graduate to set up their own law firm in Manhattan. Most of their clients are big-time real estate developers, and in the last decade of huge property deals, his firm has grown tenfold. He's pretty ruthless from what I've heard when it comes to making a buck, the sort of guy who'd sell out his mother."

She tightly took hold of Evan's arm and remembered Fox Silverworth was a disgusting man, only it was not enough to shake her perverse interest in him, and she found herself wondering if she might not have imagined that look after all.

✳ ✳ ✳

It was starting to rain. She could hear the pattering against the roofline gutters above their second-floor bedroom window. She slid out of bed quietly so as not to wake Evan and slid the window down. The bedside table clock read 4:30 A.M. She had not slept and yet did not feel tired. Making great love could do that to her. It aroused her like caffeine to wakefulness. There seemed little point going back to bed now. The children would be up in just an hour and a half. She swirled a wrap over her long strappy black nightgown and padded in bare feet along the carpeted hall to the children's bedrooms. She could see into all three of their bedrooms from this place in the hall. Their arms fell to either side and their mouths hung open, in full abandonment to the home they knew as safe. She had told them they could not eat any more candy when they got home from trick-or-treating, and she smiled now to notice her musketeers had listened only partly. Clearly they had later discussed a plan, as they did when one was needed. They had each placed their buckets below them on the floor, where they could reach for them instantly in the morning, when they had not yet been told they could not eat candy. The buckets were in the kitchen when she put them to bed.

They did that sometimes, crept around together after bedtime, thinking no one knew. Most times she did know, but she let them do it anyway. It was the innocent stuff of childhood. She loved hearing them giggling and noisily trying to tiptoe, as much as she loved their bedtime ritual. Every night of their talking lives she and they had sat up in her and Evan's bed and after reading them a story they would each tell the best part of their day. When it came to Charlie's turn those nights he would stand bolt upright on the bed, often still naked after his bath, and wave his plastic sword. His favorite toy was his little brown sword. It stayed in his hand through bathtimes and sleep (the one time she tried slipping it from his sleeping grip he woke instantly), and when he ate or went to the bathroom he laid it carefully beside him, watching narrowly lest someone try to take it. Last night the best part to all the boys' days was the same: Daddy taking them trick-or-treating.

"Tell us again how you and Dad met, Mom," Thomas had pleaded, cleverly pushing bedtime off still further.

"It's very late, boys. . . ."

"Please, please," Charlie and Nicholas had together chimed.

All three of them then started jumping up and down on the bed.

Clearly they were still on a sugar high.

"Ah-h hah, yeah, yeah, ah-hah, yeah, yeah," they chimed in chorus.

It was their invented chant like a rain dance to bring on something they wanted.

She and Evan laughed; the boys knew they had won. They scampered back under the covers, so that all five of them again rested in a line along the headboard.

"Your mother was the most angelic thing I'd ever seen." Evan looked over at her. He was grinning. He loved telling the story. She felt herself blush slightly.

"She was in her final year of the two-year analyst-training program at Morgan Stanley, where we both worked at the time."

"Your daddy was much more senior than me; he was an associate investment banker then. I was still in the training program fresh out of college. He'd even been to graduate school. Do you remember what an M.B.A. is?"

"Who's telling this story?" Evan put on a mock face of indignation.

"We want Daddy to tell it!" Nicholas shouted. "He tells the best stories."

"Okay, okay." She smiled.

"Your mother was stepping out of the elevator one morning with a take-out coffee from this café down on the ground floor. I was so entranced I just followed her back to her desk, to see where she sat. The next morning I went down to the café and described your mother to the owner and asked was she a regular and how she took her coffee. Well, this guy just smiled at me and you know what he said?"

"I know," Thomas announced proudly. "He said, 'Join the line, buddy.'"

"That's right, Tom."

"Every morning when your mother would get her coffee she would chat awhile with the owner, and most times after she walked out, there would be some guy drinking his coffee in the café who would ask him, 'Who was that?' So I handed this owner a one-hundred-dollar bill and he made me a coffee just the way she liked it."

"Wow, one hundred dollars!" Nicholas marveled. He never got over how much money it seemed. It took him a year to make just eight dollars by searching the floors around the drink machines at the tennis club for dropped coins. And he had to suffer his mother all the while nagging him to please, please get off the floor.

"That's the way the real world works, little buddies. You've got to have money to be in the game."

"Evan . . ."

"All right, all right, your mother's getting cross with me now. So I stood in front of her desk and handed her coffee to her and asked would she join me for dinner. She seemed a bit shocked at first, and then she regained her composure and said with the most beautiful smile, 'Hi, my name's Nora. And you are?'"

"I know what you said then, Dad," Thomas said in a rush to beat his father to it. "You said to Mom, 'I'm your future husband.'"

"That's right, little buddies. It had seemed to me when she stepped out of that elevator that first day like she was a delicate little bunny rabbit popping its head out of the burrow, and I was damned—"

"Evan . . ."

"There was no way I was going to let any of the foxes out there snare her."

"So you snared me yourself!" Nora laughed, and although she made fun of him, she was recalling how her first reaction to *him* had been similarly overwhelming, and not just because of the way he looked, or because of his charm and dynamism. Though she had never resolved the question of whether certain souls were fated to join for some higher purpose, the elation Evan effected in her being had brought her then closer to an answer.

Nora closed the boys' bedroom doors quietly and felt her way down the stairs, grateful for moonlight through the windows at the top of the double-story entrance foyer. In the kitchen she toasted a slice of bread. Dry toast was her only reliable remedy for the morning queasiness. That, and ginger. She could eat a whole bag of Australian crystallized ginger at a time when the nausea got bad, and it did get bad, often. In the first trimesters of her other three pregnancies the nausea had virtually incapacitated her. She had needed to avoid stores that sold food. In her own kitchen she had sealed her nose with a swimmer's clip. Just the trace smell of coffee or anything fried had the effect on her of poison. Her stomach would seize, her head would cloud, and her vision would blur so that there was no escape even in television. The condition was compounded during the first pregnancy by worry that something was wrong; surely no baby could survive this. *She* could barely survive it. But then she read it was healthy for a pregnant woman's sense of smell in the first trimester to become sensitive to food potentially toxic to a new embryo.

The rain had begun lashing. An inspired wind was making miniature twisters of sodden fallen leaves. She would have liked more toast, but she dusted her fingers over the sink and started through the rooms to check the windows. She thought she heard car doors closing out front, but it must have been claps of thunder or a tree branch knocking at the roof. A window in the laundry had been left open and she slipped on a circle of rainwater on the floor. She steadied herself against the wall, but felt shaken for a moment. She closed the window and threw some towels over the puddle and thought about warming milk and going back to bed for a while. But the telephone rang and she went back into the kitchen to answer it. She presumed it was Evan's car service confirming a car en route; she would need to make Evan a coffee and get him under the shower. But when she put the phone to her ear she heard only a dial tone. She idly took a bite of cold toast, expecting whomever it had been to ring back momentarily. Then the ringing sounded again, only it was not the telephone at all. It was the doorbell; Evan's car must be in the drive.

In the entrance foyer, she turned on the front porch light and looked through one of the glass panels alongside the door. The porch light sparked like a firecracker, then went out. It did that sometimes in bad weather. She kept meaning to have the wires looked at. She had expected to see a man standing respectfully on the doorstep in a driving cap. Instead she made out a group of dark figures standing under umbrellas, their flashlight beams darting about like a light show. She could not believe that people were still trick-or-treating. It was almost morning. And in this weather! It was unusual to see trick-or-treaters at their door, too. The drives in this part of Bedford were too long. By the time children walked from one house to the next, they could have mounted ten porches in Katonah. Perhaps that was why the people outside were still at it! They had yet to make their candy quota! No, more likely now that she thought of it seriously, this was a good family salvaging Halloween for their children who had not been able to trick-or-treat last night. She had heard of a family doing this before. She looked at the clock. It was just after five A.M. Many people rose that early around here, or earlier even to be in Manhattan by seven A.M. These people were likely neighbors. "Just a minute," she said, padding back to the kitchen to find treats for their buckets.

She pulled her wrap tighter and opened the door. A scattering of raindrops blew into her face. She started to hold out the bag of Kit Kats, but something was wrong. There were no children. The adults—men, all of them, she realized now, some half dozen—all wore the same costume: windbreakers over polyester suits. One had his jacket open. She saw a gun in a holster. Everything about them seemed too real. She clutched her wrap tighter. The metallic taste of fear sat heavy in the back of her throat. She inched back inside the door. The men all stayed where they were. She noticed how tall and broad the man in front of them all was. It crossed her mind that he could snap her like a twig. She drew back further and, without moving her eyes, screamed in a shaky voice, "Evan!"

"Nora Banks?" The voice of the man in front was loud and authoritative.

How did these people know her name?

The man held up some type of identification.

"We have a warrant here for your husband's arrest."

She heard the words but did not understand them.

"We're FBI, ma'am."

The light outside was turning yellow.

"Where's your husband?"

Her hand hurt from gripping the doorknob so tightly.

"Ma'am, step to the side. Where's your husband?"

He stepped forward so that there was only a sliver of space be-tween them. He smelled of cigarettes and damp wool and something minty that was the gum she now noticed he was chewing; she could even hear it squelching between his teeth, the workings of his jaw purposely exaggerated and intimidating.

A sense of outrage brought her up abruptly.

"Get off my porch. My husband's done nothing wrong."

The man pushed past into the foyer. More men in suits followed.

"Evan!" she screamed again. The voice seemed to come from some-where outside her now. Then, to the men, "Get out of my house."

Eyes looked up the stairs. She followed them. Evan stood at the top in his bathrobe. She half registered Beatriz standing in her night-dress on the landing a long way over to Evan's right. Beatriz had stayed over in her old room. They had arrived home too late last night for her to drive home.

"Evan! Tell these men they are mistaken, tell them to leave, Evan, tell them to get out of our house."

Evan said nothing.

"Evan!"

Still he said nothing.

She saw Evan's face really for the first time then. It was ashen, his eyes almost absent. Why, he is sick! she thought, and she moved to go up to him. But she stopped when Evan said very quietly to the man beside her, "Just let me dress." This was not the Evan she knew when his wife was in danger. He had instinctively always jumped through fire to protect her. He would jump through fire to protect her from needing to be protected. She started to say something, but no words came out. Evan was looking at the men. He seemed unaware that anyone but they were in the room. All at once Charlie appeared, rubbing his eyes next to Beatriz and asking for Mommy. A new panic rose; the children could not see this. But Beatriz instinctively thrust her body between him and the scene. She pushed Charlie's face into her ghostly nightdress and shuffled him away.

Beatriz's absence left a void. Nora felt strangely more alone.

"Evan Banks, you're under arrest."

"No!" she yelled, grabbing at the sleeve of the man in charge. "You're wrong, you're wrong. Evan, tell him he's wrong. Tell him, Evan!"

The suit brushed her off like a fly.

Why wasn't Evan saying anything?

One of the suits had climbed the stairs and was leading Evan by the elbow back toward the bedroom. He wedged his hands under his armpits at the door and watched as Evan disappeared into the room. The suits in the foyer looked around, oblivious to the muddied rainwater spreading out from their feet. One on her right rested his hand on his Glock. "Nice place," he said, not bothering to look at her. "Bet he had to steal a lot to afford this!" She looked away from him. Evan emerged in jeans, a blue sweater, his olive rain jacket, and those boots he wore when they went hiking. His lips were tight. He had not combed his hair. It stuck up like a crest at the back. The suit outside the door patted him down. Her hand clutched her throat. Words that would no longer come were tearing at it from the inside. On the way down the stairs Evan looked at the carpet. It was then she registered that none of this seemed a surprise to him. At the bottom of the stairs, the head suit told Evan to put his wrists behind his back. A pair of handcuffs snapped around them. The wrists were her husband's. Just hours ago they were wrapped around her in bed.

A suit started to lead Evan out. Evan raised his head and looked at her, terror and sadness in his eyes. He did not take his eyes off her. Tears streamed down her face.

He said defeatedly, "Call my criminal attorney, Jarvis Finch. His number's in my cell phone."

He had a *criminal attorney*? She bit her bottom lip.

And then Evan was pushed so roughly toward the door that he stumbled.

He looked back for a moment and said, "I love you, Nora."

The suits then formed a tight semicircle behind him and stepped off the porch.

She started to follow them out.

"Stay inside, ma'am." The head suit was looking back at her. Her arms were now wrapped about her body to hold herself up. Her nightgown flapped like sails behind her in the wind. He then smirked as he added, "Don't worry, we'll have him back to you in twenty years."

WINTER

Four

Nora had been keeping up appearances for two months since the arrest when the exhaustion of the effort and of all she was now managing alone swelled to the feeling that a blood vessel would burst if she didn't rest. A stomach virus had struck the boys the previous night and she had spent the moonlit hours shuffling one and then the other to the bathroom, changing sheets and pajamas, showering soiled bodies, wondering as she armloaded laundry into a brief, dark calm at how life had not turned into a dead end, but into a desperate, endless, solitary swim through treacle. She had left when Beatriz arrived only because she needed respite from the stench of her life even more than rest. It had astonished her that the boys were then recovered. She had agreed to their pleas they still be allowed to go to school for end-of-semester celebrations only because to ask Beatriz to drive them would put an end to any more discussion.

She fastened her umbrella as she entered Phillip's and slid it into the stainless-steel stand. It had sleeted in Bedford for two days straight, icy cold finding its way between neck and scarf, inside cuffs not elasticised around wrists. Winter's bitterness had crept up early this year—for which she couldn't have been more grateful: The cold stopped everything from growing so that the grounds no longer needed mowing. For now, the estate didn't reveal how bad things were financially. And the women of Bedford *would* be scrutinizing her estate. If they went out of their way to drive past the addresses of new parents in the school directory to determine their level of wealth, they would most certainly be keeping the closest of eyes on a troubled stock already in the portfolio. She dreaded the snow, when she would have to do for the most part without a snowplower, and the spring, when the grass would almost be seen growing—unlike her landscaping, which would likely fail to flourish at all. She had told the landscapers not to repair the damaged deer fencing. She had canceled the painters she had scheduled six months ago to paint the house in the spring, too. She had hesitated before that call, conscious that the painters maintained the area's best estates and word would get out that climbing mildew at hers was not just an overlooked matter.

The café was empty, but she found a tucked-away seat nonetheless, delaying the inevitable. Again today she would be looked at that way: She was still the scandal *du jour*. She fumbled in her pocketbook for her compact mirror and dabbed at her cold sore. A part of her wanted to wipe the cover-up off again, to give the mothers later an inkling of her stress. She would push out her belly to emphasize her pregnancy at the same time, though pregnancies were too common to elicit solicitude—unless you suffered serious nausea, something she had not experienced beyond the first weeks this time, strangely. But she did not stop dabbing, for it was hopeless to expect compassion. That virtue registered about as much in this world as working mothers. The thing was to keep imperfections of every sort at bay at all costs. As she felt the effort of it all now, though, she clung again to a certain hope: A general Bedford mind-set might just save her and the boys. That mind-set was this: What mattered at the end of the day in Bedford was that you had money. In her case, *still* had money. And there was this in her favor: Nobody knew for sure

whether she did or not. Newspapers had printed no more on the subject of their finances than that Evan Banks had pleaded guilty to wire
fraud and had agreed to a prison term of two years and a restitution and punitive fine together amounting to $29 million. None knew
that they were not worth quite that amount. She suspected that accounted largely for the continued school-crowd looks, eyes still darting her way from all directions, straining to reexamine her since the
arrest, searching in the absence of clarity for clues. Of course, there
was also relief in the looks that this had not happened to them, and
surprise, so much surprise that she had not curled up and died. In the
same looks was also the unmistakable hint of respect for a restitution
and fine that could only come from a sizable life. But all it took to understand the redeeming value of money in Bedford was the memory
of how the women had responded to Pamela's quip on that jam-
making day in the summer when nobody cared whether Martha Stewart was then on house arrest: "Why would we? She's still rich. Richer
than any of us."

She, Nora, could not manage hefty checks to the right local charities just at the minute, but if she could just keep up the front for
long enough . . . well then, she might have back just in time a good
amount of her money.

An idea she could justify by what she had found in the safe.

She was filled at once with hope and the bone-chill of a remembered nightmare whenever her thoughts went back to the day she
discovered the safe—the day Evan was arrested, the day his attorney
told her that Evan preferred her not to attend the bail hearing, the
day she learned by television of her bleak future, the day journalists
began and friends stopped calling the house, the day the boys started
asking with a note of anxiety, "When's Daddy coming home?"

That day, Beatriz told her about it.

"*Señor* made me promise to tell you only if something happened to
him. I had thought he meant if some physical harm came to him—"

"A safe?" she had snapped. "What do you mean, a safe?"

She had felt angry enough that so many journalists, federal agents, lawyers—strangers all—had seemingly known more about her life than she had, and then even Beatriz knew something that she had not. Somehow Beatriz's composure also bothered her. It made her feel all the more frantic. She felt like she was fading, while Beatriz stayed steady, sturdy, like a rock she gripped gratefully but resentfully as the waves beat her this way and that, her color and vitality ebbing as the rock glistened, untroubled. Though she was dimly aware at the same time of the absence of superiority in Beatriz's calm.

"Why didn't he tell *me?*" Nora had raised her voice to try to regain some semblance of control. Her voice was the only power remaining in a life that had overnight been wrested from her grasp, though that voice sounded even to her as weak, trembling, fragile, insignificant. It was the unheard scream of someone drowning alone at sea.

"I cannot know, *señora,*" Beatriz had replied with a kindness that was so disorienting for coming from a whole new dynamic between them, disorienting even though she was shocked at the contrasting uneasiness and unkindness of so many others. Her mother had phoned early on her cell phone—at least the journalists did not have that number. Her stepfather had seen the morning news in their condo in Florida. "How is Evan?" her mother had asked. Not, how was her daughter, or how were her grandchildren, but how was the man who had done this to them. Her mother would never change. She idolized men with money; they could do no wrong. Her stepfather was less impressed with Evan's money. It diminished in his wife's eyes his own net worth. If Evan had been poor and in trouble, her mother would not have asked about him. She knew this because of the way her mother had treated her father; she had not ever tried to hide her disdain for his inability to earn any real money as a musician. Her mother had resented their spartan life in an apartment in

Providence. After her father died, her mother remarried quickly. Her stepfather was a marketing director of a shoe company in Boston at the time, a man with an expense account.

"I'm sure he'll work this all out," her mother had said of Evan that fateful day. "Dreadful business, dreadful. Oh, well, let us know, of course, if there's anything we can do. Just don't call at seven P.M. That's when the girls come over for bridge."

At least her mother had made a phone call, she supposed, which was more than the Bedford mothers had done. There was no way that even one of them could not know what was going on. It only took one to know for them all to know. Even if one or two had been overlooked in the chain of phone calls invariably looping all about town, had not seen the morning television reports, surely their husbands would have phoned through the news from their offices. It was the Wall Street story of the day. "Fuck 'im," she imagined so many Wall Street men were saying. It bothered her, the inevitable schadenfreude out there. And it bothered her that it bothered her. How could she be feeling still such a powerful sense of protective loyalty toward Evan, while her rage at him so consumed her that it took every ounce of restraint not to burn his belongings in the fireplace? She had almost twice snapped, "Never!" to the boys' repeated question of when Daddy was coming home. She had kept the boys home that day, had kept them away from the television, too, until she knew what to tell them. But Charlie had let slip that some men came early in the morning for Daddy, and all day their mother had been a wreck, bloodshot puffy eyes, wavering voice, alternately shouting into the phone to "Stop calling here!" and hugging them too tightly. They knew something was wrong. Even the deer seemed to eye the house curiously.

"Perhaps the answer to why *señor* could not tell you about the safe will be inside it," Beatriz had suggested. "*El señor* said you would know the combination if you remembered the place he proposed."

The evening Evan proposed. When he knelt before her at the same Central Park bench on which they had first kissed, it felt natural and expected, never mind that they had known each other only three months. One giddy day after making love in the open country air, he had asked her if she wanted to have children. He was excited to become a father, unlike so many men his age. He was not then even thirty, though he was in a better financial position than most men his age. He had left Morgan Stanley just a few months earlier to start up his own hedge fund, and all early signs indicated great success. She had never thought about children. She had been too busy struggling to pay her way through Barnard while maintaining high grades and then working long days and weekends at Morgan Stanley. But all at once, with this man, having babies was all she wanted to do. They had been conjuring images of those children, the evening they became engaged on their bench, when a taxi swerved out of nowhere toward them. It squealed to a halt at their feet and a spotlight shone on them. The driver climbed out and walked forward. Evan stood up instinctively to protect her. The buffed, mustachioed man in jeans flashed a police badge and then a photograph. "We're looking for this man, have you seen him?" After they had shaken their heads and the plainclothes policeman left, she and Evan had burst into laughter over the odd encounter. It was the first of many funny stories that had grown over the years into the repertoire of a life together.

How could she have known then that this first unlikely event they experienced together would prophesy possibly their last, the authorities coming for Evan in the end? How could she have known that evening, either, that she was willing her life to a man who would put her and their children one day in such a position? But she knew that Evan had not been thinking of all this when tasking her to remember the place he proposed to her. He had meant her to think of the bench. He had dedicated that park bench to her, for five thousand dollars paid to the Central Park Conservancy. He had told her many times that his life began on that bench. The bench dedication had been to her, "My life." Six letters, *m, y, l, i, f, e*, numbered in the alphabet *13, 25, 12, 9, 6,* and *5.* That was the combination to the safe. She had not solved that just then on the spot. The day he dedicated the bench to her, he had laughingly said that if ever he was kidnapped and she needed to verify with his kidnappers that he was still alive, she should ask him to relay those numbers. She had been so happy that day to be thrown back into the childhood world of codes and intrigue.

That happiness seemed so distant now.

The first thing she noticed when she opened the safe was the wads of cash. Her stomach seized when she took them out. Things were seriously bad if Evan could only get money to her this way. She suddenly felt like a mobster's wife; she understood Evan had hidden this money from authorities and she knew she had to keep it. The words "Wall Street tycoons going down" and "Fortunes being seized" had played over and over on the television and in her mind. What else was she to do now; how else was she to feed her children, keep them in school?

Beatriz had appeared at that moment, her mouth shaped into a small smile. "The *señor*," she said. "He is a good man. He still looks after his family."

She threw Beatriz a look. We are in this position exactly because he *didn't* consider his family, she wanted to say. But she could not tell Beatriz anything Beatriz didn't already know. She had heard Beatriz turn on the television in her room that morning.

"May I please have some privacy!" Nora demanded.

She pulled a clump of hair from over her eyes and turned back to the safe.

Beatriz slipped quietly out of the room.

Beneath the wad of cash was a stack of papers. She sat cross-legged on the floor in the jeans she had pulled on earlier and began to read. On top was an old copy of her own bank statement showing the wire deposit that was her inheritance from her father's estate when she turned twenty-one. It had not been a large amount, only $50,000. Regardless, why was this document here? She turned the page and found herself reading investment statements showing how she had grown her inheritance on the advice of some M.B.A. students at Columbia she had met while at Barnard into $200,000. She had felt so proud, making that money then. She had not thought of it in years. She thumbed a series of transaction reports, backward and forward, following the numbers. It appeared that not only had Evan always kept her money separate from his and their other investments, but that he had turned her $200,000 during their engagement year in a series of legitimate commodities and currency trades into $3.5 million.

So where was that money?

The plaster dust irritated Nora's nostrils and she sneezed, surprised and relieved that her body still functioned. The telephone was ringing nonstop, the calls cut off she knew by a voice mail full of journalists' names and numbers and promises to report the human side of the family's story impartially. She made a mental note to unplug the phone; everyone she knew had her cell phone number.

The jerk of her body when she sneezed had shifted the papers. Now an envelope poked out. "My Life" was scrawled across it in Evan's handwriting. She knew it was his, anyone would. He had beautiful handwriting, unexpected in a man, though it had never seemed incongruous since his romantic side loomed so large for her.

Nora put down the financial documents and peeled back the envelope flap.

She read a page and dropped it, then read another and dropped it, then another and another until her crossed legs were covered in a blanket of sheets torn from a legal notepad.

She stared blankly at the hole in the wall and tried to take it all in. Three million of the three and a half million dollars had been used to purchase their estate ten years ago. It appeared Evan had reinvested the other half million and had grown it more over the following years to pay both the renovating bills as well as taxes on the investment earnings. Taxes. She had not prepared or even read a tax return since she met Evan. Every year Evan would hand her a joint return prepared by their accountant to sign and while pinning the telephone to her ear with her shoulder or bouncing a baby on her hip or shuffling with a child around her leg she would scrawl her signature trustingly and feel good about addressing the interruption so expediently. Not that she had been wrong evidently to trust that the returns were accurate. Evan was not being charged with tax fraud. It was just that not having read any returns had left her in the dark about all monies. It seemed now that she had paid for her own wedding gift and its complete renovation, Evan's investment of her money having made unexpectedly more than his new business that first year. He had not wanted to admit it at the time, having assured her that his business was booming, when in fact it would take another year to flourish. But it turned out now that the government had no easy claim to property owned by her and purchased entirely with her own money.

Though it would likely still try to make some claim, having months ago placed a *lis pendens* order on the property. This apparently prevented her in the meantime refinancing or selling it.

This would now all go to court.

To *court!*

She should have felt relieved, that possibly not all was lost, but all she felt was shocking incredulity. One moment her life had been hers, the next it became a battle to keep it. After staring numbly at the wall, something broke in her and she balled the sheets of paper in her fists and hurled them violently across the room. Fuck, fuck, fuck! The fucks came out as dry guttural sobs, bursting all about her like balloons of desperation swollen too big. She didn't even know when her throat became empty. She felt more tired than she had ever been. And that was just the first day.

✳ ✳ ✳

When Nora entered the café that morning, she had not noticed the owner, Phillip, in the kitchen doorway. But as she made her way through his modern-style café with its stainless-steel stools and bright lighting to a square, resin corner table, he had watched her. He wondered for a moment as he often did whether his customers were as aware as he of the incongruity of a man like him in a setting like this. He had told the designer his story: that he originated from the Australian bush. His love of baking had started in the outback, in fact, where he had baked in the coals of campfires. He had been designated "bush telly [campfire] cook" in his group of bushie mates, and along with bunya nut cakes, roasted such bush tucker as witchetty grubs on pieces of wire—"Nuh, it takes like peanut satay," he had explained when the designer screwed up her face—native lobsters called yabbies, snake, goanna. He had been an outdoorsman there through his twenties, making his living at different times as a cattleman and horseman and drover, sharing his bed at night with another outdoorsman, whom he thought he loved until the man left him for another man. He came to America lovelorn and married an American woman and stayed married and a construction worker through his thirties. They divorced in his forties without children, and he became so spent in his fifties—while training formally as a baker and then setting up Phillip's—from various relationships with men *and* women, that in his sixties now he had sworn off relationships altogether. He would "cark it before he had any other type of hottie in his bed again than a hot water bottle." He had offered all of this in his typical casual manner without a care that any of it would compromise his masculinity—why should a tall, broad man like him with swarthy squared features and a wry smile that could stop people dead be worried that anyone would doubt his masculinity? Indeed, the designer had completely disregarded his story in her concept for his café. She had insisted that in a shopping hub like Mount Kisco for surrounding affluent northern Westchester communities that prohibited chain stores, the look was more about development than preservation: The austere look was needed.

It was the first time he had seen Nora since the arrest. When she took her seat and he could see the profile of her face, he noticed how thin she had become. Her expression looked stricken, bewildered, lost. His jaw had dropped when he saw the reports on television. He had wrestled for days over whether he should take some Kakadu Plum jam over to her. He had long ago introduced it to her. They had built a loose friendship on their common interest of baking. He had visited her summer kitchen once, musing it would be his dream to have one. He had resolved to visit her after overhearing the private-school mothers one morning in his café. He could still remember all that was said.

"So Nora came up to me in the school hall yesterday and said . . ." At this point the long-faced olive-complexioned woman tried to mimic Nora's voice. "She said, 'I'm afraid I'm going to have to pull out of the committee.' How does she think I'm going to replace her at this late date? I'm going to have to do her work raising funds myself! It's just not done. She made a commitment. And then you know how she excused it?" Nora's accent was mimicked again: "'I'm just swamped.' Like I'm not! Well, I called her on it. I said to her, 'I'm at a loss, Nora.'" The woman switched back to Nora's voice: "'Pardon?' she asked all innocently. And so I said, 'Well, what really do you have to do? I fail to understand why you're so swamped just because your husband is away, so to speak. I mean my own husband is in Europe at the moment.'"

As the women laughed, he had shaken his head in disbelief.

"I bet she's enjoying all this," one of the other mothers had said.

Another responded, "She's always loved being the center of attention. Remember how she controlled everything like she was running her own cooking show at her jam-making day in the summer?"

His heart had gone out to Nora. So why had he waited out the overdue delivery of the jam from Australia before visiting her? Why hadn't he just damn well gone empty-handed? Now the recognition of a bad decision dammed in his chest.

He set down a tray of éclairs and moved toward her table.

He startled Nora when he appeared before her. He towered over her in his Driza-Bone hat he wore inside and out no matter the season. Nora had supposed once or twice that his hair was silver like his brows, but there was no knowing since his hat never came off. It wouldn't have surprised her if he slept in it.

"Mind?" he asked, gesturing toward the seat opposite her.

"Please," she said, making a determined effort at a smile.

He took a seat and flicked back his hat to reveal such warmth in his pale blue eyes that Nora found herself comforted by his mere presence.

He said, "You don't have to smile for me if you don't feel like smiling."

"If I don't feel like smiling?"

"I wouldn't feel like smiling if I was carrying your load."

It didn't surprise her that he knew; everyone knew. Rather than dropping her smile, she laughed, and her laughter had the anesthetic effect on her of a tumbler of brandy. Her inhibitions reduced, she felt a compulsion to confide in this kindly man.

"Smiling is the least of it, Phillip." She revealed all her pretenses then, everything from not wearing spandex to school drop-off anymore, lest anyone ask if she was heading over to the Saw Mill Club, when she had needed to cancel that membership, to washing her car more regularly: Only the ostentatiously rich could carry off a dirty car as a status symbol.

It probably all sounded ridiculous to him. But his gentle expression didn't change at all, and he seemed to be considering seriously her confession.

He said calmly, "It helps that your pickle is beyond the comprehension of your mates, I imagine. It's so far removed from how any of 'em live that it'll take something glaring for 'em to get the pic—leaving the school, say, or losing your house."

"Which will happen over my dead body!"

"You planning to go back to work, then?"

"What? I couldn't possibly. I haven't worked in ten years. I wouldn't know how to work any longer. And it would look as bad as losing the house! Hardly a woman I know works. And if I went back now it would be obvious that I *needed* to work."

"Nah, you'd be a quick study, and would anyone have to know?"

"Well . . . I don't know. Well, of course, people would know!"

"Not necessarily."

She was struck again as she often was with his rubbery nose. It seemed to change shape with his every new expression.

"What if you worked night shift?" he asked.

"Night shift!"

"I need a new head pastry chef: It's just occurred to me you'd be perfect!"

"I wondered how long it would take you to tease me."

"I'm serious."

"You're firing yourself as head pastry chef?"

"Business has slumped and what's needed is new talent."

"If talent is what you're looking for, you should be looking else-where."

"Yeah, right! And who better to know the tastes of my customer base?"

Phillip's face had lit up.

Nora felt she was letting him down, but there was nothing to do but refuse. Baking was hardly the solution to her money problems. She would make pennies relative to the millions they once had, and to bake as a hobby was one thing, but to do it professionally was, well, what it was was blue-collar work. This conversation had taken quite the wrong turn. She was a fool to have confided in Phillip. Now she felt worse both for Phillip's hopes having been raised when she had no intention ever of working in a bakery, and for the offer having driven home in a new way the wretchedness of her circumstances: These people who once served her thought nothing now of approaching her with jobs like theirs.

He looked at her with sudden concern. "You look like you're gonna chunder."

She *did* feel nauseous.

Phillip called after her, but she beetled out without looking back. As soon as she closed herself into the chrysalis of her car, anguish oozed from every pore of her body so that her skin grew clammy. For the rest of the morning she drove around aimlessly behind the big sunglasses she went nowhere without now.

Five

She was no more prepared to face the "mother crowd" when she turned off the car's engine several hours later in the school parking lot. She would have wished for anything but to have to endure yet again the effervescence of the gathering cluster of women outside the school entrance desiccate with her approach.

Thankfully, she would be partly saved today from the strain of light conversation. Another aspect to winter about which she had become both conscious and grateful: the necessary runs on days like this from car door to school door and more importantly from school to car. There was no lingering once the school doors opened. Returning to the plush warmth of vehicles took priority over social concerns. Of course, once there, mothers called one another on cell phones programmed into cars so that no headsets were needed. The acoustics of the speaker systems and background rush of vented heat created the perfect pitch of hurriedness. It complemented well the breathless voices used to ensure it was understood that life was busy, busy, busy, in all the appropriate ways of course. Busyness was worn like a badge of courage, excusing the women also from any self-reflection. But she would not have to steel herself either for any car conversations: Her phone rarely rang anymore. There would be no exceptions today, certainly: She had only managed the minimum fifty-dollar contribution to the boys' teachers' class gifts, though she knew one hundred and fifty was expected of parents for each teacher, and that volunteering class mothers who bought the gifts compared "parent generosity."

Gradually, she summoned the mettle to reenter the fray.

But no sooner had she climbed out of her car than the rear window of the chauffeured Town Car she had just at that moment noticed parked alongside her lowered to reveal Fox Silverworth, lounging in the back with a newspaper over his lap. Her first reaction was envy. How much easier to be a man and live oblivious to the mother scene!

And then he grinned in a way too familiar and he had her again as he always did, both enthralled and exasperated.

He said, "I must say you have an intriguing look when you're deep in thought."

He had been watching her as she summoned her mettle! She felt herself blush. She lowered her umbrella to refuse him the satisfaction. The man was odious.

"Why were you watching me?" she asked, looking at a dripping umbrella-spoke.

"You interest me."

She raised her umbrella and scanned the parking lot to be sure there were no other mothers in earshot. It would hardly do to be heard receiving such attention from one of their husbands. It would be bad enough to be seen talking alone with him.

She turned back to him. His eyes glowed to the same degree as his skin, the result in the latter case of some moisturizing product undoubtedly. She thought of a slippery seal.

"You don't think I would wantonly compromise your reputation, do you? Please give me more credit than that. I know how these women would pull into a coven if they thought you were putting claws into one of their husbands. Rest assured you're safe with me."

She was glaring now. "What does that even mean? That you are complimenting me but not propositioning me, or that you are propositioning me but assuring me of discretion?"

He laughed. "I had meant that I wouldn't be so presumptuous."

"And yet you tell me quite forwardly that I interest you."

"Does that interest have to be sexual?"

Again he had made her feel she had imagined more than there was! She didn't have the energy for this conversation.

"I'm going to collect my boys now."

"Don't you want to know why you interest me?"

"Not really."

"I'm going to tell you anyway. You're not like the other women up here. You're not from the same mold."

"Really," she said sarcastically.

"Well, I don't imagine my wife, for instance, would be walking around with so much genial dignity if I'd done to her what your husband did to you. I couldn't see any of these women"—he gave a nod toward the cluster outside the school entrance—"holding up as well in your place. Your strength doesn't surprise me, of course. I've always sensed something different in you. But it's interesting to behold."

"Things aren't always as they seem."

"By which you mean you don't feel strong."

She said nothing.

"My talking to you right now tells you that you are. I only bother engaging with people I have no doubt are strong. There's no fun to be had otherwise."

"But you just a moment ago implied your own wife wasn't strong."

"I don't engage with her."

"You mean you never talk?"

"Barely."

"Then why did you marry her?"

He laughed heartily. "Dear Nora, you are strong, but terribly naïve." There was a silence while he grinned at her. "I'm going to call you," he said. And then he leaned forward to tell the driver up front whom she had forgotten, "Pull up directly in front of the school, will you, so that I don't have to get out in this rain."

Call her? What was he talking about? The man was insufferable.

Nora went to move off, but then he laughed again.

She wheeled back.

He said to her with an expression of incredulity that she hadn't seen the obvious: "I married my wife for the money, silly goose. How else would I have been able to set up my business?"

She couldn't imagine marrying so coldly for money, and even worse was to gloat about it shamelessly. She decided there and then that she hated this man. As she crossed the road to the school, she made a mental effort to deposit all thoughts of him in an imaginary box and then pictured that box buried under one of the tall oaks in the far reaches of her property, never to be stumbled upon again and more effort than it was worth to uncover. And then with Fox Silverworth out of mind, she composed her expression and squared her shoulders for the next minefield.

The campus looked suddenly small, nondescript, a horizontal ranch-style at front, multiple levels in the rear, simple gray-painted brick and clapboard, white trim. A paved space big enough for just visitors to park set the entrance back from the side road, a tall wire-mesh fence separating the playground from the main road into the more populous town of Mount Kisco. It surprised her to see it, think of it as diminutive, this school that had loomed so large for so long in her consciousness. But perhaps it was the weather that did it. This incessant sleet made everything slump. The icy cold alone bent things out of shape, piercing as a blade so that bodies pulled inward.

The women had evidently not noticed her as she approached under her umbrella, for she heard Thomas's name mentioned before she stopped a short distance from them.

"Pardon?" Bonnie asked the mother who had spoken, the mother of a boy in Thomas's class, and the current chairperson of a committee formed of Presbyterian Church members to raise money for Christmas gifts for orphans. The Presbyterian Church was one of the three points on the Bedford Holy Trinity. The other two points were the Bedford Golf and Tennis Club and the private school. If you belonged to all three, you were "entrenched" and a certain glow was bestowed you. If you only belonged to one or two of the three, a fat checkbook went a long way toward making up for it. This mother ran her committee when not writing her customized Spanish-English cleaning guide so there would be no confusion and no need for repetition when new maids replaced old ones about how exactly she liked her cushions positioned.

"Did you know that Thomas's birthday party is the same day?"

"Oh, is it?" asked a third mother, the mother as it happened of Thomas's best friend. "I've already RSVP'd."

"How tragic," said Bonnie. Despite the cold, Bonnie was wearing the flip-flops they sent you off in after pedicures at Fashion Nails on the Village Green. Her toes were separated with cotton wads to keep her wet nails from rubbing against any neighboring toes. She was blowing her fingernails dry. "We're doing an Egyptian theme for Chloe's party this year. We're bringing in six camels to ride, and dancers and acrobats, and the musicians will be playing traditional harps and lyres and lutes and oboes and drums. We're even hiring an exotic dancer to drape guests as they arrive with wreaths of flowers, and the waiters will pour wine from ancient jugs for the adults. I told the caterers I wanted the banquet, 'Lavish, nothing short of lavish.'

Such a good word, isn't it? I think I'll make it my 'me' word. Oh, what a shame you'll be missing it. Though I guess you have to go to Thomas's, he being your son's best friend and all."

The mother of Thomas's best friend looked conflicted. She spoke in a voice more hushed, but hardly hushed enough, "And I do feel badly for Thomas."

"Yes, I know," sympathized Bonnie.

"Having lost his father and all."

"I'm sure you'll have a lovely time," said Bonnie. "What's Nora doing for the party again? Oh, that's right, pizza and cake at a bowling alley."

"You got an invitation, too?"

"Nora invited everyone in the second grade."

The mother of Thomas's best friend hesitated. When she spoke again it was as softly as a tiptoe. "But you still planned Chloe's party the same day?"

"I'd already made far too many plans by then to change anything."

"What did you say when you RSVP'd?"

"I told Nora she should think about changing the date of Thomas's party."

"Well, why do you think she hasn't?"

"She said the bowling alley didn't have any other openings around Thomas's birthday. I have no idea why she didn't just cancel the bowling and do a party another day at the house. A few phone calls and a few thousand and it'd be all handled."

The first mother said, "Thank goodness I haven't RSVP'd yet to Thomas's! I heard that simply everyone's going to yours. It's been the buzz all morning."

The mother of Thomas's best friend bit her bottom lip.

And then the first mother said to Bonnie, "Oh, I almost forgot, Bonnie. The girls and I extend an enormous thank-you for that extraordinarily generous contribution you made to our fund. It will make a lot of children in unfortunate circumstances so happy."

"Well, of course, anything to help."

Nora had stood beneath the cover of her umbrella all this time feeling grief-stricken for her boy at the hands of such brutality. God, who did these women think they were? Her fury was so hard she might have spat in their hypocritical faces if Thomas hadn't run up and hugged her, for then she looked down at his happy, unknowing face and a great protective tenderness infused her.

As she held him tightly with the arm not holding the umbrella above them, her eyes fell on the playground to the left of the school building. A wind had picked up, elevating clumps of rotten leaves. Over the sodden sandbox and up high into the naked, shivering limbs of a towering tree, a squirrel scampered on a reaping mission. It tucked into a bend like the crook of an elbow to devour its harvest. The playground looked so abandoned, so forgotten under the already darkening afternoon sky without bright-cheeked children racing tricycles or swings squeaking as they arched high and heavy with child in the air.

She felt a growing sense of aloneness with her children.

Thomas had called over his best friend.

"Can we have a play date?" Thomas was begging her.

The mother of Thomas's best friend appeared behind her son. This mother had made the task of hiring nannies a profession, and other mothers went to her for copies of her frequently revised "nanny contract." She preferred live-in nannies from the Midwest, and her contracted arrangements seemed mostly to work. Her relationship with the current nanny had worked so well that she had kept her on for company for herself now that her children were all in school all day—and so she could go at night to lectures on how to prepare your elementary school child for admission into Ivy colleges.

"We'd love to, Thomas," she said, "but we have to drop our dog at

Northwind Kennels." Northwind Kennels was the almost ten-acre wooded vacation resort for pets in the Bedford Hills estate area where they served gourmet dog food in temperature-controlled kennels into which they piped classical music. Everyone put their dogs there when they traveled to exotic locations to eat their own gourmet food and hear their own piped music. Their pets' vacations cost plenty—but that was still less than the veterinary bills over the year for every sneeze or hiccup or ingrown nail.

The mother looked up at Nora, ruffling her son's hair.

"My munchkin has always wanted to see the Eiffel Tower and so I thought, 'Why not take him over to see it this Christmas?' Of course, my husband can't come as usual. Ever since he became a partner at the firm, we never see him. It's such a drag having to travel with the nanny everywhere. I sometimes refer to our nanny as my husband!"

She found this funny and laughed.

Nora smiled, remembering that at least this family was coming to Thomas's party.

And then this mother's voice went up an octave and she spoke rapidly, "Oh, and Nora, I feel so absolutely terrible about this, I really do, but I believe that hopeless husband of mine promised Bonnie some time ago that we would of course attend Chloe's birthday party when it was planned. I didn't realize that when I RSVP'd to Thomas's, but of course since we promised Bonnie first, we're sort of obliged. . . ."

It was on the tip of Nora's tongue to say, "So when you said that your husband wasn't around anymore, you meant except to handle children's birthday invitations?"

But the woman's son cut in, "What! I can't go to Thomas's party? But Mom!"

His mother put her hands on his shoulders, the strain showing on her face now. "Maybe next year," she told him.

Thomas looked up at his mother with imploring eyes that salted the wound of Nora's impotence. She clenched her fists tightly to keep from embarrassing her son.

The mother could not look Nora in the face now. "I'm so sorry, Thomas. I'm sure you'll still have plenty of fun, and of course we'll drop off a present for you."

Nora took Thomas under her arm and held him close.

This mother was evidently waiting for Nora to say the expected, "Oh, never mind, I completely understand. Husbands! It's not at all necessary to drop around a present."

Instead Nora's smoldering silence shifted this mother from one foot to another.

Looking mortified, the mother mumbled holiday wishes, and hurried off with her son.

The rain saved Nora then. It began to fall heavily suddenly, wind whipping it in so many directions that umbrellas were pointless. Her boys all loved stormy weather, rolling clouds portending things unknown and spooky, and Nicholas and Charlie skipped ahead over the school crossing and toward the car and the holidays without cover or a care in the world. Only Thomas stayed behind, walking beside her, his heart drowning in tears too heavy to rise to his eyes. His wobbly chin gave him away. There was little Nora could do but hold him close and consider how she could still make his birthday special if she had to cancel the party. Indeed, how she could protect him from knowing that it was because of a lack of attendance? Other children now ran ahead of their mothers, too, their squeals of glee as they splashed in puddles drowning out their mothers' commands to get off the road. These mothers might have been covering their heads with jackets, or holding down the flapping rims of designer umbrellas, but their carriage and bearing was no less confident for the rain. Nora's and her son's humiliation weighed on her: She felt like a bending willow tree, straining against her nature to stand tall in a forest of elegant oaks.

Two mothers behind her were discussing their plans to vacation in the Caribbean.

One of their children piped in, "We're not going to Little Dix Bay again, are we?"

Little Dix Bay was a luxury resort in the Virgin Gorda.

The child went on, "That's such a dump. The Four Seasons is much better."

The mother responded, "But they don't have a Four Seasons on Virgin Gorda."

The child said, "Then why don't we go back to Nevis, where they do have one?"

"Isn't he cute!" the mother said.

"Adorable," the other mother replied.

Nora held Thomas close, her arm covering his ear. She didn't want him to feel on top of everything that they were the only ones not going away for the holidays, though it seemed that was the case. No sooner had she taken him under her wing than the women started discussing how to angle for play dates with Richard Gere's son when he started at the school next year.

She wondered suddenly how she was going to survive Bedford intact, and wished all at once she could just move on and leave it all behind, but of course she was legally prevented from selling her house and she couldn't afford to live elsewhere. And there was more than herself to think about. No, she must keep focused on fitting in this world. Her children's lustrous childhoods were at stake.

She drove home slowly along West Patent Road, past Daisy Hill Farm on the right with its frozen rolling hills and grazing horses blanketed caringly against the weather, icicles already arrowing downward from the gutters of its meticulously maintained barns, and over Guard Hill Road running end to end through the estate area—and as such rarely empty of cars. Some belonged to gawking outsiders, others to construction companies heading to the latest work site, the rest either real estate brokers showing off the area to customers or insiders taking the most efficient route to the village or the Bedford Golf and Tennis Club or the private-school middle-school campus. And then sometimes there were the Clock Winders, a group of neighbors who took turns winding the historical clock in its tall brick tower on the corner of Guard Hill and Succabone. Its chimes sounded accurately every hour over the surrounding bucolic scene. The Bedford Historical Society owned the Sutton Clock Tower, as it did the Bedford Oak. The society also owned seven historical buildings in the village. This venerable group attracted sizable donations, the preservation of Bedford's historical character being a foremost concern of its residents. The society had invited Nora to become a board member before Evan's arrest, her interest in kitchen antiquities and her preservation of her summer kitchen having piqued the board's interest, but she had politely declined after the newspaper stories and television reports. She imagined that was the right thing to do.

By the time she and the boys pulled into their drive, the heated confines of the car now steaming, a bead of perspiration wending down her temple, the boys had turned restless. At first, she didn't register the shift in mood. Her addled mind had begun scratching again for solutions to the problem of one of her trees that had fallen in the storm the other afternoon on to the roof of the caretaker's cottage on a neighboring estate. The tree still lay where it had fallen, a tormenting reminder each time she drove in or out of her property of her dismal circumstances. She could neither afford the deductible, if she claimed the cleanup on insurance, nor the thousands it would otherwise cost. The neighbor had already accused her of being unneighborly for not immediately putting up the money. Not having money here equated with not having manners. The neighbor knew of Evan's arrest, had been watching that fateful morning. It was incredible to her that he did not just have his caretaker chainsaw the tree and be done with it given the circumstances, though his miserliness should not have surprised her. How many times had mothers positioned themselves in the line at Phillip's so that she would end up paying for their coffees? Even after Evan's arrest they would exclaim before moving off to another table, "Oh, Nora, I hadn't realized . . . well, thank you." Not once had anyone paid for hers.

"Mom, my ears are hot," Nicholas yelled, unraveling the scarf from around his neck and flinging it between the two front seats so that it landed on the dashboard.

The flying scarf startled her into registering the commotion in the car.

"And my socks are wet inside my boots."

"Mine, too," echoed Charlie.

"Mom, how do you spell 'video'?" Thomas asked all of a sudden.

Just then one of Nicholas's boots came flying toward the windshield.

"Nicholas!" she yelled, half turning to ensure another boot-projectile was not about to launch. She caught a noseful of smelly-sock smell. Nicholas had undone his seat belt and had zinged himself over the passenger-seat row headfirst into the cargo hold.

"Nicholas, you're not allowed to take off your seat belt until we have stopped!"

"'Video,' Mom, how do you spell 'video'?"

"Just a minute, Thomas."

She slowed to a crawl up the drive. Short of stopping the car and getting out in the rain, she could not get to Nicholas. And he knew it. In the rearview mirror she could see his brilliant blue eyes sparkling on the high of mischievousness gotten away with. Nicholas suffered from three conditions: allergies to mosquito bites, intolerance to heat, and extreme fluctuations of blood sugar. The latter two were affecting him now, she understood. There would be no reasoning with him until he was cooled and fed.

"But Thomas was elbowing me! You should be yelling at him!"

"Was not!" Thomas defied.

"Were so!"

"Mom, I wasn't. Nicholas is lying!"

"I need to go wee-wee!" Charlie yelled urgently above the fray. She glanced up again into the rearview mirror and noticed all at once how chapped Charlie's lips were. There was a feathering of blood on the bottom one. She had completely forgotten every one of these bitter days to put lip balm on any of their lips. Also, his nose was running. He was swiping at it with the back of his sleeve. Then, for whatever reason, he took up his feet in his hands in one of those poses particular to children and dancers and she saw, too, that his shoes were on the wrong feet. How had she not noticed that this morning?

"We'll be inside in a minute, darling," she tried to console him.

"But I need to go *now!*"

"Mom, where's my water bottle?" demanded Thomas. "I'm so thirsty I'm going to die." He made a sound to imitate someone choking to death, like that was how someone would die of dehydration.

"Mooooooom! I need to go wee-wee!"

Nicholas screamed, "Hey, I've got a wobbly tooth!"

"What!" Thomas swung his head around. "No, you don't!"

"Do, too."

"Show me!"

Nicholas leaned over the seat and opened his mouth right on Thomas's face.

Thomas pulled away. "Gross! Gross, gross, gross! Mooooooom!"

She turned off the engine in the garage and closed her eyes. Now her own mood had changed. Her children felt like clothes on a drowning person, weighted, tangled, clinging, impossible to remove, impossible to survive. Before, three children had seemed par for the course. But with sleeplessness and an inhuman load having worked on her nerves like a cheese grater, she wondered sometimes now what she had been thinking to have three. How was she ever going to manage a fourth? She had never imagined life could be so hard. Hell, most divorcées had it better. At least they got child support and a rest every other weekend. She knew there were lives far more tragic than hers now, children losing limbs in wars in Africa, gang families with every male member incarcerated, but those worlds were not her reality, and in her reality life hardly got worse.

She wanted to scream at the boys to give her a chance to catch her breath; instead, she strained to meld the cacophony into a sheet of indecipherable background noise while she guided everyone inside and took off her coat and their coats and shoes. While Beatriz marched them off to towel their hair and retrieve sodden lunch boxes, Nora opened the refrigerator. There was no better reminder of a mother's straits than a bare refrigerator. But she wouldn't think of that now. Something would give and save the day. The worst was behind her. She had hit rock bottom. Things just had to look up from here.

The boys were running back into the kitchen for their snack; she was grateful to be relieved from having to think again about her money problems.

"We're having crepes stuffed with cinnamon apples and topped with sweet butter," she told them, devising the menu on the spot.

"Yippee!" screamed Charlie.

"Thomas, you're in charge of setting the table; Nicholas, you need to choose me five of the best apples; and, Charlie, you help Beatriz get drinking glasses for milk."

"Come, my little Charlie," Beatriz said, taking his hand as they walked to the other side of the kitchen. "Can you remember the name for cup in Spanish?"

Charlie shook his head.

"No? Thomas, Nicholas? Do you remember?"

It was while Nora was making pensive loops with a wire whisk through a heavy creamlike batter of farm eggs, buttermilk, flour, and salt that the phone started to ring. Instantly she thought, Could Fox Silverworth really be calling? Surely he wasn't serious. She wished he would leave her alone.

She went to her office at the other end of the house to answer the phone. By the time she reached it, the machine had picked up the call. She heard her greeting, and then just as she reached out, that familiar automated voice. She drew back sharply, her hand going to her chest as her body went cold. She stared at the machine, listening.

"This is a prepaid call. You will not be charged for this call. This call is from . . ." And Evan's voice sounded, "Evan." Then the automated voice again, ". . . an inmate at a federal prison. Hang up to decline this call, or to accept dial five now."

She knew she should pick up and press five. She knew Evan had probably stood in line for an hour or more to use the one pay phone to make this call. If she didn't pick up he would need to stand in line all over again. She listened to the long pause, knowing Evan was hearing it, too, that he was right there, sensing her, too, probably.

The system disconnected the call and then there was just a droning dial tone.

She continued staring at the machine, unable for her shaking rage even to press the delete button. Every time he called, every time she heard that automated voice she knew would forever haunt her, hate rushed through her. She was incapable after that of speaking to him civilly. If the children were there she would usually pass the phone directly to them. If not, she would often take advantage to call him the worst names she could summon, which left her exhausted and full of still more venom when she was interrupted again by that damn automated voice reminding her that she was on a call with a federal prisoner—as if she were not utterly aware of it. The call often disconnected before she was finished, because the allotted fifteen minutes for calls had expired. Sometimes she would keep slapping around her words into the dial tone like a fish out of water. Now she felt like there just weren't any words for what he had done to them—and though she knew the boys would have loved to talk to him, she simply had no strength to manage anything more today. The boys would just have to do with their crepes.

When she returned to the kitchen the boys were all sitting at a beautifully set table playing guess-the-word-in-Spanish with Beatriz. Thomas became annoyed that Nicholas said *leche* before he managed it when Beatriz took a dramatic sip like a mime artist of raw milk, but then Beatriz had them all laughing again when she drew a mustache over her upper lip with a finger-point of cream. "*Bigote!*" Thomas yelled through his laughter. The happy scene registered as somehow distant from her, as though she were looking through a window into the home of some other family. She didn't speak Spanish, she had lost the ability lately to engage the children the way Beatriz seemed always to do so effortlessly, and she felt excluded all of a sudden, forgotten, as though she really was just the cook.

She set butter and sugar to warm in a sauté pan, and then turned to core, peel, and slice the apples, the sluicing sound of the knife against the crisp flesh of the fruit giving her whirling mind finally something to clutch. She dropped the apples into the pan, shaking it gently by the handle to coat the apples until they were slightly caramelized. Then she added a splash of cider and let the buttery, sweet liquid reduce before seasoning with cinnamon and pouring the softened apples into a serving bowl. She leaned over the bowl as she customarily did when making cinnamon apples to breathe the earthy-sweet aroma. Normally the aromatic airbath would push aside all mental clutter. But today she was sensitive to the steam, the heat, and pulled her face quickly away. It felt like her face was burning.

She looked over at the children, laughing, engrossed now in games of naughts and crosses, all three of them against Beatriz. They had forgotten even that they were hungry.

She turned back and stared at herself in the stainless-steel back-splash electronically raised behind the island range. The steel reflected her as formless, faceless, a drawn blur of washed-out color. It was as if life was seeping out of her.

And in fact it was.

At first she felt just woozy and thought she needed a glass of water. She gripped the edge of the counter with one hand and with the other poured water from a jug into a glass. But before the glass reached her lips it slipped from her hand. It splintered over the floor at the same instant as she doubled over with a scream. Intolerable spasms shot across her abdomen and down her thighs. She felt all at once insane with pain, then with nausea, too, and then, oh God, no, don't let it be, a flood let forth between her thighs. Bent over still, gasping for breath, she frantically pulled up her skirt and reached up.

Her hand came out as she dreaded it would: smeared with dark, clotted blood.

Six

The combination of rain and sleet had still not let up the following day. The light through the partly opened curtains was so weak when Nora awoke that she couldn't determine the hour. But then the voice floated up from the kitchen over clattering silverware, Beatriz demanding the boys get down off the table she was setting for lunch. A heavy sense of dread descended upon her. As her mind began searching for what had happened recently to make her feel this way, she went to sit upright. It was an effort to move. Her body felt as heavy as . . . what was it? Dead. She felt like a dead weight. As she used every bit of her strength to raise herself up from her pillows, a weak cramp gripped her womb and she began to remember.

A chill overcame her as she recalled how she had crawled late yesterday afternoon over the kitchen floor toward the back porch. She had heard as if through layers of sleep her boys screaming, "Mommy, Mommy, you're bleeding! There's blood all over the floor!" and Beatriz urging them all calmly to go to the playroom while she helped their mommy. A single determination had overtaken her to get outside. She had reached up to open the door and had crawled into the icy rain. Beatriz had tried to lift her back inside after failing to

restrain her, but she'd refused to be moved, balling tighter into a fe-
tal position to will her body heavier. She hadn't cared that her skirt
had ridden up to her hips, that rain washed the blood into a swelling
pool beneath her of red. She couldn't feel the rain, the damp, the
cold. From the darkness inside the ball she had made of herself she
just listened. It was as if she could hear every one of the raindrops
falling, splat, splat, splat. She imagined each one washing another part
of her away, tier after tier of emotional shock gone until nothing was
left to hurt.

The chill stayed with her as she now remembered Beatriz's kindness. Beatriz had eventually helped her inside, and after the doctor
had visited, she gave her a sponge bath. She had brushed her hair and
dressed her in a fresh nightdress. "I wish I could spare you this,"
Beatriz had said while urging her to drink a mug of steaming
chamomile tea, sip by slow, protesting sip. She began to sleep after
that, exhausted from the pain and shock, vaguely conscious for a
short while of the boys banging on her door and calling for her until
Beatriz encouraged them away.

Now the thought that she had lost her baby was too terrible to be
alone with. She feebly rose out of bed and dressed warmly. She was
so deeply cold that her teeth chattered. Slowly, she made her way
down the stairs, finding no joy even in the decorations. Beatriz had
twisted lengths of realistic-looking evergreen around the banister,
and had decorated the tree she had taken the boys to buy, but none
of it enlivened the flat mood of the house. Even though they had
spent all their previous Christmases abroad or skiing or at a beach
resort, the season was always full of voices, laughter, plans, a camera
flashing to catch coy poses, the rustle of presents being wrapped.
This year, she had forgotten even to buy wrapping paper.

In the kitchen, she saw that Beatriz had scrubbed the blood from
the waxed floorboards and had soaked out the bloodstains from her
skirt: It lay pressed on the pile of folded clothes in the laundry

basket. The house was immaculately clean. It would be good having Beatriz live with them again. She would be moving back at the end of the month when her lease was up. They needed her now more than she needed her own apartment, she had said. Beatriz had refused two job offers to stay with her and the boys. She had said she did not recognize the school mothers who made the offers after the arrest, and probably would not recognize them again, but Nora suspected Beatriz was saving her feelings. Beatriz had taken a financial risk, staying on without any questions in such uncertain circumstances, but Nora had put aside enough for her wages for a while.

"You should not be out of bed, *señora,*" Beatriz scolded. It was the first time she had spoken since Nora's appearance. Beatriz's greeting had been an ushering into a chair at the table and a scurrying about to set a bowl of soup before her. Now Beatriz stood in a posture of maternal reprimand, hands on hips. The pose belied her petite size and made her seem daunting. Beatriz's brown eyes were large, so that it was apparent when she narrowed them. And she narrowed them, as they were now, when she didn't approve. The familiar, practical Beatriz had usurped again the soft, tender Beatriz of last night.

"Really, I'm fine, Beatriz," Nora insisted with an attempted smile.

"You do not look fine, *señora.* You look much too pale and there are dark smudges beneath your eyes. And your lips! They are so dry and cracked." She moved forward and dabbed at Nora's lips from a miniature pot of homemade balm she took from the pocket of her apron. Nora was too weary to protest—and it gave some delusional comfort to be tended as though she were a child again.

To be young and safe again! Something about the idea resonated deep within her. Her mind's eye pictured the day her brow was tight with adolescent worry and in an instant everything was all right when her father's supporting arm went around her and he said, "There, there, stop worrying. These problems are solvable. We'll work through them together." She longed to hear those words now. It was a relief to visualize her salvation, to know it was a father figure she needed, though it was empty relief for its impossibility, and it brought on new heartache. It was as if she were hearing the news a second time that her father wouldn't be coming home again.

Beatriz was right. She was not fine. She could feel depression taking its hold.

"You should be resting," Beatriz was saying. "Why else am I here?"

Nora nodded vaguely when on a gust of chill wind the boys blew inside in their dripping yellow raincoats and rain hats and matching mud-caked galoshes. They were bursting with the news that three huge trucks like moving vans were trying to reverse down their drive. The rush of cold and activity brought Nora swiftly out of her thoughts, though she didn't give the boys' words much more weight than Beatriz's advice. At first she thought the trucks must have the wrong house. All she registered was how her boys' faces looked like adorable painted puppets, their cheeks and the tips of their noses blooded circles on complexions frozen otherwise white and stiff.

"They're not very good at it," said Nicholas.

"Not very good at what, darling?" Nora asked absently.

"They're all in a muddle out on the road. They can't seem to work out how to turn the trucks around to back in. The back tire of the first one is stuck in the ditch."

"Well, perhaps we should find out where they really need to go," Nora suggested.

"Maybe it's a carnival," Nicholas said hopefully.

"What?" asked Thomas.

"It said 'action' on the side of the truck. Remember that cool carnival with safari animals we went to last summer called Action Attraction?"

"It said 'auction,' stupid, not 'action,'" Thomas chided.

"No, I remember it was Action Attraction."

"Not the carnival, the truck. It doesn't say 'action' on the truck. It says 'auction.'"

"My God!" Nora cried, raising anxious eyes to Beatriz, a rush of fear bringing her fiercely to her senses. The determined expression Beatriz had already taken on told Nora that Beatriz also understood that the trucks were in the right drive. The government-commissioned auction house Nora had vaguely registered would one day come was here now on this of all days to seize all their household possessions.

Nora scanned the room. She stopped at the sight of the silverware she had earlier heard Beatriz laying out. "They'll take all that and everything else," she cried. The red drained instantly from the boys' faces. They watched her now with startled eyes.

"You have no choice but to let them," Beatriz said, though she was worried. The evidence of what she had done last night would still be wet. There was no time now to do anything about it. She prayed silently her actions would not be discovered.

"The money!" Nora squealed. All at once the memory surged to the surface of how she had climbed up into the attic yesterday morning to count out three hundred dollars from the cash box she hid there when a spider had startled her and she had taken the attic stairs down two at a time swearing she would never go up there again. "To hell with the electrical bill," she had said to herself in a moment of irrationality. "To hell with money! It's all too much trouble." She had left the cash box open on the attic floor.

What if these men checked the attic? They'd report the money and there'd be no more food on the table. She'd be begging for food stamps before the week was out.

"*Señora?*" Beatriz asked with concern now.

But Nora was already on her feet and hobbling as fast as she was able toward the staircase. She stopped momentarily and looked back at her boys' faces huddled around the table. In a calm voice now for them, she said, "Beatriz, take the boys out to the garage to play where it's dry. Keep the garage door open. When the trucks pull up, yell as loudly as you can, 'Time for lunch!' That will be my cue. Keep the—" She refrained from saying what she was about to and said, "Guests. Keep the guests out there for as long as possible. Talk to them about anything. And then do take the boys for lunch. Make sure your car can get out around the trucks. Go to Bellizzi's, where they can play all those carnival games, and let them play as long as they like. If the trucks are still in the drive when you get back, then take them to Phillip's for hot chocolate."

"Pizza *and* hot chocolate!" Nicholas squealed, eyes now dancing.

"Ah-hah, yeah, yeah, ah-ha, yeah, yeah," Charlie sung.

Only Thomas looked skeptical, but followed Beatriz out.

In her bedroom, Nora pulled out her underwear drawer so desperately that it came off its runners and she fell backward against the opposite wall with the drawer in two hands jammed beneath her breast. The pain she had been weathering deep and low within her jerked tears to her eyes. She slid with clenched teeth down the wall until the drawer sat on her lap. She ran her hands through all the silk and lace, picking out what must have been five hundred dollars in ten- and twenty-dollar bills. She stuffed all the notes down the front of her shirt, stood with effort to replace the drawer, and waddled out and down the hall. She stopped to listen for the sound of trucks, but there was only silence. She reached up for the cord to pull down the attic stairs and yanked so hard that the stairs banged into her forehead and knocked her down, yelping. With her hand to her brow she stumbled to her feet and started climbing. At the top, she stopped dead. What had she been thinking? Beside the open cash box, she had left a loose pile of notes. Mice or any other creature she often imagined lived up here might have eaten them overnight! How could she still be so careless about money! The life that had allowed her to toss money cavalierly about was over.

With her heart racing, she packed up the cash box, adding the stash from her bra, and buried it in the darkest corner under stacks of scratchy feather-light pink insulation mats. There was nothing else in the attic. Not even one packing box. There was only one obvious deduction to make: There was nothing but air units and switch breakers here.

The sound of voices outside as she climbed down the stairs and quietly raised them made her heart race still faster. She mustn't have heard Beatriz's cue. Now there was no time to sweep for overlooked clues to the cash box. And then a slight relief wedged into her heart: At least the trucks were off the road where every passing car would see them. All her neighbors would be out of town, but it only took a passing construction worker to start the telegraphing of news. She took deep breaths to calm her heart and the fluttering in her temple, dusted herself off, and descended the staircase.

Hard eyes peered in through the glass panels to the sides of the door, trained eyes, she could tell, like those of the trooper who pulled over Evan for speeding, rapidly assessing the situation, quantifying the level of danger. At the sight of her, the eyes relaxed some; she felt and probably looked as threatening as a trapped mouse.

And then for a moment before opening the door, she stood transfixed, frozen by the surreal realization that this had all happened before. The morning Evan was arrested it had been raining heavily, too, and those dozens of male eyes had the same hardness as these. She had not understood then the other gleam in them. But now she suffered the nauseating knowledge that it was that of victory and righteous pleasure in it.

Though she had known this day would come, it was suddenly too callous, too brutal, too excessive to believe. They had taken her husband, her family name, more money already than needed to recompense those wronged, and had come back for more for their own coffers. Her fear of her only remaining money being discovered turned now into impotent, shaking rage toward these agents at her house, and when she opened the door and faced them, her casually arranged expression tightened into hate. It surprised her how much she suddenly hated the agents who had invaded her house once and these who would now—and the judge and prosecutors behind them. She should have directed all her rage toward her husband. But what concept of justice was this that willfully made children fatherless and left mothers to cope alone, and then ransacked under their noses their only means left of survival, nary a letter or phone call from any government office to direct them to financial or emotional support? She had not even received a pamphlet on how to manage the loaded issue of incarceration with her children. When Evan went away, she had suffered what had felt like his death. She understood it now as more like a Western version of a pillaging and plundering, everything from the man of the family down to the coffee grinder grabbed, leaving her alone with her children and unprotected to bear at once their impoverishment and the shame of their victimization.

It was all so extraordinarily cruel!

She knew the drill, identifications flashed, papers wielded as legal swords.

For three hours she stood by the door, watching helplessly as the men pushed past her, in with more blankets for padding and to protect against the rain and out with her heart in the form of all the articles she had painstakingly selected over the years to make her family's house a home. She wanted to claw the men's wet faces when they carried out her French Regency–style dining chairs she had selected for their cloven feet, and her custom-made tufted chairs with their canted backs and curved seats, and all the swirled-grain mahogany pieces with brass hardware, the chests of drawers, center tables, bedside tables, the sideboard she loved with its acanthus leaf motif. Her nails dug into her hands when she witnessed a greasy blanket thrown carelessly over her beloved tufted rolled-back chaise. The crystal vases, silver picture frames, artwork, her brass-bordered mirrors, even the embroidered drapes were taken while she watched on. Her work at assembling all the ducks in a row of a married life with children was rendered piece by vanishing piece to nothing but a childish art-work of muddied boot prints every which way over her floor. All those years thumbing fabric swatches and traversing city avenues from show-room to showroom and arguing prices with designers utterly wasted!

How would she ever start again? It had all taken so much time and money, and she had neither of those now! Even if she could keep the house, where would the money come to furnish it again? She was much too old to start again in any case. Why, every woman in midlife she knew had her life in order. And then a new fear sur-faced: How was she going to hide her galling depths of poverty now? She would not be able to have anyone at all to her house. None of the women visited any longer anyway, but now she could not risk us-ing even her contractors on speed dial. If any kind of plumbing or electrical emergency arose, she would need to check the yellow pages for another town. And to think that only last spring she and Evan had hosted the annual junior pre-kindergarten cocktail eve-ning, a privilege they had won against every other family positioning for such a perfect opportunity to show off their house. She could still remember the gushing compliments on her taste in design. How in-toxicating it had all been! All at once again she felt so tired. She slumped back against the door and watched with an almost numb heart as the last of the plasma televisions went past her. There had been a strange moldy smell in the air these hours, presumably from those blankets, or the men's jackets. She suddenly found it nauseat-ing. When two men came down the stairs awkwardly shouldering her Regency-style bed, it was lamely and without much care anymore that she asked, "And are we all supposed to sleep on the floor now?"

"We have no use for mattresses," was the response.

So, they would be sleeping henceforth on mattresses on the floors. All she could do was drop her head.

As she did so, a glint caught her eye. The tiny piece of silver on the foyer floor behind where the center table had stood made her smile sadly. Every week, she gave Thomas and Nicholas three single-dollar notes each for their allowances, one for a box marked "spending," one for another marked "savings," and the third for a box marked "charity." Since Charlie didn't want to be left out, she had started giving him the same, only he thought his notes play money, and she had found them too frequently cut into shapes or enlivened with crayon squiggles. She had switched his pocket money to coins, only then to find coins in the oddest places. Obviously he had hidden a dime behind the leg of the center table. But when she looked at it more carefully, she drew a sharp breath.

It was not a dime: It was the spare key to the cash box.

She had misplaced it months back and had never found it. Now she remembered she had hidden it in the center table drawer. It must have fallen out when they removed the table. Those cash box keys looked like no other keys she had ever seen. Not even the keys to their Louis Vuitton travel luggage taken out earlier resembled them. Would they ask if they saw it where the cash box was? Would her face give away that one existed?

The balding, squat, barrel-chested agent who had been directing things stood now at the bottom of the stairs checking off items on their insurance records. He stepped to the side to allow the men to pass with her bed. The key was now just to the right of his boot. The men with the bed crashed it into the wall on the way out the door. They backed up, looked dispassionately at the crumbling hole, and then continued out the door. The man at the bottom of the stairs never looked up. What did any of them care? She could practically hear them thinking, The house won't be hers much longer, either.

She took it silently, took it all, but when the redheaded, bearded man came down the stairs with an armful of portable DVD players and high-end photo printers and an assortment of other electronics, and on top of the pile was her camera, she cried out, "Not that!" Her mind reeled through the photographs of her children she had taken with that camera over the years, from the times they learned to swim in the Caribbean to their first skiing lessons in Chile. That camera was bound up with every important moment since the children were born. By God, it had even captured their births, though the boys squirmed theatrically to see those photos now, refusing with fascinated eyes to believe their own images. And the camera represented now what was left of Christmas. At least there would still be the click and the flash of the camera!

But before she could get her answer, a voice hollered up from the basement, "Better take a look down here!" The agent with the papers tucked them under his arm and headed casually downstairs. Nora followed. The musty smell bothering her earlier became suffocating. With the agent in front of her in the stairwell, all she could see ahead of him at first was the man who had hollered. He was scratching his chin. "Never had a situation like this," he said. And then suddenly Nora reached for to the stairwell walls onto either side to stop her knees from buckling. There were no longer plush Persian rugs over the carpeted basement rooms: There was no longer a floor at all. Water was so high throughout the five-thousand-square-foot space that it submerged the bottom two stairs. She slipped and her shoe became waterlogged. Bright-colored plastic toys and worn tennis balls bobbed over the surface. Floating toward them was that squeezable, lightweight, yellow vinyl ball Evan had bought with the big black smiley face on it that sent out cascades of laughter when it hit a surface. It floated in unnerving silence.

The men were talking as though she weren't there.

"This much rainwater . . . must have been seeping in for days."

The clipboard agent answered, "Yeah, gotta be a cracked foundation."

"What a big fucking clean-up job this'll be. You woulda thought a house like this'd have drainage pipes and sump pumps. I'd sue the fucker who built it."

The clipboard agent laughed. "That fucker's dead as your great-grandmother. This house is goddamn old."

"Yeah, well . . ."

All Nora heard was that the money she had saved by not painting the house and had put aside for the boys' schooling next year was now all gone, for that was surely what it would take to make such extensive repairs. She knew the house insurance didn't cover flooding. She and Evan had not considered flood insurance necessary. It was not as though they lived in a flood zone. And there was no way even to put it off. The damage was worsening and she would not have her boys become asthmatic breathing mildewed air. The money was as useless now as the Persian rugs and the gym equipment and the home-theater system and the new media-room sofas and armchairs whose price tags had made her fret only months ago lest Beatriz see them, and there was nothing she could do.

The agent with the papers now remembered her behind him.

"Lady, don't think you can claim all this stuff on insurance." He swiped at his nose with the back of a free hand and sniffed casually, proprietarily. "'Cause the government'll be making that claim. That money belongs to the government."

She felt glad for a moment that she had not taken out flood insurance, that the government would get nothing. The agent turned to the other man. "Make a list of everything that's down here. Everything you can see, anyway." He handed the man a sheet of paper, and a pencil from his shirt pocket, and turned to head back up.

It was then that Nora remembered the key on the floor upstairs.

Before she knew it she was making a scene, pretending to cry because it would turn the men rigid and buy her time, running up the stairs and slamming the basement door behind her. In that moment alone in the foyer, she plunged for the key, and thrust it deep inside her bra. She had lost a huge portion of her cash reserves in a way unexpected, but the key meant there was still something left. And then she took a seat on the stairs and dropped her head in her hands in a pose of destitution. That was how the agent with the papers found her, and that was how all the men left her, when they were presumably done, and she heard the clomp of their boots, and then the truck engines roaring to life, warming to carry off all her earthly possessions. Still, she did not move. Her pose of destitution had taken possession of the fight left in her and as hopelessness flooded her heart she could no longer bring herself to raise her head. How could she bear after everything to face her empty house and the flood. She recalled her feelings from just a few hours earlier: It had seemed incredible to her that a baby could be taken from a woman who had lost so much. And yet before there was time to recover from that, more had been wrenched from her life.

At least earlier there had remained something of a semblance of her former life. It had been easier to believe things would somehow right themselves. But now just knowing how different things would look when she raised her eyes was enough to bring home the full horror of her situation. In such a ridiculously short time, her life had completely changed. Everything on which she had once relied but her children's love and Beatriz had let her down—everything down to her ability to bear children and the foundation of her home. The cracked foundation was like some cruel joke or terrible metaphor, in fact, underscoring how all that had held her up before had collapsed beneath her.

The house phone rang. She let the machine pick it up, not even trying to decipher the words being recorded of the male voice that sounded vaguely familiar.

All she thought was, Ah, so they left the answering machine.

And then a minute or so later, Beatriz stood before her saying, "*Señora?*"

Nora looked up. Beatriz was holding out her, Nora's, cell phone.

"I took yours by accident on the way out," Beatriz said. "It is a gentleman . . ."

"On the phone?" Nora drew back from the cell phone. "Now?"

Beatriz nodded, knowing their conversation could be heard.

Nora gave an annoyed look, grabbed the phone, and followed Beatriz back into the kitchen, refusing all the way to let her eyes survey the new emptiness.

"Yes?" Her voice echoed.

"Nora."

"Who is this?"

"I just tried you at the house and there was no answer, and then your nanny told me you were *in* the house. A man might think you were avoiding him."

"Who *is* this?"

Beatriz was bringing in the boys one by one through the garage door—each one—*what on earth?*—blindfolded and on Rollerblades! They were giggling hysterically.

"It's Fox, of course. I told you I'd call."

"Fox. This is not a very good—"

"I've been thinking a lot about you."

Beatriz was whispering something to the boys. Whatever it was switched their giggles into glowing smiles. They were all looking up at Beatriz as if they could see her through their blindfolds.

He went on, "I didn't tell you this before, but I know what you're going through."

Her attention came back to the conversation. It was the first time any Bedford person had commiserated with her. That it would be Fox Silverworth stunned her.

He said, "I don't generally tell people this, but my brother went away on a drug charge for four years when I was a teenager. I remember how lonely and confusing it was. It was exactly the reason I went into law. I never wanted to feel so helpless again."

"Oh. I'm . . . I'm sorry. That you had to go through that."

"Yeah, it was pretty rough. Not many people around to help."

"No."

"So I wanted to offer you my help. I know you have one pretty big legal fight on your hands, and I'm sure you're aware this thing is kinda my specialty."

He was doing nothing more than trying to sell her his services!

She hobbled furiously through the house and into her office, anger over all the injustices exacted upon her that day now flaming within her. "Of all the low-down things. I should have known better than to think you were being kind. Isn't there anyone your own size you can drum for business, or do you like to prey on mothers on their own? Of all the indecent things people have done—"

He laughed so loudly that she had to draw the phone away from her ear until the laughter ceased. "I wasn't planning on charging you."

"Oh," she said in a whisper and sat down on the windowsill. The desk and chair were gone now and piles of her papers were stacked around the floor.

"But I'm glad you thought so for a minute, because that passionate display was quite something. I always suspected that you were—to play with the line in Charles Macklin's comedy of 1781—less demure than you came across."

Nora was caught between incredulity at his audacity and grudging admiration for his literary awareness. The two balanced each other and she sat mute.

"So, could you do with my help?"

"How did you know about the government's designs? Does everyone know?"

"Not unless they made efforts to find out."

"And why did you make efforts?"

"I didn't. I know some of the prosecutors on your husband's case. They gave me the lowdown, that the property's all in your name, all that."

"They just told you everything? Is that ethical?"

He laughed again. "Firstly, the government has a publicly listed *lis pendens* on your property, and, secondly, you'd better get rid of the idea there are any ethics in law."

Well, he wouldn't tell her that unless *he* was more ethical than most at least. Perhaps Evan was wrong about him being the type who would sell out his mother.

He took on a serious tone. "What are you planning to do?"

"I don't really know yet."

"You're kidding?"

"Well, it's all just so new, and I . . ."

"You mean to say you don't even have a plan of action?"

"There hasn't been anything to do. They haven't filed a suit yet."

"They'll be doing that soon enough. Listen, Nora, we need to talk. You don't have to use me, but I can give you some good advice. I'm down south with the family this week, and then I'll be in California for business. When I get back we should get together. I'm calling you from my cell phone, so you have my number now. If you get any legal notices, call me and I'll guide you through them."

Guide you through! We'll work through them together! It was the sentiment her father had extended. Her wish was answered: Someone had come to help her solve her problems! She swallowed as she digested the knowledge. And as it digested, the panic and despair of her terrible losses lessened in severity and a strange calm flooded her. Her topsy-turvy world was realigning itself. She was right that too much had been taken from her. Now the universe was righting things, stepping in to settle the injustices done her.

In the background of this thinking the initial memory of her father had turned to thoughts of family and those in turn had made her remember the camera.

She cried out, "The Memory Stick!"

"What?"

"The Memory Stick. It was inside the camera. It has on it a year's worth of pictures of the boys—"

"Slow down. What're you talking about?"

"They took the Memory Stick."

"Who did?"

"The government. These men came and took all our possessions today."

After a long silence, Fox said calmly, "I'll see what I can do."

Again he had said just the right thing. It was just what she needed to hear, that someone would handle things for her. A picture was forming in her mind's eye of Fox as her knight in shining armor. After they had hung up, a smidgen of renewed hope bore her back to the kitchen. She put the absence of furniture from her mind and faced the boys. They were still blindfolded and grinning, clinging from their handicap to Beatriz.

"Okay, *mis niños*, Mommy is back now," Beatriz said, removing their blindfolds.

The boys looked horror-struck at the change in their home, but then Beatriz said, "Ready, set," and they looked down at their Rollerblades and then over to their mother for approval. Seeing no disapproval at least, and not wishing to wait for that to change, they took off over the floors bare suddenly and excitingly of Persian rugs.

Beatriz explained, "The Rollerblades are my Christmas present. I was hiding them in the car, but then I thought why not give the presents today? I told them the house had been cleared out to make a roller rink for them. I thought it would help to break the shock when they came in. And it will give you time to think how you want to explain things to them tomorrow."

Nora smiled. She had always understood that Beatriz had a special faculty for celebrating the good in life. But what Nora just now realized was that Beatriz retained like a prize truffle hunter a magical ability *to recover* the good in life to celebrate.

"You're right, Beatriz, it *is* still Christmas." And then latching on to the idea like a lifeboat, she wound her way through the bumper cars of her boys on wheels without brakes, praying she wasn't going to be sent tumbling in her fragile condition, to retrieve her own presents upstairs. They were still in her closet, along with all her clothes and the bed linens. She checked the boys' rooms. She blinked in the doorways. Without the blinds, the rooms were bright, even on this dreary day. All that was left besides the mattresses were the computers worth nothing on the resale market and a television so old you had to spank it to maintain reception. She quickly pulled all the doors closed.

She couldn't deal with this right now, except to think she would have to tack sheets over the windows, to darken the rooms again enough for sleep.

"Boys!" she called above the hip-hop music now blasting from the miniature built-in CD player in the kitchen.

The boys were now speed skating around and around the adjoining family room.

Nora recalled her local roller rink growing up, the disco music and bubble gum, the double-pumps, crossovers, the Friday night crushes on boys. It seemed like another lifetime, not even her own.

"Boys, it's Christmas-present time! We're doing things differently this year."

They all fell under the tree like dominoes, flushed and breathing hard.

Only when they began opening their bags did she realize that her presents were lame. When she thought they would be holidaying as a family in the Caribbean, she had purchased fishing nets, boogie boards, snorkels, goggles, and flippers for them. So now they were receiving on this freezing wet northern Westchester afternoon the accoutrements meant for a beach.

The boys didn't seem to realize the presents were all wrong, and shifted easily into different footwear, staging flipper races up and down the stairs, testing their goggles and snorkels in her bathtub, which was oversized and like a small pool. But their not realizing the wrongness of it all made her feel even more that she was cheating them, and just like that the guilt started in on her again.

Beatriz read her face.

"Come on," she said, helping the boys already back into their rain boots.

And to the surprise of them all, she packed Nora and the boys into her car and drove them through the backcountry down to the Target store in Mount Kisco. She led them to the shelves of "everything for a dollar" items: packages with all the parts needed to assemble an American flag; flip-flops for the summer with lights flashing intermittently around the edges; glow-in-the-dark Velcro wallets; water pistols; plastic horses; tiny drum sets. Nora had never noticed the section before. Beatriz handed the boys a single dollar note each from her own purse and told them they could buy whatever they liked. The boys were as excited as ever Nora had seen them, racing up and down the aisles, trying on every hat, testing every toy, deciding and redeciding, conferring with one another as though the world depended on their decisions. It was a full hour later that they left the store, the boys' bags weighted, their eyes shining, their heads as high as kings'.

"It takes so little to make children happy," Beatriz said. "Stop feeling guilty that you cannot now give them the same childhood they

had before. You have cause to celebrate these holidays. Without the
material things you once had to fall back on, you will draw on the
more meaningful gifts of your passions and resourcefulness and creativity. You will see: You will surprise yourself as well as the boys."

But Nora shifted in her seat impatiently. The boys' happiness at
their little loot from Target was just a bit of fun. She was grateful to
Beatriz for the distraction, but what did Beatriz know about money?
There was no way she was giving up on grand childhoods for her children! And the notion of this being a consideration filled her with new
resolve. There was Fox Silverworth now and she would win her suit.
She felt around in her bra discreetly for the little key, but the feel of
it hardly reassured her. There was no pretending anymore the remaining money was going to last long enough. She stiffened her
spine some more and as she lifted her shoe to refasten her loose lace,
she thought, All right, then, I'll find a way to make some money. I'll
suffer ignominy for a while to get a foothold back into my former life.

Beatriz asked suddenly, "Why is your shoe wet?"

"Oh my God, the flood . . ."

Seven

It was a world away from her world, the bakery behind Phillip's storefront. The storefront was always empty when she arrived to begin her shift, chairs overturned on tabletops for the night cleaners to restore the floorboards for another day's traffic. But even after the doorbell had stopped jangling behind her there was never a sense in the abandoned darkness of being alone. The shaft of light from the kitchen out back brought with it each time the hum of voices and the warm, sweet smells of baking breads that impressed upon her increasingly the enchantment of this work. For yes, aside from the exhaustion that had settled into her bones since she started working nights four weeks ago, and aside from the disquieting awareness at the end of each week that her paycheck was not enough, she was coming to accept that it was boosting her self-esteem to be putting her talents to profitable use. Over the first week and a bit she had denied it, telling Beatriz, "I have to do what I have to do." But that had been the habit of her grief for her lost child talking, and Beatriz could never be fooled. Beatriz's small, amused smile had been the flag to make Nora wonder herself at her reemerging zest.

Nora had leaned on Phillip the first two weeks like a blind person on a guide dog. Phillip had shown her where everything was stored, how to anticipate what customers would desire, and how to slip something different into the menu—something that would make them think, Hmm, that sounds interesting. She learned how to maintain an inventory of supplies, which suppliers could be relied on in a pinch, and how to monitor food costs. This last was a real lesson for Nora. She had never been conscious in her old life of the cost of baking. She had never examined the invoices for the oils and butters, the creams, the bricks of chocolate charged automatically to her credit card. Now it was imperative that every nugget of sugar be accounted for. Everything leftover could be turned into something new. A few extra leaves of fresh organic sage remained after the bakers had made enough herb loaves? Turn them into sage ice cream, to serve with twists of caramel. A few loaves came out of the oven too misshapen to sell? Break them up and make chocolate bread pudding. Soon enough she was not only costing out individual pastries, but enjoying pastry baking more for doing it. It completed the very preciseness of the art, and pushed her to be even more creative.

She wouldn't admit it to anyone, but she had begun to feel grateful to Phillip for pushing her to accept this job. She had explored other options before accepting it. She had reconsidered returning to banking when it occurred to her that if she took a lower position and swallowed her pride and worked as a personal assistant she could leave every day at five to be home before the boys went to bed. She would have to neither travel, work weekends, nor meet at night for drinks. But in this new era of legal scrutiny over Wall Street, human resources investigated applicants as if they were applying for a top security position at the White House. When she learned that even the spouse's criminal and work and credit histories were taken into account, she decided it was better not to open that can of worms. She could just imagine it—being served in a bank with registered letters and subpoenas, having to take time off for court appearances and depositions. Oh, they'd just love that! And no matter how hard she had thought on it, there would have been no getting around it looking as though she *needed* to work. She had then enrolled in a real estate brokers course. She had planned to tell the mothers that she simply needed something to do now that she had more time on her hands without a husband. It was an acceptable job among the women, too, because you were privy to local real estate goings-on. Only too many had told her at the course not to expect to make anything her first year in the field. You needed to be supported meanwhile by husbands or alimony checks or some independent income.

She had an idea then to rent out her house and move them all to something less expensive. They would live on the difference after taxes. And the renters would then be responsible for the considerable cost of maintenance. It had seemed such a simple and good idea that she wondered why she had not thought of it before. It would be harder then to hide her financial straits, but she would still own the property. She could say they didn't need so much space while the boys' father was away. She even found renters, a couple sent her way—just after the idea had come to her, ironically—by one of the Bedford mothers, though the referral had been handled absurdly. This Bedford mother had inadvertently copied her on an e-mail meant for the potential renters. Newspaper stories about Evan were attached with a note suggesting the potential renters may be able to "benefit from the situation." The renters had indeed come her way, and she and they had come to an agreement, only they canceled their checks at the last minute after word reached them of the *lis pendens* on the house. Well, yes, but the government hadn't even filed a suit to follow through on that yet. Still, she supposed she should have mentioned it. But her concern had been to support her children. What impossible positions she was always finding herself in now. The twist was that the mother who made the referral was the one who then raised the alert about the *lis pendens*. The very next day and with the renters out of the picture this Machiavellian mother placed with the government a nominal offer on the Bankses' estate, in the event it moved to claim it. Fox phoned through the news from Napa Valley.

She had retreated to the bakery, never expecting to find joy there.

That night she had worked alone at the pastry station. For the sake of exacting chocolates and spun sugar turrets, it was tucked away from the heat of the bread ovens. From around the corner came the metallic clang of wire bagel baskets and bagel scoops, the rocking of the jumbo rocker knives used to cut the dough into portions, the squeaking of baker-rack wheels, the slamming of heavy oven doors, and the melody of indecipherable deep voices, a laugh rising once in a while—all the sounds that had kept her company. She was hand-dipping another chocolate and wiping her damp brow with the back of her other hand when Phillip strode in, startling her so that she dropped the chocolate.

"Us cattlemen often have that effect on women," he joked.

Nora smiled and took up a pair of tongs to lift out the sunken cube.

Phillip slapped his cheeks. "Still waking up. Overslept. Wasn't time for anything but a dingo's breakfast." (It had been like learning another language, working for Phillip and learning his native idioms. This one meant, "A yawn, a leak, and a good look around.")

"Wasn't even time for a durry." That meant cigarette. "You up for a bikkie and tea?" Bikkie meant cookie. "Haven't eaten since yesterday arvo, come to think of it."

Having recovered the chocolate, Nora removed the white nurse-bouffant cap that tucked her hair hygienically away from the food and took a seat on the stool behind her. Watching Phillip move about the fluorescent-lit cluttered space with its linoleum floors to prepare the strong black sugary tea he drank like water gave her time to think on the startling idea that had come to her during the night—that she could sell in the café provisions she baked in her own time with a shelf life longer than pastries. When she thought of it there had been a rush of certainty she could do it, and a prickling of pride in having conceived a way to make money on her own. It would double at least what she was making now. Without Nicholas it might never have occurred to her. The other day he had stuck a label, which he had found in the junk drawer, on a plastic-wrapped loaf of banana bread. He wrote on the label with a marker, "From the Summer Kitchen Bakery." She had found the gesture adorable at the time and hugged him, but something about it had evidently started percolating in the recesses of her mind, and now she was lapping at the brew like someone tasting it for the first time and wondering how she had never before tasted such ambition. She was thinking of cellophane-packaged chocolate brownies and caramel blondies and orange-and-almond biscotti and pear and oat slices and butter shortbread and Belgian chocolate truffles, marmalades, chutney, relishes, and jellies beautified in jars with black-and-white gingham hats and black-and-white ribbon tied above skirted brims. She could even sell a muesli mix she had developed, full of organic cranberries and nuts and the zest of unwaxed lemons. And she wouldn't change Nicholas's label at all. A child's handwriting impressed that the goods were homemade. She would have his design printed professionally, in black and white, too, old world, like the summer kitchen itself.

She was sure Phillip would agree to it—she would share the profits with him, and the originality of the product, if successful, would draw more business to the café. She was just about to release the dam of plans already in her head when Phillip's comment about oversleeping registered and she cried in a sudden panic: "What time is it?"

She didn't have a watch now. It wouldn't have worked to wear one in any case, her wrists being covered often in flour or dough. The kitchen clock could not be seen from the pastry station. The only sense she had of time as she worked was the span of oven timers as one delicacy or another baked, and the changing light outside the back window signalling the approach of dawn. She was turned to the window now and was seeing, as Phillip told her it was seven A.M., that it was lighter than when she usually left.

How could she have let time slip on this of all mornings!

"Oh, God," she said, hurrying to clear her station of the flat-bottomed mixing bowls and spatulas and Teflon pie weights she had used to make the maple-rhubarb pies cooling on racks. "My kids are going to be late to their first day at their new school."

"What 'new school'?" Phillip demanded.

"It has all just happened." She had not said anything the last few nights at work because she had still been working it all out in her mind, and wondering why it was that this turn had not come as quite the blow she had imagined such a turn would. Had she been hardened so that she no longer felt shocks? But with Phillip she was comfortable being candid, and by now she had confided in him everything else.

As she began frantically rinsing her tools in the sink, she told at a perspiring clip of how she had received notice in the mail just three days ago and three weeks into the new semester that the fees for the second half of the private-school year for all three boys were late. She had thought Evan had paid out the academic year, that she had time to work out how to pay the next. She had planned on quietly applying for financial aid, though even that would not fully cover fees for three. She had not planned on needing money *now,* just to enable the boys to complete the year. There was no way she could raise $40,000. Even her BMW was gone, leaving her to rely on Beatriz's car. She had sold hers last week to pay the property taxes, a deal transacted in the parking lot out back of the Mount Kisco diner because she hadn't wanted a stranger at her home and the dealership hadn't offered enough. The car had escaped seizure, having been the gift one year of a grateful client of Evan's. They only had her car in the end. Evan had not replaced his Porsche after totaling it. He had relied on his driver after that. She gave silent thanks that her property taxes were only $30,000 a year. Taxes on surrounding estates were upward of $250,000. Somehow her property had been assessed leniently and its discrepancy with neighboring properties never realized.

She explained that the headmistress had been extremely kind; financial aid had been distributed for the year, but the school would extend her credit. She had been tempted, so tempted, but going into debt terrified her more than having to leave. And so she had picked up the boys from their private school yesterday afternoon for the last time. They would be attending the public school now.

But even entering them into the public school hadn't been easy. The district had wanted to know did they own their house, what did the father do for a living, where could he be contacted, were the parents married, divorced, or separated. She had ticked yes to owning the house, though that ownership would soon be in contention, but she figured she had been paying taxes long enough without having used the school system until now that really the town owed her. She had left the father's work details blank. When the school nurse had phoned to say it was imperative that they have those in case of an emergency, she had said that he was away for a while and that it was better to contact her always. "What about grandparents?" the nurse persisted. She told the nurse none of the grandparents lived nearby. "Friends?" Right. It was then she had realized that she had no real friends in Bedford. And she had lost touch with her real friends before; it had been as if she moved into a cult when she moved to Bedford. Nobody brought in friends from outside. "We'll make new friends at the school," was all she said. She could tell the nurse had been frustrated, but she had not wanted the school staff gossiping. She had considered ticking "separated" to the question of her marital status, but then read that in the event of separation or divorce, copies of custody arrangements must be provided. She had ticked "married."

"Public school is just temporary, of course," she told Phillip now. "Until next year when I can get financial aid, possibly, or until I get back clear title to my home."

"Of course, mate," Phillip said. "Apples, she'll be."

He took the towel out of her hand. "I'll clean up. You get going."

When she reached the door out to the storefront he called to her. She turned.

He adjusted his hat. "Give 'em my name at the school as an emergency contact."

She felt tears fill her eyes and she had to tilt her head back a little and blink rapidly to hold them in. "Thank you." She paused. "For everything."

She spun quickly to make her way outside to find a taxi, but before she had crossed the café, she heard her name being called. She knew the voice even before she turned in its direction. There was no mistaking that practiced powdery sincerity. And yet her loneliness flicked a switch in her mind and she forgot how because of Bonnie she had needed to cancel Thomas's party for lack of attendance, forgot that whereas once she and Evan and the boys had spent part of almost every weekend with Bonnie and George and Chloe, Bonnie and George made their weekend plans now always with Lacy and Ned Cabot. She forgot these things and other slights for a moment and turned with a smile that told her genuine happiness at hearing Bonnie call her name.

It was then she realized she was wearing her white cotton chef's jacket and chef's clogs. She had not had time to change as she normally did before leaving—or to wash her face or brush her hair or reapply lipstick. She became conscious then that the café was busy with customers. Normally when she left it was just opening and almost always still empty. She shot a nervous look around to see whether any of the other mothers were there, but really it was too early for them still. They came in about nine, having dropped off their children at 8:15 and chatted some afterward in the parking lot. But what did it matter now? Her cover was blown. Bonnie stepped out of the line at the register and strode over, her legs looking disproportionally thin in her riding pants beneath the upper bulk of her Barbour waxed cotton jacket with fur lining and corduroy collar. Her pants and riding boots were muddied: She had clearly been for an early ride.

"You work *here*?"

There was nothing for Nora to do but to nod. It did not hurt as much as she had expected.

Bonnie looked around as though she had never noticed before this café to which she had been coming almost every morning for years. Her polite expression strained to hide an amused disapproval. Nora could tell that she was just dying to tell the mothers.

Bonnie turned back with a bright bleached smile intended to make her next question seem light and off-the-cuff. "Why?"

Nora's mind reeled for some plausible explanation, but the disingenuousness she remembered in Bonnie rankled faster, so that she felt compelled all at once to illuminate it with a contrast of plain truth. "Because I need the money, Bonnie," she said before she could think better of it. The words surprised her in their feeling of empowerment: It felt strangely *good* to be who she was, to hold her head high in a different air, and not be writhing. Moreover, she had seemingly shifted momentarily the power in this exchange. Had she imagined it, or was that awe that had flickered across Bonnie's face?

"Oh . . ." Bonnie said, clearly dazed by the unashamed response. But then she seemed to register the import of the confession, and took a step toward the door, taking a contrived look at her watch. "Well, I should keep moving." Clearly, she had lost her appetite for her coffee, or whatever it was she had stopped in to buy. "I'm planning a surprise forty-fifth birthday party Saturday night for George, and the sushi chef I was flying in to cater it has fallen sick, so I have to call Nobu to see if I can hire away one of their chefs for the night, and I still need to think of a gift from Chloe and me, though I'll probably buy this golf cart I test-drove the other day, so that George can drive rather than walk from the house up to the barn, you know, that barn on the hill in which he keeps his antique cars . . . don't tell him, of course! I mean if you see him at drop-off."

"I won't be seeing him at drop-off."

"Well, you might. He's taking Chloe today."

"Right, but we're not attending there any longer, Bonnie."

She volunteered this only because Bonnie would learn it soon enough anyway, though since she had no wish to subject herself to Bonnie's now inevitably impending scrutiny, she hoisted her pocketbook higher on her shoulder to signal she was leaving.

Bonnie tried to hold her back. "You've left the school?"

Again Nora nodded. "Sorry, but I have a bit to do myself." She hoped Bonnie registered her slightly sarcastic reference to Bonnie's comparatively less crucial schedule.

She didn't expect an invitation to the surprise party and didn't wait for one.

"Well, I'll be seeing you, then," Bonnie said. She did not move, having evidently forgotten her own hurry.

Nora gave a closed-mouth smile, and then just as she was turning toward the door, she caught the spark of an idea glint in Bonnie's eye. "Wait!" Bonnie cried. "I suppose you won't be needing your seats to the school spring charity ball." The powder was thicker in her voice. She had regained her footing. "There's this new family at the school and they're really nice—the most spectacular property over on Guard Hill—and they were told there aren't any more tickets. . . ."

"They can have my tickets."

"Oh, great; they'll be thrilled. I'll have them send you a check."

Since I can see you need it, Nora heard Bonnie thinking. "Sure."

✳ ✳ ✳

The crispy aroma of deep-frying churros wafting through the slightly open summer kitchen window had guided Nora to her boys and Beatriz. Nora had showered and dressed and was eager to know how the boys' first day at school had gone. Beatriz had picked them up so that she could sleep. She had carefully avoided telling Beatriz that she wanted to be rested for Fox Silverworth. He had called her as soon as he returned from Napa Valley to invite himself over to discuss her situation. When she heard his voice she knew she'd been waiting all this time to see him again. Whenever her mind had become mired in her problems, trying as if in a maze to find the way out, his words would come back to her in a gust of relief: "I'll guide you through."

But on the heels of this relief would come the next worry: What if he meant to meet with her only once and to send her on her way with just a few words of advice? She might be all right for a while, but then what about the next hurdle? One meeting would do nothing but stave off the inevitable and afford her a few peaceful nights. No, she needed someone she could go to every step of the way, who would help to carry her load for the distance.

In desperation and without the money to afford such attentive counsel an idea had grown. She had recalled the smile full of ambition Fox had flashed her Halloween night, the twinkle in his eyes when he told her at pickup that she interested him. He had covered up well by turning away into the shadows in the first instance and by explaining in the latter that he didn't imagine his wife would be walking around still with so much dignity in her shoes. But the more she thought on it, the surer she became that she had not imagined his attraction to her. Indeed, that she had not imagined it in any of their interactions over the years. Only a man attracted would pay a married woman and mother any heed.

"Why, I'll flirt with him!" she had said to herself.

The night she said that she had slept well. It was such a practical arrangement. Everyone would be happy. No one would get hurt. She wasn't taking anyone's husband. She didn't want to marry the man, or even take him to bed. She had thought on the plan so dispassionately at the time that it surprised her now to find that the stunned state in which she had lain down that morning, after having essentially confessed to the world of Bedford both that she had no money and that her children had become attendees at the public school, had passed in her sleep into a strange thrilling anticipation for her meeting.

But Fox was not expected still for a little bit. Now Nora stood inside the door to the summer kitchen, watching her boys gathered around Beatriz on stools, their hands by their sides in diligent obedience of her frequent cautions against burns. The boys were silent in their excitement, their necks straining to witness the strips of dough, piped through a star-tipped pastry bag, turn golden brown in the hot oil.

"Can I do that?" Charlie pleaded when Beatriz started to scoop out the churros with a slotted spoon. She lay them on a plate covered with paper towels to drain.

"This is the part that only big people should do," Beatriz told him gently. "But you could fill up that paper bag on the bench with the sugar and cinnamon mixture you helped to mix in the bowl. We are going to shake these churros in the bag until they are coated. You can eat them then while we make another batch to dunk in chocolate."

Charlie climbed down from the stool and scampered over to the counter.

Nicholas and Thomas stayed watching wide-eyed as Beatriz dropped another batch into the oil. Nora looked up at the paper chain threaded above the counter through the hanging light shades. The ends of the chain hung down to within inches of the built-in counter, itself decorated with paper place mats, their edges painted with sparkles and scissored into fringes, crayoned happy scenes of playgrounds in their middles.

Behind it all a banner hung over the glass door to the back porch. HAPPY FIRST DAY OF SCHOOL, it read in Beatriz's pretty handwriting.

Nora smiled at Beatriz's unique ability to invert what might have been a sad day into the first of a chapter that Beatriz would have you believe promised wonders. It had been Beatriz's idea for this celebration that had saved the day that morning at school.

"Why do we have to go here, Mom?" Thomas had asked, stuffing his pocket chess computer angrily into his backpack in the back of the car once they had pulled into the unfamiliar parking lot. "When can we go back to our own school?"

"It will be all right, Tom," she had tried to reassure him. "You'll make new friends quickly. What boy wouldn't want to be your friend?"

"But I want to be with my old friends!"

Beatriz had chuckled then. "Oh, Tom, this is going to be fun! This is an adventure. You and Nicholas will be the special new people today; everyone will want to meet you and know about you. And when you get home we will celebrate; we will have a party to celebrate your first day and you can tell me every detail of your adventure."

"A party! Yippee!" Nicholas had squealed. "Can we have cake?"

"Better," Beatriz had promised. "I will bake you churros."

"Churros!" Nora had gushed. "I've only eaten them in Spain; I love them! But I had no idea you baked, Beatriz!"

Beatriz had shrugged.

"What are churros?" Thomas had asked.

Beatriz had explained, "It is a pastry dough we fry into curly shapes, the inside soft, the outside ridged and crunchy."

Nora knew Beatriz was also celebrating the fact that the boys were attending public school: She had always thought that a better option.

"It will be easier to say no to them now!" Beatriz had said when Nora returned to the car after walking the boys into their new classrooms. Beatriz had stayed in the car with Charlie as he slept through his cold in his car seat. Since the first level at public school was kindergarten, and she could not afford a private preschool any longer, Charlie would be staying home now. "They will see a simpler life: Their friends here won't be flying in private jets and talking of their golf instructors and horse trainers."

Nora had laughed; Beatriz had always worried about the boys being surrounded at the private school by children she believed were being raised to be Fabergé eggs, beautifully packaged, the right school, right clothes, right address, right vacations, right tutors, right summer schools, all in all the right résumés, but eggs nonetheless, fragile, cushioned, ill-equipped to withstand the harsh realties of the world.

She herself was already reassured that the boys would be all right for a time in their new setting, and not just because the grounds and buildings were so impressive, she had discovered, for being in a rarefied district flush with high property taxes: In fact, to her shock, they were more functional in their layout than the facilities of the private school.

She had seen Thomas to his classroom first. It had torn her heart to watch him hang his backpack and coat so tentatively, to see him pull the neck of his sweater up into his mouth, hiding at least half of his face from this frightening newness. But a pretty black girl with braided hair tied back with red ribbon eased Nora's worry when she bounced over with a smile, took Thomas's hand with silent, friendly ease, and led him to his seat next to hers. Thomas let the neck of his sweater fall from his mouth.

She found when she took Nicholas to his classroom that she worried less for him; though his soul was as sensitive as Thomas's, he got on with things whereas Thomas stayed pondering them. When she had told the boys that their father had to go away for a while to fix a problem, Thomas had stared at her with accusatory eyes. He knew there was more to the story and he wanted to know it. She had explained the situation as best she could. She did not use the word *prison;* she used the term the Federal Bureau of Prisons used for the facility in which Evan was incarcerated. His father was staying in a *camp,* with other men by the order of a judge. It was like an adult time-out. He made a mistake and needed to think about what he had done. That, Thomas had understood. Charlie and Nicholas had listened with half an ear.

"Can *we* go camping, too?" Charlie had asked.

"Daddy's not exactly . . . yes, Charlie, I'll take you camping."

"Does Daddy get food at his camp?" Thomas asked after a while.

"Of course, darling; probably not as good as the food we eat."

"What if they don't give him food, though?"

"They must, Tom."

"What will he wear? His clothes are still in his closet: I saw them."

"They will give him clothes, too."

"But what if they don't?"

"They must give him clothes, Tom."

"But what if they don't fit him?"

Over the following weeks, Tom had come back with a hundred questions. She imagined him coloring in a moving picture in his mind of his father's life away from him. It was hard for him to imagine his father managing without his family, she could tell, because he was struggling to grasp how they were going to manage without his father. But all Nicholas had said was, "So when's he coming back?"

The fact of the matter was that he needed to go about things without his dad for a while.

"Can *you* play baseball with us, then, Mom?"

✳ ✳ ✳

"Mmm," Nora said now. The boys looked up. She had entered so quietly that they hadn't noticed her watching inside the doorway.

When they saw her their eyebrows popped.

"You look so beautiful, Mommy!" Charlie gushed.

"*Sí!*" Beatriz echoed. And then she turned to the boys. "It makes a *señora* feel nice to dress nicely. It is important that your mama feel as beautiful as she is."

Nora smiled distractedly, her mind now on the churros.

"These delectable smells have me ravenous," she said.

Indeed, her hunger now raged. She felt weak for it. She sat down at the bench and started to help Charlie to drop churros into the bag he had semifilled with sugar and cinnamon. But Charlie insisted on doing it himself. She let him. The cinnamon-sugar spilled everywhere.

"So what was the best part of your first day at school?" she asked Nicholas and Thomas. They were now overseeing Beatriz lift the second batch out of the oil.

There was no answer.

"Boys?"

"Mooooom," Nicholas whined. "We do the-best-part-of-our-day *at night.*"

She laughed and settled in to enjoy the churros Charlie was now offering her from the paper bag. She took a bite hungrily, never minding that there was no plate beneath to catch the fragrant granular dust. It was exquisite: fried to perfection, a soft, perfect light cake on the inside, the outside crisp and warm and sugary without being greasy. The crunch alone was the perfect pitch: the sort of crunch that potato chip

manufacturers hope for with their dollars invested in research and development. She took another bite: heaven.

"Beatriz!" she gushed. "These are divine, absolutely divine!"

She took another bite.

"Oh, they're just peasant food," Beatriz declared with customary
humility, bringing over the next batch, Thomas following with the
chocolate dipping sauce.

"No, these are the best churros I've ever had. How did you learn to
make these?"

"Ah, that is a story . . ."

"Tell it, tell it," Nicholas urged after wiping his mouth on the back
of his sleeve.

Beatriz laughed and took and finished a bite first of churro.

"When I was a girl"—she dabbed at the corners of her mouth with
a napkin and glanced across at Thomas—"about your age, Tom . . ."
Beatriz was looking at Thomas with that special warmth she reserved
for him. Beatriz adored all the boys, but Thomas had been the first,
and a difficult birth at that, and Nora had felt when Thomas's soft
dark head crowned and lifted her to some higher plane of happiness
that the moment had also gone a way to filling some hole in Beatriz's
heart. Beatriz's face had relaxed that day into an added degree of
warmth that it still retained. Forever after Beatriz had doted on
Thomas, and in recent years, Thomas had become territorial of that
affection. This dynamic in their relationship was subtle enough that
neither one was consciously aware of it.

Beatriz began to tell how her family migrated when she was a girl
from the mountains of Mexico to *chilangos*, what they called Mexico
City. They lived in the crowded lower-class area, and ate little else
but beans. It was a much harder life than they had lived in the mountains, but it was the price of her father pursuing better economic opportunities so that his only child could attend convent school. It
turned out she made it to the school on the new earnings rather of

her mother, who devised a system of employing someone to fix sewing machines discarded from factories and then selling them for a profit to homes back in the mountains. It was a lot of pressure on a girl, seeing her mother work so hard to keep her at school, seeing her father become increasingly miserable away from the mountains he loved and for lack after all of adequate-paying work, and once she ran away from it all for a day. The seductive cheers of *"olé"* drew her to the Plaza de Toros, the largest bullring in the world. Those cheers sounded so free, so happy to her that day. Of course, she had no money to enter the ring to see the *toreros* take the first passes at the bull, then the *picadors* ride in to draw blood, then the *matadors* themselves pass the cape to the cheers of *"olé."* But outside the ring was a *churrero*, one who makes churros. When the *churrero* saw her standing alone in her school uniform marveling at the cheers rising almost visibly from behind the walls, he called her over and offered her a free churro. Churros were common in her mountain home. She was taught as early as she learned to speak that the churro was so named for its shape—similar to the horn of the churro breed of sheep reared in the Spanish grasslands—that the churro was not made but created. But never had she tasted one as good as that one. It made the *churrero* happy to see her appreciate his creation. Since he had time awaiting the crowd to exit, he offered her a second churro and they talked. When he learned of her family's struggle, he told her with a kind twinkle in his eye that she trusted, "What a coincidence." He needed an assistant in the hours after school. After that, she met Don Churrero—as she came to understand he was known, so revered was he for his churros—three afternoons a week outside one or another of all the places that made the city *la Ciudad de los Palacios,* the City of Palaces. And all the while as she was falling in love with the city from behind the roadside stand, and supplementing the family income without word to her father on her mother's insistence, she was learning the secrets of the city's master *churrero.*

She did not suppose they were expecting such a story, her *niños* and *la señora*: They could not take their eyes off her now. The boys' wide eyes were full of questions, Beatriz could tell. She dunked one of the plain churros into the thick, rich chocolate, and for the moment she was the only one making any movement to eat. They spent the next while talking more of her childhood, and even more of bull-fights, they so captured the boys' attention, until they all became aware that the churros had disappeared.

Beatriz rose to lower the temperature of the oil that had become too hot to fry another batch. As she did, she noticed the pile of mail she had collected earlier from the mailbox and picked it up to hand it to *la señora*, only Thomas moved to take it instead.

"Yes!" he yelled. "A letter from Daddy!"

Nicholas and Charlie jumped down from their stools and crowded around as Thomas tore open the envelope addressed to all three of them. Their father wrote simply enough when he wrote to them that Thomas could read the letters without assistance. Thomas took pride in reading the letters aloud to his brothers. Nora's stomach had knotted at the mention of Evan. It twisted into a tighter knot when she heard Thomas reading Evan's plea for the boys to please visit him.

"Can we, can we, Mom?" Thomas beseeched, holding down the letter, distracted from anything else it might say, so focused was he now on seeing his father again.

It was clever, Evan making his plea through the boys. He had evidently seen the futility in asking again in his calls to her. She had not wanted to expose the boys to that world, never mind that Evan had assured her it was perfectly safe and relatively relaxed in the camp visiting room for the children, that there were no metal detectors or handcuffs or partitions between inmates and visitors. It was like any other crowded public place, he had told her, only half the men would be in green uniforms. Still, she had not wanted to take them. Only now she saw in the boys' faces how much maintaining contact with their father meant to them. She glanced over at Beatriz. Beatriz was nodding at her as if to will a yes for the boys.

It occurred to Nora suddenly that perhaps her resistance to taking the boys was really her own hesitancy to see Evan again. She knew one day she would have to, but not yet. She could not bear to have the feelings she was grappling with roused just now into a fire that would consume what energy and focus remained to keep surviving.

"We'll see," she said, taking up the rest of the letters Thomas had put down.

She felt a gloom pass around the room.

"That means no," Thomas said. "Every time she says, 'We'll see,' it means no."

"No, it means 'We'll see,'" she said. "It means 'I'll think about it.'"

The boys went back to their churros and she stared at the envelope on top of the pile in her hands. It was addressed to her from Evan. He always addressed those to her separately from those to the boys. He had written to her every other day since he went away. He had remembered every occasion, a card at Christmas, on their anniversary. She had not sent him even one card. She had read the cards but none of the letters, filing them in a folder marked "Evan, Prison." There was no risk that way that Beatriz would find them discarded in the trash.

She went to tuck the letter behind the terrifying pile of bills in her hand when she sensed Beatriz's eyes still upon her and she looked up and saw keen suspicion in them.

"It is nice that *el señor* writes to you so often," Beatriz said.

Did nothing escape Beatriz's attention? Nora wondered as she felt the full measure of this slight woman's quiet power when she wished to drive home a point.

"He loves you and his family very much."

The boys were now looking at her, too, with longing and expectant eyes.

Under no circumstances could she let them think their mother hated their father.

Damn you, Beatriz!

"Yes, how nice," she said, and opened the letter.

She read silently the first sentence her eyes landed upon, "One of the things I find I miss most in this dreariest winter are the little footprints of our boys in the snow . . ."

She looked up, unable to go on. Already she was infuriated. She knew well that he was trying to ingratiate himself by playing the devoted family man. He should realize that she distrusted everything about him now and that this ploy wouldn't work.

She held the letter to her chest, and told her waiting boys, "Your father misses you very much. I'll have to read the rest later. Mommy has someone coming now."

Beatriz looked her up and down then. The look acted as well as a mirror and reminded Nora of how she was dressed. She had chosen a figure-hugging, long-sleeved, vibrant lipstick-red cashmere dress, nude Wolford thigh-high stockings, and four-inch suede heels the exact shade of her dress and lipstick. Looking at the dress in her closet, she had wondered whether the color was undignified, but when she slipped it over her head, she remembered why she had purchased it and the shoes: The fabrics were so luxurious that she looked provocative in a sumptuous rather than brazen way. But it was clearly a dress to wear for a man and Beatriz now realized it.

"What? What!" Nora demanded.

Beatriz stayed committed to her narrow-eyed look.

"I know what I'm doing, Beatriz." Nora turned to her boys. "I need you now to stay with Beatriz a little while longer while Mommy talks to her visitor."

"Why can't we come?" Nicholas cried.

"Because this is an adult meeting, darling. Why don't you make Mommy some more churros? And then I can eat them with you after dinner later."

And then she went around and kissed all the boys on their foreheads and left with the letters to pick her way across the icy pavement stones toward their redemption.

✳ ✳ ✳

The best place to watch for his car was through her bedroom window on the top floor. Her bedroom suite extended the whole width of the house, and from the master bathroom on the opposite side, she could also see out back. She had checked that rear view intermittently to be sure Beatriz was not spying on her. Having seen no narrowed eyes pressed to the summer kitchen window, or any silhouette in the doorway, she had sat on the window ledge to set her eye on the drive. Fox Silverworth was late, but she was happy to wait. It gave her time to savor the strange arousal that his pending visit had stirred within her again. Actually, it was swelling within her now. A pulse beat heatedly between her legs, where she had not been touched in so long. She wiggled to try to relieve the sensation, but the movement heightened her desire. How her fingers urged to remember her whorls of soft, blood-engorged flesh, the hardness of the tiny pistil that alone could render her body delirious. She longed to relieve the pressure, to become lost for a moment, but now was not the time. It never was anymore. The last time she had climaxed had been with Evan, the night of the morning he was arrested. They had not made love while he was on bail. He had slept on the sofa each night, not even in the guest bedroom. It was as though by sleeping uncomfortably he was flagellating himself, or trying to elicit her sympathy. She had none to offer him outwardly, though she could tell he yearned for it, could tell how alone he felt, he was, in his agonizing nightmare. Here and there he floated thoughts of fake passports and chartered planes and obscure

South American countries. They could all join him, down the road, he always proposed fantastically. She understood how it was for him, living each day alone with the knowledge he would imminently lose his liberty, his children's childhoods, his wife most likely, and possibly even his life. Prison was a dreadful thing to face, particularly from a Bedford view of lush rolling land. He was remorseful, she could tell; but it was too late. Every day was a day he needed to treasure as one of his last, and yet fear had already snatched his pith. He cried out to be held and lulled; she sometimes found him asleep in one or another of the boys' beds, a collapsed storybook on his chest: There had been nowhere else to go once the boys fell asleep and he was happy clearly for someone breathing beside him, loving him unconditionally. She felt ashamed to ignore his silent cries for compassion, but anger had frozen something within her. She could no longer touch him or be touched by him or even look at him when they spoke.

Only on the day she drove Evan to surrender himself to incarceration had she shown any genuine affection. The night before he had come home at four A.M., anesthetized with alcohol. She had not known it was Evan at first. She had awoken to a loud noise outside the master bedroom. She had jumped out of bed and raced toward it in fear it was one of the boys in trouble. Instead, she had found Evan on the floor, struggling to tie a hangman's knot with a coil of rope. The rope still had a price tag attached to it. Its plastic bag and receipt lay on the carpet. It all seemed more pathetic than desperate and she knew immediately he didn't want to die, that he wanted to be saved, comforted. She had felt enormous guilt at that moment. Her husband had needed to stage a suicide to get her attention. Calmly, she had led him to the bathroom. It was while he was showering that he told her he needed to surrender himself that morning. They had both thought he had another thirty days of liberty. His lawyer had informed him otherwise the night before. His lawyer was going to try to reach the judge after six A.M. to try to retrieve those thirty days, but Evan meanwhile needed to plan to surrender himself by nine A.M. She came to wish that his lawyer had not promised to speak with the judge. It made their drive to the facility even more stressful. Evan sat in the passenger seat like a ticking bomb waiting for his cell phone to ring, or telling his attorney before hanging up to call him back when he had news. Of course, no man could wait in those circumstances for a callback, and Evan was calling his attorney himself every five minutes. Another thirty days, even one more day, one more hour, to someone going away for years meant everything. It was in a gas station almost two hours down the turnpike that he got his answer: He must go to prison after all.

Parked inside the front security gate, dazed by predawn events and then the surreal drive toward this—awaiting an escort to collect Evan and drive him to the prison deep in the back side of this federal military air base in New Jersey—she had leaned over the console and hugged him so tightly that no one looking through the window would have guessed at their recent matrimonial strain. So much time passed in that embrace that she had felt in time the thin winter sun through the windshield burning her cheek; she let it burn. She had felt so sorry in that embrace for all that had transpired between them since Evan's arrest: Her husband was about to enter prison and she had not even invited him on his last night back into their bed. Her love for him felt so intense then that she would have believed she could die of it. And Evan had felt it; his body had relaxed in gratitude. It had felt to her like he was scooping her into his soul, to last.

A tap at the window had broken their embrace.

"This is it," Evan had said, pulling himself up in his seat.

They looked at each other one more time, then climbed out their respective sides of the car to face the guard. He seemed congenial enough; tall, like Evan, older, heavy build, ruddy complexion, his full head of hair still blond. He seemed in no hurry, accustomed to the pace of government work. This was just another task on the clock.

They stood in a circle beside the car, the sun weaker in the open air, barely making an impact. Nora and Evan were shivering; the guard seemed immune to the cold.

"Ready?" the guard asked Evan.

Evan nodded.

"Got anything in your pockets?"

Evan felt around. Some coins. His keys. His wallet.

"Leave all that with the missus. Wearing a belt?"

Evan pulled up his pale blue sweater to show the leather belt around his jeans.

"Take it off. Can't take that in. Anything in your shoes?"

Evan squatted to unlace his boots, taking them off and tipping them one at a time the way he had tipped sand from his canvas loafers at the beach just last summer.

The guard was satisfied.

Nora turned to put Evan's belongings in the car. By the time she returned, the guard was patting Evan down. It was unnerving seeing Evan humiliated that way, and no doubt devastating for him to have his dignity taken in front of her yet again.

"Well, then," said the guard when he was done.

She and Evan embraced then one last time while the guard watched on. There would be no more privacy between them, she understood.

"I love you," she said.

"And I you."

There were no handcuffs, only a gun and holster on the guard's belt. He walked unaware of its threat; it was just part of the uniform to him. The guard gestured to Evan to sit in the passenger seat of the government vehicle as he himself walked calmly around to take the wheel. As the vehicle crawled deeper into the base, she could still make out through its rear window the back of Evan's head. From the stiff, alert way he held it, she knew he had forgotten she was still standing there; he was thinking of nothing now but surviving. She watched his head diminish and longed to have him back. Longed for her children to have him back. Longed for the way things once were. The awareness all the while of the impossibility of her longings made her feel so desperate that she wanted to cry out. And then she couldn't see the vehicle any longer and her husband was gone. She did not remember walking the few steps back to her car or opening the door or sitting back behind the wheel or closing herself in again, but all at once she was staring out the windshield, staring at nothing, at everything, at the government personnel moving around the base oblivious to their good fortune at being free to go about their days, staring, staring, until a guard was tapping on her window asking whether she was all right and if she was whether she would mind moving her car for another.

In the days afterward she had felt a combination of relief and bewilderment. Relief that she did not have to live any longer with the silent corrosive tension between her and Evan; bewilderment that her husband and the father of her children had *snap,* just like that, vanished. One day he was moving around their house, answering the phone, chugging down a morning coffee, the next he was gone. His office telephone line was disconnected, his e-mail account had been shut down, and she suspected the regular mail would soon stop coming for him, too. In a panic and all at once, she had tried frantically to call him at the prison. The number Evan had left rang through twice. A woman picked up on the third ring. She listened to Nora outline a situation all too common in her world and then explained in a practiced way that they could only pass along messages of an extraordinary nature such as a death. The only way to contact a prisoner was to write them by regular mail. They had no e-mail or incoming calls. Only limited authorized outgoing calls were allowed. This man who had taken up so much space over the past years, in her and the boys' lives, in people's minds, in courtrooms, in newspapers, would now take up little more space than a bunk bed in a place so removed and disconnected it might as well have been outside this world. Her anger had been easier to live with than the trauma of that realization.

And then the very next day, Nicholas collided with the corner of a wall and she found herself clasping his hand as he lay strapped to a hospital gurney, screaming while a doctor stitched under local anesthetic the bloodied head wound. The helpless screams killed her for their duration. When they stopped she rose out of herself momentarily and saw the scene from a distance: the bodies of a mother and son drenched from the storm the mother had sped through, her drowned-rat hair matted with her poor boy's blood from having carried him so close, both their ghastly faces tear-stained, clinging to each other through their eyes. The terrible aloneness of their situation hung about them as a visible, portentous cloud. That quickly, her anger returned.

Evan's birthday came and went without any acknowledgment from her.

Now she felt only this desire for a man who in every way was unlike her husband. The likelihood that his being a lawyer was what aroused her was not lost on her. She only had to become one with him and she was back on the other side of the law, the righteous side where no one could hurt her anymore and nothing could be taken. He could return to her that feeling now denied her, of being beyond reproach and untouchable, and while to know that again would be heavenly, she was now wondering why she was limiting her fantasy. Her mind was ticking on to the idea of a more permanent union. She would not ever again have to feel scared or unprotected, and while her reputation among the women of Bedford might be further tarnished for a while, they would surely get over it when she was firmly established as Mrs. Fox Silverworth. It wasn't as if he even had a relationship with his wife, and she wasn't seen that often at the school. Their nanny was usually sent to drop-off and pickup, though his wife was a big philanthropist, and so was well liked by the women—but then *she* could become a philanthropist again if she married Fox Silverworth. *All* her money problems would be resolved! And though the boys didn't need a father—they still had a father—Fox Silverworth at least knew what it was to be one. Above everything, he could return her children to their old life!

She was melting now in the heat of her fantasy.

She willed Fox through the dreary and dimming gray outside. Nonetheless, the drive stayed still, and she began to worry that Beatriz would soon bring the boys back into the house. They couldn't make churros out there forever. She stood and walked through to the bathroom to peer out back again. The lights down there had been turned on, and then just as the movement of figures reassured her, she heard the roll of tires over gravel and she darted back to see the Town Car pull up in the driveway. For a moment she expected Evan to climb out. His Town Car had pulled up every night for years just like that, and she had often waited eagerly for him just as now. How odd it felt suddenly to be waiting as always but now for another man to enter her house.

She took a deep breath to compose her beating heart, checked her appearance in the full-length mirror behind the door, and made her descent down the front stairs.

In his expensive, pressed dark suit he was holding out to her a little black box, so that her first word to him as she stepped back to invite him in was, "Oh . . ."

She noticed that his driver had not turned off the car's engine.

"Open it," he told her.

She detected gloating in his hoarse voice, and that combined with the waft of cigarette smoke as he stepped in and stood facing her dragged to mind the memory of the gum-chewing head suit who smelled and sounded the same when he pushed past her in just this spot to arrest her husband. She forced back the unwelcome image, but found herself then wondering whether she could sleep with a man who smoked. The smell of cigarettes had always sickened her.

She opened the box and cried out as she reached for her camera's Memory Stick, "How? How did you get this?" It seemed the kindest thing anyone had done for her.

Surely she could overcome her aversion to cigarette smoke!

"I told you I knew some of the prosecutors on your husband's case."

She held the Memory Stick to her heart a moment, sure that this was a sign she was doing the right thing: This was the man who could save her children.

"Do you trust me that I know what I'm doing now?"

"Trust you?" she cried. "I'm relying on you!"

She saw in his eyes that he looked pleased and it occurred to her that this might be easier than she thought. All men liked to feel needed, and her need of him was genuine. Feeling needed was likely something he missed, too, since his wife had her own money.

"You went to a lot of trouble for me," she purred, leading him to the stools at the kitchen bench. That was the only place there was to sit now. If it had not been safely built-in, like all the woodwork, the office of restitution would have taken it, too. She noticed that Fox seemed strangely oblivious to the lack of furniture. He was looking around rather it seemed at the structure of the house, his eyes rising to the ceiling, scanning the built-in kitchen appliances, his head leaning one way and then the other to peer into rooms.

"And the garage is out that way I take it?"

She thought, The garage? What did that have to do with anything? She nodded.

"I thought we might have a glass of wine," she offered, before panicking silently that perhaps there was no wine in the house. She had not had even one drink since Evan went away, her boys depending on her alone now. She should have checked the racks.

It was then he seemed to notice for the first time how she was dressed. He looked at her for a moment too long, and then flashed at her that ambitious smile of his.

The brazen look was back in his eye and she instinctively went to recoil from it when she remembered her unfamiliar role as seductress and gave a teasing smile instead.

He laughed, resting back on his stool indolently. "Well, Mrs. Banks . . ." A suave note entered his voice. "The best way to proceed here might be for you to act *pro se*."

Disappointment stirred in her. Here he was talking business already, and she thought something had been starting between them. "*Pro se?*" she almost gasped.

"It's a Latin adjective. It means 'for self.' You would represent yourself in your case without a lawyer. It might even help you, a pretty woman like you so helpless."

Now the disappointment congealed as panic.

"But I can't do this on my own!"

"Why not? You're a smart woman."

"But you said you'd help me."

"Have I said that I wouldn't?"

"Isn't that what you just said?"

"No. There's nothing stopping me if you act *pro se* advising you on the side."

"All the way through?"

"All the way through."

An intense relief swept over her and she hurriedly retrieved her poise.

"But I'm not sure I understand the difference," she said sweetly. "If you intend to advise me anyway, why not simply act as my lawyer?"

"All the difference in the world."

She looked at him, waiting for him to explain.

That ambitious smile again. And then he said as coolly as if he were still discussing business, "Lawyers aren't supposed to engage in relationships with clients."

He didn't need to add, "But if she wasn't officially his client . . ."

She swallowed and dropped her eyes as she digested the certainty that she and Fox Silverworth were going to begin an affair. It had all happened so quickly that she was suddenly not sure how it had all come about. All she knew was that somehow Fox Silverworth had wrested control from her over the outcome of this meeting.

"I take it Mr. Banks is out of the picture now?" he asked.

She looked up but found she couldn't answer him.

There was intense curiosity in his scrutiny.

"I'll make you forget him," he said calmly. "A man like that isn't worth loyalty. Certainly you wouldn't want to be going to him for advice in this case. I won't help you if I think you're taking my advice to him for a second opinion."

"I won't," she said.

"Well, then, Mrs. Banks . . ."

Was he going to kiss her *now?* She quickly put down the Memory Stick that had been in her hand all this time and prepared herself to be kissed for the first time in more than ten years by a man other than her husband. But when he rose he simply ironed the breast of his suit with the palms of his hands and ran his fingers through his hair to prepare to leave. "We'll be seeing a lot of each other, I suspect," he said.

"That's it?"

"For now."

"We don't need to discuss the case?"

"I know now what I needed to know."

While she still knew nothing and felt no closer to solving her problems.

Yes, he was exasperating.

"Haven't you any idea of the prosecutors' intentions at least?"

He was already heading toward the door, as if it were his house and he could come and go as he pleased. He turned. "Sure," he said. "They know they don't have a claim to your property, but they're planning to take a case all the way through the court system in the hopes of wearing you down emotionally and financially so that you'll want to settle and they'll that way redeem at least part of the property."

She was speechless.

"The property is worth enough for them to take their chances," he added.

She followed him in a daze, and then just as he opened the front door and she registered his car was still running, Beatriz and the boys came around the house.

"The boys need the bathroom," Beatriz explained. "The back door is locked."

The boys ran inside and scampered in three directions to three bathrooms, but Beatriz stood at the bottom of the porch and stared at Fox Silverworth. Beatriz's impudent manner surprised Nora.

Fox extended his hand gallantly. "Fox Silverworth," he said.

"*Señor,*" was all that Beatriz said before passing into the house. She did not shake his hand.

Fox smiled in her wake. "We'll meet somewhere more private next time."

Eight

He stood out, Rich Boy. They all read the papers, watched the news. There was little else to do, but walk the perimeter of the field out back, around and around and around, day after week after month after year, turning over and over and over how things might have been. They all knew him even before he got close enough for the name Banks to be decipherable over the left breast of his uniform, close enough that the fear in his guileless eyes was as large as his shoes were small: New guys were often issued with shoes too small. "Just until your size comes in," they'd be told with a smirk. A lot had that toe-curled walk coming in, buttocks clenched tight against another cavity search. Not that he was the only rich inmate. They got plenty here, only two hours south of Manhattan down the New Jersey Turnpike. A lot of the Wall Street guys getting sentenced lately had their big lawyers request this camp. Their families in Manhattan could still visit them here. Hard luck if you got sent down to West Virginia or Alabama. It happened. Harder luck if you landed this camp and then your wife dumped you. A lot of guys got served with divorce papers the first year in. They'd arrive and think it was over in a way, at least the mental prison they'd been living in. They'd known the outcome of the investigation and then the indictments would be horrible, but what crippled them was not knowing how horrible. At least when the gavel went down they knew what they were dealing with. Only then came the divorces, the bankruptcies, new tortures. Some guys staved off divorce by allowing their wives to have other relationships: Some wives couldn't take the loneliness, the ostracism, the struggle. Those guys ground their teeth in their sleep and hoped they were buying time. Other guys tried having sex with their wives in the woods out back after visiting hours, though that was more about relieving themselves than pleasuring their wives. Try going years without so much as seeing a woman naked except in magazines smeared with clammy prints from the toilet cubicles. There were no conjugal visits at Fed camps, but there weren't coils of barbed wire or circling guards, either. Sometimes there were only a couple of guards to four hundred inmates, which was why it was easy to smuggle in pornography, drugs, and alcohol—though that got a guy killed the other night. Fell out of his top bunk drunk and smashed his skull on the concrete. Bloody mess, the guys who cleaned it up said. Violent offenders weren't put in camps. They went into the medium- and high-security facilities. Stuff happened there; that's where the guards were. There were still fights here. It happens when you lock a bunch of guys up together after taking away their lives. But not killings, rarely stabbings, rarely rapes.

He was not Rich Boy because he was by any means the youngest, either, though he was still considered a kid by the standards of the old-timers, long-timers usually who had already done a nickel or so in the camp or a couple of dimes already over in medium security and wished they had the sense they did now when they were his age. Two years was a joke. They told him they'd spend more time on the crapper in the joint than he'd spend in it in total. They envied him, those guys, the chance to learn the lessons prison taught so young, then get another chance while still so young. Some of those guys were learning lessons too late; they'd be in their sixties, early seventies when they got out. Normally they wouldn't have respected a guy much who was only bidding two years. Bidding times, release dates—they defined you. They especially wouldn't normally show respect to a guy bidding only two years who had it so good on the outside. Didn't matter whether the government took all his money or not; rich was rich. Most of these guys had never been rich, never would be, though they'd tried; most were in on drug offenses. A lot of these guys came from the projects; Fed camp was a step up in lifestyle for some. One of the guys preferred camp to the streets because he was a better father in here; he was never high anymore when he saw his children. No, they wouldn't have normally respected a guy who always had it so easy. But Rich Boy was different. Not at first. At first, he just kept to himself, stayed alert, listened a lot, slept little—though he never became one of the Vampires, who prowled at night to avoid human contact, then slept during the day. God knows how they did that with all the racket; radios blaring hip-hop, rap, farting, belching, prayers aloud that their aching tooth wasn't a cavity. A tooth would rot before you got to see a dentist in here. Guys cared for their teeth like they were gold. You noticed him, Rich Boy; you couldn't help but notice a guy as bloody handsome as that. Not too many guys looked like that came in here. Wouldn't have lasted a day in state prison, a guy who looked that good. His looks combined with his wealth—that's what first got him the moniker Rich Boy; it meant trust fund baby. Someone as rich as that who looked like that had to have had it all handed to him. "Hey, Rich Boy!" they messed with him. "Gotta light?" They pretended they held a cigarette between their fingers. He'd shake his head, "Don't smoke." They'd laugh. That was the joke: Someone like that probably didn't even know how to smoke, wouldn't want to get his hands dirty. But pretty soon they began to show respect. Pretty soon *Rich Boy* took on a different meaning. That's when they started calling him The Bank.

Now he stood out because they'd seen for themselves how f'ing good he was at making money. They respected something like that;

the guy was smart. Not just in that book-learnin' way, either—though he quoted some heavy stuff sometimes they didn't always get. But he had real street smarts; surprising in a guy who looked like that. Turned out he never did have nothing handed to him. Did college somewhere upstate New York on a scholarship, then worked a few years to pay his own way through his M.B.A. at New York University. The guy's father never gave him a cent. They hadn't picked him for a guy who knew how to make a buck even in a place like this. But he worked it all out real fast, adapted: He "made moves," as they say. The two main currencies inside prisons across the country were books of stamps and mackerels, yep, cans of that oily bait: A can or "mack" sold for one dollar in the commissary. Each mack traded between inmates for something less than a dollar. Inmates offered services for mack currency. One inmate might steal the iron, and charge one mack for each item of clothing ironed for another. All guys wanted to look their best at visiting time; razors, combs, irons, they were valued as much as the Muslim prayer oils the Muslims traded to those without the M as their religion. Non-Muslims used the oils as cologne, when their wives and girlfriends visited, though the Arabian musk scent was so nauseating that the reaction from other inmates was usually something like, "Are we a bunch of fucking broads in here?" Others charged macks for the more legitimate services of tutoring, fitness training. One inmate had been a lead guitarist in a rock band; he charged three macks for a guitar lesson. A few others were artists; they charged macks for personalized birthday and holiday cards. The macks earned were then sometimes traded for black-market items, smokes usually, but anything really, even cocaine if you were into that. The Bank had only been interested in black-market food. He hung out with a physician with a Ph.D. in nutrition who was busted on insurance fraud. They talked constantly not about any financial index but about the glycemic one. That was how it all got started. The Bank and the doctor would trade with other inmates for whole-grain rice and chicken fillets and fresh fruits and vegetables, shit like that, all of which they steamed or grilled and divided into every-other-hour servings to maintain perfect digestion and insulin levels. It was like a f'ing mantra: They'd know exactly which type and how much of a food to eat before exercise for optimum performance, before reading for prime mental agility, before sleeping for the best rest. It was all pretty time-consuming, and The Bank decided to cut through the middlemen and deal directly with the inmate kitchen staff. What did they want to learn? He'd teach them in trade for the food: English, chess, math, accounting 101, whatever. They wanted to know about math and accounting; they needed to turn macks into cash. They wanted to send it home. Every dollar would help. They had kids, wives struggling.

The Bank expained that the rules of arbitrage in which he'd specialized could be applied most anywhere and to anything. He explained that if they traded macks they earned for chocolate bars and sodas bought by others through the commissary, they could sell those sodas and chocolate bars to the truckers making deliveries to the kitchen. It all depended on pricing. They would have to trade more macks than the chocolate bars and sodas were worth in the commissary or the guys with the sodas and chocolate bars could just buy macks instead at the commissary. And they would have to sell the chocolate bars and sodas for a lot less than the truckers could buy them outside. He figured the truckers would be interested if they could buy two chocolate bars and a soda for a dollar. No one worried about getting caught. The whole mack economy operated unlike Wall Street without scrutiny. The idea was not necessarily new; guys had done similar things. But its organization was. Pretty soon guys were rolling in macks and cash; well, rolling by prison standards. Must have been quite a shock for The Bank, the different value of money on the inside. A mack could buy two hours with a qualified fitness trainer inmate. The Bank probably paid hundreds for that on the outside. Probably never thought about it, either. Seen it before with the rich guys: When they had more money than they could spend it became valueless. One of the things about prison, it shakes you awake, makes you appreciate the value of things, the value of a dollar, of life, of your freedom, sanity, health, the value of your family.

The Bank never asked for nothing for boosting the mack economy. He "went hard," as they say. All he wanted was his healthy food. There was no point evolving spiritually if he didn't help his body to keep up, he explained. He wanted to stay in prime shape to play baseball with his boys again when he got out, and to keep open the chance his wife may take him back—though he knew that was going to take a lot more than a good body. God, he loved his wife. Never shut up about her, poor guy, or his kids, for that matter. Most guys went on about sex rather than their wives, sex they'd had with girlfriends, hookers, sex they wanted again with them. Not The Bank. He paid a couple of macks the other day to one of the artists to sketch a picture of his wife from his memory. It was like watching a scene with a police sketch artist.

"Is the nose right?"

"No, more delicate."

"The hair?"

"Softer."

He had tears in his eyes the whole way through.

The Bank taped the sketch to the bedpost above his pillow. When one of the guys brushed too roughly against the bedpost and the sketch fluttered to the floor, The Bank attacked the guy like he'd raped the woman. Took three guys to pull him off.

Kind of another reason the guys respect him now; turned out to be f'ing strong.

Nope, The Bank never asked for nothing. He understood he "had nothin' comin'."

Except today he sat out in the trucking bay. Sold enough to make three crisp dollar bills. He folded them like they were lace handkerchiefs, and then removed his left shoe. He untacked the heel effortlessly. The small space beneath accommodated all three bills. He hammered the heel back into place with the side of his fist and looked up. Nobody was going to tell. Nobody would cut off the hand that fed them.

Besides, it turned out they liked the guy.

He put his shoe back on and returned silently inside.

＊ ＊ ＊

Eventually cars in the visiting line started to be processed. After Nora and Beatriz had shown their identification at the checkpoint and their names were located on the inmate visiting list, Beatriz's car was directed through the gates. Nora glanced over apprehensively at Beatriz, but Beatriz seemed typically unfazed. She took her eyes off the road for a moment to wipe a smudge off the smeary glass front of the instrument panel. Beatriz had seen all this before. Several women friends when she had been drinking had done time for crimes committed under the influence. Nora turned away and looked out her iced-over window. Tall wire fences surrounding the higher-security east and west wings to either side of them were hunched at the top in the way of the shoulders of inmates behind them, hands in pockets, boots shuffling snow, or planted, nowhere to go: Nothing stood proud here. It was that, the pervasive sadness and ennui, that she found frightening. There was no color, no laughter, no texture, no sound at all but the earthquake a moment ago of a jet taking off from the nearby base. Instead, she imagined, the air resonated with the slow draining of lives until nothing remained but ghosts, ghosts of former selves, of regret. Nora could almost smell the rotten, lonely, bored misery, like the smell of a damp cellar. The smell, even if imagined, made her shiver; it seemed too close to death.

Soon both wings were behind them and they were looking at a loosely fenced paddock of snow under scattered wooden picnic tables. An inmate sat atop one, his uniform green, his arms folded against the cold: He was watching cars pull up, waiting presumably for his visitor. Or perhaps he had no visitor and was fantasizing, the way regular people imagined living in the exotic homes in celebrity magazines. Adjacent to the picnic tables and set back from the road was an army-style bungalow. There was no fence in front. To the other side of the bungalow lay a soccer field with stand seating, nothing beyond that but an unmade road into the woods. They had presumably reached the camp. To either side of the gravel road, cars had parked haphazardly. They found a spot among them. Beatriz turned off the knocking engine and Nora began to pack a Ziploc plastic bag with cash for the vending machines inside.

She had told Evan when he phoned to speak with the boys that she was bringing them to visit and he had filled her in with feverish excitement on visiting regulations. Nothing could be taken in but keys, cash, and identification. Those things must be carried in a transparent container, no larger than one cubic foot. There were so many other rules and regulations she had to remember that she forgot she had felt so sad just a moment earlier for Evan. She found herself feeling irritable that she was here, brought to this, packing a Baggie with cash on some slushy road in the middle of nowhere while her boys slept cramped in the back of a car not theirs as a means to see their father in prison: in prison, for God's sake. How had she come from a regular upbringing to be a prison wife? "Goddamn him," she said without thinking.

Beatriz smoothed the front of her skirt.

"Do you think, perhaps, *señora,* that you are being a little hard on *el señor?*"

Nora bridled and glared at Beatriz. *Hard* on him! In her agitated state she could almost have slapped Beatriz. "You're supposed to be on my side, Beatriz."

Beatriz looked up with gentle conviction.

"It is not about sides, *señora*. It is complicated for everyone. Only *el señor* is a good man. What he did, it was not so bad. I have seen men do far worse things, violent things. But I have never seen a man love his family as much as *el señor* loves his."

"If he loved us so much, Beatriz, he wouldn't have put us at such risk."

"He did something foolish. We are all flawed. I was flawed when I came to your home, and you did not judge me. Why do you judge *el señor* so much more harshly?"

"He deceived us, Beatriz!"

"In his mind, *señora,* he was protecting you."

Nora did not answer but bent for her coat balled on the floor at her feet. She meant for the conversation to be over.

Beatriz would not be deterred: "It is possible, *señora,* that things could be easier if you stuck together as a family, if you and *señor* helped each other through this—"

"I don't want to talk about this, Beatriz," Nora snapped, opening the car door now and climbing out into the cold even before she had struggled into her coat.

"As you wish, *señora.*" Beatriz sounded understanding but unrepentant.

Beatriz shrugged herself into her coat and climbed out, too, and they each leaned back into the car through opposite rear doors to awaken and unbuckle the children. Charlie slowly awoke on Beatriz's shoulder as they all picked their way through the puddles to the bungalow. A blast of overheated air almost knocked them backward as they entered.

"Phew, it smells like girls," Nicholas said once the security officer at the Formica table inside the door had cleared them all into the visiting room.

He meant the malodorous cheap perfume the girl ahead left in her wake. Nora had noticed the scent while they were in line, too, though all she smelled now was microwaved food and the musty scent of damp wool and the greasy dust of old heating ducts. She looked around. She was reminded of a Third World airport, a tangle of civilian men in uniform and woman and children and other men in regular clothes, some milling in front of the vending machines on the far wall, others settled into couples or groups on the green metal benches bolted to the floor in rows facing one another, playing cards with worn packs or chess with missing pieces, security cameras watching all the while. Almost everyone was engaged in conversation, but for the few who had run dry and were watching the television hanging high in the corner. A handful of children knelt around a grubby yellow plastic child table. They alternated their focus between the television and the tabletop mound of mismatched Lego pieces while their parents presumably snuggled amid the crowded benches and tried to put out of mind the unkind fluorescent lighting.

While "Banks 18954-053" sounded through the public-address system, Beatriz looked for a place for them all to sit. She found it at the end of a bench next to two nervous elderly Caucasian parents visiting their son presumably and across from a party of four black men and women and a black inmate tucking into a plate of fries. No one acknowledged them as they stacked the coats, gloves, and beanies they had removed at the door into a pile at the end of their bench and took their seats. Beatriz understood: These people retained like dwellers of clustered city apartments what privacy they could.

"There's Daddy!" The boys made a sudden beeline for the father. He was entering the room from a door on the opposite side to the visitors' entrance. The boys tripped over two sets of knees and nearly sent a plate of chicken wings flying in their rush. Beatriz hoped they remembered to pardon themselves, but sent out apologetic looks just in case.

Nora was hardly thinking of her boys' manners. She was glaring across the room at her husband. He looked good: not a sign he had been presumably to hell and back. He looked in the best shape she had seen him, in fact. It was clear he had been working out. Her response to the fit of his shirt over his torso in her irritable state was to realize the truth of the idea that had plagued her the day their possessions were seized: that it was the wives who were punished, the families who suffered most. These men, they faced none of it inside, not the ostracism, the paucity, the overload. There was no worry about how they would keep the lights on: They never flicked a light switch much less received an electrical bill. There was no approaching any point of collapse from becoming the sole body on which so many lives depended in impossible circumstances; they had nothing to do but sleep and read and dwell on a misspent life and *exercise*. When had she last had the time to *exercise*!

Evan had Charlie in one arm, Nicholas in the other, Thomas draped over his back by the time he stood in front of her and Beatriz. The boys were laughing. Beatriz felt sad that they missed this rough-and-tumble now, missed this man in their lives strong enough to lift them all at once; neither she nor the *señora* could give them that kind of play. She gave Evan a warm smile, and he returned it, rocking the boys like they were in a boat. His smile came easily, she noticed. So often these past years he had forced it, forced the appearance of happiness for his family. It was not so much that he now seemed happy, but that he seemed at ease in his unhappiness, his soul no longer tortured by secrets.

He kept his eyes averted from Nora.

"Why do you wear green in here, Daddy?" Nicholas was asking.

Evan's long-sleeved green polyester shirt was tucked in at the waist of his matching black-belted trousers. His black shoes were polished to a sheen that would pass army muster. His cut hair, trimmed nails, pressed uniform, clean shave, it was all for Nora, Beatriz understood, though she shuddered to think of the silent torture he must be quietly enduring, appearing before his family in prison fatigues.

"Because green is manly, buddy!"

He tickled them all in turn. "Grrrr."

The boys all squealed in pretend fright.

"Control your children!" the guard yelled from the front desk.

"Indoor voices only, okay?" Evan said more quietly.

"Okay. Can we go play over there?" Thomas asked, pointing in the direction of the other children gathered around the yellow plastic table in the corner.

Nora felt herself seize with panic. She had not anticipated being with Evan without the buffer of the boys.

"Sure, buddies," Evan said, taking a seat next to his wife.

They all watched the boys scamper off, flashes of color appearing and disappearing and appearing again between the playground of coats and limbs.

Beatriz stood and announced that she was getting the coffees.

"Sorry I can't get them for us," Evan said. "We're not supposed to touch cash."

"I know."

She headed toward the vending machines; Nora knew she would take her time.

She and Evan both stared after her as they had after the boys: Nora grateful for a reason not yet to have to speak; Evan because he was admiring Beatriz. As he watched her thread her way through the throng with unfazed ease, he remembered the dignity on which he had thankfully relied on her. His gratitude toward this woman that he had no meaningful way any longer of expressing felt at times intolerable. Though what felt equally intolerable was his continued need to have to rely on her; it felt emasculating having to accept the money she wired into his commissary account so he could pay for the phone calls to the boys, and for the stamps for *his* letters to them and his wife, to await without control the frequency of *her* letters with news of the family. Once while unbuttoning Nora's blouse years ago he had scoffed at Nora's decision to hire without scrutiny a woman straight out of an alcohol treatment program. Now this woman was his only link to the world, the only one to step forward to care for his family. He felt as indebted to her as humbled by her honor and loyalty, though prison was illuminating the futility of pride.

After losing sight of Beatriz, Nora took in the scene between a boyish-looking man and an attractive, petite, blond woman she recognized from articles she had read in newspapers as Ralph Harris and his wife. The former Connecticut mayor had been sentenced to nine years some years back on charges he sought payment in return for steering city business to friends and associates. So this was where he was incarcerated. They were holding hands and including their three children in their intimate discussion. He let go his wife's hand a moment to tousle a son's hair. The son laughed and tried ruffling his father's hair back, only his father had lost most of his hair. They laughed harder. Nora marveled at how tight the family seemed. How was it possible a wife could forgive and continue loving a husband who had brought upon her family the humiliation and hardship of which she, Nora, now had a good idea?

Finally, she and Evan turned to each other, her face stony, his eyes imploring.

"How are you?" he asked as politely as if they were strangers.

She gave him an incredulous look. How did he think she was?

He took on her look, let it sit with him a moment.

"Happy Valentine's Day," he said with strained hopefulness, while measuring his unhappiness at looking at his wife on such a day here rather than across the deck of the fully crewed private yacht he had chartered for them only two Valentine's ago. The Valentine's before that he'd gazed at her across the deck of their private dock at that private-island resort in Belize. The resort had served their custom meals on that dock and they had never seen another guest. They had spent three days in Turkish robes, Yves De Lormes sheets, and pellucid water. The year before that it had been a road trip along the quiet (for that time of year) Amalfi Coast in Italy, and it must have been the Valentine's before that when he surprised her with private cooking classes at the Ritz Escoffier School while staying for a week at the Ritz in Paris.

Nora started. She had not registered it was Valentine's Day. She had known the holiday was approaching; she and Phillip had been hand-dipping chocolate hearts for a week, shaping pastries into cupids, icing cakes in the shade of strawberries. She had even sent the boys to their new school on Friday with cellophane bags of chocolates Phillip had insisted she take home for them to distribute to their classmates. And the boys had returned home with reciprocated chocolate gifts, and in one case a red pencil threaded like an arrow through a hand-cut red cardboard heart that she appreciated as she might not have so well in her old life for its resourcefulness. But not once had she related any Valentine sentiment to herself, or remembered that the holiday was this Sunday.

She half-smiled uneasily at Evan but didn't return his wish.

He leaned forward, rested his elbows on his knees, his hands dangling between his legs, and looked down at the floor. He needed her love back. Though he also understood that perhaps it was too late, that perhaps too much had happened. That daily tussle between his emotional need and his rational thought drove him near crazy. A few times he had cracked his head against a wall. A few of the inmates had kept their distance after that.

He looked up to search her face for what to say next.

She was looking away at the children.

"I'm sorry about the baby," he said. Beatriz wrote to him about the loss. He hadn't been able to say anything, lest Nora learn Beatriz was writing to him. It was not like he could pretend his lawyers had told him, as he'd done after Beatriz wrote to him about Nora having been refused entry into their city apartment building when she went there to collect their personal belongings, agents having earlier been there to change their pied-à-terre locks, building management instructing staff afterward to treat the Banks family as undesirable. He had to grieve alone for their baby; feeling guilty for his grief, as though he had lost even the right to that. Nora had let him know weeks later when he phoned the boys. "By the way, I lost the baby," she said, and hung up. He had called back, but she hadn't wanted to talk about it. Her not wanting to talk about *anything* had become a pattern in their communications: He would finish speaking with the boys, they would hand the phone back to their mother, and she would demand again to know why she now had to handle so much alone, as though he had some power still to help her that he was cruelly withholding. He always just listened.

The mention of the baby had caused Nora's facial muscles to twitch.

"I'm sorry about all of this," Evan continued, his eyes moist now.

She turned on him with narrowed eyes.

"Sorry doesn't cut it!" she hissed, before turning sharply away from him again.

He stared back down at the floor, a concrete floor worn smooth by so many lives unraveled. He had no idea what to say anymore. Whatever he said made her angry. He wished he could just make her understand, but he'd tried explaining more times than he could count that he hadn't told her about the investigation because he hadn't wanted her to live with the fear he'd been living with. The anticipation of an FBI raid, of an indictment: Those had been terrible, all-consuming fears. His behavior—the carelessness, the sleeplessness, the exuberance—one day he'd be fractured, the next delusional. How could a man put his family through that, he had asked her over and over. Besides, there had been a chance it would all go away before she had to know about it. His lawyers were in settlement discussions all the way to the end. And from time to time they had prevailed at least in unfreezing his accounts, so that he'd been able to stop the credit cards being declined again, so that she and the children hadn't needed to go without anything. Of course, the lawyers had their own incentive for unfreezing his accounts: Enormous chunks were wired into escrow to cover future fees in the event he was incarcerated. That night, Halloween, he had thought it *had* all gone away, that a settlement had been reached. The Feds had wanted him to think that. They'd wanted him off his guard when they made the arrest, had wanted him to be home and not fleeing.

Her usual retort to his attempts to explain all of this was to remind him that it had also been easier not to tell her: He hadn't had to face her or his children, had he?

"You're right," he'd begun to say after she'd driven the point home enough that he'd come to understand her point of view. "It was wrong of me not to tell you."

"Yes," she would invariably answer. "As wrong and self-interested as what you did to cause the investigation in the first place."

At first he'd chafed against those words. He had done it for her, for his family. The world of wealth had been a trap. Living any other way stopped being an option. And the cost of keeping apace in that world had continued to escalate. It hadn't been enough to vacation regularly; they had needed to vacation in more exclusive parts, and to travel to those parts by more exclusive means. It hadn't been enough to landscape; they had needed to add a gazebo, a fountain, an orchard. A guest parking lot had been next. Their yearly cash-burn rate had grown to exceed $3 million, which meant he needed to earn approximately double that before taxes, at least. The monthly credit card bill alone was more than $100,000. There had been no end, but there had been a limit. When the market turned for a bit and a few of his deals went south and the cost of their life outpaced his earnings for the first time, he had lost all appreciation for the rarity of his lifestyle, had become so habituated to it that he believed his family actually needed it. And so he had overreached for the brass ring.

But recently her words had struck a chord. Perhaps it was a different way she said them, or that she said them at a different place in his processing of all that had happened, but his arms had broken under his shirt into goose bumps. He had done it for his family, yes, but also for himself. It had been like an addiction in some ways, driving the stakes higher and higher, reaching for greater and greater glory. And New York City had enabled his addiction. The end-all, be-all of existence in that city was money. Become affluent enough at a young enough age and you're a rock star. People hung on his every word. How many times had he walked into '21' or Peter Luger's or Nobu or the Four Seasons and seen people pointing him out and whispering? He had even heard word on the street of other hedge funds copying his moves. It hadn't taken long for it all to intoxicate him. It began to mean nothing when someone tried teaching him something, since it was clear to him that whatever way he already had of doing anything was innately right. And if anyone didn't get it—or didn't approve of it—there was something wrong with *them*. It was true, the expression that all self-made men worshiped their creator. He had been forever thinking, Look what I've done! And when he finally upped the ante to borderline transactions, he believed still that what he was doing was clever, that he was smart enough to win—and this: that Nora's goodness would carry them both and more than make up for a little deviancy on his part.

What a young fool he had been.

But it was useless confessing all this to Nora again; she had long ago stopped listening, had not wanted to listen since his arrest.

And really, although there were explanations, there were no justifications for what he had done. No explanation could absolve him of responsibility.

He glanced over at her hands, clasped tightly on her lap.

"You're not wearing your ring."

"No."

"Did you sell it?"

"Not yet." She had considered it before pulling the boys from the private school—the government having been forced by law to let her keep her engagement ring—but then what would she have used to pay for their next year? But also something else was holding her back from selling it. She had no desire to wear it anymore, and not only because of her cold fury. It simply no longer looked right. Her hands were those of a laborer now. They were always dry and cracked and red, her nails often chipped and always unpolished for lack of time or money for the ninety-dollar manicure-pedicures that were once part of her weekly routine. But still, she could not bring herself to sell it, let go of it.

He sighed, looked up at her. "Look, Nora, you're still young, you have a life ahead of you. It's clear you no longer want to spend it with me." He bit his bottom lip, pausing, hoping she might disagree. Silence. "I'll sign whatever divorce papers you send."

She turned her tight face back on him.

"You think I have time to manage a divorce! And what do you think that's going to change right now anyway? I already have sole custody of the boys by default while you're in here, and there are no assets left but the house, and that's even in dispute."

"So now you're even angry that you can't get an ordinary divorce!" He tried to sound angry, to be a man still, but there was not much force to his voice.

"Right! There's no ordinary way out of any of this for me."

She was stopped from saying any more by the sight of Beatriz approaching. Beatriz held out a honeycomb tray of coffee cups.

Nora took one, thanked Beatriz, stood, and headed without word toward the boys.

Beatriz took Nora's seat, handing Evan his coffee.

A young black man with dreadlocks shuffled past. He held a bag of potato chips. An attractive young black woman followed him.

"Recognize that guy?" Evan asked. "That's John Forté."

Beatriz looked blank.

"He performed with the Fugees before the group disbanded in the late nineties."

Beatriz still looked blank.

"The Fugees, you know, that band that fused hip-hop with soul and reggae? Well, anyway, he's Carly Simon's godson. She pulls up in her limousine every few weeks or so to visit him."

"Ah," Beatriz said. She peeled the plastic lid off her cup. "Why is he here?"

"Got fourteen years for accepting a briefcase of cocaine at the airport."

Beatriz blew over her coffee to cool it.

"He gives guitar lessons here Monday nights," Evan said. "I've signed up."

She laughed, though Evan stressed that he was serious.

After a bit, he peeled back the plastic lid on his coffee cup and took a sip, disregarding the scalding heat. "Thanks," he said.

She gave a small, warm smile.

They sat in silence a moment, each looking down into their cups.

"She hates me, you know," Evan confided.

Beatriz looked up. "She is finding herself, *señor,*" she said gently. "Finding her way out of her rage and into her own power. These things take time, two steps forward, one, sometimes two or three back, another few forward. Give her the time she needs."

He nodded slowly, feeling the rise of a little hope. "How's everyone holding up?"

Beatriz laughed.

Her laughter startled him.

"*La señora*, she will be okay," she said, and then she told him the story of how *la señora* had started selling her own delicacies at the bakery. Customers had noticed their label, their melt-in-the-mouth uniqueness. They had begun asking who made them, and *Señor* Phillip was only too happy to tell them. "Nora Banks?" some of those customers had asked. "The same Nora Banks . . . ?" "The same Nora Banks," he told them. These same women then asked that he pass along their regards. *La señora* had laughed when *Señor* Phillip told them. "Their regards!" she chortled. "Where were their regards four months ago?" But she started taking catering and private orders when the phone started to ring.

Beatriz held back from telling him that she, Beatriz, had been baking churros each morning for Phillip's since he had tasted them when he came by the house once to talk with Nora; she knew it was Nora whom Evan needed to talk about.

"She's taking private orders?" Evan asked.

"She says the women need the sweetness!"

Evan laughed. "That's my girl. And when she wins back clear title to the house she can refinance it so that she and the boys can again live as they're accustomed to living. You can tell her I'll pay back the loan as soon as I am out and working again."

Beatriz shook her head. "I believe that *la señora* considers debt just another complication, *señor*. I believe she intends to keep working to cover the bills."

"But she can't be earning much just by baking."

Beatriz looked at him. "Have you ever noticed how *la señora*'s face lights up when she bakes? Baking is who *la señora* is. Since she is on the right path she will do brilliantly. Riches of one sort or another will surely follow."

He looked over at Nora and the boys, gnawing now on the inside of his cheek. "Well, if Nora has it all worked out . . ." His tone had the panic of one whose usefulness had run out.

"You are still needed in your family, *señor*," Beatriz assured him. "Your boys adore you and miss you. And perhaps whatever relationship comes between you and *la señora* of this, it will be better for *la señora* finding herself. Perhaps she needed you for things she did not have within her. Perhaps you needed her for things you did not have within you. A relationship can be richer when the partners are complete and look to each other only for love and companionship."

He turned back. "She won't even talk to me, Beatriz!"

"Because your old relationship no longer exists."

He looked stricken. She touched his arm lightly to reassure him.

"To go on, it would need to be a different type of relationship."

He stared at her in silence, his eyebrows knotted.

She explained no further. He needed to come to his own understanding. She said instead, "As for the case with the house—"

Beatriz's face seemed to Evan at that moment to close down.

"What is it?" he asked, every muscle in his body snapping to attention.

"I think *la señora* is making a mistake."

"What d'you mean?"

"I know a bad apple when I see one."

"Beatriz, what are you talking about?"

"That lawyer she is talking to, there is something about him that smells."

"Literally?"

She smiled.

"I didn't even know she'd hired a lawyer," Evan said. "I was going to have my criminal attorney call her to refer her to someone. I guess she found someone on her own."

Beatriz nodded.

"Thanks for telling me. I'll have my attorney check him out. What's his name?"

"Silver something, Silvermoney, I think, no."

"Not Fox Silverworth!"

"*Sì!*"

Evan raised his hands to his face.

"You know him?" Beatriz asked.

Still Evan did not lower his hands. He clenched them tightly rather over his closed eyes. Finally he looked up, crossing his arms over his chest and jamming his still-hard fists under his biceps. "I know just who is he—and just what he is! He's a piece of garbage who doesn't move a muscle except to rip people off." Suddenly gripped by a thought, he swung around to face her. "When you say you know a bad apple when you see one, have you met him, has he been to the *house?*"

She nodded, her heart bleeding for his impotence. At the same time her stomach seized with guilty responsibility for his anguish. She had had no idea he knew the man.

Evan was staring beyond her at nothing. "Fox Silverworth in my house with my wife!" he said angrily to no one. "What lawyer goes to a woman's home when she is alone unless he has designs on her?" He had forgotten he had just offered his wife her freedom to find another husband. But he would never have stepped aside had he known his rival might be Fox Silverworth. Fox Silverworth! That overmoussed gigolo had walked across his floors and shared air with Nora and possibly his children with that grin of his that laid claim like the flag in the moon.

The picture of it filled him with murderous impulses.

There had to be something he could do, but then he became conscious again of his surroundings. His rage turned to a cold sweat. He had thought there was nothing left to fear, but this fear was worse than any other—to watch helplessly as the devil moved in on your family, unable to protect them, in that you are essentially chained, unable even to warn them because to your wife your words no longer have weight. Not only would Nora pay him no heed, she would likely act contrary to his wishes to spite him.

Beatriz was asking, "What can I do?"

He turned blinking eyes to her, digging his hands into his pockets. And then the echo of her question clapped in his mind like thunder.

"Beatriz!"

"*Sí, señor?*"

"Beatriz, I think I know just what you can do to help."

"Anything, *señor.*"

"Beatriz, I know how men like Mr. Silverworth think and he has presumably told Nora something to make her trust him. I need you to find out if you can what that was."

He could elaborate no further, as Thomas had run over, Nicholas and Charlie climbing in his wake over stretched adult legs. Nora was further behind still. Evan noticed for the first time the strain of fatigue in her face. The way she walked now was different, too. He remembered how she had glided around before so lightly and freely that it had almost been a dance. Now she moved the way people did when they carried a weight, more slowly, cautiously, as if running on reserve power. Her wrung-out state made him worry that a man with shoulders to carry her load would trap her as easily as a web a fly.

"Dad, those boys aren't sharing the Legos!" Thomas complained.

His face had lit up with their return and his voice took on a theatrical note. He said, "I have something even better for you boys." He moved his coffee cup under his seat. "Just wait a moment. I have something in my shoe."

Beatriz and the boys watched him curiously as he maneuvered his way through the crowd toward the inmate toilet. Nora's face openly bore her impatience.

When he returned, he carefully positioned his back to the closest security camera. The boys were all seated in anticipation and looked at their father expectantly. Like a magician, he produced from his sleeve three neatly folded bills.

"One each," he said, handing out the bills as discreetly as forbidden candy.

"Money!" Charlie squealed. The group on the bench opposite glanced over. Evan looked sharply at the inmate among them, then turned back to his children.

"Shh," Evan insisted. "You must keep it a secret until you get back to the car!"

He watched his boys' glimpsing their prizes and the beauty of their excitement struck him. Their lack of any sense of relative value was adorable at their age. One bill excited them as well as one hundred would have: It made no difference to them. At what age did the lack of any sense of relative value stop being adorable and become dangerous?

Only back in the car did Nora think, My God, Evan hasn't changed: He just broke the law again to give money to his children. He could have made things even worse.

There and then she resolved to be done with Evan.

At that same moment on his bunk, Evan thought, That was stupid.

There and then he grasped fully the wrongness of his ways, and it felt as if he'd finally reached the top of a mountain he had been struggling determinedly to climb, and he breathed easily and relished the view. Life, like the climb down, would be easier now.

Nora had never imagined the relief of mentally severing herself from her husband, but by the time she arrived home some hours later, her tension was loosening. Reuben was in the drive as they pulled up, unloading a crate of beets. Digger was with him, running circles around Reuben's truck, his tail wagging. No matter his age now, Digger always seemed as peppy as a puppy when he visited.

Nora smiled to see them both and turned around to the boys.

"Look who's here!" she said.

"Digger!" Nicholas yelled from the back of the car, pushing himself up on his hands for a better view through the window. Thomas craned, too. Charlie needed only to turn his head from his booster seat. Digger's visits were the boys' favorite play dates. The boys had even set up a dog's playground in the stripped-bare basement. Last time, the boys had wrapped him in a winter coat and taken him down the snowy slopes out back one time after another on their sleds. Once they even harnessed Charlie's sled to Digger, and Digger had pulled Charlie on a ride.

Perhaps it was because of the boys that Digger showed so much pep.

Reuben and Digger had been visiting more lately than when she had been one of his best customers. She had told Reuben that the quantities of anything she could now afford would not even cover the cost to him of delivery, surely, but still he came with eggs from his chickens and rutabagas and quinces and leeks. Sometimes, as now, he showed up with something delectable out of the blue. He had even been snowplowing her drive before dawn after each major snowfall. She had wondered who had done it, the first morning she awoke to a trail through the heavy overnight accumulation. But then she had found the crate of parsnips on her doorstep.

For a while she had considered that perhaps Reuben was simply lonely, his divorce having recently come through, and that he needed connection with another family. And then she realized that it was not for her that Reuben came.

She glanced at Beatriz as Beatriz pulled her car up alongside Reuben's truck. Beatriz looked flushed all of a sudden and fumbled with the keys after she turned off the ignition, pulling at them a little frantically as though they were jammed.

Nora smiled to herself.

They all grabbed their hats and gloves and pulled their coats around their shoulders and climbed out. Reuben's eyes went to Beatriz. There was a yearning in them so intense today that Beatriz could not possibly be unaware of it. Nora followed Reuben's eyes and saw Beatriz through them for the first time. A cold wind had lifted Beatriz's skirt and Nora found herself staring at Beatriz's legs. How had she not noticed Beatriz's legs before? They shimmered now in her stockings, legs slender and curvaceous at once, legs that moved so seductively. As Beatriz walked across the drive in her heels to pet Digger, Nora also noticed the hypnotic sway of Beatriz's hips, perfectly proportioned, curvaceous hips, the sort of hips she imagined men yearned to grip, the sort of hips she imagined made men think of lovemaking. It came to her then: Beneath the tightly twirled hair and stiffly buttoned blouses there was fire in Beatriz.

Reuben watched Beatriz but said nothing, and after Beatriz had petted Digger, she stood and awkwardly smiled her hello to Reuben and headed inside.

Nora turned her attention back to Reuben. He looked so gallant, braving the deathly cold without gloves or jacket or hat, his blunt hair combed back, holding his offering of purple gems as steadily as his hope of winning love.

The earthy aroma of the beets was strong. She found herself being drawn forward to breathe in more. She breathed in deeply and deeply again, feeling less and less tense, the prison becoming more distant, and then, the familiar rush of love of good food. In the heat of the moment she decided to use that love to bring love together.

"I can't possibly keep accepting these gifts without paying you," she said.

"No, really, I—" he started to protest.

"I thought perhaps you might like to stay for dinner," she interrupted. "We could think of all the different ways of cooking beets and have a beet feast."

His face lit up. "Well, if it's not too much trouble . . ."

"Of course not. We would love to have you."

He nodded gratefully and then, just as he was about to follow her inside, he remembered the envelope in his hand. "This was hand-delivered for you while I was waiting," he said. "The caretaker for a woman named Bonnie drove it over."

"Bonnie?"

She took the envelope and opened it while he waited for her.

It was an invitation to Lacy Cabot's fortieth birthday on the first day of spring next month. Bonnie had attached her own handwritten note on pink heart-shaped paper.

> *I do hope you can come. I am hearing the most marvelous things about your baking. I was at a wedding reception the other day and the bride was gushing about how her wedding cake was exactly to the specifications of her childhood dream. And then she said you had baked it—and that she was given your name by a board member of the John Jay Homestead who said that you were catering desserts for their upcoming ball! I phoned Lacy straightaway, of course, and she and I both said how much we miss you!*

Driven away by adversity, attracted by success, Nora thought. Bonnie chose the wrong word for herself, when she chose *lavish* as her "me" word. *Insubstantial* would have been more accurate. She had no intention of being Bonnie's latest pet project, which was all she was without money of her own. No, she would wait and make a grand reentry into that world when she had money again and stop them all dead with the most lavish child's birthday party any had attended. How wonderful it would be to put them all in their place when she was rich again and untouchable. But as she went to push the invitation back into its envelope, she felt the faint rise in her breast of excitement, and then the thought causing it pushed forward: Fox Silverworth would be there!

She hadn't seen him since he came to the house. It seemed he lived most of the time in Manhattan. She couldn't imagine anyone looked forward as she had of late to some legal notice arriving. If she called him without an excuse like that, it might seem she was too eager. But his wife was friendly with Lacy. There was no way Lacy would not invite the Silverworths.

When she looked up at Reuben, she knew her eyes were glowing.

SPRING

Nine

Eyes turned to her when the maître d' showed Nora along the highly polished floorboards of the Glen Arbor Golf Club's rear balcony. They were headed toward the far end where a good number of the men and women of Bedford had gathered around a roaring outdoor stone fireplace to celebrate Lacy's birthday. The balcony overlooked the course and surrounding wooded folds of Bedford Hills. The spring dusk air smelled of freshly cut grass and smoldering logs. A warm glow from the fireplace circled the guests like a halo, though for a few moments the illusion broke when the burning wood crumpled and sucked back its light and an attendant stabbed the coals with a poker. Everything gleamed, from the windows of the silvery set room where they would later dine, to the smiles directed at one another in complicit acknowledgment of this bounty that was theirs.

It was indeed a spectacularly seductive setting, though Nora struggled to push down an uneasy contempt for it all. She was simultaneously experiencing a déjà vu moment: Nothing about this world had changed. Everyone seemed even to have forgotten how it all was merely a few months ago. Evan was dead to them and they had all moved on. But as she drew closer she realized that there *was* something different.

Was it just that she was seeing these people from a different perspective for all that had happened to her? There was that certainly but there was also something more. The immoderation of their airs and graces had intensified. And this observation shed light on the increased number of construction trucks she had noticed moving about town, and on the spectacular brick mansion on Guard Hill being demolished while a newer replica went up on the same grounds just ten feet back: They had moved on with enormous end-of-year bonuses. But the irony of having lost everything in this great bull market did not deflate her— perhaps because she was confident now she would have money again.

She scanned the faces, looking for one in particular.

She was conscious of a pattern in the way the eyes turned to her. First the men noticed her, and then one by one, the women by their sides noticed something in their husbands' faces and followed their eyes to her, too. Many of the women lifted themselves on their toes a little higher than their heels already provided to whisper in their husbands' ears. Many of those husbands then allowed themselves to be led over to other couples needing apparently to be greeted that very moment, or their faces simply obediently shut down. It was understood that extramarital lust was to be kept outside of Bedford. And Nora realized that she was a threat to that social moray. Not only was she arriving unaccompanied, she had made sure to look spectacular. She was wearing a slinky white ankle-length gown by La Perla, tied into a deep-cleavaged halter, cut in the back below her waistline. The gown draped in exactly the right places, so that her hourglass figure was accentuated with elegance. And she had curled her hair into waves as soft and feminine as the makeup she had applied to look naturally beautiful without further ornamentation, such as the jewelry she no longer owned. She had even grown her nails a little, though had stopped short of painting them. She didn't want to draw attention to the redness of her hands that seemed to have become permanent. The legal toxicity that had once kept everyone away also no longer existed, but then neither did her financial ambiguity. Certainty had replaced that: She had nothing! But really that was not altogether true. What she had now, from what she had learned from Bonnie's note about her baking, was evidently a new mystique.

All at once Bonnie stepped forward and enveloped her in high, powdery words of endearment and a light but heavily perfumed squeeze. Nora noticed the other women's icy looks melt some and their husbands' faces radiate relief.

"And how *is* our newly famous baker!" Bonnie asked loudly enough for those few couples in the immediate vicinity to hear and be drawn into the conversation.

Nora smiled and nodded her hello to each in turn.

"What's this?" one of the husbands Nora had met once or twice at functions over the years inquired. He was a wiry-haired, distracted man, tall, thin, and rumpled. He appeared always as though he had slept in the streets rather than on his fifty-acre equestrian farm with its innumerable outbuildings for its staff. He was not one of the men who had looked her way when she entered. Nora understood from the jokes his wife had often made that the only thing that turned him on was money. Nora suspected now that his interest had been piqued by the words "newly famous." He had boasted once at a dinner party of how he had made a fortune buying up Krispy Kreme donut stock after tasting one right before they became commonly known, and likely he was wondering whether she was about to go public, too!

"Haven't you heard?" Bonnie asked with a teasing note of condescension. "Nora has set up her own little business, selling privately and through Phillip's the most delectable baked goods. You should taste her blondies!" She lowered her voice. "Though you've probably tasted a few in your time, Morris." Bonnie laughed at her own innuendo. Morris's brown-haired, attractive, petite wife, Ticky, gave a bored polite smile. She was familiar with the sexual bantering that passed the time at these functions. Something tickled Nora about that smile. Nora knew Ticky as the stepmother of Morris's daughter from his first marriage, who was in the ninth grade at the private school. The second husband in their group now looked away, and the third looked down and shuffled his feet. Their wives did not seem to notice and were laughing with Bonnie. But Morris's chest visibly puffed. Probably he was the only man among them who had never tasted a blondie, and was surprised at how good it felt to be mistaken for one who had. Bonnie had won him over by playing him like a harp.

Nora just gave a gracious smile. She knew as the only blonde among them, and an unaccompanied one at that, not to find the joke too amusing. Dealing with married couples as a single woman was more perilous than the mother-scene minefield.

She felt a light tap on her shoulder and turned to find Lacy smiling her greeting as though they had never stopped being great friends. "I'm *so* glad you could come," she gushed. Nora wished her a happy birthday. The maître d' had taken her gift basket to place with the other gifts. Her baskets were quickly becoming their own booming little business. She would place baskets full with provisions and preserves in the centers of enormous sheets of clear cellophane wrap and then gather up the corners around the basket and tie a tight neck under them with silky white ribbon so that they sprayed like petals over a stem. She would then add one silky black ribbon to the swirls of white and would carefully center one black-and-white Summer Kitchen Bakery label midway up the bulk of the basket. The effect was as dazzling as a diamond, with the promise of more inside, and the women had been ordering them by the dozens for luncheon party favors. It never occurred to them that Nora was this way learning of all the luncheons to which she was no longer being invited, but Nora was too busy now to think on that for long.

Standing with Lacy was Pamela Hanson, a slightly slimmer but still heavyset Pamela Hanson. Pamela had forever been going on and off diets, but it was hard for her to stick to them when she roamed the house until one every morning to avoid advances from the husband who had left her twice for young assistants. She had taken him back both times because money was too important. It was a tricky business holding on to a husband for his money and at the same time avoiding sex with him. And lonely at times—which was why she often reached for ice cream while waiting out the late hours for the sound of snoring. Pamela did not greet her effusively, and said nothing at all in fact. Lacy was fingering a bejeweled necklace. She saw Nora notice. "Oh, this," she offered. "This was my birthday gift from Ned. It was quite a surprise. Ned is such a dunderhead normally. Somebody must have helped him. You would die if you knew the things he did wrong putting together this affair for me!"

A man Nora had never seen appeared beside Lacy and wished her happy birthday. Lacy kissed him and then said to her and Pamela in explanation before moving off with her guest, "I've known Marc longer than I've had a black American Express card!"

Pamela trailed Lacy's departing figure with her eyes and then turned to Nora and with great seriousness said, "I've been very angry with you!"

"Excuse me?"

"You didn't even say good-bye when you left the school."

Nora did not know at first how to respond to this. It seemed incredible that Pamela could have expected a good-bye, when Pamela had ignored her for so many months before the boys left the school. Pamela had been capable of walking past her in the hallway without even saying hello. And in the early days after the arrest she had been one of those to extend an empty courtesy, a promise of regular Friday night dinners with the children that came to nothing. But then all at once she understood. Pamela thought that she had been charitable in her empty promise. In return, she had expected supplication from Nora and a front-row seat in her life. But Nora had slipped away and had not to Pamela's mind kept up her end of the bargain.

Smart retorts rushed to mind, but boredom checked them.

All she said was, "I guess my thoughts were elsewhere."

She excused herself and threaded her way toward the bar.

Nora noticed Morris engaged in heavy conversation with someone obscured by a potted plant over in the far corner of the balcony. Ticky was turning from the bar with a fresh glass of white wine. They smiled politely and Ticky asked how Thomas, Nicholas, and Charlie were. The considerate inquiry took Nora off guard after her interaction with Pamela, and she found herself gushing about the first-place trophy Thomas won at a chess tournament, of how Charlie had begun already at just four to read, of the vegetable garden Nicholas was planting with their family friend, Reuben.

"I admire you," Ticky said, readjusting her light-pink cashmere wrap around her shoulders with her free hand. The wrap was so delicate that Nora doubted it kept her at all warm in her matching light-pink, strappy, ankle-length, silk gown. Nora herself was feeling the chill of the evening, though both the fireplace and heating units in the ceiling attempted to heat the balcony. Ticky's readjustments caused the wine she held high in her other hand to topple and spill some down her wrist. She stopped rearranging her dress and stretched the glass away from her body to avoid worse spillage. But even then her wine hand trembled. Nora wondered whether this was far from her second glass.

Nora gazed back at her expressionlessly, a little more guarded all at once.

"I would never have been able to do what you've done," Ticky went on.

"You will likely never have to," Nora said with considered care.

Ticky had not answered her, but was gazing blankly at her husband. She turned back to Nora. "I'm sorry I wasn't there for you, Nora," she said.

Nora wasn't sure what caused her stomach suddenly to constrict, the unexpectedness of an apology from one of the Bedford women, or the sudden wrenching backward into the dreadful pain of that time. She had gained such mental control, rarely let her thoughts spiral, that it had begun to feel as if she had shed that time like a snakeskin. It seemed some remained to tighten around her again with just a word.

She took a breath and focused on steadying herself.

"I'm not as strong as you, Nora," Ticky went on. "I followed the crowd back then. But a lot has happened with me since then. . . ." Ticky lowered her eyes and gripped her drink with both hands, as though needing something to clutch. "I'm glad you didn't move away."

"That was never an option for me," Nora answered.

Ticky lifted her eyes, but lowered her voice. "It made of lot of these women angry, you know, that you didn't. It would have saved them all the trouble of having to try to work out how to peg you. There was a breath of relief when Bonnie told everyone you were working the night shift at Phillip's and that you had left for the public school. They had a peg for you—no money, public school—and justification for withdrawing the friendships they'd wanted to withdraw from the start: They simply never crossed paths with you any longer. But now that you are rising, they are outraged all over again. These women know they don't have inside them what it's taking you to survive—and they don't like to be reminded of it. But what frightens them as much as you do now is being out of step with social consensus, and somehow beyond the control of any one member of the community, the consensus has become that your baked goods are the new hot thing."

Ticky paused to take a long drink.

With an amused smile Nora said, "So they hate every bite of the cakes they love."

Ticky nodded. "Pretty much."

They both laughed. After a bit Nora said, "Ticky, you are stronger than you think: You can only see so clearly by standing apart, and it takes courage to do that."

The amusement dropped from Ticky's face. "There's a lot I'm still not apart from." Her eyes flicked warily toward the corner of the balcony where her husband still had his back turned. Her face twisted almost undetectably and for a moment into misery. But as she looked back, she had recovered and was unreadable again. "You were freed from it. You had no choice. It's harder to free yourself of it."

Nora replied with gentleness now, "I imagine."

"And whatever would I do?" Ticky went on. "I don't have any special talents like you. You see, you are so lucky in so many ways—" And then all at once she became flustered, as though she had forgotten that others were in the room. She grabbed Nora's arm clumsily, a little too tightly, and whispered, "You won't tell anyone, will you? I mean that we talked like this, that I said these things?"

"You are free to speak your mind, Ticky."

"But you won't, will you?"

"No, Ticky, I won't."

And then she begged that Nora forgive her but that she should leave her before she said any more. She started to head off only to turn back for a moment. "Just be wary, all right?" She hesitated and then spoke so softly she was almost inaudible. "Bonnie knows people at the town offices and has made inquiries about whether you need a permit to run your baking business from your summer kitchen. But don't say I said so."

So Bonnie had invited her up to this extravagant hilltop setting to drop her again.

And then Ticky was gone.

"What can I get you?" the bartender was asking.

Nora blinked at him. "Tonic with a twist of lime, please."

He handed over the glass damp with beads of fizzy perspiration. She looked at the wedge of lime balanced as perfectly as a tightrope walker over its brim. As she peeled off the napkin stuck to the bottom, a familiar movement caught her eye. She looked over to see that the figure previously obscured behind the potted plant talking with Morris was Fox Silverworth. He was heading straight for her. And then she noticed that in order to reach her he needed to pass Bonnie. Bonnie's group had become loud and animated. She could hear Bonnie telling another woman who had admired Bonnie's new Manolo Blahniks that George never minded her buying anything beautiful. Nora flashed back to one of Bonnie and George's dinner parties. George had worked into her conversation with him that he earned between one and five million a year. George wanted the world to know it, and Bonnie worked full time trying to achieve that end. Both times George had been fired over recent years (Bonnie confided that also over those cocktails), Bonnie spun it to the school community that George had "retired" and then "retired again." George got an ear pierced and took to cruising around in one of his antique convertibles during the second retirement to drive home the point.

She could not have Bonnie derailing her plan to snare Fox.

She handed her glass back to the bartender, pretending not to notice Bonnie's sharp eyes suddenly watching curiously. "I think I'll change my order to champagne." He poured her a glass of Veuve Clicquot and when he handed it to her she said, "Do you see that man heading this way?" He looked over her shoulder and then turned back and nodded. "Would you tell him that the woman in the white dress was feeling chilly and went inside to retrieve her shawl?"

Fox found her, as she knew he would, in the coatroom.

He was dressed in one of his dark Italian suits, powerful shoulders tapering to a narrow waist. He had an impudent air about him. He didn't say hello but casually leaned against the wall and kicked the door shut behind him with his foot. She was imprisoned by his clearly ardent intentions.

Their eyes locked in silence.

And then he said, "I'd like to slide my arm around your waist and pull you into me." But he made no movement to slide his arm around her waist or pull her into him. "You'd feel the taut muscles of my torso against your breasts as I slid my tongue into your mouth." Still he did not shift from his position a foot away from her. "I'd send a charge through your body that would stand your nipples erect." My God, he was making verbal love to her. She felt unnerved for a moment and then she thought, no, this was just going to be different. She downed her champagne, bent to place the glass on the floor, pressed her back up against the wall. His sardonic smile made what they were doing dirtier and more arousing. As the champagne hit her, she caught on his breath the smell of beer and red meat. It carried her to some vast, masculine place she found herself lost in. "Handful by handful, I wind up the hem of your dress. My fingers plunge inside you from behind, so cold, so shocking. You take a small step to the side to open yourself to them. I know you don't have panties on. The back of your dress is cut too low. You reach for my hand and push it in deeper. Your dormant desire becomes unquenchable. You scoop one leg around the back of my thighs, pulling me in closer, rubbing against my hardness, and I'm pushing and you're rubbing, pushing and rubbing, pushing and rubbing, and my hand is drenched and you're begging for me to push deeper and you can't press close enough into my body, and then, *ah*, you're digging your nails into my back under my jacket and pulling away from my mouth to muffle your cry against my shoulder." She was no longer looking at him. She had closed her eyes and was moaning as though she *had* climaxed. It was some time before she realized he had stopped talking. When she opened her eyes he had gone. She stood abruptly upright and stared at the door. He had left it wide open. Anyone might have seen her. She quickly closed it and sat down in confusion on the velvet-upholstered lounge.

It was almost as if she had imagined what had happened, well, imagined that he had been in the room with her. Did he intend to come back or had he just teased her? This man was beyond exasperating! But, oh, how much she wanted him now. Her desire for him only increased as she waited. And then she understood: He was not coming back, at least not that night. He wanted her to want him.

She had been staring at the back of the door all this time willing him back, and now she noticed a lock on the inside. Before she realized what she was doing, she had stood and turned it. If she could not have him physically, she would have him mentally.

And she knew now just how he would take her.

She lay back on the lounge, raised her dress, opened her thighs, reached down. And before she had closed her eyes, she was no longer there but in a hotel room.

It was small, but the bed king-sized and high with crisp, white, fluffed pillows and matching sheets folded over a duvet, its cover a design of royal yellow and khaki, the same heavy fabric used to make the drapes. The covers had been folded down, two individually wrapped chocolates on the fold. The chocolates were the supermarket variety. This was a middle-range hotel in a business district, comfortable and with the pretense of respectability but there for sex. She walked in and sat on the bed. She heard the door shut and then he was kneeling before her, pushing her dress up to the top of her thighs. In one movement it seemed, he slipped off his jacket, pried open her legs, and lifted her thighs over his shoulders so that she fell back onto her elbows. She gripped the bed linens as his tongue shot into her and rolled expertly about, and when he drew it out to flick at her like butterfly wings while his fingers pressed down inside her, an orgasm climbed within her. He felt it, pushed her farther up the bed, and stood up, looking down with an expression of simple intent at her womanhood.

"Not yet," he told her, dropping his clothes to the floor.

His body was toned, hard, perfect; she longed to run her tongue over his washboard stomach, the gentle mounds of his pectoral muscles.

"Please." The pulsing between her legs was turning to a pounding.

He smiled down at her then. He was making her wait of course.

He climbed up onto the bed and knelt between her thighs, teasing her with the tip of his manhood. Circling her waist with his arm, he flipped her onto her stomach. He pulled a pillow under her hips and drew her apart. And then . . . and then nothing. Only the creak of the bed. She expected his touch, but it didn't come.

She felt his breath all over her excitement. His chest was obviously flat to the bed, his face almost touching her. He was looking at her, really looking at her, at her hairless smoothness, engorged, trembling, and the thrill of it, of knowing he was looking, but not being able to see him looking, the anticipation of being touched, made her body burn and quiver. She felt him breathing against her. She lost track of how long, how long she lay there in a frenzy of anticipation, not knowing would he touch her, would he plunge right into her. She felt her dampness spreading across the pillow beneath her hips. When he did finally touch her, so lightly, just a finger, exploring her, she cried out. It was almost unbearable. And then the creak of the bed again and he filled her. She lifted her hips higher to meet him, and he pushed her dress up higher to take her hips bare in his hands and pull her closer. He ground into her desire like the base of a palm kneading dough, pressing, lifting, pressing, smoothing her with the perfectly timed and pressured movements of a master into something light and delicate and trusting and pliable. He bent one of her legs and lifted the spiked heel of her stiletto so that it dug into his chest, turning her in that movement onto her side. Then he slipped her lower leg around his hips without her heel on that foot even touching him and twisted her. Without his having withdrawn even once, she was on her back looking up at him, knees pressed back to her breasts still scooped in her dress. She reached for him, but he shook his head. *He* wanted to control this. He lifted her stilettoed feet onto his shoulders, and with two parted fingers closed her eyes. He spread her arms. And then he drove himself into her with such force that it hurt. And then again, and again. She could have opened her eyes, pushed him back, regained some control, but something in her wanted this. She had needed for so long to be so strong, so impervious, it felt an incredible relief to have her vulnerable femininity driven home.

He did not uncover her breasts afterward, to stroke them, acknowledge them, or hold her hand, kiss her mouth. He stood up and retrieved a washcloth from the bathroom to wipe the inside of her thigh of his release. He cleaned her and then bent for his clothes. She closed her eyes. She heard the shower. She lay there alone for a long time, listening to the flow of water, prolonging the fluttering sense of physical fulfillment, the wonder at the reaches of her womanhood, the astonishment of a man other than her husband smelling of her, until she heard . . . a knocking at the door.

"Is somebody in there?"

Nora sat bolt upright. She had forgotten altogether that she had locked herself in the coatroom. Now someone was on the other side of the door.

"Just a minute."

She rolled off the lounge, smoothed her dress, and took her brush from her evening purse. She had left it in the coatroom. In the mirror, she reapplied lipstick. She could do nothing about her flush.

But then why would that matter?

She had done nothing wrong: She and Fox had still not even kissed.

✳ ✳ ✳

Nora and Beatriz had risen early the following morning to try to make headway with a dessert order for an Easter luncheon fundraiser. Nora had suggested chocolate crème brûlée napoleons, a white chocolate sauce drizzled on top, dark chocolate shavings atop that. Coffee would be served with her signature iced orange strips covered with rich, dark chocolate and dusted with pure cocoa. The fund-raising committee had requested that she also make one chocolate bunny for each of the 250 guests to take home. Nora and Beatrix had been casting bunnies all week, Nora's chocolate recipe the finest, nothing but pure, organic ingredients: cocoa, sugar, cocoa butter, vanilla, lecithin, ground wood-oven roasted hazelnuts. The bunnies were stored in the cellar, ready to lay at the last minute on tissue paper in individual white boxes tied with copper-orange ribbon. The cellar maintained the perfect temperature, never too warm to melt the chocolate, never too cold to turn its surface brittle.

Nora was sipping on red tea from the southeast of China, a green tea ripened to heighten its medicinal properties, among them its legendary ability to cure hangovers. But what was bringing her back to life more that morning was the thrill of feeling like a woman again. Unknown to Nora was that Beatriz was experiencing the same thrill. Since Reuben had stayed for the beet feast, he had been visiting family in San Salvador. But he had written to invite her and *la señora* and her *niños* to the orchard the following weekend when he returned. The excitement of seeing him again had an arousing effect upon Beatriz. Neither woman knew of the heightened sexuality of the other, but anyone less distracted might have surmised it. The air in the summer kitchen was charged with feminine energy and creativity and camaraderie—and oblivion to the increasingly obvious repairs needing to be made: a windowpane cracked by a baseball; knobs fallen off cupboards and put aside to screw back another time; a malfunctioning oven light; an expanding patch of damp ceiling that exposed a leak from somewhere above.

While the boys kicked around a soccer ball in fields damp with dew out back, the two women dressed in white chef's coats hummed as they went about experimenting with chocolate crème brûlée napoleons. The truth was Nora had conceived the dessert on the spot when she made the proposal. Now she needed to make it work. Earlier, she had baked dozens of three-inch squares of puff pastry on parchment paper–lined baking sheets. After letting them cool on the rack she had separated each square horizontally into three layers with fork tines. The chocolate crème brûlée had set and she had just finished cutting it into three-inch squares with smooth runs of the tip of her chef's knife. Now she and Beatriz began layering the first napoleon: pastry square, strawberry sauce made from last summer's stored strawberry jam, crème brûlée square, pastry square, strawberry sauce, crème brûlée square, pastry square.

She held it out to Beatriz on a wide stainless-steel spatula and peeked out the window to check on the boys—though she could hear their laughter all the while along with squeals of glee and intermittent but short-lived fights. Beatriz lifted the wobbly mass to her mouth and tasted it.

Nora turned back, rested one hand on her hip, and watched her.

"It is good," Beatriz said, wiping a glob of crème brûlée from her chin. She licked her finger clean. "It is certainly very good."

"But?" Beatriz had not closed her eyes to savor any exquisiteness, had not flushed with pleasure. Her response lacked enthusiasm.

"It is not uplifting," Beatriz explained.

Nora regarded her. Beatriz all at once had a dreamy look. She went on, "The way great lovemaking can be uplifting." She looked intently at Nora. "Surely we can make a dessert that lifts people like that, that makes their body pulse with excitement, something that penetrates their very being?"

Nora laughed. "You want to invent an aphrodisiac? Well, alcohol would certainly help!" She recalled the warm rush of the champagne last night.

"Then let us add alcohol," Beatriz said matter-of-factly.

"I was joking, Beatriz. Really, we shouldn't be creating something that's going to require you to be around alcohol."

"I have this mental exercise. I just have to imagine the smell of the alcohol, and then picture myself being completely unaffected by it."

"When did you devise this?"

"It's a technique I've been using for years." She smiled. "How do you think I would have managed otherwise around the wine you enjoyed every evening all those years with *el señor*?"

Nora looked surprised and then ashamed. She had not been aware of the temptation she was placing every night before Beatriz.

She had been clueless about so many things back then.

Nora said, "Well, all right, then. Let's at least experiment. What if we made the fruit sauce hard?"

Beatriz shook her head. "Not enough. Not nearly enough. It will not penetrate. This should overpower almost, be something for which you should need a license."

"You want to get people drunk?"

"I want to give them a rush."

"Would a hard filling *and* a hard sauce satisfy you?"

"I will not be the one eating it, but I think that would work."

Nora raised her palms in surrender. "Let's get on with it, then."

The two women threw themselves into the task after that, once Nora had made a note to advise the fund-raising committee of the change before the menus were printed the next day. Nora remembered the exquisite napoleonbakelse one of her mother's distant relatives had made on her only visit from Sweden, where Nora's maternal grandmother was born. The napoleonbakelse was the Swedish version of the napoleon pastry. Custard replaced the pastry cream, jam replaced the sauce, and the top was often glazed with currant jelly. Now Nora adapted the recipe for the custard filling. Rather than regular sugar, she added sugar that had been stored in a tightly sealed container with vanilla beans. Beatriz stored her vanilla beans this way to preserve their shelf life, so that she would always have a ready supply for the braised chicken with vanilla that she loved and made often for the boys. The dish was a specialty around her mountain hometown. The sugar took on an especially intriguing vanilla flavor. Nora was trying for custard that tasted of truffles, as truffles paired beautifully with the liquor she had in mind to add. Along with the vanilla-sugar, she stirred into the tempered mixture of heated whole milk and whisked farm eggs a proportion that felt right of pure cocoa. After pouring the mixture through a strainer, she stirred in powdered wood-oven roasted pecans—and her favorite sherry.

Beatriz used the sherry in her mother's recipe for fried plantains. The plantains were sautéed in butter until golden brown on both sides, placed in a shallow baking dish, and kept warm enough to dissolve the sugar sprinkled on top while a topping was made to serve with them of whipped cream, vanilla, sugar, and sherry. This sherry from the chalky-soiled area of sea breeze–cooled southern Spain was what made the dish special. The memory of its aroma of nutty brown sugar with a hint of citrus in the plantain dish Beatriz had once made had given Nora the idea it would be the perfect addition to their napoleon.

Nora found the forgotten half-filled bottle in a cupboard.

While the dish of custard baked in the oven, Nora and Beatriz descended again to the stone cellar to explore in the dim light of the bulb hanging from the ceiling the shelves of marmalades they had made the previous summer. There were so many to choose from to make their hard sauce: cherry, fig, lemon, orange, raspberry, strawberry, peach, apple (they had made that batch in the fall, with an experimental pumpkin marmalade that was exquisite on fresh scones with whipped cream). Nora reached for the cherry marmalade, Beatriz for the orange. Nora imagined instantly how they could use both. They could make cherry-chocolate napoleons, and orange-chocolate napoleons, and alternate servings of each around the tables. After coating their tops with a dark chocolate glaze, she would dust the cherry napoleons with shavings of dark chocolate mixed with shavings of sugared orange peel, and dust the orange napoleons with shavings of dark chocolate mixed with fine strips of crystallized cherries. One plate would flash red beneath, orange on top, the next orange beneath, red on top, the effect opulent and festive. To make the sauces, Nora simply strained the marmalades into separate pots and added the sherry and a little more sugar to taste, and stirred over the flame until the mixture thickened again. She knew the stove heat would burn off some of the alcohol—as the oven heat would burn off some in the custard—but enough would remain to bring a flush to cheeks.

When Nora tasted the napoleon, its crisp, light pastry against the creamy custard with its slight nutty texture, a thick, rich palate of truffle and cherry in this case with the punch of the nutty, sugary, citrus sherry, she could not help moaning.

Beatriz was as proud of the reaction as a mother of the success of her child.

Nora smiled. "Beatriz," she said. "This came of both our labors and both our cultures. We'll call our exquisite invention here the 'Spanish Napoleon'!"

They both laughed. And once their laughter eased into smiles, Beatriz realized that now was the time: There was something she wanted to talk to *la señora* about, and *la señora* seemed in the perfect relaxed mood to hear it. She said, "I have a proposition."

Nora had set the pastry down and turned to make tea.

Beatriz went on, "You know how I was taking, until everything happened and I moved back in here, those business courses at nights?"

Nora turned with the bag of tea leaves in hand and gave Beatriz her full attention. "I'm so sorry you had to give those up, Beatriz. You've made a lot of sacrifices for us."

"No, no, it was the right thing to do in every way. I may have never found what it was I wanted to do if I had kept my head in the books and not moved back to help you."

Nora felt her stomach seize. Was Beatriz about to resign? She put down the bag and faced Beatriz with hands clasped at hip level. "What is it that you want to do?"

"We work very well together, do we not, *señora?*"

"Very well."

"I mean at the baking."

"Yes, particularly at the baking." Nora meant it. Beatriz had a natural instinct for baking—her perfectionism helped—learned quickly, worked hard, and had a savvy business sense, Nora had been surprised to discover. It was Beatriz who had convinced her to charge what had seemed at first too exorbitant an amount for the private orders. "The more expensive it is, the more exclusive it seems," Beatriz had argued. Beatriz had read that the country's most renowned preparatory schools followed this model. And the women of Bedford were the same clientele to which these schools pitched their business. These women wanted only the best, and they measured the best monetarily.

"Well, there is a way of making a lot more money than you are making supplying your products to Phillip's. What would you say to opening your own bakery-café?"

Nora laughed, partly with relief that Beatriz was not leaving them. "Right, Beatriz. With what money?"

"Mine."

Nora was startled.

Beatriz went on, "I have been saving since I started working for you eleven years ago. What else was there for me to spend my money on? I am not after all supporting a child." Nora noticed a shadow pass across Beatriz's face. "And my father's medical bills long ago became more manageable. You have always fed me so well, and then I lived in a commercial district. I could have afforded to live better, but I wanted to save. I knew one day there would be an opportunity like this. I have one hundred and fifty thousand dollars put away safely. I had intended to loan you some of it, if things got really bad for you. Now this is what I would like to do with that money."

Nora looked at Beatriz. Aside from the house, Beatriz was now richer than her. For a moment before Beatriz's idea sunk in, Nora felt disoriented by the shift in their positions, Beatriz being the one now to offer her, Nora, a job and money.

Then she thought of dear Phillip. "I could never do that to Phillip," she protested. "He has been so good to me; I couldn't just turn around and take his clients."

"Of course not," Beatriz said. "He could join us. We would need more money than just mine. And he has invaluable expertise. He could be the third partner."

"Beatriz . . ." Nora now knew the idea was unrealistic. "Why would he do that?"

"Because you are a rising star and *Señor* Phillip's star is fading; because your bakery would be high concept and his is not; because without you in his kitchen, and your products in his café, his business would decline."

"How do you know that?" Nora asked. She had never told Beatriz that Phillip had confided when he first offered her the job that his business then had been suffering.

"He said as much the day I met him when he tasted the churros and asked me to make them for his café. You remember, he said, 'Without Nora I would be doomed.'"

"He was just saying that, Beatriz."

"No, I saw the truth of it in his eyes."

"Even so, Beatriz, asking him to give up Phillip's—"

"Well, that is just it; he may not have to. It could be Phillip's the bakery that becomes a partner to the Summer Kitchen Bakery. It continues to sell its own bread, but the Summer Kitchen Bakery would provide the pastries and provisions. *Señor* Phillip could save on employing pastry chefs, and the Summer Kitchen Bakery could simply make a delivery to Phillip's each morning. And, of course, as a partner of the Summer Kitchen Bakery-Café, he would help to run that and profit from that, too."

Nora's hands began sweating at the same time as the rest of her body had broken under her clothes into goose bumps, and she recognized the feeling rising in her as panic.

She folded her arms under her breasts to hold herself steady.

"It is not a bad idea, is it?" Beatriz went on, leaning in, almost unrecognizably excited as a child. "Of course, we would need to find a location. We could continue baking wholesale here, but we would need a storefront, a café. And it would have to be a place where we could do it on a shoestring. . . ."

Nora closed her eyes to a dizzy spell. She felt the confused sensation of her body swooning under the hot-lipped kiss of ambition while her mind struggled to remind her that the point of working temporarily was to get her through to a position of no longer having to work. Starting a café would commit her to a working life.

She opened her eyes, though her spirit and mind still fought.

Beatriz sat back. "You don't like the idea?" she asked.

"It's a great idea in theory, Beatriz, only it's so much, such a big thing to do. A bakery-café would be a whole new can of worries and complications."

"Yes, but they would be of your own making, and within your control; and inside that can would also be satisfactions and rewards, all of them yours, too."

Nora's look turned thoughtful. "Who would mind the boys?" she asked.

"That is the beauty of this; this sort of work we can do with the boys around."

Nora walked over to the window. She looked out at the fields of blossoming wildflowers, each like a gem centered in glistening diamonds of dew. A few feet from the window, a small bird was lifting twigs in its beak, one after another from the ground up with a fluttering of its wings to its nest in the birdhouse her landscapers had once installed at eye level. She could just make out the tops of small blue eggs in the nest.

"*Señora?*" Beatriz asked after a while.

Without turning back, Nora answered, "I was just thinking on how quickly the seasons turn, one day life disappears, the next, it seems, it all starts to regrow."

Ten

The boys were helping Reuben farther down his orchard toward the barn, and Beatriz had gone exploring in the heels she refused even for this Saturday picnic to forgo. On the strip of freshly mown grass at the top of the hill separating the rows of apples from the rows of cherries, Nora was sitting cross-legged on a spread blanket. She was taking the opportunity of time alone to try to call Fox Silverworth. They had spoken almost every day since the party last week, though not one conversation had been the least bit provocative, since they had all taken place while he was at his office, and she had called in the first place each time about the lawsuit. The government had filed its suit and she now had to answer it. The work of that alone was proving impossible to manage between her night shifts and her private business, and Fox had explained that this was just the beginning and that she should give up one of her two jobs for a while. But she had already been considering resigning her night shift, because her private baking was becoming more than a full-time job, and *that* she needed to keep doing for the money.

Certainly setting up a bakery-café was out of the question already.

On top of it all she had received a visit during the week from a town inspector. He had spent hours making notes to which she was

not privy on whether or not she satisfied the town's residential business ordinances. She had thought all that would be required was the
board of health permit she had been granted. The inspector had
seemed satisfied that she displayed no external advertising, that the
area of the summer kitchen did not exceed the limit for a residential
business of 25 percent of the first floor of the main house, that there
was only one resident employee and one assistant, that there was only
one occupation being practiced, and that she kept no outside storage
or equipment. But the call could be made either way on whether her
baking caused any "odor," whether her hours were "conducive to the
neighborhood," or whether the delivery trucks to her house now
constituted "unreasonable traffic." The Bedford community was ob-
sessive about preserving its quiet bucolic surrounds. The inspector
had told her that the board would need to meet to discuss her case
and so she had been left dangling. She had consulted Fox about this
problem, too. He had asked if she knew anyone at the town. She
had answered that she did not, but what did that have to do with
anything?

"When are you going to stop being so naïve?" he had asked impatiently.

That was another thing worsening her panic: Fox seemed to be
retreating emotionally. A note of irritation had underpinned his professional tone all week and this backstep had fanned her feelings
of desperation and neediness. That in turn had tipped her toward
carelessness. While baking late one afternoon, she had let slip to
Beatriz that she was worried about her arrangement with her lawyer.
At least she had not voiced aloud her bigger concern that either she
had lost her power over Fox or she had been delusional in thinking
she had any over him.

"How is it you trusted *Señor* Silverworth as the person to help in
the first instance?" Beatriz had asked with that same penetrating
look she wore when meeting him.

"More than anything else, he knows a little of what it is to be in my shoes."

Beatriz raised her eyebrows.

"His brother did prison time," Nora explained.

In the concentrated pause, Nora felt that Beatriz was writing a mental note. Nora reminded herself to keep her mouth zipped in the future. Things were wretched enough without having to defend decisions and suffer cross-examination in her home. It was too much already to think Fox might not provide enough help.

Last night in a storm of anxiety she repeatedly called his cell phone. He neither picked up nor returned her calls. Her nervousness had compounded and her preoccupation with reaching him became manic.

Now on the hilltop blanket she was so lost in the vague solace of the ringing that she was startled when he answered.

"I got your messages, Nora." His caller ID had obviously displayed her number.

"Fox!"

Though she had spoken breathlessly, he didn't ask her what was wrong, nor did he even pause with a greeting. It was the same business manner she had suffered all week.

"I've thought about your situation and I have a suggestion," he said.

The way his voice lowered at the end of the word *suggestion* frightened her. If he had raised his voice, it would have suggested excitement. But she sensed something final in the way he spoke, as though his suggestion was the only option remaining.

He went on, "There's a way for you to be done with all this and still have money at the end of the day. And I'm willing to help you at my expense to accomplish that."

She was listening so carefully that she had almost stopped breathing. At the same time her mind was racing—she did mean something to him! He had not withdrawn emotionally. He had just withdrawn mentally this week to mull over her problems.

"Now, this would be a lot of trouble for me to take on, but I'd be willing to write you a check for three million dollars for your house and then spend another two or three million settling your case with the government. I'm sure that with the contacts I have in the prosecutors' office, I could get them to accept that."

Nora shivered and the winged creature within her that had just a moment earlier taken flight now landed heavily. Her mind clutched her property close to her. She found herself recalling the day she fell in love with it at first sight and the three years she threw herself into renovating before she had Thomas. She had virtually rebuilt that house on her own. Now it became clear why the arrival of the lawsuit sent her spiraling so quickly. The notion of losing it possibly had become as real suddenly as its dearness to her.

"I can't leave my house," she said quietly.

"You wouldn't have to. I could rent it back to you."

"I can't."

"You can't take three million dollars when the alternative is to be left possibly with nothing? Think clearly now, Nora. I alone can help you. You can't sell it otherwise because of the *lis pendens* the government attached to it. And if you can't keep up the fight—which you can already see will be a big one—then it will all be taken."

On one point Nora was now thinking clearly.

"Even if I could conceive of selling it, the house was appraised at twelve million dollars. It says so in the lawsuit. Three million would be giving it away."

"I'd give you more if I could, but my money's tied up."

"I see."

"Three million would get you back in the saddle."

She wished he hadn't said that. It was not the way a man who had designs on some kind of future with a woman spoke to her. It felt like he was sending her off riding.

But just as her heart contracted more, he seemed sorry for his error of speech. A kindly note entered his voice finally and his words felt like a hand stroking her hair.

"You know that I only want the best for you, Nora. My God, I know firsthand how hard all this is for you. Harder even than my own experience because you have children. I think how much three million dollars could help those boys now and I feel good that I can do that for them. You could re-enroll them in the private school."

The winged creature lifted faintly at the idea.

"And you never know . . ." That teasing note she had missed all week was back in his voice. "Perhaps your landlord might move in one day and you'll own it again."

The winged creature was airborne. She was coming to feel this might not be such a bad plan, after all. They could stay in the house and refurnish and resume their old lifestyle and she was feeling surer that she could in the end also have Fox Silverworth.

And yes, maybe then her house back.

"Can I think about it?" she asked him.

"Sure, but I can't leave the offer on the table forever. There are other things I could be doing with that money. How about I feel out the prosecutors about a settlement, and if I can get that in place and you agree, you could come over to the house to sign the papers the week after next." He then added after a pause, "My wife will be away."

* * *

Reuben was spreading compost under the apple trees. The compost contained powdered oyster shell to raise the soil pH level, and gypsum to improve its level of calcium. It gave off a slight salty, metallic odor that made a heady mix with the earthy aroma of freshly turned soil. He wore a navy T-shirt loose over his jeans, and a navy bandana knotted around his head, his usual attire in the orchard on warmer days. As he guided his rake now to within an inch or two of the trees' drip lines, he was telling Thomas the story of Johnny Appleseed. Thomas was poised atop a ladder under one tree, dressed also in jeans, but with a long-sleeved, button-down lemon shirt over his white T-shirt, pruning branches the way Reuben had shown him, to keep the trees open to air and light to prevent disease. His mother had initially hesitated, claiming the ladder was too high, the shears too sharp, but Reuben had reminded her that Thomas was eight, and in the time of Johnny Appleseed, boys of eight were not only pruning but as part of their farm chores chopping down trees. The thought of an ax in her son's hand had made the shears seem less dangerous, and so she had agreed to Thomas helping so long as Thomas wore the thick gardening gloves Reuben provided.

The gloves were oversized and awkward, but Thomas understood they were the price of his being allowed to have this much fun. He liked that Reuben trusted him, that Reuben let him do this himself. His dad had been that way. His dad had let him handle the oars that time they went canoeing, and had once let him take the canoe out by himself. His dad had told him to keep that from his mom. His mom would never have let him do that. She was always so worried he would get hurt. "Don't go so close to the edge," she would say, or "Stay in the drive with your bike, don't go out onto the road." Their dirt road was great for biking, and there was hardly ever a car, and it wasn't as if he wouldn't see one coming. But he listened and stayed on the drive. He didn't want to upset her. It was his job to look after her, look after things, with his dad gone, he supposed. He was the oldest, after all. He saw how pleased it made her when he helped to teach Charlie to ride his bike or learn his alphabet, when he listened to Nicholas read his readers while his mom and Beatriz never stopped moving. He always carried the groceries in from the car, the way he had seen his dad do it, and took a broom to cobwebs in the garage when he found them, since he knew how spiders scared his mom.

He felt proud helping his mom, though he got so angry at her at times, like at how she made excuses for why they couldn't go see his dad again for a while. He kept imagining horrible things were happening to his dad and he wanted to check on him. He was also still suspicious about what really happened with his dad. Sometimes he suspected his mom had caused his dad to get into trouble. She only spoke of him when he or Nicholas or Charlie did, and it was never the way she used to talk about him. It wasn't anything she said. She always said nice things about his dad to them, but sounded angry when answering his calls. He wasn't supposed to hear; his mom always took the phone into another room. But he heard her yell sometimes. And the tone she used when she talked of their dad was different. He couldn't remember whether she sounded that way before, but sometimes he wondered if his dad made his mistake because his mom had stopped loving his dad.

Other times he felt angry at himself. Maybe *he* should have done something different. Maybe if he had been different somehow. Maybe then his father would not have gotten into trouble. He wished he could better remember what he might have done wrong. He wanted to ask his dad. He had meant to when they visited him. But he had been so excited to see him that he forgot. And then those kids playing with the Legos had distracted him, and then his dad had given him and his brothers that money. He kept that dollar bill in his special hiding place. He had discovered that if he took the bottom drawer in his closet off its runners, he could put on the floor under the drawers his special things like that credit card he found in the parking lot at the supermarket. Once he reinserted the drawer, nobody could get to his stash without taking out the drawer again. And who would think to do that? There were so many things he wanted to ask his dad, things he didn't want to ask his mom. Like how he was supposed to act when his friends asked him what prison was like. He knew his mom thought that none of the kids at his new school knew. But what was he supposed to say when his friends asked why only his mom and never his dad came to soccer games? And it had kind of made him famous. His soccer friends thought it was cool. They had even googled his dad on the Internet. They printed out this article they found and brought it to school.

"Thought you said your dad was a bad guy?" they questioned him.

"I said he was in prison."

"Same thing. Then why's he doing this?"

They held up the article and Thomas snatched at it.

He could read enough to understand that his dad was running workshops for guys in jail on how to be better dads. The article said he had successfully requested funds to purchase enough books on fathering to devote a section of the library at his facility to the subject. It said his Father Involvement Training was the first initiative of its kind in the prison system, where workshops if held at all were almost always for job training. He was lobbying the Federal Bureau of Prisons through the press to start FIT workshops in all their facilities. His dad was quoted as saying, "There's no more important job a man can have than establishing and maintaining healthy relationships with his children. Understanding the crucial role he plays in his children's psychological and developmental well-being helps a man make sound choices, which in turn helps his children to understand what it is to be a positively engaged parent. Being a good parent is where everything starts and ends."

His pride had felt like it would burst through his skin, only he didn't let it show because his friends preferred the idea of his dad being a bad guy. He had just shrugged and walked away. Had he done the right thing? He wanted to ask his dad that, too.

And he wanted to ask his dad if it was okay to show the article to his mom.

Nicholas and Charlie had run back over from the mounds of compost they had been climbing with Digger and were now loading Thomas's prunings onto the back of a tractor. Digger scampered off to drink from the pond. Reuben had shown them earlier how to load the prunings. He had explained that rot spores would form on the cut branches if they were not removed. Thomas had wondered aloud when Reuben had counted all the enemies of the fruit trees why he even bothered. Reuben had dug his mud-encrusted boot into the ground. "Because of a fierce loyalty to this land and way of life. This may be hard to understand, but when I work with the land I feel in harmony with it, I feel connected to the world. Think about it sometime when you're walking barefoot on the grass. Notice how much more peaceful you feel inside, compared to how you feel walking on a floor in shoes. A physical connection to the earth grounds you."

Nicholas immediately removed his rubber boots and socks. He grinned at Reuben and then went about his work barefoot. Charlie copied him, so that four boots, two red, two yellow, and four navy socks were flung about.

"Your mother's going to kill me."

A branch that Thomas had just pruned fell on Nicholas's head.

"Tom!" Nicholas protested, shooting up an annoyed look.

Reuben laughed, and then so did Thomas, making Nicholas more annoyed.

Reuben rested his rake against the tree and reached behind his head to tighten his bandana. "Well, I'm getting hungry, boys. Let's go find your mom and Beatriz."

The boys and Digger took off, running between the rows of apple trees on the incline above the pond. Reuben liked mowing the grass around that pond. He had befriended a deer over the years, and it would come up close when he mowed, scraping the dirt with his hoof, as though saying, "Hi there." He had made a point of remembering every physical detail of that deer, so as not ever to mistakenly shoot him those rare times he hunted for venison to eat. He shot turkeys more often, and prepared them to roast the way his mother had taught him as a boy. He laughed when he saw turkeys in the supermarket, packaged with labels marked *Fresh*. Nobody would eat them if they knew how a real fresh turkey tasted. His dream was to be completely self-sufficient, which meant that at some point he would need to invest in a hive or two of bumblebees, a few cows, and a goat for the cheese he loved on crackers with the fig and walnut spread Nora made with his figs. For now he traded with local farmers for what he did not produce himself.

"There you are!" Nora said when the boys and Reuben emerged from behind the last apple row. She was lying back on a blanket on her elbows and had been admiring the span of a hawk's wings against the clear blue sky. Her racing heart had quieted since the phone call and she was finally noticing the beauty around her. The boys were grubby, barefooted—black-footed in two cases—and beaming on a sunny hilltop against a backdrop of fruit fields with a devoted dog at their heels, a picture postcard of boyhood. She felt inside her breast an eruption of perfect happiness. She ascribed it to a growing surety that she could give them this and so much more again.

"Where's Beatriz?" Reuben asked with forced casualness.

Nora blinked as a flash of sunlight off a moist silvery leaf caught her eye and told Reuben that Beatriz had headed down the rows of cherry trees. Nora was sure she would be back soon, since it had been a while since she left. Reuben said he would go to look for her. Thomas threw him a narrowed look, and said he wanted to come.

Reuben smiled gently. "I need you, Thomas, and Nicholas and Charlie, to stay here to protect the cherry trees from crows and raccoons. Last year I even had a bear take down a cherry tree. Can you do that for me? It's a job for brave men."

Thomas looked skeptical. The cherries were still not even ripe. But he agreed, and sat down on the blanket next to his mom and started to rummage for something to eat while Nicholas and Charlie went searching for sturdy sticks to fight off marauding bears.

After a while—full enough on rice crackers and homemade hummus, his mother's eyes closed for spells as she seemed to soak up the sun like a sponge, his brothers noisily discarding good sticks for better ones—he disappeared quietly into the rows of cherries as Reuben had. It did not take him long to find them. He had expected that. What he had not expected was that Reuben would be kissing Beatriz. His stomach knotted like it had the morning his dad woke him up and told him that he needed to go away now like they had discussed and to be strong and to mind everything his mother told him and to never forget how much his father loved him. He had wanted to cry, but his dad was crying and so he had been strong. But the knot had never really gone away, only faded a little. Now he felt it back, intense like it had been, painful, unbearable really. He sunk back behind one of the trees, but he could not take his eyes away. Beatriz had her arms around Reuben's shoulders, and one of her knees bent at an angle so that the heel of her shoe on that leg plunged like a straight nail into the trunk of the tree she was pressed back against. Reuben cupped her face as he kissed her, his body pressed tightly into hers. Thomas wanted to run up and pull Reuben off her, but there was something about Beatriz's face that seemed so serene that it made his impulses by contrast seem dark and wrong and knotted like his stomach and so he stayed hidden.

It was hard for him to believe he was sitting cross-legged with the others on the blanket not so long after that as though nothing had happened, Beatriz and Reuben sitting beside each other, but being careful it seemed not to touch, Beatriz's legs folded neatly to one side, her skirt pulled over her knees, her back as straight as he imagined it had always been at the convent. Her face glowed as though she had seen Jesus. The top button of her blouse was undone and a strand or two of hair was loose from her braided bun. He thought he saw his mother notice, but she hadn't said anything. They had all gone about piling their plates as Reuben told how he protected the strawberries in winter by covering them with straw.

"So that's why they're called *straw*berries!" Nora gushed. "Isn't that interesting, boys!" She looked around at them. Nicholas and Charlie were busy eating. Thomas nodded slightly, then looked away a moment, as if to examine the strawberry field, though really he could not have cared less if Reuben covered the strawberries in manure.

"Is that?" Reuben drew up his head like a turkey, it seemed to Thomas, craning to look over the rise toward his barn below. Reuben put down his plate of food and stood, dusting his hands on the front of his jeans. "A customer's just pulled up." He turned back before heading down the hill. "Save me some, boys, okay? I won't be long."

The trunk to the Bentley outside the barn was open and a large-framed woman wearing tan riding breeches, tall black boots, and a white ratcatcher-style shirt with a stock tie was bent over the private garden to the right pulling up a rhubarb plant. She turned when she caught sight of him and said, "Do you have something I could put this in? These stalks are the perfect color for my windowsill. My tea towels are exactly this shade."

Reuben picked up and handed over an empty plastic pot. He was too aghast to think what else to do, though he kept meaning to plan retorts for this kind of behavior. A few years back he opened his orchard on summer weekends to the public, had invited them to pick their own berries for the "country experience." Mostly it was the wealthy Westchester folk who pulled in en route north to Millbrook, the rural version of the Hamptons. A lot kept horses up there. He had learned that the more expensive the car, the more fruit its occupants would eat on the sly while picking.

"My husband and I were passing on our way to a show jumping event and we saw your sign for apple wood." Reuben glanced at the car. A man sat behind the wheel. "We're having a function at the house tomorrow and apple wood would be the perfect thing to burn in the fireplace! I said to George, 'Wouldn't that aroma be perfect!' So would you mind?" She gestured toward the trunk. "Just fit in there as much as you can."

And then she turned back to the garden and pulled out a second rhubarb plant.

The woman was sitting back inside the car with her two rhubarb plants on her lap when Reuben was done. He closed the trunk and walked around to her window. Her husband was on his cell phone setting up a golf game for the following weekend.

"How much for the apple wood?" the woman asked.

"Twenty-five dollars should do it," Reuben told her.

She didn't offer to pay for the plants and Reuben let it go, as he always did the illicitly consumed fruit. In the end he felt sorry for people who lived feeling entitled. It closed them off to the world and to the texture of humility that made life worth living.

The woman asked, "Mind if I write you a check?"

The husband was presumably distracted on his cell phone when he peeled out to the road, as his wheels spun before catching and taking off, leaving black rubber marks on the ground.

Reuben glanced up the hill and saw Nora look down.

And what Nora saw surprised her.

As the newly released Continental Flying Spur sped off, she caught a glimpse through the open passenger window of Bonnie.

"I feel like I'm the victim of a hit-and-run," Reuben said when he joined her. He was laughing and shaking his head. He bent for a water bottle and as he chugged it down he noticed Beatriz and Nicholas and Charlie squatting to examine some insect on a strawberry plant, Thomas behind them kicking up stones with his boot.

"It's funny you should say that," Nora said.

"How so?" He pushed down the spout on the top of the bottle.

"That woman is a mother at the boys' former school, and after Evan was arrested she confided something in me. I've never repeated this and I know you won't say anything, but before she was married she hit and killed a man while she was drunk behind the wheel and then left the scene. The police found her the next day."

"Dear Jesus! Did she do time?"

"No, she told me she cut a deal on the morning of the trial. She admitted her guilt, became forever after a felon, and served community service and three years probation."

"That's it? For leaving someone she killed for dead? Dear God, and your husband gets years for a crime that affected only a few other rich deal-makers!"

All at once who did not go to prison and who did and for how long did seem to Nora rather arbitrary, and she found herself recalling in a new light a conversation she had overheard shortly after Evan's arrest in the service waiting area of the Mount Kisco BMW dealership. Two men in suits waiting for their own BMWs had been discussing an editorial in *The Wall Street Journal* about how the prosecution of financial crimes had become politically and judicially fashionable since all those moms and pops lost their savings in the 2001 Enron scandal. One read aloud excerpts from the editorial about how the government passed a new law in 2002 increasing white-collar sentences to keep voters happy, and about how New York State Attorney General Eliot Spitzer was riding into the governorship on a platform of combating the white-collar excess that millions felt cheated by.

One of the men had said, "A guy can't afford to sneeze on Wall Street anymore."

"Yeah, you wouldn't wanna screw up now. Spitzer's nailing guys for any goddamn thing. The *Journal* put it that he's hanging Wall Street heads like trophies. And the sentences judges are handing down are out of control. It's a fucking witch-hunt with the whole nine yards of politically endorsed mob lynching."

At the time her mortification at her husband being one such trophy had impeded a proper grasp of what the men had said, but now she saw the injustice of targeting certain groups for harsher sentences because of voter trends and political ambitions.

Was it even strictly legal to prosecute for political advantage?

It startled her to think it, but she was inwardly acknowledging all at once that, wrong as Evan had been, he had also been treated unfairly by a morally questionable system.

Reuben had been deliberating and now asked, "When you say she 'confided' this in you, how is it that nobody knows? Surely her crime is all a matter of public record."

"Sure, but under her maiden name, and in an altogether different state." Nora picked up her hair and tied it into a knot at the nape of her neck. "She's created a whole new identity up here, and she's married to a rich man besides. Who looks past that?"

Reuben shook his head. "Imagine living such a lie."

"Hmmm." Reuben's comment struck a chord in her.

Reuben went on, "I guess you were safe to off-load to back then."

"I think she regrets having told me. I think that's why she's trying so hard to destroy me. I have something on her and she's frightened."

"Guess she's never seen *The Godfather Part II* or she'd be keeping her friends close and her enemies closer." He bent to put down the water bottle. "What do you mean she's trying to destroy you?"

But before Nora could tell him about how Bonnie had reported her business to the town, Charlie cried out in a way Nora knew was not simply about some injustice exacted upon him by his brothers, and she turned and ran to him. Reuben followed. It turned out Charlie had stubbed his bare toe on a rock. She picked him up and sat down on the ground with him in her lap, comforting him through the pain.

"My fault," Reuben admitted. "I'll go back and fetch their boots."

Thomas said firmly, "I'll go with you."

The day had grown warmer and Thomas stopped every few steps to slap madly at the gnats that now stuck too close to his eyes.

"Reuben . . ." Thomas started.

"Yes, Tom."

"Why were you kissing Beatriz?"

"Ah. So you saw that?"

Thomas nodded.

"Because I think I love her, Tom, and my wish is that she will love me."

Thomas's face tensed and his ears and the part of his throat exposed above the first button of his shirt reddened slightly.

"Tom," Reuben said.

Thomas pressed his lips tighter.

"Tom, I know you've lost a lot, your dad, your friends, a lot of your stuff."

Thomas was struggling, Reuben could sense, to hold back his tears.

"But there are some things that no one can ever take, like your mom and dad's love for you, and Beatriz's love for you. They will be yours alone forever."

"Not if Beatriz loves you instead," Thomas blurted out, tears now running down his cheeks. He wiped violently at his face with the backs of his hands.

Reuben dug his hands into the front pockets of his jeans.

"People can love a lot of people, Tom. Their love for each person is different. You love a lot of people. Your dad, your mom, your brothers, Beatriz."

"Exactly," Thomas said. "Beatriz can't love two people the same."

The violent wiping of tears had turned into a mad slapping again at the gnats. "I hate it here," Thomas said.

Reuben did not try to fill the silence. Nor did he try to stop him as Thomas slashed a handful of leaves from a tall weed and turned to run back.

Eleven

The sun shone brightly that Friday morning two weeks later as Nora drove out of the public-school grounds after seeing the boys to their classes. She had been worried about Thomas. He had not been himself lately. He seemed distracted, unusually quiet, and was doing only the minimum work that school expected of him. But the beautiful day now seemed auspicious after a week of unusually severe spring storms that caused roads all over town to be closed for days while cleanup crews chainsawed fallen trees and restrung electrical wires. All about was the gentle, greening hint of summer. Worries about Thomas and doubts that had rattled her during the night shift about what she was now about to do melted in the sun's buttery warmth through the windshield. As she turned Beatriz's car with one hand in the direction of Fox Silverworth's estate, she turned with the other the radio dial until she found a song to fit the new mood taking hold and stopped at Simon and Garfunkel's "The 59th Street Bridge Song."

What added sparkle to her state of mind was the prospect of the consummation of a new relationship. Fox had been true to his word in finalizing a settlement with the government in time for her to meet with him to sign the papers while his wife was still away visiting relatives. She had dressed that morning after her shower in a black velvet-lace bandeau baby-doll and matching thong and sheer black thigh-high lace-top stockings beneath a Wolford mocha merino rib dress with deep cleavage that fit like a second skin. Beatriz had been waiting in the kitchen clutching a thrice-folded page torn from a legal notepad while the boys finished their eggs. She narrowed her eyes when she saw the dress.

"You had best read this first, *la señora*," was all she said. She handed Nora the page and then took Charlie by his hand to dress him for their day together.

But Nora had just then glanced at the kitchen clock. It was the exact minute that the bus pulled up at their drive. She remembered then that she told Beatriz last night she would take the boys to school on her way to her meeting. She thrust the paper into her pocketbook to read later and hurried Thomas and Nicholas with toast still in hand as they hoisted backpacks over shoulders out to the car.

Now as she reached Fox's estate, she was conscious of having the next five hours free of further obligations. She would otherwise have slept and was doing without, but the taste of relief staved off tiredness. Before turning into the drive, she stopped to check her appearance in the rearview mirror. Her smooth glossy lips and long dark lashes and silky flowing hair were enough to overcome her paleness. She gave off the scent of the last of her Chanel. She started through the open gates and looked about the walled garden. A caretaker's cottage overlooked the parklike grounds. To the left of the ivy-covered redbrick Georgian manor sat a tennis court and a guest house. Men were everywhere, tending to the garden, laying fresh gravel on the drive, painting the window shutters, replacing a presumably storm-damaged section of fencing around the tennis court. Things had been that way before at her property, the management of it all having been her job. It occurred to her that this arrangement to rent back her house would oblige her to resume such a management role. The idea made her recoil for a moment. Lately, a faint sense had nagged her that she actually enjoyed the scaled-back life. It had seemed uncivilized and she had told no one, but really she missed none of the seized possessions. Secretly, she savored the freedom in no longer having to insure things, clean things, rearrange things, update things, or worry that Beatriz would see the price tag on things. It was the same way with her property. She had not expected her necessary neglect of its upkeep to feel so liberating. But now she checked the impulse with a cool hand of reason: This was part of the life she had fought all this time to retrieve, and how else would she spend her time when she no longer had to work?

She was looking at the workers uncertainly for a second reason: She had not anticipated anyone seeing her here. She pulled up directly in front of the house and kept her face averted as she approached the front door, but no sooner did the door open than she was looking into the eyes of another witness. The maid dressed in uniform seemed to be expecting her to Nora's surprise and showed her into "*Señor* Silverworth's office." Nora's heart beat rapidly in excitement at sinking into a deep leather armchair amid Fox's personal effects, but she composed an unconcerned air for the sake of the maid and politely refused her offer of a refreshment of any sort. The maid left quietly and closed the door behind her. Nora slipped off a heel and massaged her foot. She returned the foot to its heel and followed the same routine with her other foot. She had grown unaccustomed to heels while working at the bakery all these months in comfortable clogs. She detected in the room the subtle scent of scotch and the more pungent smell of lingering cigar smoke. The mahogany desk beneath the stacks of manila folders gleamed. She had a less distinct impression of the books filling the mahogany bookcase lining the wall opposite, since the long drapes over the window were pulled closed, and only the weak light of a desk lamp lit the room. She stood and moved closer to the shelves and saw that most of the books were about real estate. To pass the time she drew one out.

It was an oversized glossy volume and she opened it as it happened to the title page. An inscription was scrawled there in pen. The writing seemed to be hurriedly written, but she concentrated and made out the words "To my rogue bro on his birthday." It struck her as odd that a brother who had been to prison would be calling his brother the lawyer a rogue, but then perhaps Fox had more than one brother and this was just the way the brothers had of talking to one another. Outside the door she heard the murmur of a male voice and she closed the book and put it back. But when she turned to the door she realized the conversation on its other side was one-way, and as it passed and dimmed she understood that Fox was on a phone call. She returned to her leather chair, folded her arms, crossed her legs, and wiggled her foot. After a time some of her excitement deserted her and restlessness crept into its place. She decided with nothing else to do that she would sort the contents of her pocketbook and she lifted it from the floor onto her lap. Sitting there at the top of the bag was the thrice-folded paper Beatriz had handed her that morning. She felt grateful for it all at once. It was something to occupy her mind. She took it out and unfolded it and then her body startled back: It was a letter in Evan's handwriting. She looked up from it and stared unfocused. Why would Beatriz force on her a letter from Evan? Surely she understood now that even the sight of Evan's handwriting aroused in her all the pain she otherwise managed to keep lidded?

But the letter was in her hand now and there was no place to run from it. The firmness of Beatriz's expression when she had handed it over had her faintly curious now besides. She took a deep breath and let her eyes fall back on the page. It was addressed to Beatriz and explained that what he had to write about was so urgent that he could

not risk writing it to Nora when he was not sure she was even reading his letters. Nora suffered a flush of embarrassment, as though
Evan had faced her with her manila folder of his unopened letters.
Evan got straight to the point. He wrote that Beatriz must tell Nora
to have nothing to do anymore with Fox Silverworth. Nora lowered
the letter, shocked that Evan knew of Fox, and then she remembered
that Fox knew the prosecutors in the case. Something must have
been mentioned to Evan's lawyer. She felt indignant suddenly. How
dare Evan think he had a say any longer in how she lived her life!
There was no need for her to read on. Evan's urgency was nothing
more than his desperation to keep her from moving forward. She
went to fold the letter, but caught sight of the word *brother*. Neither
she nor Evan had a brother and the only brother related to this issue
of her and Fox was Fox's own. It seemed odd that Evan should know
of him—unless the man was back in prison! All at once the lamp-
light touched like a highlighter two underlined sentences: "Fox Silverworth only has one brother and he has never been to prison and is
in fact a county judge. No person can become a judge if he or she
has done prison time."

    She bit her bottom lip and looked over at the volume she had
taken down from the shelf. Surely Evan was making this up. She was
sure of it—but then why couldn't she tear her eyes now from the in-
scribed book? She would put an end to this. This was ridiculous.
Evan was still deceiving her. Fox was a lawyer! *He* was the good one.
She stood and took down the volume and reopened it to the title
page. The brother had signed his inscription. His name was Daniel.
She replaced the book and took a seat behind Fox's desk at his computer. She googled Daniel Silverworth. The first ten hits were about
Mahopac Judge Daniel Silverworth. She thought, There must be some
mistake; there must be two Daniel Silverworths. She scrolled down
title bar after title bar. But all were about the same Daniel Silverworth.
One was a personal profile by a local magazine. She opened it and

within the minute her palms were pressed to her cheeks. There in front of her was her humiliation doubled over: "Daniel and his brother Fox were the only sons of Frank and Beryl, who live together still in Mahopac." She scrambled for explanations. Perhaps his father had an affair and Fox had an illegitimate brother! Perhaps it was the second marriage for his mother or father and he had stepbrothers!

When the door opened and Fox looked askance at her in the un-expected position of power now behind his desk, she was too dazed to arrange a calm expression, and she blurted too quickly she knew, "How many brothers do you have, Fox?"

He looked at her a long while and then said slowly, "Why?"

A chilling understanding gripped her. If he had nothing to hide, he would have answered freely. It would have been an innocuous question. But now she saw that he had lied about his brother to gain her confidence. What an utter fool she had been not to see before how much he had to gain. What would he have made when he went to sell her property? Probably six or seven million dollars, after pay-ing her just three and settling with the government. Now every inter-action with him took on a different hue. Even his recovery of her Memory Stick appeared in this new light as nothing but a trick. What was it he had asked when he handed it to her? "Do you trust me that I know what I'm doing now?" It had all been part of his plan. She understood now why he had examined the structure of her house when he had visited, indeed why he had suggested they meet at her house in the first place. No wonder he had his driver keep the car running. If he had not considered the property a worthy invest-ment, he would not have bothered leading her on sexually, and could have made a quick getaway. The running engine had excused him, even so, once he knew what he "needed to know." He had needed to know that the property was spectacular and that she was vulnerable to his charms—and that she wouldn't consult her husband! He knew he couldn't fool Evan. It was pure hogwash that she should not retain him because ethics precluded him from engaging in an affair with a client. They would preclude him rather from encouraging his client toward a settlement that would land him her property. She recalled what he had said to her in the parking lot: "I only bother engaging with people I have no doubt are strong. There's no fun to be had otherwise." She had been nothing to him but a challenging part of a potentially profitable game. His verbal lovemaking in the coatroom had been simply a move in a bigger strategy, designed, it was clear to her now, to leave her wanting him so badly she wouldn't see straight. He *knew* his professional distance the following week when the government filed its suit would make her panic. He *knew* she would suffer then a combined fear of losing both him and her suit without his help. Of course, his "offer" then had come to her as a relief. He was brilliant. She would give him that. He had even softened his tone when he felt her nibbling. "You know that I only want the best for you, Nora," he had said. And the sweetener: "Perhaps your landlord might move in one day and you'll own it again." And she had fallen for it all.

He was still staring at her, trying to assess the situation.

Her stare, she knew, had turned to one of pure loathing.

Without taking her eyes from him, she stood.

"You will never have my house!" she snarled.

There was a long silence while she glared at him and then he spoke with a slow calmness that surprised her. She couldn't have known that he was clenching a fist in his pocket so tightly in frustration that its knuckles had turned white. Aside from a new tightness around his jawline, and the lack of any teasing light in his eyes, his face was an unreadable blank. "I think I understand now. This is about what I said about my brother. I admit I lied, but I only wanted you to feel less alone and it doesn't change anything. You still need money and I can give you that and do away with the lawsuit for you."

But her mind had become crystalline. Already she was struggling to believe she had almost given away her property. What delusional state had she been in not even to put up a fight? How could she have believed Fox Silverworth to be her only hope? It was not even like her to attempt to enter a sexual relationship for financial gain. It had once sickened her to learn that Fox Silverworth had married for money. Now she could feel the abhorrent stranger she had been coming at last to her senses. And she could sense something new entering her heart: courage. She didn't have a clue yet how she would put that courage to use, but in this very moment it dissolved her fears. She felt the growing resolve of one who has been beaten too many times and refuses to be beaten again. She could almost feel herself catching the fist of life that had caused her to cower inwardly before.

"You should be disbarred!" she spat at him. "I should report you. You're nothing but a con man of the most despicable kind. You drive around as the big man of Bedford, but you make your money consciously preying on helpless women and children."

His look of supplication died out and as lucidity entered his eyes he shifted to a defensive strategy, preceding it with a deep and unnervingly calm mock laugh intended clearly to make light of things. "Prove it," he sparred with her.

She realized then just how conniving he had been. There was not one document to prove any of what had taken place between them. He had not even shown her yet the papers she was there to sign— and would not now. What would they show anyway? Only that he had made an offer. She said, "Spending any more of my time on anything to do with you would be an utter waste."

As she went to push past him to take her pocketbook from the leather chair and leave, he grabbed her hand roughly and spun her to face him.

She tried pulling her hand free. "Let me go or I'll scream."

"I had been looking forward to hearing that scream today. I had always felt even before all this that you would be quite a number in bed. I suspect your anger might make a little tryst now even more heated. What say we put aside our differences for an hour or so, and then later you can hate me and I can hate losing six million dollars today."

She wrenched her hand free and grabbed her pocketbook.

"You're beyond words," she said, "and I won't waste those on you, either."

She didn't even waste energy slamming the door, but left it and the front door wide open behind her. Before she shut her car door, she thought she heard him laughing.

She shook as she drove through the gates, but her mind was still clear and she stopped at the bottom of the drive to look both ways and wait for a black four-wheel drive to pass. Its driver peered down at her through tinted windows, but Nora couldn't determine who it was, and in a flash the car had passed and she was turning in the opposite direction. She was aghast to see by the clock that only an hour had passed since she had dropped the boys off at school. There were hours to go before she could hug them and tell them how sorry she was for what they didn't know she had almost done. Even Beatriz and Charlie would be at Muscoot Farm by now seeing the new piglets and a puppet show.

The notion of being utterly alone in a silent house with no plan yet for how to save things made clear the enormity of her situation, but a comforting thought stopped the ebbing of her new courage: She still had her baking. In the end it may be all she would have with her children, but all at once that seemed a richer life than that of the morally impoverished man she had just left—and frankly of the Bedford life she now finally understood as so empty and corrupting. As she appreciated for the first time the dark underbelly of money and the price to be paid for it, she experienced the intoxicating relief of a circuit breaker interrupting the faulty current of her thinking. She felt her head rise and her shoulders fall back and then the astonishment of really seeing herself for the first time. She really did prefer living a simpler way. Perhaps the preference had existed even before she had yielded to the magnetic pull of materialism and the pressure of acceptance. For hadn't she once been happy just to read? But after a while her possessions had become her identity, and the charities, cars, vacations, children's schedules—it had all mattered. She had been so sure to be by the standards of that world so appropriate, had striven so hard to achieve again that position to save her children, that she had lost sight of the worth of being good in the sense of being simply authentic.

Her conforming had bridled her like a horse these women rode. Now it was as if she was taking her first breath in ten years of unbridled air. And what she wanted to do now that she could do anything was go home to her summer kitchen. If the idea of reclaiming lustrous childhoods for her boys was no longer an incentive, she understood now she would fight to keep her property for her summer kitchen. *That* was where she belonged, where she could give her boys all that mattered, her true, happy, present self, and the abundant, easy love that flowed from that.

By the time she turned into her drive she no longer shook, but rather felt utterly emancipated, and determined that there would be fresh-baked shortbread when the boys came home.

❋ ❋ ❋

But Thomas did not come home.

It had been arranged that Beatriz would pick up Thomas and Nicholas in her taxi with Charlie en route back from Muscoot Farm. Now the taxi screeched to a halt outside the garage, Beatriz, Nicholas, and Charlie pale and wide-eyed in the back. They hadn't said a word during the ride from school. Beatriz paid the driver and then to save time waiting for the garage door to open, she and the boys took the path to the front porch. She opened the front door and paused, the boys shrinking behind her skirt. They understood as well as she did. This would be worse for *la señora* than *señor* being arrested.

"Beatriz?" Nora called.

Beatriz became aware of her keys—there were so many, to her car, the house, the summer kitchen, Phillip's now—jangling like bells. She looked down. Her hands shook.

She and the boys moved into the family room and faced the kitchen. *La señora's* eyes were awaiting them.

"Beatriz, what's wrong?" Nora asked, a note of alarm in her voice. "You look stunned." What she meant was "uncharacteristically ruffled," which was what stunned Nora, as much as the stillness of her boys. They usually filled the house with noise and activity the instant they arrived home. Beatriz's look shocked her all the more for coming so soon after the happiness of her announcement last night.

"Tell me, tell me, what is it?"

"It is Thomas . . . I do not suppose he is here?"

It was only then that Nora became aware that Thomas was not with them. "*Here?* But he was at school; he should be with *you*."

Beatriz clenched her keys, to stop her hands trembling. Her words came out in a rush, high-pitched, frightened, pleading. "The school was surprised when I went to pick him up. Thomas had not come to school."

Nora hugged herself hard.

Beatriz's sentences came at Nora after that as blows to the stomach. "The school thought he was sick. I told the school his mother dropped him at school herself that morning." She was barely managing to go on, her breathing ragged. "They asked might his mother have come back to get him. I told them that his mother had phoned my cell phone only an hour ago to confirm I would be picking up him along with his brother. They asked about his father. I told them it was not possible. The school has called the police. I said I would tell you my-self."

Nora found herself in a state of paralysis. She felt like she had turned to stone against the blows, heavy and cold, only with a thou-sand fissures now wending through her and threatening to split her at any moment into little pieces.

And then the words "The school thought he was sick" came back to her. Maybe he wasn't feeling well. Maybe he had walked home and no one had heard him. The possibility of a simple explanation brought her back to life and she took off through the rooms and up the staircase. She was aware of Beatriz and the boys following, Bea-triz now taking shallow, tentative, anticipatory breaths that made the air seem that much more brittle. They searched every room, calling Thomas's name, hauling covers off mattresses, sliding clothes to the ends of racks, pulling linens off shelving, checking behind every door. Nora knew before they were finished he was not there. She could not sense his presence, and there was not much in the way of furniture left to hide behind. On the upended crate that was her bedside table she saw the list she had made of best ways to use the three million dollars she had been sure that morning she would pos-sess by this time. She tore it to shreds. She already had what her children needed and she hadn't seen it.

A movement outside drew her eyes to the window. Reuben's truck was pulling up. Nora looked to Beatriz with sharp hope. Was it pos-sible Thomas was with Reuben?

Beatriz shook her head at the unspoken question.

"I called Reuben. He was close. He said he would come to watch Nicholas and Charlie so that I could take you back to the school where you are needed."

Beatriz could not follow the drive down to the curb outside the school's entrance for all the police cars. A child's disappearance was taken seriously anywhere, but in a town like Bedford where the most

serious offense on the police blotter was usually bored teenagers bat-
ting down mailboxes, the entire force seemed to be present. That
presence had the effect of reassuring her and of making more keen
the reality of Tom's disappearance. Nora was out of the car and running down the embankment before Beatriz had drawn to a stop. She
ran so fast that she knocked the backpack off the shoulder of a man
who was holding it for his son while they stood watching with held
hands. She became aware of a lot more school parents watching with
their wide-eyed silent children. She heard a loud crack behind her,
and stopped to look back. Beatriz had driven into a rock. But Beatriz
paid no attention. Flinging and leaving open the driver's door, she ran
to catch up, her lips moving in what Nora took for silent prayer.

"Are you the boy's mother?"

Nora turned. She had seen this policeman before; he had a son at
the school. She nodded vigorously, and grabbed the policeman's arm.

"Please," she said, "find my boy, please—"

Then all at once, like a miracle, a deep male voice piped up,
"We've got him!"

Heads twisted suddenly in the direction of the policeman striding
toward them, a radio still stuttering in his hand. A roaring in Nora's
head left her dizzy and sightless for a moment. She had to wait for
her blurred vision to clear before she could make out the policeman
again. "He's okay," he said, standing before them now. It seemed to
Nora all at once that his voice vibrated like music. "He's in New Jersey. A trucker called it in. Found him in the back of his truck." He
looked directly at Nora. "Your son said he climbed in on his own. The
truck made a delivery here at the school this morning. The truck's
been making deliveries ever since. The trucker was amazed the boy
could have stayed hidden a whole day. Had some credit card with
him in a different name. Said he found it once in a parking lot. Any
idea what he might have been doing?"

Nora had her palms layered over her heart.

"Was there a sign on the truck?" she asked, her voice choking on conflicting emotions, relief, worry still for Tom's well-being, a new, awful guilt.

"I assume so. It was some New Jersey Paper Products Company. Why?"

"Do you think it actually said the words 'New Jersey'?"

"Why?"

"It's where his father is."

* * *

Nora drove to pick Thomas up from the station in New Jersey. Beatriz was in no state to drive and sat on the passenger side. When the policeman had told them Thomas was safe, Beatriz had collapsed into tears. Nora had thought at first that she wept with relief, only her wailing became a body quake and brought on a worrisome heaving of her chest. She had not managed a word while Nora took down directions, just shook her head violently at the suggestion she be taken home. Even now, twenty minutes into their drive toward the George Washington Bridge over the Hudson River and into New Jersey, Beatriz was inconsolable, her heels kicked off on the floor, her stockinged feet clawed over the edge of her seat, her arms held tightly about the skirt pulled over her knees. Her shaking shoulders had loosened the unbraided bun she had worn these past weeks so that her hair was now knotted at the nape of her neck in the style of Nora's. Nora had still not said anything. Part of her mind was on the road, ensuring she didn't miss any exits, a larger part was on Thomas, frantic to reach him and hold him, and the rest now believed Beatriz was undergoing a post-traumatic purging, one *she* would likely undergo when it was all over. And if this purging was needed now, it should be respected and not interrupted. Even a hand on Beatriz's arm would likely startle like a knife in a consciousness whose edges were blurred. All Nora had done was press beside Beatriz a travel pack of tissues.

All at once Beatriz choked something out.

"I could not have handled losing another boy," she rasped. At least that was what Nora thought Beatriz had said. But it made no sense.

When Beatriz stopped crying and looked up, Nora took her eyes off the road a moment to examine her. Beatriz's eyes were bleary and her paled, puckered face was splotched so badly it looked as though she had broken into hives.

Nora turned back to the road.

"I have a son, you know," Beatriz said so quietly it was almost a whisper.

Nora was too taken aback to think of what to say. Her blinker had been on to shift lanes, but she snapped it off now and stayed where she was behind the slow car in front.

"Had a son. Have. Had. Both."

Nora wanted to say something, wanted to reach for Beatriz's hand, but she gave her space.

"He would be fifteen now," Beatriz struggled, her eyes now fixed on the cars ahead. "The last time I saw him he was two months old."

Tears welled in Nora's eyes, imagining the loss. It had been hard enough losing a child in vitro. It was clear now how Beatriz had known then how to care for her so well. The car ahead had increased its speed and was some way ahead now, but Nora remained at the lower speed.

"Every day I wonder what he is doing, how he looks, if he is happy, healthy, does he have friends, does he like his school, what his dreams are. Every day I send him thoughts so I will be in his heart, though I doubt he remembers me. His father probably never mentioned me, probably long ago destroyed everything about me. . . ."

"He is still *alive?*" Nora gasped.

Beatriz turned to look out the side window. She was having trouble talking.

"I had no idea," Nora said gently.

"How could you have?" Beatriz's voice was muffled for being directed away. "I have never spoken of my son in this country. Not even when I was expected to bare all in that treatment program."

"The pain, Beatriz. I don't know how you've managed it."

Beatriz said nothing.

"Tell me, Beatriz, tell me what happened."

And so Beatriz pressed the base of her palms into her eyes for a moment and then after a deep breath told of how, when she was eighteen, she met a man in Mexico from Buenos Aires. He had bought a churro from her at the roadside stand she was tending for extra money that first summer after she graduated. Not long afterward, he bought an apartment. The man came from a very rich family and traveled frequently between his family company in Buenos Aires and Mexico. And then one day her breasts had felt unusually tender, and the next day the smell of frying churros had caused her to dry-retch.

The birth of her son had filled her heart with a happiness it could almost not contain. But she had become ill after the delivery. She could not accompany the baby's father when he took their son back to Buenos Aires to meet his family. He was meant to be gone just a few days, but that became a week, which then became two. In the third week she had taken a drink. It was the only way she knew to quell the pain of separation from her son and the furious incredulity at a man who could keep a new baby from its mother. Whenever she called Buenos Aires, the maid who answered the phone told her coldly that the baby was fine and out with his father. Not once had she received a returned call.

When her son and his father finally returned four weeks later, she was adding vodka to her orange juice at the breakfast table. She was barely even aware by then of how much she was drinking. Certainly she was unaware of how similar and quickly the patterns of her days had become to those of her father. It had felt as if she had fallen into some psychosis and was operating on automatic pilot. Her son's father had pleaded a delirium from his love for his son and she had forgiven him, though her son seemed no longer to know her and cried every time she picked him up. He cried even when she did not pick him up. She was frantic to soothe him, but nothing seemed to work. His father stayed but a day and left once more for Buenos Aires. She took her son to the pediatrician, tried soothing him with cooled chamomile tea. She took him on walks in the stroller, sang to him, bathed him, swaddled him, cradled him, sustaining herself on teas laced with whatever was in the liquor cabinet. The only thing she did not do was tell her mother. Her mother was worried enough about her father. Nothing seemed to help, and she began to cry with her son.

One hopeless night, after a week of sleeplessness, her stomach hollow from lack of food, her head swimming from potent teas, she cried until she forgot.

When she awoke her son was gone.

She found a note. Her son's father had returned home the previous night. He had found their baby crying in a soiled diaper, his mother intoxicated and unconscious, an open bottle of vodka on the kitchen table. She was unfit to be a mother to any child, the note said, and there was no way she was going to mother his.

She tried calling and calling Buenos Aires, to no avail. She could not imagine where else he might have gone. She took a flight to Buenos Aires. The guards at the family compound refused her entry. And then she caught sight up at the house of her baby! With his father—and another woman! She screamed for her son. His father went inside. The guards came outside. The police came then and took her to the airport. They had orders she must leave the country.

A lawyer she consulted in Mexico told her she had little chance of getting her son back. He was in a foreign country and surrounded by lawyers and money to pay people in high places. She had nothing and was accused in addition of child endangerment. One lawyer after another told her that her case was hopeless. She drank more and over time began to believe she *was* an irresponsible mother and that her son *was* better off without her. In this state of mind she signed the custody papers and flew to America, though starting a new life was not simple and there was nowhere in the world she could hide to escape her torment.

Nora had crossed over the George Washington Bridge and was nearing the precinct where Thomas was. She was not sure how she had managed to keep driving. The effect of Beatriz's story had been to rend at once her heart and mind.

She finally managed to ask, "Does your son still live with his father?"

"How can I know for sure?"

"You've never tried to see him again?"

Beatriz was staring fixedly at the road ahead.

"I flew again to Buenos Aires before I signed the custody papers. I was turned around at the airport and put on a plane back to Mexico. Since then I have written my son a letter a week every week of his life. I always write a return address, so that he will know where to find me. I have neither received any of my letters back nor any response."

"There has to be some way, Beatriz."

"When he is older."

"But he is old enough to understand now. You could hire someone to go to Buenos Aires for you. You could use the money you want to invest in the café."

"No!" Beatriz came out of her trance suddenly. She looked over at Nora. "That investment is for my son. I need to make something of myself so he can be proud of me."

"He would be proud of you as you are, Beatriz."

Beatriz shrugged. "Besides," she said, "what would my son do, anyway? He only knows one family, has friends, a home. It would be selfish and unfair to unsettle him."

Beatriz lowered her stockinged feet to the floor and smoothed her hair, not bothering to pin it back atop her head. Nora glanced over. For all the splotches still on Beatriz's face, she looked prettier suddenly for having unbuttoned her secret, more relaxed, less constrained. Nora suspected she was seeing Beatriz now for the first time in all her flawed, honest, pained realness. Beatriz looked over and said, "You know, it has occurred to me more than once that our positions are not so different. We both have unresolved relationships with people loved and lost to us." And then she unclasped a locket from around her neck and opened it to show Nora a picture of her son.

Nora pulled over to the side of the road for a moment to look at it.

The rosy-cheeked baby was the very image of Beatriz.

Nora took Beatriz into her arms then and together they wept.

Twelve

Beatriz was standing in her heels on a stool in the summer kitchen reaching up to the antique-beam shelving when Nora walked in the following dawn. Beatriz had decided after baking the Saturday churro order that this was as good a day as any to bring out from hiding the pastry-making antiquities. She had hoped to surprise *la señora,* have up on the shelving again before she came in the decorative tea tins, pottery bean pot cookie jars, vintage copper kettles, the wooden egg crates with their dovetail corner designs, the hanging kitchen scales, the biscuit cutters, nutmeg graters, jelly molds, tea caddies, and ice-cream scoops. And she had, within a hairsbreadth, managed it. She had just now slid into place the last of the albums of collected traditional baking recipes.

"What . . . on . . . earth?" Nora was wearing khakis, a maroon cotton sweater over a white shirt, and white ankle socks with white canvas sneakers.

Beatriz climbed down and hand-pressed her pleated skirt.

"I could not let the authorities take these," she said matter-of-factly.

"But I thought they had taken them."

Beatriz moved the stool back to the island bench.

"What would you have done if you knew that I had hidden them?"

Nora said nothing.

"My guess is you would have done the right thing," Beatriz answered for her.

"But they will find out that they're missing; they have our insurance records."

"Look . . ." Beatriz pressed a palm on the countertop, rested the other on her hip. "It's been five months since they seized your belongings. You would have heard by now. Besides, they are not going to miss a few things here and there. We are not talking about jewelry or bonds. They got the majority of your belongings. And they will only know you have them if you sell them. I did not hide them for you for that. I know how much these mean to you. They are irreplaceable to you. You would never sell them."

"When did you do this?"

"After you lost the baby, the night before the seizure. You had lost enough."

Nora nodded hesitantly. "But where did you hide them?"

Beatriz gave a chuckle. "Why, behind the same wall *el señor* hid the safe! The plaster was still drying when the men came to take everything: I was so worried one would notice, but their trucks were gone when we got back and I knew it was okay."

Nora gave a little smile herself then. She had not been into her husband's office since the day he was arrested when she had opened the safe. She hadn't kept the cash or documents there because the safe was obvious once they had opened the wall in front of it, and if they plastered over it, they would not be able to access it.

"I knew there was a lot more space behind that wall," Beatriz explained. "Certainly space enough for a few boxes. I have plastered up holes there often enough."

Nora nodded. "I know."

Beatriz hesitated a minute. "You do?"

"I always knew about the holes, just not about the safe." Nora walked over to the bench, took a seat on a stool across from where Beatriz stood. "I just didn't want to know." She gave out a heavy sigh. "There were so many signs that something was wrong, Beatriz. Evan putting his fists through walls was just one. The credit cards being declining, keeping the insurance money rather than replacing the car he totaled, late-night meetings with lawyers and insurance carriers . . . I'm not stupid. I didn't know he had done something illegal, of course, but I knew there were problems. It was just easier to pretend it wasn't happening." She dropped her hands to the bench, tapping a row of fingers, following the rhythm with her eyes, conscious vaguely of Beatriz taking the seat opposite her. "I am as responsible as Evan for what happened, you know. If I had asked hard questions and not been afraid to hear the truth, I might have been able to stop things before they went too far. But did I do that? No, I did absolutely nothing. Instead, I pushed in the other direction, throwing lavish luncheons, planning vacations, a guest parking lot, getting pregnant. . . . I put more pressure on Evan when I should have been helping to relieve it." Nora shook her head. "It was the pressure I put on him all the way through our marriage that partly led to all of this, you know, always complacently expecting credit cards would be paid, checks would be covered, never asking if we had enough, never questioning if we needed so much, never stopping to consider the real cost of it all. I was utterly financially irresponsible."

Beatriz let the silence between them sit a moment. "But did *señor* ever discuss with you money problems or ask that you cut back on the lifestyle he wanted for you?"

"No, but neither did he ask me to give up work, to give up my old life and friends, to shut my eyes to signs that things weren't right. I became the blindly extravagant Bedford wife and mother on my own. That Evan happily supported that role just made it easier."

Nora's gaze shifted to a trance. Her remorse for her part was so heartfelt now for finally having read Evan's letters last night. Thomas had unknowingly encouraged her to read them. When she had felt Thomas's heart beating alive in her embrace in the station house yesterday afternoon, she had found herself saying to him, "You need me to forgive your dad, don't you, Tom?" She had felt his body slacken, the tension gone with a few words. With the idea of forgiveness in her breast and a gratitude to Evan for having seen through Fox Silverworth where she had not, she had sat to read Evan's letters on the edge of her mattress, a "bed" she had come to refer to as hers, but that she remembered then had also been her husband's. For three or four years it had been "our" bed, and for seven years after that until recently, "Mommy's and Daddy's." She still slept on her side of the mattress. Suddenly she wasn't sure whether this was from habit or to keep his place.

His letters expressed the debilitating pain of being at once worried about and separated from his family. She had better understood then the horror of a life being taken while alive to feel and know it, and it sickened her that she hadn't considered before all that the father of her children was enduring. It had been then that the truth had emerged from deep within her confused mistakes of late. Beatriz had been right about her that first time visiting Evan: She *had* been too hard on him, way, way too hard, throwing him just scraps of herself as he starved. She had not once listened when he had tried to talk about what had happened. She had not once asked how it really was for him in there.

She had felt so sick then that she had wondered whether it was her fear of that sickness that had kept her so angry, distant, cold. As long as she didn't care any longer what happened to her husband, she could stay above the agonizing commiseration whose weight would pull at her and consequently the children. But his spirit, she realized from his letters, lived still. He quoted intelligently philosophers and authors whose works he presumably devoured in the prison library, and wrote of his incredible inner journey to an understanding of the purpose of his suffering. He wrote of how he had learned from having done things the wrong way how to do them the right way, how he felt so privileged to not yet be forty and still to have had the opportunity to survive the fire and learn mindfulness. Prison not only hadn't obliterated him, he seemed to be coming to triumphant terms with himself and life. He seemed headed, in fact, for a brilliant future. And so perhaps she needn't desperately guard against a more charitable perspective.

Perhaps it was time to summon the courage of compassion regardless.

When Nora's vision cleared, she found Beatriz's eyes upon her still, full of compassion. All this time Beatriz had understood this virtue better than she.

"So are you going to keep it all?" Beatriz asked.

Nora looked up at the shelving and then back to Beatriz.

"Thank you," she said, standing and pushing up her sleeves. She could either sit wishing to change what could never be changed, or she could get on with things with her new resolve to handle things herself now. She had doubted the breadth of her shoulders when her shoulders were plenty strong.

A knock sounded just then at the door. She went to answer it, sure it was one of the boys—though it was odd they would knock.

At first Nora didn't recognize the figure on the doorstep who was dressed down in sweatpants and a long-sleeved polo shirt, her hair caught up messily in a barrette. But the figure was fixing her collar and the gesture took Nora's mind back to that moment at the golf club party when Ticky had been awkwardly readjusting her pink cashmere wrap.

"I've got no one else to turn to!" Ticky blurted out.

Nora blinked at her.

"No one else would understand."

Nora reached for her hand and led her inside.

"I'm going to make some tea," Nora said.

Ticky nodded and climbed on top of the stool that Nora pulled out for her.

"I was just leaving, anyway," Beatriz said. "I have to deliver my churros."

"*You* make those?" Ticky asked, her voice straining to stay steady. Beatriz nodded.

"They've become the chic cure for hangovers," Ticky told her. "The mothers have even coined a phase for mornings after dinner parties: 'It's a churro morning!'"

Nora and Beatriz laughed, though Ticky had no spirit for laughter.

Nora made the introduction. "Beatriz, Ticky. Ticky, Beatriz."

They shook hands and then Beatriz left.

Nora could see that Ticky was ready to cry and moved the tissue box closer.

But Ticky just wrapped her arms about herself.

"Are you cold?" Nora asked, lighting the gas jet. "Can I get you a cardigan?"

Ticky shook her head. Her dark oversized sunglasses pushed up on her head fell to the floor. The clattering sound startled her, and just as though a plug had been pulled, the tears surged forth in a flood. She pulled out a tissue and blew her nose.

Nora settled the kettle over the flame and walked around the counter to pick up the glasses. She set them on the bench beside Ticky and gently rubbed Ticky's back.

"I need to leave Morris," Ticky sputtered. She dropped the scrunched tissue on the counter and drew another to wipe her eyes. She then tipped her head back with a sniff to settle her tears and running nose. When she lowered her face again, there was a trembling fear in her eyes. Nora reached out to draw a clump of hair from Ticky's face.

Ticky went on, "But with his malicious nature and all his powerful lawyers it will be a long, long time, if ever, before I see any money. And I don't know how to live without money or how to make it. It's just the reason why I haven't left him sooner."

She started tearing off bits of tissue.

Nora felt her chest tighten, seeing herself the day of Evan's arrest, everything she knew gone in a flash, the vast unknown ahead; and what if Ticky didn't find herself in time, and the enormity of the change defeated her first? Nora knew now that one could not conceive the difficulty of being alone until one was, could not fathom the massive emotional shock of losing one's accustomed lifestyle until one did. But she didn't speak the caution she had intended. For all at once she had faith in Ticky: If time had come for change, then change should be embraced. Ticky would not wither and die. She would suffer for a while, but life would go on. She would continue running errands, and sorting her mail, and filling her coffee mug, and one day the sunshine on her back would soothe and the wind would bring the fragrance of a flower and she would find herself standing taller and marveling at what she was seeing and understanding. She would realize then that those pains were growth pains, without which she might have simply stagnated.

Nora said gently, "Would you like to tell me what happened?"

Nora gave her time. The kettle steamed. She returned to the other side of the counter to prepare the herbal tea, wafting its soothing fragrance toward Ticky. She dug a teaspoon into a cereal bowl of honey and set it between two odd-colored steaming mugs.

Ticky turned a teaspoon of honey slowly through her tea and said quietly, "I told Morris before he left for the office this morning that I wanted a baby."

Nora climbed on top of her stool and took her mug between cupped hands.

"That would hardly free you of your marriage if that's what you want."

"Perhaps not altogether, but it would free me to love. My step-daughter barely visits from her mother's any longer, she has that much homework and that many activities, and she's off to boarding school anyway next year, and I thought perhaps Morris might be will-ing finally to father my own child. I'm not getting any younger; I'll be forty this year." She stirred her tea some more, then looked up with a flushed face. "Do you know what that bastard said? He said if I needed a friend, to go and buy a dog."

She set her teaspoon down, wrapped her arms about herself again, and shut her eyes. Then she looked up abruptly through new tears. "It's funny, but I realized at that moment I've never known love. I was raised by a series of nannies, put out into the world with good wishes and a trust fund, dated men I didn't care about to fill the time because I didn't need to work, and then married because it seemed the right thing to do. At which time my parents considered they had no further obligations and withdrew the trust fund and most remaining involvement in my life and left me to what was a new cold home."

Nora said gently, "But had you not lived that life you may never have come to understand how important love is to you. Now you un-derstand and now you are perhaps being given an opportunity with the collapse of your marriage to go out and find it."

"But the idea of losing all the money terrifies me."

"Once you've lost it, the fear of losing it can no longer exist."

"But I'll still have nothing."

"No, you'll have the realization that you must begin anew. And if you don't let that overwhelm you and you embrace instead the possi-bilities inherent in it, you will find what it is you're looking for and a whole lot more besides."

Ticky gazed meditatively at Nora, her face slightly calmer for some-thing new to contemplate. When she spoke again her voice was a little steadier.

"How is it possible to do that in a world in which money is all that matters?"

"Live life on terms true to your heart and shuck everything else off."

"But how do you know what your heart is saying?"

"You listen."

"But how do you know what you hear is right?"

"It feels right."

"How does that feel?"

"It will be easier to pay attention when there's less noise in your head and you find how to be still with yourself. It takes time. I've only recently found that stillness myself."

Ticky raised her eyebrows, but her suffering drew her back to her own misery. "But how do I get rid of the noise?"

Nora set down her cup and reached for Ticky's hand. "A good first step might be to eat something." She let go of Ticky's hand and stood to walk over to the refrigerator. "I'm sure you haven't eaten and it's hard to think on an empty stomach. I need to prepare breakfast for the boys, anyway." She peered inside the refrigerator. Looking back around the door a moment later, she said, "You know, I decided something last night that might help you, too. If I want happiness, I decided, I must insist upon it. In the same way I once worked out my body, I'm going to train my mind. If you leave your marriage, life will be hard for a while, but I don't believe you need to be unhappy. It seems to me that the more you insist on happiness, the more you repeat that way of thinking, the more naturally your emotions follow. It will take time and mental effort, but the point is to work your mind into a groove, so that a positive perspective will become instinctive." Nora saw that this was a lot for Ticky to take in. It had taken *her* long enough to grasp it. She put her head back into the refrigerator.

"How about a warm rhubarb-and-muesli crumble?" she called out.

The basic reality of good food calmed Ticky. Closing her eyes, she said, "Mmm." When she reopened them she was holding her head a little higher and experimenting with a happier expression. She asked directions to the bathroom. She returned with lipstick freshly applied and the question of what had happened to all the furniture in the house.

"The mats of sea grass and oversized floor cushions and bright-colored yarn tapestries—that *is* our furniture now," Nora said cheerily. "The boys have been spending their afternoons with Beatriz learning to weave and decorate." Nora had been struck all the while they did that at how things turned: Beatriz helping to create a home for them now in need, the way she, Nora, had so many years ago created one for Beatriz in need.

Ticky nodded and watched Nora preparing the crumble, but when the silence became too much, she lowered her voice to a conspiratorial tone and said, "Speaking of love . . ."

Nora looked up.

The small smile on Ticky's face told her that Ticky meant what Nora thought she did.

"I'm afraid everyone knows already," Ticky explained kindly, seeing she had caught Nora unawares. "You know what that Bonnie is like. I suppose you should know Bonnie is saying you betrayed Evan. She and George both are saying it, actually. Bonnie brought it up at a rather large dinner party last night, how she'd seen you leaving the Silverworth estate when Susan Silverworth was away and only Fox's car was there, and then George picked up her lead and assailed your fidelity."

Nora asked, "How do they know I wasn't just there to get legal advice?"

Ticky responded, "I asked that myself. She said you looked far too disheveled. Bonnie told the women that they had better keep a close eye on their husbands with women like you out there. I dragged Morris home at that point, but not before warning Bonnie and George to be careful throwing stones from glass houses. Morris was furious with me, of course. 'What the hell did you mean by that?' he asked in the car. I told him it was something Bonnie had told me once about George. He said, 'Keep a lid on it next time!'"

Nora laughed. A sexually active single woman in an enclave of tenuously married couples seemed to be more threatening even than a wife of a felon!

She said, "I'm just sorry that Bonnie will probably disparage you next. But it was good of you to stand up for me. Thank you. And see? You're already starting to live your life on terms true to your heart!"

Ticky nodded. "So tell me, then, what is it with Fox?"

"Nothing, nothing at all."

"Well, then you need to stop Bonnie from spreading falsehoods."

Nora laughed again. "I don't give a hoot what people say anymore, but Bonnie will stop soon enough. She doesn't realize this yet, but not only that, she's going to go out of her way to help me. She's part of my plan to reclaim my life."

❊ ❊ ❊

The first step in that plan was to seriously address the prospect of the Summer Kitchen Bakery-Café, and true to her new determination, Nora had within weeks secured both Phillip as a partner matching Beatriz's funds, and a lease. Signing Phillip on was easy. The Summer Kitchen label had become so lucrative for his business that he had been about to suggest that Nora take on overhead and supply him from her summer kitchen. He had grinned when she presented her offer and told her he could not believe his vision for the future of her label and his involvement in it had been so limited.

The space had been the challenge. Nora had her heart set on finding a location in the village—the southeastern hamlet of Bedford Village's "Village Green"—but the village was so small that there had been nothing available. She had viewed nearby barns to lease, though they were all zoned residential and she knew she would have trouble getting permits. The word already was that she was likely going to be denied a permit to keep baking in her summer kitchen—the next issue to address. She didn't need to create any more issues. None of the barns had felt right in any case. Beatriz had suggested looking in Bedford's other hamlets, Bedford Hills and Katonah, but Nora was quick to make the point, such was her love of old things, that Bedford Village better retained its old-world feel. It had the longest history, too, having been founded all the way back in 1680. She had considered waiting until space became available, when late one afternoon driving past with the boys and Beatriz, she had seen moving trucks pulling out from in front of the village saddle shop.

There had been speculation two weeks earlier about whether the business would renew its lease. It decided it would and that option had closed. But it looked suddenly as though the owner had yet another change of heart. She made a U-turn and parked. Outside Beatriz's car while Beatriz helped the boys out, Nora paused to set in her mind a picture of this village she had a feeling now would be home after all. The village was little more than a quaint row of meticulously preserved white buildings, their shutters and awnings regulation black or hunter green to match the patches of lawn or potted plants out front. The stores and galleries were locally owned. There were no malls or chain stores in Bedford. Nor was there yet a village green café-bakery. The buildings faced a swath of green space designating the center of the historical district. To the right of the green were the nineteenth-century Historical Hall, used now for private events, and the burying ground planned the year following Bedford's purchase. The tombstones so close to the road provided a perfect backdrop to the annual Halloween parade. To the left was the one-room village schoolhouse from 1829 to 1912, known locally now as the "Stone Jug."

The row flanked by its redbrick pavement began with the reaching white Presbyterian church tower behind which preschoolers attended weekday programs. Their little rooms overlooked a parking lot full at drop-off and pickup times of black four-wheel drives that were only a year or two away from being among those dropping off or picking up at the private school. Alongside that was the post office. This Greek Revival–style historical building was once a harness shop, but had served as the village post office since around 1900. Things ran in that post office now as though it were still 1900. Locals drove miles out of their way to the post offices in Bedford Hills or Mount Kisco and *still* saved time, the service in the village was that slow. Two up from the post office was the firehouse, its mini–attack truck always at the ready to address brush fires, its dive team the canoeing accidents at Black Heron Lake. The station sounded a foghorn each of the approximately five hundred times a year its volunteers were called out, to let the town know to pull in and prepare for activity. The foghorn was so loud it distracted construction crews miles away, and had children sometimes crying for its duration at the preschool. The Bedford Free Library sat next up the row, an early nineteenth-century building that was until 1902 the Bedford Academy, one of Westchester's first classical schools. The library was leased from the historical society for one dollar a year. It sat back further than the other buildings, behind a white picket-fenced garden. Children skipped up a charming garden path to return their books, or to attend a reading of *Mother Goose*. Beyond that were various stores—a few boutiques, galleries, a delicatessen, the Bedford florist, a store selling cookware, more real estate offices than anything else, and at the far end just before the historical occupied houses started again, the charming one-theater Bedford Playhouse and the meetinghouse restaurant for dinner after the movie. But what stood out to her was the historical Lounsbery Building that the saddle shop had it seemed just vacated. As she and Beatriz and the boys climbed its three steps between rounded columns, she felt wobbly with anticipation. There was a sense in the portico's shade before the heavy green door that something wonderful was about to happen.

Inside, the boys took off to explore. The room was wide and deep and empty. The leather smell of saddles and the dry, fibrous scent of blankets lingered, underpinned by the papery whiff still in the air of cardboard boxes. Scattered over the antique wood floor dusty with boot prints were scraps of hay presumably from decorative hay bales, and half-used rolls of moving tape. Nicholas had found a spider cowering in a corner and the boys all hurried over to look. A bit of tape had stuck to the bottom of Charlie's shoe. The rapid squelching sound he made was almost musical, echoing off white-painted walls and a vaulted ceiling edged with decorative cornice molding. The only modern alteration was the high track lighting, but its light was as soft as that of lanterns. Otherwise the light was natural and dust-mottled, filtering through latticed windows facing the street. She knew instantly this was the place. At the heart of the room was a stone fireplace so vast that children could sit inside its cavity and gaze up the chimney throat at constellations. Its similarity to the one in her summer kitchen gave her the idea: Not only would she model the café on her summer kitchen, but all their products would be made in the traditional way, using old-world equipment and slightly modified old-world recipes. They would become food artisans. The products would be labor-intensive and expensive, but exceptional and unique—which was exactly what the women of Bedford demanded.

The only issue was money. But since she had taken a new breath of resolve, the ideas had been sparking. After learning that the space was indeed available for lease, she made a presentation to the building's owner, the Bedford Historical Society. The society ladies were hesitant at first. They knew already of her business, but they knew also of the scandal. She piqued their interest with two words, *preservation preserves*. She proposed designing or naming many of her products after historical aspects of the town, cookies to resemble the face of the Sutton Clock Tower, for example, Bedford Oak chocolate trunk bars, in exchange for the society signing a percentage lease, accepting as rent a small portion of overall profits. Her café would also support the society's objective—to promote the virtues of a past time in Bedford—by preserving the memory of summer kitchens. She could tell the ladies were excited, though they asked would she allow them time to confer. Their smiles told her on her return that they had an arrangement. They even added sugar to the deal. If she would also open her real summer kitchen for their bimonthly historical kitchen tours, they would allow her bakery one year's grace on the rent. They understood there was a risk the café would not last beyond a year, but they wished to help the remarkable venture however they could.

It was the break the fledgling business needed.

Now she, the boys, Phillip, Beatriz, and Reuben were celebrating in the new space with rounds of Reuben's cider.

"Can I be the register?" Nicholas asked excitedly.

"You mean the cashier," Nora corrected.

"No, the register. The register makes all the money."

They all laughed, though Beatriz kept laughing long past the others. She could not contain her happiness. She was already making, between her churros and her part in the Summer Kitchen Bakery, more than she had ever made, and before her was the prospect of making more—all while being in love with a man who was also in love with her.

Beatriz had brought a fresh batch of Spanish Napoleons. As Phillip and Reuben tasted them now for the first time, Nora told the story of how they had come about.

"We've gotta serve these in the café," Phillip said, wiping the corner of his mouth with the back of his hand. He tipped his hat. "We could make 'em regular size and mini."

"I love the idea of making them mini-size!" Nora gushed.

A moment before, Beatriz had been too preoccupied with her happiness to notice the glow about *la señora,* but as she noticed now she understood all at once the recent changes in *la señora. La señora* had always had a relaxed look, but a polished relaxed look, her hair always blow-dried, lifted often into the perfect French twist, her hands bejeweled, her nails painted. Even her jeans were designer label. But lately her polished relaxed look had become a natural relaxed look. She let her mane of hair air-dry, tying it into a loose knot at the nape of her neck, and her typical outfit now of khakis in gray, green, black, or white, white shirt, cotton sweater, and white canvas sneakers was as practical as the nails she now kept short and unpainted. Far from letting herself go, she accentuated this natural look simply; a dab of perfume, a bracelet, lipstick, and what Beatriz now realized was new confidence. She, Beatriz, had told *señor* at the prison in winter to give *señora* time, to find her way out of her rage and into her own power. It seemed *señora* was now coming into that power.

Reuben said, "Mini Spanish Napoleons should be your signature pastry. Think about it, all three of you have contributed now to its creation. Like the Summer Kitchen Bakery-Café, they've come out of your partnership."

"Yes!" Her fingers in midair about a Spanish Napoleon, Nora looked over at Beatriz. "And Beatriz," she added. "It's time you started calling me Nora."

Their celebration was interrupted just then by the ringing of Phillip's cell phone. The woman who served behind the front counter at Phillip's needed to leave to pick up her daughter from after-school care: She had come down with a fever. Phillip said he would return immediately to relieve her. He explained this to the group, and Beatriz told him she would go. A good-natured argument set in—"Nah, nah, it's very kind of you, but—" . . . "But nothing, you're still eating your napoleon!" . . . "I couldn't ask you to do that!" . . . "Do what, it is nothing!" . . . "Well, then I must pay you." . . . "Good heavens, put your wallet away. We are partners now; you would do the same for me!" . . . "You're too much, Beatriz!"—until Reuben said that he and Beatriz and Phillip would all go together so that they could discuss, while Nora stayed with the boys, the renovations that would need to start immediately if the café were to open in summer.

The interaction between Phillip and Beatriz had the easygoing quality of an old married couple. They often made Nora laugh, though now in the wake of their little scene and after they had all left and the boys were exploring down in what would be the kitchen, she suffered a feeling of loss. Today Beatriz and Phillip had made her think of her *own* marriage. For she and Evan had once been that way, finishing each other's sentences, then huff, huffing that that wasn't exactly what was meant, but, well, yes, possibly it was, really. Once they had even bought each other the same Christmas present, which had been endearingly hopeless, since what would they do with two sets of arrangements for a pair of massage therapists to come to the house late every Sunday evening for a year? They could not even move one set to another night. Sunday was then the only night they could be sure of no other engagement.

Was she actually missing Evan?

Did she actually want him here to share in her success?

"No," she argued with herself.

"Are you sure?" she asked herself back.

"Sure!"

"Then why are you rubbing the base of your ring finger?"

Nora looked down at where she had once worn her wedding ring.

"Well, okay, a little, I guess."

She had been having this dialogue with herself often since discovering inside the envelopes of Evan's letters separate folded pages to the general letters. She had taken them out to find that they were love letters, gentle, sometimes funny letters expressing such deep, refined feeling and coming back so often to the simple, sad, beautiful sentiment that he missed her that tears came to her eyes. It was only then and for the first time in her life that she understood just how much he cherished her. All this time she had perceived it differently due to her rage. But he loved her so much that he had no choice but to keep loving and fighting for her. For how much easier it would have been for him to cast her and all the grief he must face with her aside. How much easier to start again, after he did his time, with a woman with whom he had no past. Evan had told her years ago the story of how one of his brokers had cheated on his wife and when the wife learned of it and confronted him he silently packed his bags, walked out the door, and never turned back. He did not leave for the woman with whom he cheated on his wife. That had only been a one-night stand. He ended up meeting and marrying another. He left to avoid the fallout. How much harder to wade back through his own radioactive dust for the woman he loved.

All this time Evan had been fighting to the death for his marriage.

His love for her moved her then and now in the same measure it wadded her up, though now at least she understood why that was: All this time that she had been fencing with the more obvious hardships, she had been battling inwardly a bigger challenge—that to her heart. What frightened her suddenly about that struggle was that she had no strategy for it.

※ ※ ※

Nora did not hesitate as she drove the next day between the horse farm's yellow stables and grazing horses to find Bonnie. She knew she would be practicing on the property's show jumping course for the late-summer Hamptons Classic Horse Show. Nora was herself riding that early afternoon—on a wave of solid successes. She had just now come from her latest, one she had fashioned of surprising cunning. Determined not to let the government take advantage of her lack of time and financial resources, she had filed a motion to accelerate the schedule for her case. She had researched how to do it at the Columbia University law library. At the scheduling conference that morning she had balanced Charlie on her hip and forced tears as she emphasized with a fragile voice her vulnerability as a single mother. All counter-arguments had seemed merciless and calculating against her act, and the government had known it and had encouraged the judge to look upon Charlie's presence in the courtroom as a prop. To which she had inquired whether they would also name as a prop, if asked by the *New York Times* journalist sitting in the back of the courtroom, the worn shoes of an immigrant worker trying to recover in court unpaid wages. The judge sat back at the mention of the journalist. The government heads twisted violently. The journalist had reported on her husband's arrest. Nora had called and told her there might be a follow-up story in the government's subsequent tactics to claim property not rightfully its to claim. The judge seemed suddenly to take in the scene before him from the point of view of the press. After a thoughtful silence so as to seem as if he had come to the decision himself, he had said that he saw no reason why the case could not be dealt with expediently, and ruled to fast-track it.

Now that she had left Charlie with Beatriz, she was prepared for her next prestidigitation. She could hear with her window down the soft roll of her tires over loose gravel, and the intermittent echo of a woodpecker either signaling his territory or locating insect larvae. When she rounded the bend the dust was as thick in the air as the grave sounds of tall thoroughbreds making big, brave leaps over show jumping fences. This was the women's weekday inner sanctum. Everywhere women in beige breeches and tall black boots and tucked short-sleeved white shirts tended to things equestrian. Nora looked upon the scene as if upon another world. The conformity of their attire and patterns shed an even brighter light on the frightening conventionality of their lives. The women seemed to her now like marionettes in a gilded toy store looking, if at all, through protective glass upon the real world of struggles and triumphs.

A horse at that moment knocked down the topmost horizontal bar of a fence. The clanging drew her attention to Bonnie. Bonnie and her horse were dressed immaculately, the horse in a white, square saddle pad with an English saddle, a figure-eight noseband bridle, running martingale, open-fronted tendon boots on its forelegs, and fetlock boots on its rear, and she erect on its back in the same costume as the other women, but with an additional dark-colored coat. Nora had not recognized her at first because her hair was tucked beneath her riding helmet, but now the figure riding a well-planned line to the next fence became familiar. Nora parked her car and walked down to the edge of the ring to watch her. Again and then once more, the horse that must have been twenty hands high jumped cleanly, his rider beaming with pride and then looking about as she drew rein as if to see who had been watching. She was startled when she saw that her audience was Nora, and then a look of defiance slowly came over her face. Nora was standing where the horse would be led out and back to its stable and there was no way that Bonnie and her horse could avoid her. Nora could see that Bonnie was assessing this and she seemed then to dismount slowly and to become overly preoccupied in combing through her horse's mane with her fingers. Nora waited patiently, her eyes concentrated on Bonnie.

Finally, Bonnie led her horse toward her.

"It's so good to see you, Nora!" Bonnie had drawn up before her with the reins hanging between two hands. The horse breathed heavily and gave its head a dusty shake.

Nora stood her ground. This was no time to be scared of horses. She reached out and stroked the horse's neck. "And you, Bonnie, are just the woman I want to see. I need your help."

"Oh."

Nora went on, "I understand you have town contacts."

Bonnie's face drew tight.

Nora smiled sweetly and said with a calmness that was coming naturally, "There's a meeting next week on whether or not to issue me a permit to bake commercially from my summer kitchen. It's all quite ridiculous as there's really no good reason why I shouldn't be allowed to continue, but I would be most appreciative if you would put in a positive word for me with your contacts just to be sure all goes well."

At first Nora saw relief in Bonnie's face, relief that Nora didn't know after all that she had already gone to her contacts with the opposite intent. The traces of a smirk appeared around Bonnie's mouth as she said, "Of course I'll try to help, though I'm not sure my little voice will impact what the town believes is best for the community."

"You're much too modest, Bonnie," Nora responded. "Your philanthropy has earned you a great deal of influence. And I know how well you will press the point to support me. Oh, and did I mention I saw you the other weekend? It was the funniest thing. That was my friend's orchard you pulled into to buy apple wood, and after you and George took off so fast, not only with the apple wood but also with a few of his rhubarb plants, he very lightheartedly said he felt like the victim of a hit-and-run."

Bonnie suddenly gripped the reins so tightly in her hands that her knuckles turned as white as her face. She seemed to grip them for dear life. As she did so, she cast a hurried look about to see whether anyone had overheard. Though there were people all about, they were all out of earshot, which did not stop Bonnie checking again.

As Nora took all this in, the balmy blossom-scented air of spring encompassed her, and the smells of new life seemed all at once the truest perfume of victory.

Nora added, "It struck me as so uncanny that he would use that expression."

A long silence ensued wherein Bonnie took the full measure of Nora's intent, and then slowly Bonnie composed herself and said with the return of the familiar powdery tone, "I'm sure you're right, Nora, and it's kind of you to say so: Perhaps I *can* help you, after all. I'll call some people I know tonight, and I'm sure they can be persuaded to understand your *harmlessness*."

Bonnie raised her voice at the end of the last word, and to the question she made of it, Nora answered, "Completely harmless, I assure you, if the permit is issued and there are no further complications down the road."

Bonnie gave a slow nod, acknowledging their tacit agreement.

"Well, good, then," Nora said jauntily. "I'm so glad we had this chance to talk. Do be sure to let me know if ever you need anything baked for any of your functions. I would be so disappointed to learn of you ever hiring another dessert caterer."

That fleeting look of awe she had seen pass across Bonnie's face at the bakery back in winter when she, Nora, spoke the truth of her situation for the first time now passed across it again. Nora knew then that she could count not only on the permit but also on more business. Walking back to the car, she surmised from the silence behind her that Bonnie was standing leaden, watching.

But already Nora's mind was picking up to a gallop toward the next fence.

SUMMER

Thirteen

Thomas's mom had never ridden bikes with him and Nicholas and Charlie before his dad went away. Yet that morning she had ridden Nicholas's bike right up the drive, standing high on the pedals to exert more force to the wheels. He and his brothers had moved on their own bikes and scooters to the side of the drive to watch, glancing at one another to be sure the others were seeing this. "Whee!" she had squealed on her way back the first time from the end of the drive. She was sitting down then on the bike seat, her legs flying out to the sides like wings. "It's fun, isn't it!" he had shouted. She had nodded her head excitedly as she flew past. "This is what we do!" he hollered after her, elated to be finally showing her the world he and his brothers had created these past months while hanging about the fringes of all the baking and activity that had been going on.

He later gave a tour of the vegetable garden Reuben had helped Nicholas start. They planned to hold a vegetable festival when the seeds sprouted. They had even unearthed a rope fire-ladder and had assembled it over a rock ledge. "We can hold a rock climbing competition," he had explained, "and give out prizes of baseball cards and shiny rocks and turkey feathers." They had fashioned teepees from saplings, too, in which people could rest after the competition. But his mom's favorite had been their garden Christmas scene, a real pine tree in the center, garlands of wilting daisies draped over sun-glistening pine needles, twig boxes tied in ribbons of grass beneath like presents.

Feeling such joyful surprise at the opportunity to share his world with a parent was a new thing. His dad had often played outside with him and his brothers, kicked around the soccer ball, batted a few pitches, wrestled on the grass, assembled new toys. He remembered one summer evening when they had set up a tent in front of the house and waited inside it on bean bags past twilight to spot bats. Not that he wanted to be taken wrong. Before his dad went away, his mom had done things with them, too, took them to lessons and parties, places on weekends, but he could never have imagined his mom waiting to spot a bat. She had usually been so busy arranging those lessons and trips, and then on her cell phone during them arranging others.

After his dad went away, his mom was no longer busy on the phone or with guests, but even more of her seemed lost. There had not even been Beatriz to go to after a while, since she became busy with his mom. He had wondered whether what he had begun feeling was loneliness, for there were not many other children left in his life. He had not seen his old friends since he left that school. He kept asking his mom for a while if he could have play dates with them, but she always said probably they were busy. Eventually he gave up, though he understood there was more to it when he overheard his mom talking to Beatriz about why she had really canceled his party. So his old friends weren't friends anymore, and if he wanted to see his friends from his new school, his mom needed to drive him, or their moms needed to drive them. The arranging of it either way was beyond his control, and he felt he was imposing to ask, his mom had that much to do, or was forever saying she did.

For all that he loved his property, he had begun to wish they lived on a regular suburban street like those streets in Australia where play dates happened naturally. He and his brothers and Mom and Dad had spent a few months in Australia a few years back, in a rented house on a street close to a golden sand beach where he and Nicholas learned to ride surfboards. His mom and dad had wanted them to have an authentic Australian experience, living among the locals, shopping at their open markets, eating Vegemite sandwiches and sucking the juicy interiors out of the thick, hard skins of passion fruit ripened to a deep purple on the vine. They had lemon trees in their back garden, too, and squeezed them every day to make lemonade. The houses in that inner coastal suburb were all close together on small plots of land. The "yard" was either the beach or the street. The street was closed at one end, and so only local cars drove through, and slowly because of children at play. Every afternoon the kids along that street emerged from their houses the way men in suits emerged en masse from buildings around five o'clock. For hours until the sun went down late they would ride their bikes up and down the street and play chase and other games that they would invent.

Here in Bedford he couldn't even see his neighbors' houses, and the neighbor to one side in any case was that miserable old man suing his mom for not having had that fallen tree moved off his property. The boy to the other side was a few years older, and had only emerged a few times recently, once to cut the tops off his mom's flowers—the potted ones he, Nicholas, and Charlie had helped her plant in the spring when he had first felt her coming back. They had smeared one another's cheeks with so much dirt that by the end of that day, shirts untucked, twigs through hair, they resembled a family of scarecrows. The other time the boy next door emerged was back in winter to throw stones at their garage door. His, Thomas's, mom caught him at it. The door never opened properly now, and his mom was forever getting out of the car to jiggle it. She tried fixing it intermittently, whenever mice found their way in again through the gap created by the door closing now on an angle. Once she stuffed the gap with rubber, but the mice ate right through it. So she set traps after that, glue ones she stabbed with a stick to lift with their open-mouthed catch into plastic bags.

He was happy most of the time playing with his brothers, though he was always cleaning up after Nicholas, and Charlie followed him everywhere. He often needed to teach them things, too, like when Nicholas had thought *suffer* and *suffocate* meant the same thing, or when Charlie had wanted to know where the trees went to sleep. He didn't even mind all the stuff they used to have being gone, the plasma TVs and video games and pinball machines and battery-operated cars to drive up and down the drive. The only times he missed those things was when his mom told him to "quit asking me what you should do," or "think of something yourself for you and your brothers to do," or "imagine your own way out of your boredom." But soon enough he and his brothers would invent some game or project, and it was always worth it for Beatriz's pride in their resourcefulness. He had come to appreciate the simpler life she had been showing them all along. It was way more fun building forts, climbing trees, spotting cloud-animals, dredging dead fish from the pond, though that was more Nicholas's area. Nicholas had stashes around the house now of discovered snakeskins, beetles, tadpoles, bird nests, wasp wings— trophies from their free time spent now finding their amusement around the property. But that fun he was having outside until the mosquitoes started nipping and they would hurry Nicholas inside was not enough. Really he missed his dad *and* his mom. And then Beatriz and Reuben announced their engagement the night before he ran away and he felt so miserable it had been all he could do to play chess with Reuben.

Charlie had climbed onto Reuben's lap, wanting to watch, but he kept grabbing Reuben's pawns, refusing to return them.

"Charlie!" Thomas had screamed.

"Charlie, don't touch the pieces," Reuben had tried reasoning.

Reuben gently rested a bishop from Charlie's clenched fist, ducking his head from one side to the other around Charlie's squirming body to see the board.

Suddenly Charlie jerked backward, smashing Reuben's nose with the back of his head. Reuben's face clenched shut in pain at the same instant as Charlie's flailing feet sent half the pieces scuttling to the floor. Thomas felt something within him erupt. He snatched a piece remaining on the board and hurled it at the wall on the opposite side of the room. The wall at least was his intended aim. Somehow, though, the king left his hand at a sideways trajectory and came crashing down to the floor with shards of glass after an echoing crack like a whip. Silence hung a long while in the air.

Quietly he told his mom, "You can use the money from my piggy bank to fix the window." His anger had shattered with the glass.

He pretty much understood without being told they had been scraping by.

His mom had not wanted his money, but she had given him a time-out. He was happy to do it, happy to be by himself. He felt even more miserable than before the chess game. In his bedroom he took out the drawer under which he kept his stash. He took up the one-dollar bill his father had given him and fell back into the bean bag in the corner. In the absence of anything else to do, he examined the bill. He read the name Washington under the picture he recognized from the history section of "What Your Second Grader Needs to Know" that his mom was reading to him before she went off to her job at the bakery. He turned the bill over and wondered what the words *Annuit Coeptis* meant on one side of the Great Seal, and what *E Pluribus Unum* meant on the other side. He started counting the letters in the mottos. Thirteen in one case, thirteen also in the other.

Then he counted the layers in the pyramid under the eye, all under the motto *Annuit Coeptis*. Also thirteen. He wondered what to make of the thirteen theme. There were still crease lines in the bill where his dad had folded it into a tiny square to hand over to him. He tried to picture his father folding it as precisely as origami, or like a note. Wait a minute: In the crease lines there *was* a note. He sat upright and looked more closely. The writing was tiny. It appeared in the crease as a black streak. But when he snapped the bill straight he saw there were a series of words in perfect block letters. He tried to make them out. "I'll," he read, "be mone"—no, that wasn't it— "home." Then, "Soo-soon." He had it. "I'll be home soon, my son."

He read the words over and over, his heart singing now as though his dad had suddenly materialized. He *was*, he *was*: He was coming home. He had started counting the days down when his dad first went away, but he could not recall what number he had been up to the day he forgot to keep counting. Surely it could not be long now. It had felt like a hundred years already. He fell back again into his bean bag, his arms spread now to either side, one hand still clenched around the bill, his dreamy gaze up at the ceiling, and tried to imagine how it would be when his dad came home. Would they pull up like in the movies to find him standing outside the gates, waiting with his belongings hanging from his hand in a plastic bag? But then his dad had told him he had no belongings in prison but his toothbrush, and in any case he had said he would be going to some place called a halfway house first. And what after that? Would he live with them again? Where else would he go? He tried picturing his dad walking in from work at the end of the day, he and his brothers jumping all over him before he had set down his keys, his dad and mom then kissing hello and then everyone sitting down to dinner. He even tried imagining how his dad would get up from the table to get him and his brothers more milk and jump at the slimy goo they would have stuck as a gag on the refrigerator handle. They would howl with laughter. Wouldn't they? Somehow the images refused to take shape easily.

The fact was his mom and dad didn't get along anymore.

He turned onto his side in the bean bag and buried his face under a crooked arm. After a while he heard his mother calling that his time-out was over and that he could come back downstairs if he liked, but he stayed where he was and he must have fallen asleep, for the next thing he was half aware of was being lifted by his mom into bed.

When he woke in the morning he went to return his note to his stash, but instead slid the note and his credit card into the pocket of the clean pants he had put on. After his mom dropped him and Nicholas at the curb running along the school façade, he had found himself standing rather than moving toward the front entrance. Up ahead yellow buses stood in line taking turns like atomizers spraying out boys and girls. Beatriz's car had disappeared behind the buses and now emerged again heading out behind the parking lot on the mound, then disappeared again behind a truck entering the school. He had seen the truck at the school before. He liked the pictures on its sides of a table set for a party. He also liked the words "New Jersey." They made him feel close to his dad the way the note had on the dollar bill. Nicholas had been calling to him to come on. He told Nicholas to go ahead without him. Nicholas had shrugged and then got lost amid other heads. The truck parked in the second lot up to the right. The driver in a green uniform like the one his dad wore now began piling boxes from the back into a hand trolley. He knew what was in them. He had seen them being opened once in the cafeteria: paper cups, napkins, plastic cutlery. He waited for the driver to wheel his load down the hill and into school and then he walked up the mound casually and climbed into the opened back of the truck.

He had thought for a while that someone would come to get him. But then the doors slammed shut and he heard a bolt locking into place and soon the hard cold floor beneath him started vibrating like he was

on the seat of a bicycle riding over rocks. The roar of the motor rever-
berated loudly in the back of the truck. It occurred to him no one
would hear him even if he shouted. And so he tried instead to settle
into his adventure. Intermittently he wondered where they were. When
he started to hear swishing traffic he guessed they were on I-684. That
was the way he remembered they had gone to New Jersey. After a long
while they stopped for longer than for what he had earlier presumed
were traffic lights. He heard the driver's door slam and then the driver
whistling as he walked to the back of the truck. The click of a bolt, and
then sunlight. It stung for a moment the way suntan lotion did when it
mixed in the summer with his sweat and dripped off his brow into his
eye and he found himself blinking. The whistling continued as the
driver unloaded more boxes, but just as he had blinked away the stinging in his eyes and was thinking this was the time to declare himself
and to see how far he was from his dad, the door shut again, and the
bolt clunked. For a long while he heard nothing, and then voices, male
voices, two.

"What's all that red stuff around your lips?" one asked.

"Had a kids' birthday gig last night," the other responded. "Takes
days to get this damn clown makeup off."

"Whatcha mean, clown makeup? You a fuckin' clown for a second
job?"

"That's Mr. fuckin' clown to you, jackoff!" And then he gave a
clown's laugh. "Hyuk, Hyuk, Hyuk."

Thomas suddenly had trouble breathing. Tears pricked his eyes.
Ever since he had seen a bit of a film called *Killer Klowns from Outer
Space* at a play date a few years ago when his friend's older brother
had been watching it, clowns had terrified him. Now he imagined on
the other side of the truck a man with big feet, pointy teeth, a creepy
expression that never shifted. Was that the same man driving this
truck? He couldn't be sure. He pulled his knees tighter to his chest,

sure now that he was going to die. He stayed that way through more vibrating and jolting and two more stops, moving only to reach reluctantly for an empty jar in the corner to pee in, until at a stop again, the truck was opened and hands reached for the box behind which he crouched.

He didn't open his eyes again until a new voice announced itself as a policeman and asked him where was home. When his mom had run into the police station exclaiming, "Tom, Tom," as she opened her arms wide, he had wanted to cry with relief. They had just clung to each other.

In the car, his mom had talked of forgiving his dad and he had relaxed finally and closed his eyes, and for a while before sleep came he had floated on the comforting melody of his mom giving Beatriz directions. And then Beatriz drew his mom's attention to the yellow and purple wildflowers blanketing a field to the side of the highway, a pleasant contrast apparently to abandoned auto parts rusting a mile back among roadside weeds. His mom had responded that the only difference between a weed and a flower was perspective. Beatriz had asked what she meant. After a silence so long he thought his mom wasn't going to answer, his mom had asked another question, "How do you really judge someone? How do you judge between good and bad?" Beatriz didn't answer. His mom continued, "I had it all wrong. I was the one who was bad. I was bad because I was so good. It was so important to me to fit that I betrayed myself and my family. And Evan: He is not a bad man at all, but a good man who did a bad thing. Only judgment made him a bad man."

Thomas had opened his eyes slightly then. Beatriz glanced over her shoulder briefly at his mom. He closed his eyes again. His mom talked more, her voice deeper, softer, calmer. All this time, his mom was saying of herself, she had been as judgmental of Evan as the women of Bedford. She felt ashamed to realize it, yet at the same

time liberated. In fact, it seemed to her suddenly as though the residual icy angst within her was melting to water—soft, pliable, flowing.
"And able to accept things as water does," Beatriz had contributed.
After a moment, his mom had said that yes, she supposed that was
it. She had come this night finally to accept—as her boys had accepted all along—that what had happened was simply what had happened.

"Hurray," Beatriz had said.

"What?" his mom had asked.

"Acceptance," Beatriz had answered. "You've finally arrived."

"Finally? You mean you've been expecting it?"

Beatriz chuckled. "A recovering alcoholic knows better than anyone that the key to peace, strength, forgiveness, all, is acceptance. I
found my footing after stumbling many times the day I accepted finally what I could never change and what I still could."

He had slept late the next morning, a Saturday, and after he woke
and his mom had said good-bye to her friend Ticky, he and his mom
began to talk. Not in any way they had before. Sitting on floor cushions with the sun bathing them through the window and the house
quiet for Beatriz having taken Nicholas and Charlie to the playground,
his mom had brought up all the uncomfortable subjects whose questions had been eating at him. She had explained that his dad had not
left because of him, Nicholas, Charlie, or her. He had no choice. She
had explained that whereas once they had more money, now they had
less, but that money was fluid and came and went in life, and that
when it came back to them they would not build their life around it
again, for that was like building a house in a flood zone. That was not
where security was to be found. She had told him that she had lost
friends, too, but had made better ones, and so would he, and that
though she was busier than ever, it was in a good and focused and
happy way now. She had said it was good for him to see how someone
could love working like a fool at something they loved, though she had

also become mindful of involving him, Nicholas, and Charlie. When they took a walk around the property, they were still talking and asking of each other a lot of "How comes?" There were also a lot of "Mmms" and "I sees." And they had shared their wishes.

"I wish Daddy would come home," he had said.

"I wish I could bring him home for you right now," his mom had responded.

They had sat in silence awhile after that.

Then he had asked, "Did you mean it when you said you wanted to bring us into what you do? 'Cause we want to help you, Mom, Charlie and Nicholas and me. We want to help with the café you told us about, help you in our own way pay for things."

"I could do with three smart helpers," she had said.

That day with his mom had been a golden day.

The following weekend she had taken him to see his dad. Nicholas and Charlie stayed home with Beatriz. His mom had said that Thomas needed time alone with his father. The others had protested that so did they. His mom had promised to take them each alone in coming weeks. He had been so happy just to be molded into the comforting crook of his father's arm and to watch his mom and dad interact in a quiet, new, easy way that felt nice to be around. His dad had come out in his pressed green uniform and smooth-shaven face to join them with a look at his mom that at first seemed shaped as a question mark. But his mom had answered it with a soft smile that made his dad bite his bottom lip and nod as his eyes moistened. Something was understood between them without words.

He had experienced this easiness about his mom again just this past weekend—when she took him and his brothers swimming in a country stream. In they waded in one hitched group. The water was ice-cold and felt good in the new heat, and soon enough he and Nicholas and Charlie were scampering over the rocks, slipping on the mossy ones here and there, splashing madly to regain a footing, and then laughing and doing it all over. He had expected his mom to say, "Be careful!" or "Watch!" or "Not so deep!" but instead she waded in deeper and called to them to follow. "You'll be fine!" she hollered above the echoing rush of water between rocks. They hesitated at first, with disbelieving grins. "Come on, boys!" One by one they made it over to her, and found she had discovered a pool, wide enough to swim across, in just a few strokes, but only as deep as up to Charlie's chin, so they could all stand. They scooped up armfuls of water and splashed one another, and his mom dove under and tickled their ankles, so that they squealed thinking it was fish. They did it to her then and she squealed even louder. Even when it showered briefly, they stayed in the water, practicing blowing bubbles and floating like four-pronged stars and diving for glossy pebbles until their skin wrinkled and the sunny bank grew more appealing. The rain shower had stopped by then.

It had been his mom's thirty-seventh birthday the day before, but her plans to join Beatriz, Reuben, Phillip, and his mom's new friend, Ticky, at that dinner place were spoiled when Charlie threw up all over her black dress and she had stayed home to care for him. "We'll come to you!" Beatriz had insisted from the restaurant. Beatriz and Reuben had gone there from Reuben's home. "No, no, no, I have no idea if it's contagious." His mom had insisted the others go ahead with dinner. The restaurant had delivered four cupcakes, each with a single candle, and Beatriz and Reuben and Phillip and Ticky had called to sing "Happy Birthday." His mom had put it on speakerphone: "One candle for the first year of your new life!"

His mom told him that it had been the strangest but most heartfelt birthday she had ever had. He and Nicholas and Charlie had given her grass floor mats they wove themselves for the secondhand canary-yellow Volkswagen Beetle they had known their mom had made arrangements to buy for herself for her birthday. His mom had taken them for a drive, Charlie still wearing his Spider-Man costume with a ski hat for a mask because he had lost the mask. Nicholas had brought his Rubik's Cube. The car was a convertible and his mom had folded back the top. Nicholas yelled, "Whoo-hoo," over the noisy engine as they bumped over the dirt roads. After that they all joined in with their own whoo-hoos. It was like being in a deafening open-air ride over at Rye Playland Amusement Park: You never knew when you were going to go fast or slow or be bucked.

His dad had sent a book of stamps. "He's helping the only way he can," Beatriz had said. His mom had nodded, tears in her eyes.

Digger had given her a card with his name signed by himself. He and Nicholas and Charlie had held a pen in his paw and had guided the paw in the shape of the letters. They were practiced at doing this with Digger, since they often sent letters to their dad from him, the letters recounting all that was happening in Bedford from Digger's view. They signed them with Digger's paw-print.

Nicholas had given her an extra present. He had covered his teepee in bark pulled from dead trees, not live ones—lest he cause the tree some infection—and gave her a voucher for one night's accommodation. He had even promised to sit outside on watch all night, to make sure no night creatures bothered her. She had suggested they run a noise machine instead, to scare the animals away, but Nicholas had said, "No! That might hurt their poor ears!" Besides, he had said, "Imagine how many wishes I can make on stars over a whole night!"

Beatriz and Reuben had given her Reuben's two-hundred-year-old wood-burning oven. He had built a fireplace in the barn to keep it warm in future winters when the electricity failed. He and Beatriz thought the oven would be perfect for roasting nuts at the café.

Ticky had arranged and prepaid the birthday dinner at that dinner place.

Phillip had arranged for a crate of Kakadu Plum jam to be sent from Australia.

A vase of flowers was delivered with a card his mom read aloud. "Happy Birthday, Love, Bonnie. P.S. Why didn't you tell me you were opening your own café!"

His mom just laughed.

Charlie was fine again the following morning and so his mom intended to celebrate her birthday properly at a special stream. She had made a giant hummingbird cake, damp with pineapple and mango pieces mixed throughout, all covered in thick, sweetened, cream-cheese icing. As she marked enormous portions with a knife while they sat cross-legged on damp grass in towels wrapped around their shoulders, Nicholas spotted a rainbow. A second stretched fainter behind.

"Mom, can you take us to slide down the rainbow one day?" Nicholas asked.

"Well, darling, rainbows aren't really there."

"Yeah! Jack at school said so. He said he slid down one once. So can we? Some people say there's a pot of gold at the end."

"Ah, the Irish leprechaun's pot of gold. Well, it's certainly a good hiding place, because no one can ever get to the end of the rainbow. Try it! Whenever you walk toward a rainbow, it will seem to move farther away."

Nicholas jumped up and starting running up the embankment.

"Shoes!"

But Nicholas didn't listen. He and Charlie stood up then, too, and they all took off up the embankment and over the field beyond.

He became aware that his mom was catching up to them.

He stopped and turned. When she reached him she stopped, and put her arm about him. "You know, Tom," she said, panting a little, though her voice still sounded, as it had begun to of late, kind of lower, softer, a bit fuller. Somewhere close a bird began to sing. "The rainbow is a symbol of peace, a sign that the deluge is behind us."

He smiled because his mom's happiness seemed so big.

"We're in bare feet," his mom went on, "chasing a rainbow! In bare feet chasing a rainbow! It's over! It's all over! Come on," she said then, "I'll race you!"

And she took off that day last weekend with as much life as she had that very morning on his bike on their drive, her legs out to the sides like wings as she flew past.

Yes, his mom was back, and more.

Fourteen

Nora pulled up in her Bug that same warm late June Saturday morning outside Joe's TV store on Church Street. Beatriz and Phillip had insisted she take a couple of hours for herself. She planned to drive over to Phillip's and sit like a regular adult with a tea and a newspaper. A newspaper! She had not read one in so long! She looked forward now to that simple pleasure the way she had once anticipated a week in the Caribbean. But first she needed to buy a new three-pronged thingamajig that connected the TV to the DVD player. At least that was what she thought was needed. This past week she had not been able to get a picture on the TV when she turned on the DVD player, no matter how many times they all spanked the TV. A bell jingled as she entered the store. No one else seemed to be inside. The store smelled of dogs. Indeed, two dogs suddenly jumped up against a plastic safety gate between the store and the office out back and barked. They gave Nora a fright and she started. "Down, boys," a woman's voice called out from deeper inside the office. Nora stared into the office. On the desk was an empty jar of Hellmann's mayonnaise, a mangled plastic dog bone, and an antiquated radio, the type with a big dial on the front. A man on the radio was discussing the backlash against SUVs. Nora picked up a

hard candy from a bowl on the counter. It had been stuck to a cluster. The candies had seen better days. Still, she popped it into her
mouth. The voice presumably belonged to a dough-faced woman
who sidled past the dogs, shutting them back in. She was so heavy
she shuffled rather than walked. She wore an oversized frayed man's
shirt, tucked into an oversized pair of man's pants.

"Hi," Nora started. "I think I might need—"

"I'll be with you in just a minute," the woman said in a friendly
tone. "Just gotta finish this one thing I'm doing. My husband's out in
the field, you see, and so it's just me here." She brushed some crumbs
off the counter onto the floor and set down some device she had
been carrying in her hands. She poked inside it with a pair of pliers.
There came one and then two plinking sounds. "Funny business, this
TV business," the woman went on, her head lowered now almost inside the device. She did not seem bothered by the thin strands of lank
grayish-blond hair in her face. The woman's hands fascinated Nora.
They were enormous and steady and capable. "Quiet one minute, busy
as anything the next."

Nora smiled to herself. "I've never noticed this store before," she
said. She shifted the candy with her tongue to the other side of her
mouth. It knocked against her teeth. "If a man I work with hadn't
told me about you, I'd never have known you were here."

"We're tucked back a bit, that's true. Better that way. Don't get so
busy. More time for our dogs." She gave a little chuckle. "And each
other."

Nora wondered how it was then they got customers.

As if reading Nora's mind, the woman said, "Enough people know
about us." *Plink.* The woman looked up suddenly, setting the pliers
down on the counter. "And enough is plenty," she said. "Now, what
did you say it was you needed?"

Nora studied the woman intently. In her former life she would
have considered this woman . . . well, likely she would never have

come across a woman like this in her former life, but if she had she would have considered her a hard-luck story.

She had it all backward.

"Yes, it is," Nora said after a moment. "Enough is plenty, isn't it?"

On her way out of the store with the plugs the woman had pressed into her hands—"free of charge, since it's such a small thing"—a group of children the approximate ages of her own caught her eye. They were playing some game on the pavement. She found herself heading over to them. It was so hot already that the pavement was giving off radiant heat. She felt as though she had entered a painting: She had only seen this street of small, close homes and tiny, proud gardens through the frame of her car window. She passed the only other store on the street besides Joe's—a tiny grocery with wooden crates of fruit and racks of newspapers out front. She paused to let a construction worker with a tool belt hanging around his waist step out, a steaming Styrofoam cup in his hand. "No, no, after you," he said with a smile before greeting someone behind her. The people along Church Street seemed so happy, and she was beginning to understand why: They had something more than money, something none of her neighbors could buy—a genuine connection with other people.

On a porch across the road a young woman sat in a rocker knitting as the cooing of a baby sounded from a bassinet beside her. A man walked out to join them, the spring-hinged screen door slamming behind him, and stood beside the woman. Absentmindedly, he stroked her hair. An ache of longing overcame Nora so that for a moment she fought down tears. No one but her children touched her so familiarly anymore. The man pointed over at a verdant elm on the fence line before the next house. Nora followed the line of his arm. The man was evidently discussing the new-looking plastic baby swing roped from one of the elm's high branches, but Nora's eyes landed beyond the swing at the next house. A quality about it, ram-

bling and dignified at the same time, captured her attention. The
house reminded her of one of those old ladies so graceful that they
hardly seemed old at all. It was small, the size really of those little
outbuildings on grand estates, though its irregular shape and unusual tiered height gave it largesse. It was built of stone, with wood-
framed windows to match a wooden porch, and on either side of the
front door were panels of intricate stained glass. The flowering garden around the half-tennis-court square of clipped lawn before the
pavement was equally colorful, but charming more in its modesty
than in its intricacy.

The street was so delightfully humble: It was hard to believe this
was still Bedford. It was as if she were seeing the town suddenly
turned inside out, or rather she had been looking at things inside out
before, for now it seemed she was seeing everything in its true form.
This street all at once felt like the town's true heart.

She reached the children. "What are you playing?" she asked
them.

Another child was approaching on a bike. She heard him before
she saw him. He was ringing his bicycle bell excitedly to warn her.
She stepped back onto someone's lawn to let him pass, plastic stream-
ers flapping off the back of his bike in his wake.

"Jacks," one of the children on the ground answered her. He didn't
look up.

"Oh! I used to play that when I was a girl. I'd forgotten all about it!"

She watched as the children took turns cupping the little stones
they were using as jacks, flipping them onto the back of one hand,
then back to their cupped hand again. A Hispanic girl dropped the
least and so she went first. She scattered the jacks over the circle of
ground in the center of all the children, bounced a small rubber ball,
and then madly picked up as many jacks as she could before the ball
bounced again.

"Do you know other variations of the game?" she asked them.

They all looked up at her blankly.

"Toad in the Hole? Snakes in the Grass? Threading the Needle?"

They continued staring at her.

"Would you like me to teach you?"

They all looked at one another and shrugged.

"Sure," said an athletic-looking white boy about Thomas's age. He wore a baseball cap with the brim to the back. "What's your name?" he asked.

"Nora, and yours?"

"Lukey, but they call me Lucky because I always win everything."

Nora laughed.

And then she sat down cross-legged in a space they made for her in their circle, put aside her funny-looking plugs, and started teaching them Over the Line.

❊ ❊ ❊

As she strode an hour later over the village green toward the booth she and Phillip were manning that day for the Family Baker competition she had arranged, she was still floating on the ecstatic disbelief of having revisited in a manner her childhood. So she was caught off guard when a woman unknown to her standing idly by stopped to ask her could she believe that the proceeds of this competition were to help children of incarcerated parents?

"I mean couldn't the people running this have chosen a more local cause? There are so many of them, the John Jay Homestead, the Westchester Land Trust. . . ."

"Well," Nora said, "I'm sure you wouldn't want to forget about that other very local institution of ours at the far end of Harris Road's line of horse properties?"

At first the woman did not seem to know what Nora meant, and then it must have occurred to her, for her face flushed and she shifted the bag on her shoulder.

Nora added with a light note of sarcasm, "The children of women incarcerated in the Bedford Hills Correctional Facility may not be as prestigious a cause as maintaining old buildings or preserving Bedford's bucolic beauty, but surely families and children with real problems right in our faces are considered worthy by the women of Bedford? And surely you've considered that some of the children needing the help of that other favored charity—the Boys and Girls Club—are in fact children of incarcerated parents? Maybe even children of mothers up at the far end of Harris Road, which happens to be the largest women's prison in the state of New York."

She left the woman standing red-faced and stunned.

"Grrr," she said to Phillip in greeting, wondering at the same time whatever the woman must be thinking, seeing her, Nora, now behind the booth.

"No need even to tell me," Phillip laughed.

Nora smiled. "Thanks for my break," she said.

"No drama," he said. "Anything for a mate." He hoisted up his togs (swimming trunks), and refitted his bare feet into his thongs (flip-flops). He had come directly from a three A.M. surf over in Long Island. There was still sand crusted to his toes, and his nose was white with zinc cream. Why he needed zinc cream at three A.M. Nora wasn't sure—or perhaps that was a recent addition: The sun was blazing now. He still wore his Driza-Bone hat. He placed a hand on Nora's shoulder. "You've helped me a lot, too—though that stands out like a shag on a rock, doesn't it? I'm a whole different fella now, aren't I?"

Phillip *had* seemed revitalized of late. Nora had never heard of him surfing at three A.M. before, for instance.

Nora stood on her tiptoes and kissed Phillip's cheek. He smelled of the strained Greek yogurt he had started eating for breakfast lately with raw almonds and honey.

He shuffled his feet and dug his hands into the front pockets of his togs.

Nora looked over the table. "I see we have quite a number of entries already."

The soon-to-be-opened Summer Kitchen Bakery-Café had invited local women to enter either cookies or a pie baked according to their favorite family recipe. At noon Nora would taste them all and select the best. When the café launched, she would name the winning cookies and pies after their family—Kittlebrush Family Pie, for instance, or Griswald Family Cookies—and sell them for a month, with all proceeds benefiting the group she was founding. It seemed she had been right to count on bragging rights to encourage involvement, but that was fine if it helped to raise money and awareness.

Phillip said, "Yep, so many have been by that the deviled eggs you asked me to put out for them have all gone. The hubbies love 'em. One ate five while his trouble-and-strife [wife] gave me an earbashing about the history of her family recipe."

"So let's make more." Nora tied on a black-and-white checked apron, wiped her hands on a damp cloth, and retrieved the wire baskets of preboiled eggs from the cooler.

"You know," Phillip said, clearing a space on the table of entries for them to work. One pie tipped a little over the edge in his rush and he jumped to upright it. "Something I've noticed today. I do believe that these sheilas have taken to dressing like you. I mean, these private-school sheilas have been coming into my café for years now, and I have never, I mean never, seen any of 'em in khakis and T-shirts and white canvas sneakers. Yet three of 'em this morning were wearing just that."

Nora laughed. She set the baskets down on the table and handed

Phillip an egg to peel. She took up another one and started peeling it herself. "I'm sure it's coincidence."

"I don't reckon," Phillip responded. "It makes sense. Hear me out . . ."

Nora plopped her first peeled egg into a bowl and picked up another.

"I mean they didn't look *exactly* like you," Phillip said. He plopped his egg into his bowl. "Only there was something contrived about their appearance. Their T-shirts were tucked in and belted, and their sneakers looked straight out of the box. Really everything looked straight out of the box, you know?"

"You mean their pants and sneakers weren't smeared with butter stains and splattered in crusted bits of chocolate and dough as mine always are?"

"I mean they didn't carry the look with the same casualness you do."

"Phillip," she said. *Plop.* "I'm not trying to carry any look."

"That's just it."

She peeked over into his bowl. "I'm beating you," she said.

He picked up his pace again.

"You don't care," he said.

"That I'm beating you?"

"Nuh, nuh." *Plop, plop.* "You don't care to live up to a myth any longer, to waste your energy keeping one alive. I bet these sheilas expected you to try to win your way back into their society, but instead they eat your desserts at functions now, and have to listen to their hubbies moaning. Every time they drive through the village they likely see you running in or out of some mysterious café about to open. Now you flit about in this convertible Vee-dub that is the complete antithesis to the gas-guzzling machines they all drive. And then they have to read your quote in that local *Record-Review* article about how the café will use only small, local suppliers, to support the very idea of a self-contained lifestyle that meets the need for comfort but is not excessive. You fly in the face in every way of their avid con-sumerism and yet seem utterly unconcerned. You instead wear this tremendous relief for not having to be any longer what this commu-nity expects."

This was a long-winded spiel for a man of few words, though his frankness was hardly new. Nora had stopped peeling eggs and was staring at him a bit uncertainly.

Phillip kept peeling and plopping and talking.

"That style comes of being free to be yourself—and of being ex-ceptionally unembittered at the end of the day and what would seem to be increasingly self-fulfilled. I bet you London to a brick it's allur-ing to these sheilas exactly because such completeness eludes 'em. Since it's inconceivable for anything not to be acquirable, they've set out by way of emulation to purchase it. Of course, I doubt they're conscious of all this—"

He was cut short just then by that familiar powdery voice.

"I hope I'm not too late?" Bonnie called from a little way across the green.

She reached them and set a platter of cookies down on the counter.

"They look lovely," Nora said, knifing her eggs in half lengthwise and then pressing the yolks through a miniature transportable food mill into a bowl.

"I couldn't not contribute to your little charity!" Bonnie said with characteristic breathlessness. "Though I did have to stay up very late to get these done. George didn't get home until ten o'clock last night, and I would never eat without him. We weren't done with dinner until midnight, and then the strangest thing happened. I went to put his briefcase in his office for him as I customarily do each evening, and realized that there was something different about it. 'Did you buy a new briefcase?' I asked him. 'Because this one'— I had looked at it more closely by then—'because another name is engraved on this one.' He had brought home another man's brief-case! I mean how in the world . . . I don't know where these men's minds are!"

Phillip shot Nora a look. She avoided it, not wanting to embarrass Bonnie, though she knew what Phillip was thinking. She had won-dered the same thing since she had noticed George once at a cocktail party slipping a very attractive young male waiter a moony look when he presumably thought no one was looking. The waiter had met the look and held it and later at the bar she had seen the waiter handing George his card. George had caressed his breast jacket pocket after slipping the card into it.

Phillip's look eluded Bonnie. "So I tried to open the briefcase to see whether there were any contact details inside for its owner. Of course George didn't like that I wasn't paying him attention any-more, and took the briefcase back and said he would address it in the morning. But meanwhile the owner of this briefcase likely had George's! Well, he hadn't thought of that, had he! Once George went to bed I found a cell phone inside the briefcase and scrolled through the stored numbers to find home. I found George's cell phone and office numbers stored in the phone, and concluded naturally that they were business associates and that the briefcase owner was prob-ably only just getting home himself and that it would be a simple matter of arranging for a courier to swap the briefcases overnight. I wanted to surprise George with his in the morning! Anyhow, I call the owner of this briefcase, apologizing of course for the hour, and af-ter I said, 'This is George Taggart's wife calling,' there was this long pause before he said, 'You'll have to talk to George . . . I don't know . . . umm . . . look, I've got to go.' Before I knew it, I was listening to a dial tone. He hung up on me! I mean, how rude! I couldn't believe it! I had to have a glass of wine and by the time my nerves had steadied and I had resolved to have George call in the morning to give a piece of his mind, it was getting on to one o'clock. But still I made these cookies for your little charity!"

Nora had been avoiding all of Phillip's looks.

"Well, I'm sure—" Nora started. She was going to say that she was sure it was all some misunderstanding, but just then Bonnie's cell phone rang.

The cell phone was in Bonnie's hand and she looked at her caller ID.

"Oh, this is George now! I left him sleeping this morning. He always needs to know exactly where I am at all times. . . ."

It was true. Whenever Nora had been with Bonnie in her old life, Bonnie had received George's calls it seemed almost constantly, and Nora had understood even back then that those who were untrustworthy themselves were often most vigilant of others.

She had never said anything, though had felt grateful Evan was never that way.

Now Nora turned to blending scoops of her own brand of mayonnaise into the pureed yolks. She added a little of her own chopped pickle and salt and pepper. She then scooped the mixture into a pastry bag with a fluted tube.

Bonnie's voice on the phone became instantly like prime skiing snow. She told George where she was and that Chloe was with Carmelita somewhere in the house and then she started to say, "George, I've got to tell you—" but he must have cut her short, for then she just said, "Oh, okay, well, all right . . . oh, I'm sorry about that . . . oh, and that, too. Actually, we've run out of the other sort. Yes, I'll pick some up this morning." And then he must have hung up abruptly, because she looked startled before recomposing herself and then quietly took the phone down from her ear and closed it.

"He's off to golf," Bonnie said flatly to no one in particular, adding almost self-chastisingly that she had mistakenly laid out non-golfing clothes for him ("I should have thought!") and the wrong type of jelly for his toast. Then suddenly she noticed Phillip and it was powder again. "But how rude of me," she said. "How *are* you, Phillip? Yes, I did read that you and Nora had become partners! How, well, wonderful for you both!"

"Beatriz, too," Phillip reminded her. "It was all her idea."

"Yes, of course."

A nanny chasing desperately over the green after a group of escaped children caught Nora's attention just as she had started piping the yolk mixture back into the whites. Bonnie followed Nora's look to a group led by that private-school mother who had turned her role as volunteer coordinator for the Bedford Youth Soccer League into a full-time job as self-designated town crier. She kept a running directory of e-mail addresses for all those with esteem in the community, and sent out en masse almost daily news not only of soccer but also of school bake sales and town shopping fairs and every other manner of neighborhood chestnut. It had surprised Nora how long it had taken this mother to realize after Evan's arrest that her mass e-mails were still going out to Nora and Evan. It took at least three weeks for the e-mails to cease.

Bonnie turned quickly back to Nora. "Let me help you," she offered sweetly.

"No, no, I've got it," Nora responded.

"Really, I insist," she said with indeed more insistence, and moved around the booth and almost elbowed Nora out of the way. Nora handed over the pastry bag and Bonnie began piping filling into the whites just as that town-crier mother reached the booth.

"How clever of you, Bonnie!" the woman said. "I'd never have thought to *pipe* deviled-egg filling back into the hardened whites. Very artistic!"

Bonnie claimed the compliment with a completely unashamed smile.

The funny thing was, Nora was not surprised. A moment earlier she had happened to look down and notice that Bonnie was wearing khakis and white canvas sneakers.

✳ ✳ ✳

The café renovations were well under way when Nora walked in that afternoon after having packed away the booth. She drew up inside the door from the suddenness, after the summer quiet outside, of construction noises—the squelch of a wet paint roller, the rubbing of sandpaper, the clank of pipes somewhere in the walls, and various conversations in Spanish that rose in volume every half minute when a hand drill whirred, and then sounded too loud when the hand drill suddenly fell silent. Behind it all a paint-splattered radio on the floor was tuned to a Spanish music station. It all felt so communal and exciting that she felt like dancing, though for now she intended to make a nourishing meal for everyone.

But then she felt a sneeze coming on and she shifted her grocery basket to her hip.

"*Salud,*" said the Guatemalan carpenter putting the final touches to the counter. He spoke with a quiet politeness that fit his tidy, unassuming manner. He never tucked his carpenter pencil behind his ear, but kept it protectively in his left shirt pocket like a pet mouse. He wore a clean, pressed T-shirt tucked into belted jeans.

She sneezed again.

"*Salud y dinero.*"

Then came a third.

"*Salud y dinero y amor.*"

She laughed. She had picked up enough Spanish from Beatriz to know she had been wished her health for the first sneeze, health and money for the second, and health, money, and love for the third. "I haven't heard that before," she said.

"It was a good thing you did not sneeze a fourth time. Where I come from, we wish allergies for the fourth sneeze. It is our way of saying, 'Oops.'"

She laughed again.

She so liked these men. The only place she had noticed men like them in her old life was in the parking lot outside the Mount Kisco train station. They gathered there early in the mornings, stamping their feet in the winter cold to stay warm, to await any contractor pulling up to offer work. They would haggle for a few minutes over wages and hours presumably, the driver and the laborers both looking over their shoulders, and then climb in and drive off if no immigration van pulled up first. Their faces had always seemed so hard, though now she understood that they were simply tight with worry. Many of them had wives and children back home, or living with them here in overcrowded housing. The hours were long, the work hard, the pay poor, and the risks of employer deception or deportation hung heavily over them.

They loved it whenever Reuben pulled up, looking for men to help him up north at the orchard. Reuben drove them back at day's end with above-average wages and bags of whatever was best and in season. So when Reuben had pulled up looking for men to help renovate his fiancée's new café, he got the best men at minimum wage—a wage that seemed incredible to Nora against the invoices she paid the branded construction companies years ago to renovate her house. Living in an affluent area, being naïve about construction, and laissez-faire about bills, had cost her plenty.

These men renovating the café came with Reuben to the real summer kitchen first thing every morning. There, along with Beatriz, Reuben, the boys, and herself, they would breakfast around the bench. Nora always cooked warm, hearty breakfasts, because renovation work took energy. Twice breakfast had still been cooking when the men arrived. They had waited out the first time changing lightbulbs, screwing cupboard knobs back into place, fixing the oven light so it shut off when it was supposed to, and investigating the ceiling leak. The second time they *fixed* the leak, and then repaired the water damage. The summer kitchen was not only fully functional again, but was even more alive for the rowdy breakfasts.

Once one of the workers brought along his wife and children. Beatriz had become friends with the wife. Her name was Ana and Nora saw her over by the café's fireplace with Beatriz now, both wearing aprons and gloves and scrubbing soot from the stonework with stiff brushes and a watery solution from a bucket between them. The woman's children stood at the base of their father's ladder with Thomas, Nicholas, and Charlie, five pairs of eyes following a paint roller. Beatriz was chatting effusively, her eyes brimming with excitement for a new friend, though when Reuben walked in she had eyes only for him. He cast about waves and smiles and then headed directly to Beatriz. He crouched where she sat and kissed her on the lips. Beatriz kissed him back a long while. Reuben and Beatriz kissed each other now a thousand times a day, and it filled Nora every time with a sense they belonged together, and also with a certain envy: There was nothing like that intoxicating high of being swept away by another.

A voice sounded in Nora's ear from the side, "I'm glad it's not me getting married!" Nora turned to face Eve. Eve was the president of the board of the historical society, a small-framed, effervescent, no-nonsense elderly lady with green eyes as intense as her confidence and a thick silver bob in the style of actress Joanne Woodward—there was a strong resemblance, actually. She had taken a particular interest in the café. She often stopped by in her stylish but practical pant suits to wonder about its fabulous future. She had just now ascended the staircase from the basement space they were transforming into the kitchen and cellar. If it weren't for the noise, Nora would have heard her. Eve never went anywhere quietly. No one but Eve could have looked as stylish as she now did in denim overalls with wood shavings in her hair. Nora would never have suspected that the dignified matron, who had headed the table around which the society ladies had gathered to hear her proposal originally for the café, would also be so hearty and curious.

Nora gave her a playfully suspicious look. "What are you up to now, Eve?"

Eve's eyes lit up with the excitement of a child. "Come and see what I've done."

Nora followed Eve back down the narrow, creaky wooden stairs stained black like the hand railing. Nora set the basket down on the counter already covered in marble and turned to see that Eve had erected rows and rows of shelves along the walls of the small room they were turning into a pantry.

"Oh, they're perfect!" Nora walked over to examine them. "Thank you!"

She stood admiring them for a while longer.

"The wood, the braces . . ."

"All authentic."

Nora shook her head in amazement.

Eve was heading over to the basket. "What have you got in there? I'm famished. I got into this groove and kept working. I simply can't remember when I last ate."

Nora washed her hands in the sink purchased with the other appliances from a secondhand dealer in the city. She then set out the tomatoes, peppers, cucumbers, garlic, and onions grown by Reuben, along with preboiled eggs. Also, two crusty loaves of bread she had turned out of her Aga oven before anyone woke that morning. The striking colors of the vegetables against the black marble made her wonder all at once at the realness and simplicity of good food. Had it ever occurred to her she had been drawn to food in the first place for those qualities it turned out she valued the most? She supposed it had, in a vague way. From the beginning she had associated her love for baking with her love for her father, a love true and uncomplicated. Now she wondered whether the pleasure of food had been working on her all this time as a grounding influence.

"So what are we making?" Eve asked.

"I'm sorry, what?"

"What are we eating?"

"Oh, gazpacho soup."

Nora refocused her thoughts and began slicing the bread.

"How do you know how to do all these things?" she asked Eve.

"The shelves?" Eve was crouched on the floor now packing a toolbox as ably as she did a pocketbook. "Why shouldn't we women be able to do all these things ourselves?" she asked cheerfully. "It's all a big fallacy that we need men."

Nora tapped her serrated knife on the cutting board to loosen the crumbs in its teeth.

"Well, I couldn't have had Thomas and Nicholas and Charlie on my own. . . ."

"Of course we need them for children, but beyond that we're better off on our own."

"But the children would then need a father."

"Don't confuse what children need with what you need!"

Nora was now peeling the papery skins off the garlic cloves.

"Don't get me wrong," Eve went on. "I *love* men, I *enjoy* men. I just don't *need* men. I don't believe any woman does, though most *think* they do. But just imagine how powerful we would be if we considered ourselves whole in ourselves and not as a half person without a man and thought of men rather as 'friends with benefits.'"

"Benefits?"

"Sex—friends with whom we have sex when we're in the mood. Oh, I've been down the marriage path before. Men require so much of you. You must follow them around in their careers, pretend they're not being condescending, put up with their flirting and drinking, then hide your disappointment when they don't turn out to be who you thought they were. It just horrifies me, the idea that my time and energy could be spent that way again. I love my life now, who I am. I wouldn't want to compromise myself again, and that's exactly what most marriages are for women, a lifelong compromise. The worst of it is that women often don't see it coming. One day they wake up and wonder who they are, who they might have been . . . I've seen that happen to too many friends."

Eve stood up with her packed toolbox. "I'm going to take this out to the car and then I'll help you," she said. Over her shoulder, she tossed back with a laugh the mention of a study she had read. "The happiest people in the world are single women, the second happiest are married men, the third are married women, and the least happy are single men . . . just goes to show that men are the ones who need marriage, not women!"

Nora shook her head in bemusement, but as she started coarsely chopping the vegetables, it struck her that she herself was falling head over heels for her new self-sufficiency. She felt at certain moments just ridiculously, intensely, overwhelmingly happy with how she and her sense of worth and purpose were actualizing. Might a partner now, any partner, compromise that, lose her all that? And frankly, she liked that her life hinged now on her own decisions independent of another. She liked there being no one to disrupt her groove, none but her boys' manageable moods shifting her own, no one around to whom to complain, so that she just got on with things. And she had grown to relish the solitude she found late at night. She had begun to feel at one with it, felt its peaceful healing powers pulsing through her, making her feel so sure about her life—not about its outcome entirely, but certain that she and the boys would be all right no matter what life had in store for her.

It had never occurred to her before that a future without a man was a choice.

Fifteen

S ome party you must be throwing," the party rental delivery-man said to her before the summer kitchen door slammed into the back of the stack of bamboo folding chairs hoisted on his shoulder. He turned to look as though that would fix any new dent, and then shifted forward to let the door close behind him. "They told me I'm to leave a hundred of these!" The phone had been ringing all morning with orders for goodie bags for the weekend parties held by the women of Bedford every summer in their beachfront rentals and it rang again just then. The latest batch of sweet-smelling cherry marmalade needed removing from the stove top, too, and now a new head poked inside following a chinking of bottles outside to ask, "Where do you want the champagne, ma'am?" The splashes coming from the buckets about the floor made it hard to hear him. Nora had been at the fish market in the Bronx at four o'clock that morning, buying enough live lobsters to prepare for the guests coming at twilight. It was a normal day running the business and planning the café opening, except it wasn't every day Nora also prepared to host a wedding.

It was Nora's gift to Beatriz and Reuben, their wedding. Their desire to be married so soon after the engagement had left precious little time for adequate planning, but Nora's life was guided now by optimism. She had asked Beatriz and Reuben to write a list of adjectives best describing the wedding they envisioned. There were three they had both used: *simple, elegant, natural.* She had pictured fruits and flowers of the season as the theme, giant glass bowl centerpieces filled with lemons as brilliant as sunshine, sunflowers spilling from pummeled tin buckets, loosely bunched bouquets of the small, round, lime-colored, tangerine-scented fruits of the calamondin. She would serve simple summer dishes. "Leave it to me," she had told them. The only snag was that she had in mind an outdoor wedding, yet Roman Catholics were traditionally married in church. "When was the last time you saw me going to church?" Beatriz had laughed. "God is with me wherever I am."

Nora addressed the party rental man, "You can take the chairs back outside, actually. There won't be any rain today." She told the champagne man on the other hand to, "Come on in and set the crates down in the cellar." It turned out the two men knew each other. Presumably they were often called to the same parties. "God, what about that last party!" the rental man said to the champagne man as they passed each other. "Jesus, you too?" the champagne man responded. Nora had no idea what they were talking about. She was also expecting a flower farmer with the white calla lilies she had requested. So she thought it was he knocking at the door after she had set the cookies on a cooling rack and was finally tending to the marmalade. Not so: It was a middle-aged woman heavy in the hips with shoulder-length blond hair wearing riding breeches and tall black boots. She seemed vaguely familiar, though Nora couldn't place her.

"S'cuse me, ma'am," the champagne man said, squeezing through the door in front of the woman. The woman gave him a disdainful stare.

"I see you're busy as usual," she said to Nora.

There was something so entitled in the way she said it that helped

Nora place the horsey face. This was her neighbor on her opposite side to the neighbor suing over the tree (that neighbor had not withdrawn the suit even after Reuben had finally taken a chain saw to the tree and turned it to firewood: He claimed he was still owed compensatory damages for all the inconvenience). This was the mother of the boy who lopped off her flower heads and dented her garage door. Nora had only met her twice before, the first time when she and Evan were new and the woman had driven up ostensibly to introduce herself but really to find out who was moving in. A year or so back she had shown up on the doorstep again to wonder whether Nora and Evan would install a drainage system at the bottom of the slope running into her property to save her having to drive through puddles when it rained. Nora had done the proper thing and had obtained quotes, but one of the contractors had told her frankly that the problem, if there really was one, was the black plastic sheeting laid on top of the soil and under the mulch to prevent weed growth. It may have been preventing the soil absorbing the water. She hired him to rip it all out and, until recently when she had let the weeds take over, it had cost her a fortune to keep the slope weeded.

The woman was never heard from again, not even for a thank-you.

"Would you like to come in?" Nora asked her. "I've just baked a batch of cookies for the boys. May I offer you one with a cup of tea?"

"Oh, no, I can't stay long enough for tea, but I will come in for a moment."

The room was hot, though the fan rotated overhead, and Nora opened a window.

The woman might have commented, as so many others would have in her place, on the sweet smells in the kitchen, but she headed immediately to her point.

"There are some concerns," she said.

"Concerns?"

"Well, every morning I see all these Central American families coming in here, and they're clearly not working on the house because they leave an hour later, and well . . ."

"Well, what?"

"Well, the house doesn't seem to have been worked on in a while."

"Ah, you mean the dented garage door!" Nora said, though there was no point driving home that this woman's son had caused that unless she, Nora, wanted a shrill and indignant and unrelenting denial—which was the last thing she had time for this morning.

"I hadn't noticed that so much as the house paint and the garden."

It was true that mildew had climbed up the exterior walls and that she had allowed the garden to take on a more natural look. The pond at the front had silted in the summer heat and become more akin to a swamp. The orange trumpet creeper that had always clung so prettily to the old wooden horse fences about the property had started making its way up the mountain ash and elm trees. Crows had mauled the crab apples before she could pick them this year to make crab apple jelly, the grass everywhere but for directly around the house had grown so tall it would need a tractor to cut it down now, and boughs sent flying in winter storms had dismantled in parts the stone fence separating the paddock from the preserve. But for all that the grounds were still colorful and fragrant. Sunny red plants flowered to either side of the porch despite patches eaten by the deer, and black-eyed Susans bloomed in the circular driveway island bed.

"Is your concern then my house paint and garden?" Nora asked.

She understood perfectly well that their neglect bothered this neighbor.

"No, no," the woman insisted.

"What then?"

Outside the window, the champagne man and the rental man had resumed the obscure conversation they had started when passing each other earlier at the door. "So that leftover food those folks at that last place gave out when I was picking up the equipment and you were taking back all the unused bottles gave you loose bowels, too!" the rental man said. "God-awful," said the champagne man. "Gave the whole family the runs. Stunk the house up like a sewer."

The woman's mouth tightened. She pointedly avoided looking toward the voices.

Nora suppressed a smile.

"It's all these Central American people. I assume they're employees in this business you're running, but were you aware that the other morning they were all kicking a soccer ball around? I looked up the hill as I was riding back to the barn and felt like I was living in the projects in the Bronx. Is this something that's going to continue?"

The cushioned *thud, thud* of the bamboo chairs being stacked against the exterior wall all at once stopped and the voice Nora now identified with the rental man picked up again outside the window. "Only one other time I've had the shits that bad . . ."

The woman placed her hand over her chest and gave a tight little cough.

Nora bit the inside of her cheek to keep from laughing.

The male voices outside the window stopped midsentence and the voice of another woman asked whether the lady of the house was home.

"Inside," the champagne man said.

"Hello-o-o."

"Eve?" Nora asked.

Eve stepped inside. "Nora! I'm so glad you're here. I went to the café first. But, my, is that you, Chauncy?"

So that was her neighbor's appropriately horsey name!

"But of course, you live right next to Nora! Funny, I'd not remembered that before. Aren't you lucky, to live so close to such an exciting project! You must savor the most delectable smells!"

"Well . . ." said Chauncy.

But Eve had already turned to Nora. "Chauncy and her husband are so supportive of the society," she explained. "They come to all our functions." She turned back to Chauncy with a smile. "And we just love having them."

"Anything we can do," Chauncy responded, a flicker of pride in her expression.

Nora said, "Chauncy dropped by to ask about our friends who come to breakfast."

"Your *friends*?" Chauncy touched her hair.

Eve regarded her and then glanced at Nora. Nora winked discreetly. The wrinkle of a smile appeared around Eve's mouth. She turned back to Chauncy and said, "Whatever would Nora do without them? But you'll meet them tonight at the wedding!"

"The wedding?"

"Beatriz's, of course," Eve said.

Chauncy looked at Nora.

"Isn't your nanny who waits for the school bus named Beatriz?"

"One and the same," Nora answered. "We'd love to have you."

The rental man popped his head inside the door to say he'd be off now and would return after the wedding to collect the chairs. The champagne man must already have left.

Eve clapped her hands again.

"So, the reason I'm here, Nora, darling, is that I have some wonderful news. A position on our board has just opened and I have come with the board's unanimous approval to persuade you to reconsider our invitation to you last year to join us!"

Chauncy's face became a study in disbelief.

Eve continued, "But, of course, you're much too busy to give an answer now. I only came because I could hardly tell you during the wedding when everything must be about the bride, and I wouldn't have been able to wait until tomorrow. Now that I've told you, we'll leave you to it and we'll be back tonight." She then led a dazed Chauncy out by the arm.

"Toodle-pip," she called before the door closed behind them.

Nora's amusement soon shifted to concentrated activity. It was hours later, after Nora had cooled and refrigerated the prepared seafood, and while arranging with hands stinging from the rub of oyster shells ingredients for the cake, that Beatriz appeared with a platter of sandwiches. She was wearing a simple blouse and skirt. Her feet were bare, her face still not made-up, her hair braided loosely down her back.

"The boys have been fed, and are setting out the tables and chairs— and tiki lamps with Ticky." Beatriz smiled, a nod to the poetry of Ticky's tikis. "Then they are heading over to her house to pick up the china and glassware and silverware she is lending us. I told the boys they could go. It will keep them occupied while you are busy." Beatriz set down the platter on the bench. "I thought you might be hungry." She took a seat opposite Nora. "What can I do to help?"

"Nothing," Nora said. "It's all taken care of. Besides, aren't you supposed to be making last-minute alterations to your dress?"

"No, I decided to leave it the way it was."

"Taking a long bath then, fixing your hair, painting your nails . . . ?"

"There is time," she said flatly.

"Is anything wrong?"

Beatriz sighed. "I just feel so surprised when I think that tonight I will be married while you are still managing on your own. It has always been the other way around."

Nora bandaged a cold towel around her hands to soothe them a moment and took a seat. "Has it occurred to you that perhaps this is the way it's meant to be now?"

Beatriz raised her posture suddenly. "No," she asseverated. "It has never occurred to me that you would be better on your own. That would only be better if your other option was an unhealthy relationship. And I know there are plenty of those—but . . . and I ask of you on my wedding day to please, please listen now and to forgive me if

I take liberties, because I will not be around in your home life much longer to say this again . . . you and *el señor* have very obviously to me come together in this lifetime to liberate each other. The universe will never give a more important person to you. He raised you up and brought you down and in doing so made you look at yourself and change your life. If he did that and continued to make you miserable, it would indeed be time to thank him for all he taught you and to move on. But your relationship is special: Not only has he been traveling a separate but parallel path of growth and awareness to you—I have stayed in close enough touch with him to know this—but you are both still *helping* each other to grow. You are learning forgiveness and compassion, and he humility and responsibility. Most important, you both know now what is inside of yourselves and each other. How many partners can you say that about? You have to see someone in impossible circumstances truly to know them. I believe at the end of the day you will have between you a unique, tender, nourishing relationship that will work the way you both need it to, a relationship cleansed of the doubts and fears of most relationships and just true and honest and moral. Of course I cannot know this for sure, it is a hunch, but is it not worth waiting for what may be a perfect love?"

Nora supposed she was looking as she felt, overwhelmed and uncertain, for then Beatriz asked gently, "You do not believe relationships can have incarnations?"

"Well, sure, I've been explaining to the boys that our relationship with you will not end when you move in with Reuben tonight, but simply enter a new phase, as it will enter yet another one when the café is up and running and you'll no longer work as the boys' nanny."

"Marriages that are not stagnant have many lives, too, if you are meant to stay around long enough to see them born again. I have seen that happen with my parents'."

"You make it seem like fairy-tale endings are possible."

"Why not? You deserve it. *El señor* does, too. You have both suf-fered and worked for it. Besides"—she gave a little laugh—"there's something kind of sexy about a man who has survived an experience as tough as prison, do you not think?"

Beatriz had Nora laughing now.

"You had best save those sorts of thoughts for your wedding night!"

"I have plenty to spare!"

Nora did not doubt it. "You look at ease and happy, Beatriz."

"I am, so happy that I cannot believe it."

Nora smiled.

Then they looked at each other a moment and said together so that the words blended into a song, "Thank you."

There was no time and no need for anything more.

"Now get out from underfoot and go and get ready so I can get this cake done!" Nora chided teasingly, and Beatriz regained her excite-ment and disappeared.

As Nora ran the zester over the first pomelo, the fragrance of the Chinese grapefruit peel not only absorbed the fishy odors from her fingers, but had such a deliciously calming effect on her mood that she found herself not the least stressed by the enormous task ahead. The cake would be four-tiered, each tier a different citrus flavor, pomelo at the base, then orange, then lemon, and lime at top. Each of the round white-frosted cakes would be shaped in decreasing size upward and each would be separated between the separator plates with glass cylinder bowls filled with actual pomelos in the first case, oranges in the second, and lemons in the third. A single lime carved into a replica of the whole cake would sit atop the creation. It was a twist of a similarly designed cake she had seen once by Maisie Fan-taisie at a wedding she and Evan had attended in London. Her intent with the stunning arrangement of height and natural, vibrant color was to halt all clutter and noise in every guest's mind as they regarded it. The gift was to experience a simple beauty, to experience what it was to be truly alive. She would strew vines of kumquats and loose lemons and limes around the cake so that the arresting scent of citrus would accompany the visual feast. She hoped to enhance the moment by creating cakes themselves so delicate in texture and subtle in taste that nothing but the experience of that texture and taste would matter at all.

Soon enough she was lost in her work and strangely overcome with a sense of romantic love gushing from her, as though the cake was being born of her romantic heart. The relief of it had the awakening effect of smelling salts, and it was then that it occurred to her: Her tender energies had not shut down but were dammed up. That was why her heart had been so blocked and undecided. And then the next realization unleashed itself within her. She stopped in midcircle stirring the batter. At some point she would need to love again. Her body could live alone, her mind, but not her heart. Not forever. Her creativity had floated her for a long while, but it did not fulfill her in the same way. Her heart, very obviously to her now, teemed with a compulsion to be shared. She knew then with thunderous certainty she would not take Eve's solution of casual lovers as needed. This she also knew would be the hardest part of her journey: learning again how to love intimately. For she believed she would cry now at the feel of a man reopening her heart, it felt suddenly that pent up with bravery and desire.

How incredible it would be to be touched that way again.

And then immediately after that thought came thoughts of Evan.

Could Beatriz be right? Could the trust be rebuilt, could they each accept and respect who the other had become, might there be a perfect love to be discovered there?

Could she fall in love again with Evan?

Might she have always been still in love with him?

Though finally she pulled herself out of this line of ruminating: Here she was preparing to host a wedding within hours, and instead of sending all her thoughts on their day to the wedding couple, she was wondering about her own future with a man who would be gone for yet another year and who knew where *she* would be in a year?

By that time, it would be like meeting new people for them both. She refocused on the cake.

The guests began gathering in the garden just before dusk. Nora had made the last touches to the preparations just in time. She had bathed and dressed the boys and was now looking down from her bathroom window as she blow-dried her freshly washed hair. She laughed as she spotted Charlie crawling out in his suit from under the long buffet table, Nicholas in his wake. She could just picture these little ushers with grass-stained knees helping to seat the guests! Ticky wore a pale pink, sleeveless, knee-length cashmere dress and was setting oyster forks on the buffet table. She jumped as the boys emerged from beneath, but then bent and kissed their heads. Charlie stood up and performed a spontaneous dance and then hurtled off in search of more fun. Reuben stood over to the side chatting with the priest: He looked incredibly handsome in his white, open-necked shirt and cream linen suit, his contrasting dark hair combed neatly back, though he was clearly nervous. He kept rubbing his palms together and glancing back to the house, from which at some point his new life would emerge. Thomas stood beside him, affecting an exaggerated grown-up air in his new fitted suit. Reuben had asked him to be his best man. It had been just the thing to distract Thomas from the fact of the marriage. For days he had been consumed with thoughts only of his special role. He had barely left Reuben's side, kept checking his suit pocket for holes, lest the rings fall out on the special day. And there was Eve over by the guitarist. He was playing Norah Jones's "Come Away with Me." She could just make it out now that she had turned off the dryer. In a silver twin-set to match her hair, Eve stood familiarly with a handsome man at least twenty years her junior! That Eve was such a card. Who could the man be? And was that—Yes, that was her neighbor, Chauncy, standing and chatting with them! So she *had* come.

The workers looked sharp in their suits, the suit lines accentuating muscular bodies. Their wives in colorful dresses and lipstick might have been movie stars. Bobbing about them, their sons and daughters, also in suits and dresses, were a show of fireworks. The head baker and his assistant from Phillip's were supplying a good deal of the conversation in a group of men in clean jeans and shirts. She presumed they were Reuben's Hudson Valley farmer friends, though they could as well have been his famous chef or restaurateur-clients. One of the gallery owners from the village was stubbing out a cigarette on a tree trunk. She saw the two wives she had met visiting their husbands at the prison standing alone as a twosome while their children ran after Charlie and Nicholas, but then the historical society ladies walked over and introduced themselves.

The garden looked magical, swimming in the light of lanterns and candles. Here and there fireflies emitted their courtship flashes, an unexpected romantic touch. There were twelve set tables in all, strings of flowers woven through lavish pyramids of fresh fruit in their centers, giving off the smells of summer. The bamboo chairs faced the canopy of Shasta daisies under which Beatriz and Reuben would receive first the Sacrament of Reconciliation and then the Sacrament of Marriage. Someone had wired Beatriz's wooden crucifix to the top of the canopy. On each chair was folded a paper fan the boys had made to wave off the humidity during the ceremony. Even mosquito coils to save Nicholas from getting bitten had been remembered.

Nora finished her makeup, slipped into a fitted spaghetti-strap gold dress and high strappy gold sandals, and started out to check on Beatriz. But as she went to open her own bedroom door, she caught her reflection in the long mirror behind it and stopped. She was taken aback by how young she still looked and, well, yes, sexy. She gave the unexpected reflection a playful wiggle, and then went down the hall to Beatriz's room. But just as she was about to knock, a deep, softly exploring voice behind her startled her.

"Pardon me, but . . ."

She turned to find a tall, toned, olive-complexioned man a decade or so older than she in a lemon linen shirt climbing the stairs, the same man she had seen out in the garden with Eve. He really was terribly attractive, though in an offbeat, disarming kind of way—his angular face tilted slightly downward, so that his big brown pools for eyes lifted upward through a soft dropped lock of grayish-blond hair. Though something about his face bothered her faintly. She was suddenly sure that she had seen him somewhere before tonight. The woody scent of his cologne nagged the partial memory.

He combed the dropped lock back with his fingers to reveal a twinkle in his eye and went on, "I wonder whether you might direct me to a bathroom? The one downstairs seems to be occupied. I hope you don't mind: A woman named Ticky sent me up here."

He extended his hand. "I'm Oliver," he said.

And then she remembered.

"You're that architect."

He smiled a beautiful, playful smile. "Which architect would *that* be?"

"The politely unavailable one. I visited your office some ten or more years ago when I was looking for an architect to renovate this house and you told me that you were sorry but that you couldn't take on any more projects."

He looked at Nora for a long, languid moment and said, "That was clearly a mistake. But if I can make it up to you, I am politely available now . . ."

This man was making a pass at her!

A tingling that might have had to do with the air-conditioning brushed her skin.

Nora was the first to look away when the matron of honor, Beatriz's new friend Ana, opened Beatriz's door just then and tentatively said, "Oh," when she saw them standing right there. She then said to Nora, "I was just coming to tell you that she's ready."

The moment between her and Oliver was gone and Nora directed him to one of the bathrooms.

It took half an hour, but Nicholas and Charlie finally got everyone seated with a little assistance from Nora. A hush descended over the garden as Beatriz appeared on the rear deck of the house on the arm of Phillip. Beatriz had invited her parents, of course, only her father was too unwell to travel or to be left alone by her mother. Nora had not seen Phillip in the garden; he must have arrived just now at the last minute. He was mouthing something toward her that she discerned after an effort as "Aussie rules footy game," and then she remembered that he had told her he might be a bit late because he needed to catch the replay on cable first. "Did your team win?" Nora mouthed back. He grinned and gave her the thumbs-up. He looked dapper in an olive-green suit. The color suited both his olive-brown Driza-Bone hat and the natural colors of the setting.

Beatriz appeared in a long, strapless, lightweight slip dress, a slit all the way up the side to give a glimpse of shimmering bare leg. Her silky dark hair draped over bare shoulders and spilled with her locket into her ample cleavage. She wore in place of a veil a simple crown of garden flowers, complementing the loosely bunched bouquet she held, so that she gave the impression of having just taken a country stroll. When the guitarist started playing Bach's "Sarabande in A Minor" and she began to glide toward her beloved as only Beatriz could in four-inch heels on grass, it was all Nora could do to keep from marveling at how far they had all come from that dawn not a year ago when Evan had taken a walk of a different kind down the drive in the rain.

The ceremony flowed flawlessly, its seriousness lightened with laughter even at just the right moment by a raft of wild turkeys running past cackling—far more spontaneous than the kuh-koorring

white homing pigeon release she had considered but that had been
too expensive for the birds having been trained selectively to find their
way home. She might have gone to a vendor using cheaper white ring-
necked doves, but that was never an option—ring-necked doves had
no homing ability. They lost their way after release and became easy
prey. As the ceremony ended Nora gave her attention immediately to
setting out the food. The role took her past various conversations. Over
the guitarist playing something else by Bach, she discerned that the
discussion in the threesome of Phillip, Chauncy, and the Guatemalan
carpenter was of horses. It turned out the Guatemalan roofer had
grown up on a horse farm in his home country and had ridden them
to school. He was advising Chauncy on what to do about the common colds her horses seemed continually to contract. "Keep them
outside more. Their respiratory tracts will grow stronger than if they
are more often stabled." Phillip added another remedy he recalled
from his horseman days, "And push a fresh clove or two of garlic into
an apple for 'em once or twice a day." Chauncy was listening intently
and nodding gratefully. Nora then overheard Ticky telling Eve—out of
earshot of the wedding couple—that if she had known how ghastly divorce could be, she would never have married. "How is it that no one
ever tells you when you marry just exactly what you're entering into
with marriage?" she asked rhetorically, though Eve answered anyway,
"For the same reason people don't tell a pregnant woman quite how
difficult childbirth can be. No one wants to dampen the excitement
and there's always the chance theirs will be the rare exception." Ticky
responded, "Well, mine certainly wasn't the exception!" She told then
how both her and Morris's lawyers had advised them not to move out
from the marital home yet. All the while he had told the staff not to
take instruction from her anymore. He even held dinner parties in the
dining room for their old friends to which she was not invited! During
one she had been making herself a sandwich in the kitchen when a
guest walked in. "My, that looks good," the woman had said before

asking to be reminded of directions to the bathroom. Not, "Oh, Ticky, how awful this must be for you!" or "I'm so embarrassed about this I can't tell you!" Nothing like that: Loyalties went unashamedly with the money. "And it's clear I don't have that: He gives me just three hundred dollars a week now—and then insists I buy my own groceries. He labels and measures what's his in the refrigerator."

"Think of it as a swimming lesson," Eve told her.

"Pardon?" Ticky asked.

"What happens when you throw a dog in the water?"

Ticky's expression lit with understanding. "It paddles."

"Exactly. After this you'll be able to swim through anything."

Nora smiled. She liked Eve. What an eclectic, colorful group of real friends she was gathering! She had become conscious as she awakened to the truth of things of the fingerprints of energy people left in their wake. Fingerprints of the likes of Bonnie penetrated like poison. She intended to surround herself now only with those who left positive imprints.

She started to bring out the trays of seafood. Oliver came up behind to help.

"Shouldn't you be paying attention to Eve?" she asked him.

"My mother?"

"Your *mother!*"

And then she laughed.

"You thought she was my date?" And then he laughed, too. "We have different last names because Mom kept her maiden name. A good thing, too, since she's gone through two divorces since my dad!"

They started talking and eventually sipping glasses of champagne. The potent bubbles made Nora instantly light-headed on an empty stomach, and aware of how exhausted her work of that day had left her. When empty shellfish shells smelling like a fresh breeze at the seashore had started to pile up on the tables with juiced lemon wedges, they were still talking. Neither of them had eaten.

Charlie gave her leg a big hug.

She dimly registered that Oliver tensed a little at the intrusion.

She lifted Charlie onto her hip. He asked, "Is it time for the cake, Mommy?"

It was this that awoke her to the different light and piled shells. She jumped. *She had neglected her guests!* Though when she looked around, everyone seemed perfectly content, languidly sucking at juicy fingers—lobsters were a messy business, after all—intermingling as happily as, well, people flushed with champagne and seafood under stars and lanterns on a warm, clear night conversing and playing with laughing children and listening to guitar music. But the smaller children would tire soon, and Thomas as best man still had a speech to deliver. With the help of the boys, she cleared the plates and set out giant bowls of berries and platters of cut watermelon and ribbons of lemons and limes and pomelos. The delicious quiet for which Nora had hoped came over everyone for the second time that evening when she and Ticky carefully carried out the cake. She let the silence surround her along with the balmy moonlight. Only when the crowd began sputtering into appreciation did Nora clear her throat and introduce Thomas.

He looked up at her nervously and she nodded that it was okay to procced. He then looked over at Beatriz and Reuben sitting so happily together in their place of honor. His voice was soft and hesitant, but he maintained perfect bearing and eye contact with the bride and groom and held his notes without shaking too much.

"I asked my dad what I should say today," he said.

The surprise and sweetness of that had Nora blinking back tears.

"My dad wrote me back that the best thing you could wish for a newly married couple or for anyone was happiness and he sent me a quote he had read recently about happiness that he said was the truest thing he had ever learned. I asked him whether he would mind if I read it today and he said it would be fine."

And then Thomas apologized in advance if he mispronounced any words—though he didn't think he would because he'd been practicing—and read slowly from his paper.

"'Happiness is the greatest paradox of nature. It can grow in any soil, live under any conditions. It defies environment. It comes from within; it is the revelation of the depths of the inner life as light and heat proclaim the sun from which they radiate. Happiness consists not of having, but of being; not of possessing, but of enjoying. A martyr at the stake may have happiness that a king on his throne might envy. Man is the creator of his own happiness; it is the aroma of a life lived in harmony with high ideals. For what a man has, he may be dependent on others; what he is rests with him alone. Happiness is the soul's joy in the possession of the intangible. It is the warm glow of a heart at peace with itself.'"

All the time Thomas spoke, something beautiful was taking place. Many were putting their hands to their hearts or biting on trembling lower lips. It was the picture of such a young, brave boy saying so effortlessly what most struggled their entire lives to learn that did it. And the spell was having a secondary effect on Nora: The notion that Evan had been growing and changing apace with his wife now grew wings, so that there spread within her another new regard for her husband.

The night took on a new mood after that. Everyone had been drawn a little into their inner worlds, and that brought a delightful serenity to the subsequent speeches and the savoring of the cake and the sending off of Beatriz and Reuben to the bed set up on Reuben's barn-apartment rooftop under nothing but mosquito netting and the stars.

And then every wedding guest went home with a single perfect peach as a wedding favor to savor when they awoke in the sunshine.

Sixteen

It was raspberry season in Bedford, New York. The local private-school mothers who had come back from their vacations in the Hamptons or on Martha's Vineyard for this day were pulling up along the village green in their Suburbans and Range Rovers and BMW X5s. Expecting them and many others besides for the opening of their mom's and Beatriz's and Phillip's café, Thomas and Nicholas and Charlie had been taking turns in the ice-cream corner all morning at the jobs of hand-twirling the ice-cream canister, keeping the barrel around it filled with ice and salt, and continually scraping down the insides of the pot. They would offer three different flavors for the ice-cream sundaes they would be serving all the children with top-pings of whipped cream, hot fudge, roughly hand-chopped oven-roasted nuts, butterscotch, marshmallows, and maraschino cherries. Earlier they had made the raspberry chip ice cream using the rasp-berries they had gathered the day before on their property. They had added the raspberry puree as the sugary cream was swirling and slowly freezing. That way the puree turned to large raspberry chips. Now Charlie was using the same method to make the chocolate chip ice cream. They oohed as the chunky chips formed. When the ice cream was ready, Beatriz removed it and hand-packed it, as she had the raspberry chip, and the cookie crumb ice cream they had made after that. They tasted each batch as she did so. Each time, the dense, rich flavor stopped them dead.

"Why doesn't other ice cream taste like this?" Nicholas asked.

Beatriz answered, "Because most ice cream is really frozen foam. Up to half of it is air. There is no compressed air in ours."

"Why doesn't everyone make it like this?"

"Because it is time-consuming and more expensive."

Thomas looked up. "That's good for us, right?"

Nicholas and Charlie looked on with huge eyes.

Thomas went on, "Because our competitors won't be interested in copying us. Why would they, when they can produce a higher-volume product with modern equipment—and air! We'll have the market for this incredible ice cream to ourselves!"

Beatriz bust out laughing.

"Why're you laughing at me?"

Beatriz tousled his hair. "I am not laughing *at* you, Tom. I am laughing because I am proud of you. You are becoming a crackerjack entrepreneur."

Thomas's hurt expression shifted as quickly as only a child's expression can to a beam. He now knew what the word *entrepreneur* meant. When he and Nicholas had pulled their all-terrain wagon door-to-door along their road last Sunday selling their fresh-grown vegetables and handing out flyers for their festival, *entrepreneurial* had been the word the adults who came to the door had used to describe them. Those adults often called to one or another of their children, whose heads were more often than not in front of screens playing video games, "*You should do something like this!*" The children almost never looked up. "Can't get them away from those things," the parents would then mutter to themselves. He had looked up *entrepreneur* in the dictionary when they returned home with their wagon empty and their pockets full of bills for the five-quart paint cans they had converted to piggy banks and a message from the man next door that if their tomatoes tasted as good as they looked, he might consider withdrawing his suit against their mom. Perhaps he was not so mean, after all.

Entrepreneur had felt so much like *his* word that he had donned it like a jacket.

Since the boys had returned to their tasks, Beatriz had taken a piece of crystalized melon from the glass jar atop the ice-cream counter. She had set the jar there herself, alongside the other jars of sugared almonds, candied dates, and crystalized cherries. Her craving today for these melon pieces was as insatiable as the craving that overcame her last week. On her way home one night she had stopped at the market and was wandering down an aisle looking for anything that might appeal to her moody first-trimester appetite when her eyes landed on a box of white rice. She had wanted to chew right into it. And then she noticed next to it a bottle of vinegar and it was as if she became possessed. She abandoned everything in her cart and went home with just the rice and the vinegar. "What are you doing!?" Reuben had asked when he found her decanting the bottle into the steaming rice cooker. "I have no idea but if you try to stop me I will kill you!" she had snapped back, pushing past him to eat. Reuben had learned to steer clear when she adopted that tone. If it was not the cravings, it was the hormones. Both of which could turn her into someone neither recognized. Parked at a traffic light a few mornings back on their way together to the café, she took such offense at Reuben's comment that her churros that morning had tasted a little greasier than usual that she had climbed out of the car. Climbed out and then stationed herself in front of it. The light turned green and horns started blowing behind, but she just stood there indignantly with arms folded. Reuben had needed to climb out of the car to coax her back in. He looked as though he had witnessed something extraterrestrial. But he was patient.

And doting.

While the boys began hatching a clever plan to package their ice cream as the Three Brothers Ice Cream from the Summer Kitchen to sell to customers who preferred taking it home to eating it straight from a sugar cone, Beatriz turned after taking yet another melon piece to finish setting things up. Fortunately, there was little left to do. The fifteen-quart copper kettles hanging from metal hooks in the hearth gleamed in the sunlight. Fine damask lace-trimmed cloths draped over the long, narrow traditional table boards that resembled sawhorses and brought people to sit together. Each place was set with cloth napkins and silver forks from Ticky's collection. The waitresses, dressed in hooped petticoats and long aprons and caps, had seen to the details. One was standing on a bench seat running a feather duster one last time over the kitchen antiquities set now on newly installed antique shelving. She had already buffed the picture frame glass, housing old-word recipes, which covered the wall space below.

Beatriz breathed in the sweet aromas that lately appealed to her. Those at the forefront were of various honeys in the wooden honey pots anchoring the tablecloths, lavender, orange blossom, and eucalyptus. But the room was a cornucopia of visual and olfactory treats. Marcona almonds were roasting in Reuben's old wood oven, and from the kitchen downstairs wafted scents of all the spices they would be offering their customers fresh over the counter in cloth bags: cinnamon stalks, cloves, anise, ground ginger, juniper berries, finely grated nutmeg. Nora and Beatriz packaged all the spices themselves. They would also offer ribbon-tied bags of Phillip's tea creations served in the café, loose leaves of lemon verbena, dried pennyroll, black tea with vanilla. All around the room, on the floor, shelves, and counters, were baskets and baskets and baskets of irresistible delights, jars of marmalades and honeys and pure, dark, sugarless chocolate pieces ready to melt with milk at home for the richest hot chocolate. Customers could even buy jars of chocolate shavings, to sprinkle over warmed pears and whipped cream, or over the whipped cream on their hot chocolates. They sold truffles white and dark, with or without rum, biscuits with every variation of nuts and spices, bars small or large of their own chocolate, and dried fruits dipped in chocolate. The chocolate-covered dried figs were normally Beatriz's favorite, when she wasn't craving the macerated or crystalized fruits.

They had done it. It was incredible, but they had done it.

She was marveling at this realization when the front door opened to a group she recognized as private-school mothers. They seemed to enter as a collective, bolstering one another's resolve. Their eyes grew wide as they took everything in. When they saw her they hesitated. She could almost hear them thinking, Is that Nora's nanny in that full-flowing turquoise-paisley silk georgette skirt with its tiers of angled ruffles, the fitted white tank with its deep crocheted floral neckline, the flat silver sandals, the turquoise concha earrings, her hair pulled into a loose ponytail? But they greeted her as effusively as if there had been no hesitation and begged to be shown absolutely everything.

"And do you do the actual baking, too?" asked one woman.

"Of course she does," answered a second mother. "They're *your* churros we buy on Saturdays at Phillip's, aren't they, Beatriz?"

"*Really?*" responded the first mother. "Well, well."

Beatriz asked, "Won't your children and their nannies join us?"

The nannies were standing respectfully just inside the door, holding the hands of their charges. The boys were dressed in variations of chinos and classic Ralph Lauren polos, the girls in cropped white jeans or Rosita skirts with Pony Tees.

"Oh," a few of the mothers said together, heads swiveling back to the door.

Beatriz walked over. Her smile was warm, her carriage confident. She remembered some of the women. "Welcome, everyone," she said. And then squatting down to meet the wondrous eyes of the children: "I hope you all like ice cream!"

She led the nannies and the children, the mothers in their wake, to the ice-cream corner. "Boys, greet your guests," she told Thomas, Nicholas, and Charlie.

The boys looked up for the first time.

"D'you want to see how we make it?" Nicholas invited.

The children let go of their nannies' hands, thrust into them their handheld video games and various gizmos, and zinged themselves onto floor cushions around the boys.

"So I see you've found my darlings!" Nora appeared behind them all in a white chef's coat over cropped chinos and chef's clogs. Her hair was loosely knotted at the nape of her neck. "Just wait until you taste their ice cream! The boys have a plan to make three different flavors every week, to serve after school and on weekends. They've become our other partners. We're letting them run the ice-cream corner as their own small business."

A camera flash popped.

All looked to see a photographer snapping a picture of the children. No one had heard him enter. He held up an identification badge hanging around his neck. "*Record-Review* today," he said, moving to take a close-up of Thomas, Nicholas, and Charlie.

"Aren't they a bit young to be running their own business?" asked the mother whose name Nora had been trying to recall.

"That's what I thought," Nora answered. "But then Thomas showed me an article about Tom Monaghan, who founded Domino's Pizza. Monaghan was just thirteen when he bought a pizza store with his brother. Less than a year later he gave his brother his Volkswagen Beetle for his share, and was opening franchises before he was twenty. There are now more than eight thousand Domino's around the world. Monaghan sold the business when he retired for almost a billion dollars. I thought, well, if that's what optimism can do, then Thomas's faith will lead somewhere, too, and really it's astonishing how quickly he and Nicholas pick up details about financing, and maintaining records, and planning. Charlie takes in every word. Thomas told me the other day that his father is the most brilliant teacher any entrepreneur could hope for. Thomas sounded like a sage old man when he said that anyone who wanted to know how to do something the right way should have as a teacher someone who did it once the wrong way."

It turned out the photographer was a photojournalist. Having overheard Nora, he had pulled out a palm-sized spiral notepad and pencil. "A natural front-page story," he announced. He began asking her questions, and she excused herself to answer him.

By the time they were done, the café was crowded, waitresses weaving in and out of loud talk and laughter with silver trays piled with mini Spanish Napoleons. Ticky was moving in and out the front door, evidently giving tours of the office upstairs that she now ran full time, the only access to it being from the door on the street. "So, what's it like to work?" Nora heard one of the Bedford mothers ask Ticky in a slightly superior tone on the way out for her tour. Ticky answered openly, "There's nothing like knowing you can take care of yourself." The mother's face glazed over and she seemed lost in thought, strangely: The women of Bedford were not given generally to self-reflection. Reuben had arrived and was singing the praises of the workers to the historical society ladies. The workers in their clean jeans and T-shirts and fresh-shaven faces and wet-combed hair smiled shyly as the ladies oohed and aahed over the authenticity of the renovations, the overall effect of which they were seeing for the first time. The workers had toiled throughout the night to finish in time. Eve was telling them she might well have a good deal more work for them and was handing out cards and scribbling numbers.

Nora found herself among Bonnie's contingent. The talk was of drapes and linens. Bonnie was redecorating her master bedroom again. She refitted it annually, though this year she was also redecorating the nursery because—she had wonderful news: She had applied to adopt a baby. Bonnie made the announcement before Nora had smiled her greeting to all, before the talk of decorating was done. The mad rush of it made it clear to Nora that Bonnie had no intention of being outdone on this occasion: She beamed in the sun shower of congratulations.

"A new baby calls for celebration," Nora said. "I'll send over a round of sherry."

"Sherry?" asked one of the mothers.

"Oh, it's so rich and smooth; it's the perfect thing with our treats today." And then she lowered her voice to a theatrical whisper: "It's one of the secret ingredients in our Spanish Napoleons, actually. You must try one of them, too."

"I already did!" gushed Lacy. "They're heavenly."

Bonnie smiled a tight smile.

"Actually," Lacy went on, oblivious to Bonnie. "This whole thing today gave me an idea. I'm heading the committee for the school fund-raising auction this year and I was thinking how marvelous it would be if we offered a day that a child could work in the bakery alongside you. The bids would be as high as for the day with our horse-veterinarian mother—higher even, probably, because . . . and don't say I said so, but I think that is getting a little worn. But God, don't tell her I said that." And then she frantically swiveled her head from side to side. "Is she here?"

She was, over with the mother/volunteer/Youth Soccer League coordinator/self-designated town crier. Lacy sent over a big smile and a wave.

"I'd be happy to do it, of course," Nora answered. "Only I would ask that a percentage of the proceeds go to a group I'm founding to support children of incarcerated parents, and I'd appreciate a small mention of the cause."

"Well, okay, sure, I suppose," Lacy responded.

"Then send me the paperwork and we'll make it all happen."

Bonnie's eyes smoldered. How glad Nora felt not to live trapped within exhausting, torturous insecurities, to be destined to searching for happiness in all the wrong places.

"The sherries," Nora remembered, and she ducked under someone's gesticulating arm behind her and cut a path happily away.

Downstairs in the kitchen, Nora helped one of the waitresses to fill another tray of copita sherry glasses. The narrow taper of these glasses enhanced the aroma. A little sherry spilled on the tray. The waitress lifted off a few glasses to wipe under them with a cloth while Nora loaded a separate tray with more mini Spanish Napoleons.

"They're so yummy," the waitress said. "People keep interrogating me for the recipe, and that freelance photojournalist, well, he said he used to work for *Gourmet* magazine. After the fourth time he swooped down on the napoleons, I heard him on his cell phone telling someone from there they should send up a critic. He asked whether they wanted him to take shots while he was here."

"That sounds promising," Nora said, and she lifted one of the glasses before the waitress whisked that tray upstairs. She took a sip. Its warm richness flowed through her. She closed her eyes to relish the experience of it. It had been her first opportunity to savor any part of the opening. She liked the sense of calm that took hold.

"We're going to need some more napoleons soon," she heard Phillip say, his voice growing closer with each word. "We're running out quickly up there!"

She opened her eyes to find him standing before her smiling under his hat.

"I know what you're celebrating on your own down here," he said. "As if there wasn't enough to celebrate today!"

"Oh, the *Gourmet* thing, yes, that was a turn of luck."

"The *Gourmet* thing? What? I meant your house!"

She looked over at the fax in a corner of the bench. She had read it when it came through that morning over and over, wondering why she still didn't feel ecstatic to have won back the whole of her property. She was a very wealthy woman again.

Phillip continued, "Hope you don't mind that I sticky-beaked. Must say, you're playing it pretty low-key. I'd have thought you'd be stoked."

"Hmm." She took another sip of sherry and sat the glass down.

"Guess now you'll be able to put the boys back in their old school."

"I'm not sure I want to do that, Phillip."

He paused a moment. "I see."

"The boys are happy at their school, and they've changed from this experience, too. They've become more creative and resourceful. They've grown accustomed to diversity. I'm not sure now that a homogeneous community would nourish their spirit."

Phillip started to say something, but Nora was giving voice to her thoughts for the first time, and she wanted to hear them out now.

"I'm not even sure I want the house any longer. I love my summer kitchen, of course. But I have this summer kitchen now, and the rest is just so . . . what's the word? Vast. And there's this house, this graceful stone house with a wooden porch and a divine little garden. I saw it at the beginning of the summer, down on Church Street. Something about it called to me. It's just so lovely, the whole thing I mean, the community along that street, its diversity, its neighborliness. Well, anyway, it's been put up for sale, the house. I saw the sign the other day. And I've been thinking that maybe—"

Just then, Beatriz burst from the stairwell.

"You will not believe it!" she told them.

They both looked at her.

"A woman upstairs just placed a ten-thousand-dollar order! Ten thousand dollars in one transaction! Says she wants to stock her beach house for the rest of the summer. Reuben is helping her carry all that she's bought just now out to her car. And a waitress is helping another woman right this minute who is also filling up box after box!"

Phillip slapped his thigh. "I knew it," he said. "We're off and running!"

"And we desperately need more of these," Beatriz said, picking up the tray of napoleons and handing it to Phillip. "Well, go on," she told him playfully.

Beatriz and Nora each hurriedly piled another tray and followed him.

Upstairs they passed Eve and a group of society board members. One of them put her hand on Nora's shoulder to stop her and said, "Eve's just told us! We're devastated, of course! Why won't you join our board?" To which Nora replied, "I was completely flattered, but I think I'm most able to make a difference by simply doing what I'm doing." She left them nodding gently. "Here," she told a waitress, handing over her tray. She could hear Thomas explaining how in the fall they would make pumpkin pie ice cream. She moved over to the ice-cream corner to watch and felt a rush of pride. They had become so confident, her boys, so proud of themselves, so able, smart, interesting, original.

All the children were sitting on cushions around a low table eating the sundaes that Beatriz had presumably helped to assemble. They hung on every word as Thomas told them, "You make it with crumbled gingersnap cookies and real pumpkin puree."

The mention of pumpkins took her mind back to Halloween, when they were all out trick-or-treating, and the boys had asked Evan about jack-o'-lanterns. How prescient it seemed to her suddenly that Evan had talked of old Jack just hours before he himself was doomed to darkness for greed. But viewed from another perspective, old Jack brought light to the world: Jack-o'-lanterns would not be but for old Jack's missteps and punishment. And all at once she understood: Evan's crime, incarceration, and ensuing misfortune had bestowed upon her and the boys great fortune.

It was incredible, but that understanding dissolved every trace of every residual regret. What a waste of time regret was anyway. Everything that had happened all at once had a purpose. There was a reason for every bit of it. It had been a good thing she had lost her money. It made her summon and realize her talent. It was a good thing she lost her husband. It had enabled her to discover on her own who she truly was. It had been a good thing she became a "single" mother. She had come to know motherhood and her children in a true and meaningful way.

Amid the hubbub of conversation so thick in the air she would have needed to drum a spoon to a glass to get anyone's attention, she felt her heart open in gratitude for the way things were. It felt to her like one of those transcendent moments she experienced with her children, when she felt connected to something bigger than herself and life became filled with meaning. Were it not for Evan having written recently to her that incarceration had been the fifth best thing ever to happen to him—she and the boys being one through four—it might have felt wrong to feel gratitude while he still suffered. As it was, her gratitude renewed her connection to Evan. And when Nicholas looked over at her just then and smiled and she could have sworn it was Evan—their expressions were so incredibly alike sometimes—she felt growing in her a longing for her husband.

It felt like such a gift, this forgotten, blissful longing, that she wanted to stoke it, pour over good memories to feed it. Had she been at home, she might have taken down the photo albums and traced with her finger that image she loved most of Evan emerging from the pellucid waters of Saint John, his torso glistening with sun-sparkling water beads, his smile for her as pure and untrammeled and innocent to the future as a baby's. She had taken that photo the day of the night they conceived Thomas. They had lain together on a darkened beach under palm trees, their naked bodies lit by water-reflected moonlight. Their lovemaking had been slow. They had joined as one, consumed with each other. They had willed Thomas, neither saying so, though both knowing. Afterward they had lain in each other's arms listening to the water lapping at their feet, and after a while he had sung Nat King Cole's "Unforgettable" to her in the deep croon he later used to sing lullabies.

She could remember that song just now because Evan had sent the lyrics to her recently. There had been nothing else in his letter, just "Dear Nora," those lyrics, and then "I miss you, Evan." The words had a different meaning now, nine years later and apart after so much had happened. It had seemed to her that Evan was saying he truly understood their import now: that true love sung on in mind and body no matter what.

But he had stopped short of completing the lyrics. The lines he left out expressed incredulity at this: "That someone so unforgettable/Thinks that I am unforgettable, too."

Evan had not sung those lines on the beach all those years ago, she knew, because a gentleman does not presume. He had not written them since, she knew, because he didn't believe them. In one letter he had told her he understood his love was unrequited now, but that he could bear that if at least she knew how much he continued to love her. All at once she wanted to tell him to go ahead and sing those words, for now that she admitted it to herself, the truth was that she had not after everything forgotten him, either.

Needing to be alone a moment, she turned to find Beatriz.

Beatriz was serving what was now a crowd of women.

Nora whispered to her, "Would you announce the winners of the pie and cookie competition for me when you're done, Beatriz? I could do with a little air."

"Is everything all right?" Beatriz asked.

"Everything's fine. I feel just fine."

She wove through the room, walked out the front door, and crossed the road. She took a seat on the empty bench under the oak in the middle of the village green facing the café. From there she could see through the café windows the colorful movement inside like spinning pinwheels. She should have felt a sense of achievement, she supposed, but all she felt was contentment, warmed by her surprise longing, and by the pastel midday sun. She kicked off her clogs and wiggled her bare toes through the grass. The street had been typically subdued for a midsummer morning, but a few bodies appeared now from cars and stores, probably for lunch.

A black Porsche pulled into the last spot in front of the green. A man got out on the driver's side and bent to direct his voice back inside the car. "Well, come on!" he said impatiently.

Nora recognized him vaguely from the private school, not enough to recall a name, or even what grade his child or children had been in. He was a significant contributor to the historical society. Eve had encouraged her to invite all the big donors. It had been the least she could do to give something back to the society.

The woman Nora remembered as his wife climbed out the passenger side.

Neither of them noticed her.

The man had obviously stepped in gum and was hopping like a mad stork now, trying to pick it off the bottom of his shoe with disgusted pincer fingers. He gave up quickly and scowled across the roof of the car, frantically flicking off whatever had adhered to his pinchers. "I don't suppose you brought me a spare pair of shoes?"

"Why would I bring you a spare pair of shoes?"

"Oh, no reason other than that a wife who has nothing to do all day might think of things like that and go places prepared. What *is* it that you do all day, anyway?"

The woman gave a nervous laugh. "So we're back to that, are we?"

"I just think you could do a better job of things. I mean, look at you. You'd think after all these years you'd have been able to lose